Maarten Maartens

The Greater Glory
A Story of High Life

ISBN/EAN: 9783337159702

Printed in Europe, USA, Canada, Australia, Japan

Cover: Foto ©Andreas Hilbeck / pixelio.de

More available books at **www.hansebooks.com**

Maarten Maartens

The Greater Glory

A Story of High Life

THE GREATER GLORY

A STORY OF HIGH LIFE

BY

MAARTEN MAARTENS

AUTHOR OF GOD'S FOOL, JOOST AVELINGH, ETC.

"So doth the Greater Glory dim the less"

NEW YORK
D. APPLETON AND COMPANY
1894

TO
WENDELA

NOTE.

HOLLAND is a small country, and it is difficult to step out in it without treading on somebody's toes. I therefore wish to declare, once for all, and most emphatically, that my books contain no allusions, covert or overt, to any real persons, living or dead. I am aware that great masters of fiction have thought fit to work from models; that method must therefore possess its advantages: it is not mine. In this latest book, for instance, I have purposely avoided correct description of the various Court Charges, lest anyone should seek for some feeble coincidence. Such search, after this statement, would be deliberately malicious. I describe manners and morals, not individual men.

M. M.

CONTENTS.

(vii)

viii CONTENTS.

THE ARGUMENT,

WHICH NONE NEED READ.

SHE came to him—the Life of his Life, the Soul of his Soul—she came to him where he sat in the loneness of the stately mansion, and she laid a gentle touch upon his bended head.

Where he sat in the loneness of his grandeur, with hands close-pressed against throbbing eyeballs, pressed yet closer, to shut out that crimson flare which was eating away his heart.

Thus she found him staring wildly into darkness, staring beyond the darkness, into that void which is more horrible than death. "Come," she said.

Then he lifted up his eyes in sluggish wonder. "Is it thou?" he whispered. "Art thou thou?"—and he took up his burden, which was himself, and followed her.

She led him down into the great hall of mirth, from whence he had but newly crept away for weariness. The discordance of its tuneless music and its joyless laughter rolled up to meet them in their coming; yet of sight there was nought to welcome them, because that its myriad candles were grown suddenly dark.

Suddenly dark and unperceivable, had it not been that, as she passed before him, the light of her eyes shone forth with spreading splendour, and by its rays he marked in dumb amazement how that the great gold cups and chargers *on the board were empty all, and lo and behold the guests sat naked, and their fair white flesh was covered with sores and they were not ashamed.*

They were not ashamed, but rather did they clash together empty goblets and raise them to their lips and drink and sing. Ay, there was drinking from emptiness and from hollowness was merriment. A cold mist, white and slow, rose across the shadows, in a ring around the radiance of that starlit brow.

He stopped beside a woman fair of face to look upon, whose leprous arms were girt with bracelets, and a serpent lay upon her breast. There was scorn in his sad eyes as he gazed upon her, and he broke into a fierce shout of laughter that beat down the tumult around.

But the woman stared back upon him as one that saw him not. In her gaze stood a sorrow, great and silent. None echoed his laugh; upon all that gay company a sudden hush was fallen. And his eyelids also were heavy with tears.

She—the Life of his Life, the Soul of his Soul—turned from where she was passing on before him. "Come forth," she said, and resumed her way.

But, ere she approached the great portal, to which her hope was hastening, one that sat low down at the table stretched out his naked arm and barred her path. "Thou art ill-favoured," he cried, "and strange to look upon. Tell thy name ere thou go."

Serene, she drew herself up to all her lofty stature. "I have many names," she answered him, "but none for such as thou. To thee let me be known for ever as an evil angel of God."

He dropped his arm with an oath and lifted one of the empty cups and seemed to drain it. And some that sat near cried shame—upon her.

Then fled they forth, these twain—he and she—into the far country, and when the stillness had enfolded them as a garment, she drew down his head upon her breast. "It was thy mother," she whispered gravely, as one chides a child that is sorry.

"My mother?" he replied, "I have never known her, if so be that she and I have met. Nothing have I known beyond the lap that bare me and the breasts that never gave me suck."

Then went they on in silence, these twain—he and she—rising swiftly into the soft night-air, sweeping forwards past many a solitary house and quiet hamlet and widespread village, over the drowsy fields, oppressed with corn and cattle, over the restless forests, that never cease conversing in their sleep. All the beautiful world, of which men know so little, lay beneath them, shrouded in darkness, and, above them, circled in light, lay the beautiful worlds of which men know nothing at all.

They arrested their flight and hung over the great city. It glowed in the abyss, a red blot through the night.

"Look down," she said. And he obeyed her. For one brief moment he obeyed her; then he shuddered away. "I cannot," he gasped. She smiled upon him, with a smile of trustful pity. "Look down," she repeated, and there was command in her voice.

And again he obeyed her. And a great silence lay between them for many moments. Then he spoke:

"It is most horrible," he murmured. "It is strangely, sadly beautiful. I would gaze for ever thus, but that my sight is failing me—— Dearest, I thank Heaven that I am blind."

And she led him far away into the desert—into the place where no man cometh except she guide him thither. On the brink of that vast precipice they stood and waited, and he felt that destruction yawned below.

"Leap!" she said, and let fall his hand. Then, as he lost her hold, the truth rushed back upon him that he was but a man, a child of earth, and that wings are given to angels only.

And he leaped.

But as he fell away into space, he realized suddenly that there was no more falling, no height, nor depth, nor distance. There was nothing but the small round earth outside him, and around him God.

And he lay silent in the immeasurable heaven.

" It is a meteor!" said the people, gathered to behold. " How brilliantly it shines! But why?"

And no one could give them answer, for the Angel of God was dead.

This is not an allegory. It is simply the whole simple story. They who will may read it. But you and I, we cannot understand it rightly, because the Angel of God is dead.

THE GREATER GLORY.

CHAPTER I.

RINGS THE DEPARTURE-BELL.

THIS is a true story. It is what they call a story of high life. It is also a story of the life which is higher still.

There be climbings which ascend to depths of infamy; there be also—God is merciful!—most infamous fallings into heaven. The wise men, who explain this world, have taught us to consider it a round one; doubtless they have wisely measured it. Then, as 't is round, should wisdom twist it topsy-turvy no one would be a whit the wiser, not even the wise men. And that, perhaps, is why—sometimes —to fools—our earthly high and low seem but a mighty matter of tweedledum and tweedledee.

Fortune, the blind old hag, in her seat by the hearth, grins down vacantly at the wise men, whom she twiddles on her thumbs—like the fools. Like the fools, they go rising and sinking, rising and sinking, till, one after another, all drop away into the fire. That, at any rate, is the end. We drop away into the fire.

Yet never a traveller paused by the roadside to look back, in weariness or wonderment, but understood, if the valley spread wider, that his path leads him up. So be. it. Presently, on the other side, the road slopes down again into another valley. But what matter the ups and downs of the journey to the traveller if his face be set firmly towards the goal? Only he feels that descent is strangely easy, and wonders why God bade him climb.

We say that the steadfast sun rises and sinks, like us. We see him do it; such mysterious eyes are ours. Yet we know that it is otherwise. We, who know so little.

In earth's tiny circle revolve earth's little high and low. God's high is a steadfast point. It is here: in the centre of this strange thing you do not understand, this thing you call yourself, the divinely-human heart.

Mine is a true story. It is a story of high life as they call it. It is also a story of the life which is highest of all.

A moment's patience! We shall be coming to the funny part presently. Is it my fault if the comedy begins at the wrong end? So much the better for the other end, the right.

The departure-bell clangs suddenly upon the silence. A score of drowsy figures creep forth from twilight corners into the radiance of a clear October afternoon.

Yes, it was on the 6th of October that the old Belgian came to Deynum. My birthday, as it happens, my fifteenth birthday. Or was it the fourteenth, Wendela?

From where she sits by the window, in the fading summer sunset, mending one of Baby Gertrude's socks, Wendela tells me that she herself was twelve years old at the time. Then it must have been my fourteenth birthday, dearest. Yet what does the trifling date concern us? It is all so long ago, but that it is to-day.

On that sixth of October, then, somewhere towards the first sink of the sun down a white-blue autumn sky, a hackney-cab drew up, with a farewell rattle, in front of an outlying Amsterdam railway-station, away on the desolate dyke. The silver daylight rested cold upon the wooden shed, upon the great grey square, with its solitary kiosque, upon the dull expanse of water beyond. Across the loneliness a cruel little wind came persistently blowing. Inside the building a sudden bell rang out, with the very insolence of noise.

"This is not enough, sir," said the cabman. He said it gently, for the Dutch remain calm under injustice.

The old gentleman who had alighted from the vehicle continued his stolid ascent of the station-steps. His servant, preparing to follow, paused on the pavement, in a confusion of wraps and traps. It was the servant who had proffered the offending coin.

A Dutch railway-station is a scene of unruffled repose, inside and out. Half a dozen porters, in white blouses and brass badges, leant immovable by the entrance, sleepily perceptive. The platform-bell stopped with a jerk, and in the stillness of the square the solitary cab stood out against its own clear shadow, with its cab-like air of sudden collapse.

"Not enough," repeated the driver, without raising his voice. The Dutch are as obstinate as they are gentle. He held up the half-florin he had received, between greasy finger and thumb, in the face of Heaven and the half a dozen porters.

"No, mynheer, it is not enough," chimed in the youngest of the porters. The elder five said nothing; they understood that information from a porter should never be gratuitous.

The valet cast a timid scowl after the receding figure of his master. Then, motioning back all slow offers of assistance, and balancing his load of luggage as best he might, he laboriously extracted a whole florin from a little black velvet purse and handed it to the cabman. The purse, with its fat embroidered cross, looked queerly suggestive of an undersized offertory-bag.

"Thank you," said the cabman, almost audibly, as he

2

drove off. He did not say: "This is more than enough." He was only a human cabman.

"Ten per cent.," muttered the servant, in French, and hurried away into the station. The white porters stared passively in front of them. They could understand neither the too little nor the too much.

The old gentleman, meanwhile, had progressed straight across the entrance-hall. There was a convenient passage to the platform here, which officialism had reserved for luggage. Sub-officialism called out.

The stranger pointed a careless cane in the direction where his servant might have been. He was a distinguished-looking man, tall and straight, well oiled and well brushed, with a magnificent white moustache, and superlatively clad in a light-yellow ulster, such as young fellows wore in those days.

"A prince," said one guard, by the gate, in an awe-struck growl.

"Pshaw," grumbled his comrade, a bilious man without any predilections. "Prince or Pope, he had no right to pass through here; barring he had been a portmanteau, which he wasn't."

"Perhaps he was an Englishman," said the first guard. "Englishmen may do whatever they like. And they do it."

The object of their unwilling admiration turned neither to right nor left. His movements were those of a man in a trance. His eyes were set in that glassy stare which sees nothing that is near.

A line of empty carriages was drawn up along the platform, waiting. He got into one of them, and closed the door. A silver-braided somebody sprang forward and opened it again. The old gentleman awoke to the action, and flushed.

At that moment the station-bell rang out afresh. "On sonne le départ," he said aloud. "Eh bien, I am ready to

go. But not thus, great God! Not *thus.*" And large
beads of perspiration stood out upon his forehead.

The deserted platform now began rapidly to fill. Little
groups went wandering by, with bags and bundles; a bright
provincial dress shone out from time to time among the
shoddy waterproofs. Presently a scrubby, shoppy individual slipped into the compartment, an open paper of
grapes in his hand.

The stranger passed out and wrenched open the first
door within his reach. But once more a conductor interposed. " This compartment is reserved, monsieur, in case
any of the directors—"

" It is the only one takable and I take it," replied the
old gentleman, still in French. "Antoine," he turned
fiercely upon his valet, who had just succeeded in finding
him, " you blockhead, where are you? Pay for all the
places, and see that they leave me in peace."

" If monsieur would but inform me where it is his intention to betake himself—" began the valet, with a slight
stutter over the word " Monsieur."

The old man hesitated on the carriage-step. " Get your
tickets," he burst out, with unreasoning fierceness, " as
far as the train goes. And see that they leave me in
peace."

No further molestation was offered him. At a few hurried words from the frightened valet, the protesting officials
fell back, with discreet glances of half-vexed curiosity.
" These great personages!" said the inspector, shrugging
his shoulders, and with his own hand he brought a card,
marked " Engaged."

" This is not for Belgium? This train?" asked the old
man, rousing himself.

" Certainly not, your Highness. The Belgian train does
not leave till 6.40. This one is just starting. Might I
ask—"

" My valet! My valet will tell you," replied the old

man, with a repellant gesture. "Morbleu, cannot you leave me in peace?"

They bustled in Antoine, still fumbling his change, and expostulating with everybody. Another moment and the train was off.

"I have tickets to the frontier, Monsieur le Marquis."

The old man took no notice. His face, under its careful make-up, was hideous with the horror of his thoughts.

The valet remained standing at the farther end of the railway-carriage, steadying himself against the side with an air of respectful indifference. Presently he drew a couple of small note-books from his pocket, and began scribbling assiduously in them. One especially appeared to claim much of his attention; it was lettered "Debtor and Credi-tor" in dull gold.

The train ran on swiftly through the ashen twilight. All around, the flat country lay brown and bleak. Not a sound disturbed the listening silence, except once when the old man broke into a shuddering groan. The valet looked up quickly, then down again, and went on with his scribbling.

"Listen," said the Marquis at last, abruptly, speaking as if he dreaded equally both silence and speech, "I may as well tell someone. I am dying."

A long stillness. "I am dying—hein?"

"I regret it sincerely for Monsieur le Marquis."

"Ha, polisson, you will regret it for yourself." Having once cast forth his secret, the sick man seemed to find relief in abuse of his companion. He heaped up angry words for some moments longer. The valet stood silent, ticking his pencil against the cover of his pocket-book. And the train ran smoothly on.

"You will gain nothing by my death. Do you understand?"

"I have always understood that perfectly, Monsieur le Marquis." And the train ran smoothly on.

Then a station was reached. During the long halt that ensued a number of inquisitive glances were attracted by the label in the window, a most unusual sight in Holland. People lingered near, a-tiptoe, peering. The valet stared back insolently, screening his master.

When the train was once more rushing forward, away among the fields, the Marquis resumed, with his eyes on the window beside him: "At least you might have asked how long."

"As it pleases Monsieur le Marquis," said the valet.

Again a heavy pause. And, beneath the deepening shadows, an increasing sense of chill. Miles upon miles of quiet meadows and monotonous cattle. The Marquis did not see them as he gazed. He saw nothing but that death-warrant he had heard an hour ago, writ large across the steadfast heavens. And the weight of his solitude became unbearable to him.

"That cabman?" he began anew. "Did you pay him more than his proper fare?"

"No, Monsieur le Marquis," said the valet.

"It is good. I should have deducted the sum from your wages."

"So I told myself, Monsieur le Marquis."

But Antoine smiled softly, as he fingered the little account-book in his pocket. And he breathed on the pane before him, and wrote "ten per cent." across it with his finger, and gently rubbed the letters out, as the smooth train flew on. He did not look round again until a quick succession of gasps attracted his calm attention. Even then he did not turn immediately. He was hardly an evil man. He was only a menial. What sympathy of sorrow should he dare to have in common with his arrogant lord?

The Marquis was lying back, faintly struggling with the tightness of his collar and cravat. His features seemed wrenched awry in the violence of his pain. "We must

stop," he whispered, "at the next station. I can go no farther. Stop!"

The valet drew near, helplessly striving to help. "But
where then—?" he began, and checked himself.

"Where? Does it matter?"—the sufferer's voice rose
to a momentary scream and immediately died down again.
"Anywhere. Only stop."

They remained facing each other in the long grey sunset, the servant uncertain, annoyed, swaying to and fro in
the continuous motion; the master crushed down among
his foppish finery, vainly hoping to beat back the fierce
flame from his breast.

At last the engine slackened its pace, and drew up with
a thud. Antoine thrust his head out into the sudden hush.
An open shed stood forlorn, amid the shadow-smitten landscape, by the glistening rails.

"This is a station—this? A village?" cried the valet.

"Jawel, mynheer," replied a voice.

"Quick!" murmured the Marquis; "open the door.
Quick. Before they start again!"

The valet still delayed for a moment, with his hand
nervously trying the lock. "And the name?" he called.

The guard came running up in astonishment. "You
are mistaken!" he cried. "This is nothing. This is Deynum."

The old man started slightly as the name reached his
ears. "Deynum," he repeated; "of all places! That de-
cides it." He stumbled to his feet. "Deynum! That
must mean little Reinout. Here or anywhere. And what
does it matter where, when the final summons comes!"

The shrill station-bell rang out its sudden warning
across the listening fields.

CHAPTER II.

" REINOUT!"

Count Hilarius went across to the window and called to his son. It was a dull, sombre-curtained window, opening out upon the long, dull city-garden of a dull house at the Hague. The room was a "study," so-named from the directories and Government almanacks which slept, uncut, on their shelves, against the wall.

Count Hilarius smoothed his fair moustache, and a flush played across his cheeks. He cast a gratified look at his reflection in the window-pane, and a still more delighted one down on the document in his hand.

" Reinout! Come here immediately. I have something to tell you. Something you will like to hear."

The boy in the distance, who had been stooping over a rabbit-hutch, turned in hasty obedience to this reiterated summons and came running towards the house. As he ran, he continued to fondle a cumbersome black bunny, which hung, jammed up most miserably against his jacket, incessantly twitching its little pink nose.

" I couldn't come at once, papa," he shouted. " This animal had got its paw caught in the netting, and I had to unfasten it. Poor beastie. Poor beastie." He squeezed the rabbit energetically. " I hate rabbits all the same," he added. " I shall give mine away on my birthday. Greedy creatures. They're no good to nobody but themselves."

" And a very wise philosophy," replied his father laughing. " Look here, Reinout; something very important has happened. You're too young to understand about it rightly. Still, you can easily see that I am pleased."

"I shall be fourteen next week, papa," said Reinout. Then a sudden burst of flame came pouring across his southern eyes. "Are we to go back to Brazil?" he asked. And dropped his rabbit.

"Far better than that—" the boy made a dash at the skipping, crouching quadruped—"We shall never leave Holland again. For here, in my hand—" Count Hilarius's voice and countenance dropped in solemn unison—"I hold my nomination to the Royal Household. Child, your father will henceforth spend much of his time in attendance on the King."

He called out the final words, somewhat crossly, after his retreating offspring. But Reinout leaped back at a bound.

"Oh how splendid!" said Reinout.

The Count smiled a complacent little smile.

"Monsieur de Souza always says," continued the boy enthusiastically, [he was quoting his tutor], "that that's what I must do when I grow up. Serve the King! There's nothing else worth doing in these days, he says. And you remember, the king can do no wrong, papa. So he will always be able to tell you exactly what is right."

"Child, how stupidly you sometimes talk. I am not to be Prime Minister, thank Goodness. I am appointed one of the Lord's Sub-Comptrollers of the Household. There; that is what you can tell your playmates. A Lord Sub-Comptroller of the Household. There are two of them. It sounds rather nice; does it not?"

And he walked away from the window, pleasantly lingering over the delightful words. Then, with one of the quick twists peculiar to his nervous figure—Count Hilarius was never more irritable than when gratified—he turned to say sharply:

"Don't talk nonsense about Brazil. You would like to

live out in the country—wouldn't you?—here in Holland, in a beautiful Castle with parks and pleasure-grounds, quite different from this poky bit of garden, where you could have dogs, and a pony, and lots of other pets?"

"Oh a pony!" cried the son, overhearing the rest. "Are you going to give me a pony for my birthday? I don't want any other dog than Prince."

"No, not just yet. But if ever I get—Deynum, you shall have one. There, run away now. I have letters to write."

"To mamma?" asked the boy.

"Amongst others. Why do you ask? Do you want me to tell her to come back?"

"No; it is not that. I was thinking she would like to hear that Prince's leg is well again."

"Oh, rubbish. You had better write to her yourself."

"I?" said the boy. "Why?" And he ran away—he always either ran or crawled—with the rabbit against his cheek, overflowing his shoulders.

At the farther end of his dusty playground he stopped abruptly. "How splendid!" he repeated, and then he sat down on the bench by the single apple-tree, to think it out.

The news had overwhelmed him, little eighteenth-century royalist that he was. Of the strange education which his parents had decreed should be his, more anon; suffice it to say at present that its central idea had been the pomps and majesties of the Crown and its dependent Coronets, the glory of the Sun and of the Stars. "Make a gentleman of him, not a scholar," his father had said to the old Chevalier de Souza. And with Count van Rexelaer a gentleman meant a man of the world.

"Tell your playmates." Reinout reflected. Boy-friends —chums—he had none. Away in Petropolis, where his father had helped, in a small way, to represent the Court of the Netherlands, his child-life had been one of absolute lordship among a confusion of servants and animals, with

Monsieur de Souza ever ready to instruct him how to use, without abusing, his birthright of supremacy. And during the succeeding half-dozen years at the Hague—school being forbidden by the ex-diplomat's theories—although he had certainly come into contact with a number of his equals, at fencing-classes, dancing-classes, riding-schools, etc., the barrier of his isolation had always been maintained. "Seek acquaintances and avoid friends," was one of his father's favorite sayings. "You want stepping-stones, not stumbling-blocks. I have known a man ruined for life by one friend."

Reinout, then, was steered clear of all compromising connections, high or low. "But I may give my old rocking-horse to the coachman's children?" And white-headed Monsieur de Souza smiled down fondly on his impetuous pupil: "Most certainly, mon petit, you must always be very gracious to the coachman's children." But that was long ago.

Reinout got off the seat again. "Prince," he called out, "Prince!" He was not intending to whisper his story to the dog, he was too old for that; but in all moments of superabundant feeling our thoughts most naturally flow out to whatever we love best. The dog did not make his appearance, however, and Reinout, after referring to his watch to make the agreeable discovery that lessons were still distant, sank back dreamily, letting the massive gold time-keeper fall loose in his lap.

With this treasure, too costly an one for his age, was connected the sole eventful episode of his dignified young existence. He loved to recall it. He loved the watch next best after Prince, because Prince was alive. But then so, to some indistinct extent, was the watch.

The first summer after the return from South America had been spent at the Belgian sea-side resort of Blankenberghe. On one broiling July afternoon, when his more reasonable elders were dozing, Reinout, impervious to heat as only children can be, had slipped out for a good run with his hoop, beneath the blazing firmament, along a quiet, dusty lane. He had progressed for a long distance, in warmth and loneliness, when suddenly a turn of the road had brought him face to face with a swiftly advancing rider. The start, and an unexpected slope of the ground, had caused him to lose control over his bounding toy, and he saw it, a few yards in front, making straight for the horse's legs. In one flash he had realized the danger to the rider and had flung himself after it, with set teeth, straining beyond his strength. Then had come a terrible rush of two seconds, a whirlwind of sand, and a great crash of thunder, as he fell aside and rolled over with the hoop in his arms. After the first moment of dazzlement, he had awakened to the fact that the horseman had drawn rein beside him, an old gentleman, high and haughty, on a magnificent charger, in a halo of dust.

"I beg your pardon, sir. I am very sorry," said Reinout, sitting up.

Of these words the old gentleman took no immediate notice. "Why did you throw yourself under my horse's feet?" he asked.

"The hoop, monsieur. I had to stop it. I couldn't— I am very sorry."

"Of course. Most children would have stood and stared. Do you always know your duty and"—with an amused smile—"risk your life in doing it?"

No answer but a puzzled look.

"Where do you come from, little fool? What is your name?"

"From Brazil, monsieur. Reinout van Rexelaer. I mean I am a Hollander. I am very sorry."

The horse gave a plunge for which, this time, Reinout was in no wise responsible. "You are a brave boy," said the rider presently. "It is good you are a small one, for I jumped you as you fell. So your name, of all others, is Rexelaer."

" Yes, monsieur," acquiesced Reinout ; " but, if you please, I did not do it on purpose."

The stranger sat looking down upon him for a moment. Then he said thoughtfully:

" I wonder—never mind. Here, catch hold! As a memento of our meeting. And remember: 'A gentilhomme devoir fait loi.' Good-bye."

Reinout remained alone in the road, still seated on his hoop, white and shabby, the beautiful watch in his lap.

" What a lie I gave him to remember me by," reflected the stranger, as he rode rapidly away. " Well, these lies are the pillars of society. A fine fellow, though I was foolish to give him my watch. Of course it is her child. The world is positively becoming too small to turn round in. I shall go back to Saint Leu to-night."

Reinout had kept his present, for—somewhat to his father's vexation—no effort had been successful in discovering the donor. By a storm of tears he had even extorted permission to wear it daily. He was immensely proud of it. And of the grand old gentleman, his mysterious acquaintance. And of: " A gentilhomme devoir fait loi."

Count Hilarius had finished his letters, and was re-perusing the last. It was addressed to his Countess, at Spa, whither she had betaken herself for a course of the waters, the state of her nerves not permitting her son to accompany her. His father was willing enough for him to remain. In his own manner, and for his own ambitious reasons, Count van Rexelaer was deeply attached to his only child and heir.

" Now more earnestly than hitherto"—the Count had written—"I shall make every effort with regard to Deynum. I *must* succeed. It has been the principal object of my life, as you know, and, at last, after all these years of economy there is money enough." " Bye-the-bye!" remarked Count Hilarius, when he came to this passage, and he rose and rang the bell. "Go to the Hotel des Etrangers, if you please, and ask whether Mynheer Strum, if he be in, could call in the course of the evening."

"To the hotel—I beg your pardon, sir?" said the man.

"I will write down the name for you; that will be better," replied his master suavely. And he did so, and then he added a postscript to the Spa letter: "At this moment I have a better chance than ever of acquiring Deynum." Then he stopped. "Pooh; she doesn't care as I do. How could she?" he said. His son's voice came wafted to him from the garden. And he smiled.

Ten minutes later he himself was on his way to the place whither he had dispatched his servant. He found the man waiting in the hotel-entry. "No use delaying till this evening," he said half-apologetically. And the servant, knowing his master, touched his cap and departed.

Mynheer Strum was in his room, an hotel-bedroom on the top floor. "If Mynheer would enter the reading-room;" but Mynheer preferred to go up. The stairs were dark, and the apartment was modest, as befitted its temporary occupant, a young country-notary who had just succeeded to his father's practice. This personage, as his visitor entered, rose lingeringly from the bed upon which he had been lounging, a big, ungainly creature, with red hair, red hands and red, spectacled eyes, his whole frame-work suggestive of bones out of place.

"I am Count Rexelaer, upon whom you called a week ago—" began the ex-diplomat.

"I remember," interrupted the Notary. "Take a seat, Mynheer the Count," and he pushed forward the one unencumbered chair, without any effort to tidy the others, as he propped himself up against the side of the bed.

"I was too much occupied with other important matters at the time to give your communication due consideration. Since then I have studied it more closely. I shall instruct my Notary to write to Baron Rexelaer, as you propose."

"Do," said the Notary, cracking his prominent knuckles. A youthful habit which his fond mother had never even observed.

Count Rexelaer's face showed a little surprise, no vexation. "If I understand the matter rightly," he continued, "you are acting in Baron van Rexelaer's interest?"

"No, Mynheer."

"But, surely, though I am sincerely obliged to you—"

"I am acting in nobody's particular interest, not even my own. As it happens, they all coincide."

"Still, I can easily conceive that the Notary of Deynum must regard the lord of the manor—my cousin, if I may so venture to call him—with feelings of peculiar—peculiar—"

"Do not say 'obligation,' Mynheer," interposed the other irritably. "I owe Mynheer your Cousin—" a sneer flashed through the last two words—"nothing beyond the deference due to his position. Me he owes—thanks to my father's good-nature—a very long bill. Please do not misunderstand me. I have nothing against the family at Deynum. On the contrary, a man does not easily break loose from his earliest prejudices, and I feel for the Baron at the Castle a good deal of what my parents have taught me to feel. I wish him well. I heartily wish to assist him. And that is why I came to—you."

There was a world of youthful arrogance in his words. Count Rexelaer rose, smiling. "Quite so," he said. "Well, I shall have the letter forwarded immediately. And I trust you to advise Baron Rexelaer for the best." He had caught the sneer; he did not again speak of "my cousin." But he smiled again.

"For the best," repeated Strum, "most certainly. Which is also your best, Mynheer the Count, as I hope you will remember later on." He got away from the bed and went, as an afterthought, to open the door for his visitor. "I must congratulate your Excellency," he said in his awkwardest manner "on the result of your preoccupation of last week."

"How do you know?" asked Count Rexelaer, stopping, in genuine surprise, on the little landing.

"I heard it talked of at the 'White' Club."

"Ah, you go there?"

"Only on business. I hate such places. My stay here is over, and I return to Deynum to-night."

"Indeed? Then I was fortunate. Bon voyage."

"I thank your Excellency."

"Not Excellency." Count Hilarius paused again, this time in the dim light of the ladder-like staircase. "That is altogether a different thing. Allow me to explain. Excellency is a title reserved for the very highest charges only. I am appointed a Lord Comptroller of the Household. There are two. But they have by no means the title of Excellency."

"I am infinitely obliged to you for the information, Mynheer the Count," replied Strum; and then he closed his door. "I did not tell him *how* they talked of it," he thought. And then he mimicked the Count's manner. "Allow me to explain. I am appointed a Lord Comptroller of the Household. Bah, what a fool my father was! And how one learns to despise them all."

Count Rexelaer, meanwhile, went skipping blithely home. "So it is talked of already," he told himself. "Everywhere. And this foolish fellow called me Excellency." Ah well, excelsior! Someday the greater glory will outshine the less. Who used to say that, by-the-bye? Oh, old Sir Percy Skefton at Rio. I suppose it was a quotation from somebody."

A few days later Baron Rexelaer van Deynum, who, by-the-bye, was in no way related to his namesake, the Count, received a letter from the Hague. He frowned over it, and crumpled it, and crushed it away in his pocket. And there he remembered it.

CHAPTER III.

On the evening which brought the Marquis to Deynum, Baron Rexelaer had been down to the village. "Good-evening, Landheer," [*] said a peasant, touching his cap.

The old Baron did not hear. He walked slowly, stooping forward, and his hands, which held a paper, were folded behind his back. He was a man nearer sixty than fifty, old-fashioned in appearance and apparel, a man of clear-cut features, which had been still further sharpened by the delicate chisel of Care.

The peasant, an old man also, turned to stare after his master with leisurely surprise. Then he shook his head lengthily as he resumed his slouching way.

The road was a long one. It came creeping down, white and thin, from the wooded hillocks against the dim horizon, and stretched itself, as one that takes possession, right across many miles of purple heath; then it broadened out, straight and hard, past the village, and curled away into nothing among the distant trees of the park.

The village lay, trim and prosperous, red-roofed and green-shuttered, in two rows, behind equal strips of narrow garden, on each side of the road. These patches of ground, though chiefly devoted to cabbages and cauliflowers, shone bright here and there in great splotches of crimson and violet. The gardens were silent. The cottages were silent. Only, occasionally, some humble figure, in white cap and print-

---

Lord of the Soil, equivalent to Laird.

gown, would come running out from a half-open door, and
hurry round to the back with a pail or a platter. On a
small green, over which the church rose gaunt and bare, a
little knot of urchins cowered, chatting sedately. They
stumbled to their feet, in a languid manner, as the lord of
the land went by, and jerked their caps in half a dozen va-
ried postures of clumsiness.

He had not noticed them. Yet, at this point, he paused,
and, slowly turning, took a deliberate survey of the village,
from the windmill which stands at the entrance, like a
towering sentinel, its great brown sails becalmed upon the
pale blue air, to the little low-thatched cottage, asleep at
the farther end, against the park-enclosure—the lame cob-
bler's cottage, which looks, in its deep-sunk humility, as if
it had pulled the roof over its eyes for shame.

It was very short and thin, this village. And around it
heath and woods spread very far and wide. An ashen dulness fell slowly settling upon all things, such as follows
when the shadows lengthen over the deep gold of a sunlit
autumn day. A chill little wind, from nowhere, began flat-
tening out the soft air.

" My village," said the old lord's thoughts; and the
paper crackled between his nervous hands. All Deynum
was his. It was little Deynum. To him it was neither big
nor little. It was all Deynum.

Beyond the village, as has been already said, the road
led away into the castle-grounds. You found yourself suddenly among the tall trees, on both sides, in the half-light
shaded and solemn. A moment ago you could still have
seen them rising, from the flat fields all around, in a great
bouquet of rounded verdure, like an offering from earth to
her Maker. The park was not large, compared to many
others, but its wide-spreading oaks and beeches were reck-
oned among the oldest in Holland. It was open to the
public road, excepting for a deep, dry ditch alongside, and
presently you happed upon the avenue, which, without

3

lodge or gate or even stone of warning, stretched broad and stately from before your sight to a dark-brown spot in the distance—the house. The owner of the place—for as such the world still regarded him—turned gently in the direction of home. It was colder here, under the great trees. He shivered slightly.

A pretty peasant-girl, bright and healthy, with a face of " milk and blood," came tripping down a side-path. "Good-evening, Landheer," she said. But she also got no answer; she threw up her dainty nose indignantly, and repeated the words in a higher key. The old gentleman started, and coloured over his thin cheeks.

"Good-even, good-even, Lise!" he said hurriedly, re-calling now the words he had at first ignored. "I had not noticed you; I am sorry for it. You look prettier than ever, little maid. How goes it with the bridegroom?"

"The bridegroom is well enough, Mynheer the Baron," replied the girl, laughing. "Were his pockets as full as his cheeks, there would be no cause to delay the wed-ding."

"Many things would be easier, girl," said the old man musingly, "did purses not run dry."

"But we hope, nevertheless, to trouble Father Bulbius before St. John comes round again." The girl had the privilege of her good looks, and she used it. "Perhaps your Worship will deign to dance at the wedding," she said.

"Yes, yes," the Baron gave hasty answer; "good-even, my child! Tell your father I have spoken to the bailiff. He can have that stroke of land he asked for. Good-bye!" and he resumed his thoughtful walk. "Dance," he re-peated; "the very word, forsooth. Other dolls will be set a-dancing,* before that time comes round."

He struck aside—half-way down the avenue—into an

---

* Dutch idiom.

alley of soaring chestnuts, broadest green, with an occasional dab of golden orange, as if an early imp of autumnal mischief had frolicked along the trees. At the farther end of this alley—"the Holy Walk," they call it—hidden away in the leafy silence of the woods—sleeps a small grey chapel, ivy-covered, fern-surrounded, an almost perfect bit of early Gothic, fairly well-preserved.

Its oaken door stood ajar; the old Baron pushed softly through, from the ashen calm of the park into the dusky repose of the sanctuary.

A little greystone chapel, with half a dozen stained-glass windows, a chapel of the dead, every available space upon its narrow floor and walls heaped up with monumental records in marble, metal or wood. A Roman Catholic chapel, as shown by its ornamented altar, which bore an ivory crucifix and two vases of pale-white roses, pure and fragrant. Over the altar, amidst a blaze of colour, and furthermore, in corners and cornices, on monuments and praying-stools,—or and argent upon a field of sinople, protruding one above the other from either side of the shield,—the two lion's paws with uplifted swords, the Coat of the Rexelaers. And under the Coat the motto: Ipsa glorior infamia. I glory in my shame.

Stumbling forward in the heavy twilight, the old noble sank down reverently at the altar-steps. He buried his face in his hands, which still held the crumpled paper, and his cheeks moved nervously, in the silence of his prayer. It was all very peaceful and hushed, but for a faint soughing, from time to time, in the trees. A squirrel peeped in for a moment, with bright, inquisitive eye, and then scampered away in alarm—awe-struck by the stillness.

The Baron van Rexelaer was praying for himself, in his weary middle age, for the few still near and dear to him, for the great name he bore so weakly. He was praying for the illustrious dead, his goodly heritage that none could take from him, for the old home, fast sinking away into the marsh of social ruin, for the villagers of Deynum, his children every one!

The little chapel was heavy with the petition.

From behind the plates on which their pompous dignities stand graven the dead lords of the soil came slipping forth, in their armour and slashed doublets, in their long robes and ruffles, noiselessly crowding together, as they rapidly filled—with bended knee and head—the small space round the last scion of their line. Reinout Rexelaer sank forward to the ground, and his prayer came fast and thick :

"Oh, let it go up, my God! Blessed saints in heaven, pray for me that it go up at last!"

The "it" was the American money-market.

Presently, his orisons being concluded, the Baron quitted the chapel, and climbed to a rustic seat a little beyond, on the top of a mound which we, in our pancake-like flatness, have dignified with the name of "The Mountain." You get a good view of the Castle from here. But by the time the Baron reached the spot, nothing much was distinguishable beyond a confused mass of angles and gables, a greater darkness against the dark, and, standing out above it all, still clearly visible,—as it often is for miles around, whenever you get a break in the foliage,—the great ball of the summit as borne by Atlas, for full three hundred years, upon his never-wearying shoulders.

A rest upon "The Mountain" formed the invariable finale of the Baron's afternoon walk. The rural postman purposely passed by it, on his way through the grounds, for of late the arrival of the evening mail had become the one important event of Mynheer van Rexelaer's long day. He sat and waited. Alas, the nights were lengthening downwards, dark and chill. Soon it would be too late to decipher anything.

No need of daylight to make out the crumpled paper

lying upon his knees. He had re-read it frequently, and always angrily, within the last three days.

" HIGH AND NOBLY-BORN HEER : I take the liberty, acting for the High-Born * Heer Count Rexelaer, my client, to re-open a correspondence which your Nobleness closed a couple of years ago. Count Rexelaer's reason for wishing me to do so is that it has occurred to His High-Born Count-ship that circumstances may have supervened of late which might modify your views of his original offer, were he now to repeat it. His High-Born Countship therefore requests me to inform your Nobleness that he is still as willing as formerly to enter into negotiations for the purchase of the Castle and Manor of Deynum."

The letter was signed by a Hague Notary, Klarens—old Klarens who did everything for the Court people in those days. It was dated October 3rd.

The old Baron knew all about Count Rexelaer of the Hague. He did not believe in Count Rexelaer.

" He has heard of Borck's offer to buy the Chalk-house Farm," reflected the Baron bitterly, for the fiftieth time. " He might have waited to hear that I shall refuse it."

And then his thoughts wandered to Lise, whose father lived at the Chalk-house Farm. He was annoyed with him-self for having overlooked her salute.

" I am forfeiting my position too soon," he said bitterly. " I must look to it. Trouble deprives a man of everything, excepting of himself."

And then the muffled tread of the postman absorbed his attention, as it came twisting up among the trees. The man stopped and slung round his bag.

" Nothing but the evening-paper, Baron," he said, " and a letter for Mevrouw."

---

* For some mysterious reason " High-Born," on the Continent, is a more exalted title than " High and Nobly-Born."

The evening-paper was all the Baron wanted. He fumbled tremulously in his pockets for a box of matches he knew to be there. He could not find them. The postman lingered, uncertain how to help.

"Go," said the old man impatiently. "Go on with your work. I mean, thank you, Jacob. Good-night."

Left in peace, he found his matches, and, bending over the wooden bench, under the whispering of the mighty trees, struck a light. He passed it rapidly down the column devoted to the day's Amsterdam Exchange.

"Down again, by God!" he said. And then the match went out, and all was dark.

CHAPTER IV.

THE REXELAERS OF DEYNUM.

THERE have always been Rexelaers of Deynum. There are still. You can read about them in the Annuaire de la Noblesse des Pays-Bas. But probably you know.

If you do not, you may as well lay down this book: it does not address itself to you. It is written for a set. Ours.

The Rexelaers have intermarried with some of the great continental families, and are well-known in Germany and France. In fact, they themselves are—or were—a great continental family. For Willem van Rexelaer (grandson of the founder of the house), who remained with the Roman King Willem of Holland all through the long siege of Aix la Chapelle, was rewarded, on the day of his master's coronation, by the bestowal of the somewhat unwilling hand of the heiress of the Hohenthals, whose father and brother had fallen on the opposite side. It was this marriage which brought the fief of Hohenthal Sonnenborn into the family, making the head of the house a Count of the Holy Roman Empire, with the title of "Erlaucht." But that exalted rank fell away from them, some two and a half centuries later, when they got into trouble with the Habsburger Maximilian. There is a long correspondence in the Archives at Brussels showing how they plotted to get it back again, and perhaps they might have succeeded, had not Anne van Rexelaer joined the Compromise of the Nobles. Good Catholic as this powerful nobleman was, he would hardly have escaped the fate of Counts Egmont and Hoorn, had he not claimed, and obtained, the protection of his mother's cousin (and his own god-father), the Great Constable of France. You may look up all that in Motley, if you care to. It is hardly worth while.

Most truly they had been an illustrious family. At the time of this story they had dwindled down to a quiet old man, his wife and only daughter. And, shameful to relate, they were poor.

Ah, those were different times when Ruwert van Rexelaer sat enthroned in the Castle at Deynum, with thirty horses in his stables, and seventeen serving-men before his side-board, in green and gold. And when Rovert van Rexelaer, his brother—the renegade; God forgive him! the *Protestant*—having followed, like his ancestor of Hohenthal, another Dutch William to the conquest of another kingdom, rejected, in his pride, the alien honours that monarch would have conferred upon him. "I will make you a peer of England," said William of Orange. "You shall be Baron Butterworth!" "Of William the Third's creation," replied Rovert, with low obeisance, and sank back in disgrace. He did not want a peerage. What he wanted, and had schemed for, like his ancestors, was the revival of the Roman Countship, not for himself but for the elder brother, whose doors he could never darken again. If ambition had prompted his secession—as some still think it did—it could hardly have been hope of personal aggrandisement.

The Rexelaers had stuck to the old faith. And, as far as enforced retirement goes, they had suffered for their constancy. Thereby hangs the tale of the strange motto beneath their arms. When Anne van Rexelaer's son Eduard found himself deprived of his dignities by Prince Maurice, successor to "the Silent"—for so did they still go dropping between two stools—he withdrew in high dudgeon to his castle and carved over its portal the sentence : "Ipsa glorior infamia." "I glory in my disgrace." They left him to

his glory. And the words may be seen this day where
Eduard van Rexelaer placed them.

The device, therefore, like most heraldic mottoes, is
comparatively modern. It seems all the more so, if you
accord credence to the story of the coat itself. You are
asked to believe—not by me, mind you, though my son has
the genuine Rexelaer blood in his veins, however spurious
mine may be—you are asked to believe that the Christian
maiden Wendela, having been confined by a heathen prince
in his stronghold on the Rhine, was delivered by a lion,
which penetrated into her chamber, a flaming sword in
either fore-paw. An eighteenth century Rexelaer, in a wig
and a Voltairean nose, wrote a pamphlet to prove that the
story had been misunderstood. It belonged to the time of
the Crusaders, he said, not to that of the Romans
(A. D. 237), and the lion in question was no four-foot-
ed animal, but a lion-hearted knight of that surname and
crest.

The other version is the prettier one. None of the
Rexelaers have perhaps ever dared to believe it as much as
they wanted to. Nor would many of them have cared to
swear by their patron saint that their name was really derived from Rex Hilarius, this same King Hilarius having
been baptised—after an unaccountable lapse of the family
into heathenism—in 500 and something by an old French
priest who had named him in pious recollection of Bishop
Hilary of Arles. It was all very beautiful and deliciously
improbable, and one clung to it and might have died for it,
but, as to believing it—well, the Crusading ancestor, the
first Willem's grandfather, was an historic fact, and surely
he ought to have sufficed for the requirements of the proud-
est, or the vainest, heart.

And what now was left of it all? The old Baron shook
his head, as he passed over the bridge to the house. Not
that he had been recapitulating, as he went, the long history of the Rexelaers. He had no need to do so. His

heart was a burial-ground of the race, on which all the windows of his thoughts afforded an unconscious outlook.

"Mon cher," said the Baroness gently, "his Reverence has waited."

The Baron winced. He was a military veteran and had seen something of life—not much—in his day; he had never yet learned to accept a reproach from a woman, without a tendency to blush. And the Baroness was not one of those who accustom you to reproaches.

"I was delayed," replied the Baron humbly. "His Reverence will forgive a man of many occupations." He offered his arm to his wife with an odd little, old-fashioned bow, and the priest, who took life reposefully, grinned a good-humoured grin over the earnestness with which his patron created a round of meaningless duties out of the emptiness of everyday squiredom. "There are men who talk in their sleep for sheer waste of activity," the good father was wont to declare. "A better thing, in an ecclesiastic at any rate, than to sleep in his talk," the Baron had once unthinkingly made answer. And then he had filled up his guest's wine-glass, smiling an apology, as his eyelids dropped obediently under the Baroness's dignified surprise.

"Come, Wanda," said Father Bulbius, crooking his arm at as wide an angle as he could manage from the rotundity of his rusty black coat.

But the daughter of the house, a girl of twelve with a mass of brown hair and big brown eyes, drew pettishly away from him. "No, thank you," she said. "You hurt my shoulder last time, squeezing through the doorway." And she ran on in front. "I don't like priests," she said to herself in the passage.

The meal was a simple one; but for its surroundings of old plate and older oak you would have called it poor. These people belonged to that daily decreasing class who can-

not live poorly; their pomp is themselves. The Baron
would have pitied *you*, not his wife, had you noticed the
simplicity of the menu. And even fat Father Bulbius,
dearly though he loved a good dinner, was happy in the
eating of a bad one amidst the quiet dignity of immemorial
pride. Besides, was there not always the " King's Wine "
nowadays, to gladden sinking hearts? You cannot miss
hearing about the " King's Wine." The Baron was always
referring to it.

To-day, however, the Baron referred to nothing, but left
to his wife the unlaborious task of entertaining their familiar guest. The entertainment was single; for many years
it had been based, by mutual consent, upon alternate monologue.

" At last then," emphasized the Baroness, slowly shaking
her white side-curls, and the white ribbons on her white
cap, " I carry out my threat of complaining to your Reverence, though I do so with the deepest regret."

She was not really an old woman, by-the-bye, not more
than five and fifty, but her hair had been a silvery white for
nearly twenty years, and she had set herself early to wear it
gracefully. She wished to be old and to mortify the flesh.
At least so she told herself and Father Bulbius.

" So far, Madame, I am altogether with you," answered
the Father. He always said that to the Baroness Rexelaer.
" And as I was telling the Baron, I cannot understand why
my celery is not a success. I have followed out his instructions exactly." He threw himself back in his chair with a
sigh, and his amplitude seemed to ooze out all around him.
" I have constantly dug it up and put it into something else.
In April I took one of my few meat-dishes for it, and Veronica made my life a burthen to me forthwith."

He stretched out his hand for his wine-glass and laughed
heartily, and wiped his mouth.

" And the school-children, if they refuse to listen, must
be made to feel," said the Baroness distinctly.

The Father had one advantage over her, inasmuch as he poured forth his words like a torrent, while she dropped hers one by one, as from a medicine-tube. On the other hand, he would invariably flounder astray in his own multiloquence, and then she saw her opportunity and took it.

" But, then, I *did* listen," he replied. "For in May, according to the Baron's instructions—" He looked towards the Baron. The Baron looked down at his plate. The old gentleman *could* not attend. "And seven eights," he was saying to himself, "one dollar; two fifty; multiply by twelve. And seven eights—"

"I emptied out my single cucumber-frame for it. And Veronica tells me she is dying for want of cucumbers. During *centuries*, it appears, they have formed a remedy in her family for some mysterious hereditary ailment. And I feel like a murderer, Mynheer, till your head-gardener comes and tells me that the celery is dying in the cucumber-frame, and must be buried in trenches at once."

The child looked across at him with solemn eyes, and spoke for the first time. "I buried my canary, too," she said gravely. "Last week. But it was dead first."

Nobody paid any attention to her. The shaded light from the old silver oil-lamp played—gently reflected from napery and crystal—upon the four faces round the table: the sallow, serious cheeks of the little girl, and her mother's calm white brow, the priest's fat double chin, with its pimple, the Baron's bent nose, bent head, bent everything.

That little red excrescence on the Father's chin was an old acquaintance of Wendela's. She used to wonder of what it was made and why. But now she knew. For, one day, in the drawing-room—she could have pointed out the exact spot—its horrid little specks and dents had suddenly resolved themselves before her fascinated gaze into a miniature face, like the Father's. She had never lost sight of the similitude. It laughed with the Father's laugh; it frowned with his frown, and all the time he was talking, it

would wink with each movement of his chin, as much as to
say: "Don't believe him." It was a little Baby Bulbius,
as she had told her great friend and admirer, Piet
Poster. "Priests don' have babies," said matter-of-fact
Piet.

"And seven-eighths," reasoned the Baron silently with
knitted brows, "seven times two and a half, seventeen hundred and fifty. Let me fill your glass, Bulbius."

"And they pop up out of their graves almost as fast as
you bury them. If there's too much of them visible, they
lose their colour: if there's too little, they choke. No. I
am very much obliged to you, dear Baron. Besides, I believe your gardener hoped they would fail."

The child had been pondering intently. "It's a riddle,"
she said now. "What lives best for being buried? What
lives best for being buried, Papa?"

The Baron aroused himself at this direct appeal. "A
great name," he said.

The child clapped her hands with elfish glee. "Wrong!"
she cried. "Quite wrong. English sedlery."

"Celery," corrected the Baroness. "I wish you would
listen to me, Father. Surely it is a terrible thought that
the children should bring down damnation upon themselves—"

"Undoubtedly," acquiesced the Father. "But, then,
fortunately, the good God has made it so difficult for them
to do it."

"I cannot imagine your condoning their laughing in
church,"—there was the faintest tinge of vexation in the
lady's tone. The first article of their unspoken contract
precluded interruption.

"Mevrouw, I condone nothing," replied Father Bulbius
good-humouredly. "I exact penance for every sin confessed. The less confessed the better. The less that require confession, I mean, of course. The better for the
guilty party, for everybody"—he yawned. "The King's

wine is the King's wine still," he said to the baron. He did not care for the Baroness to play curate.

"Le Roi est mort; vive le Roi!" replied the Baron solemnly. He threw up his hand for the military salute and touched his wine-glass with his lips. As he did so, an old servant, who stood by the side-board, saluted too.

"Le roi est mort; vive son vin," murmured the ecclesiastic, with goggle-eyes dancing over the rim of his bumper. His pronunciation was bad. The Baron frowned. The Baron thought his sentiment was worse.

"And what, I say, is to become of discipline, if they openly laugh at the priest?"

"Huh?" ejaculated the Father, whirling round to my lady. "Who laughs at the priest?" And he glared across at Wendela. He put on a most comical look of indignation, and the pimple immediately did the same. The child could not help laughing. The priest had one of those variable india-rubber countenances which remain comical even when they cry. They are made in a limited number of tints. His was purple. The olive-green are best.

"I have been striving for the last ten minutes," said the Baroness complacently, triumphant in her ultimate success, "to tell your Reverence that of late the village-children in the gallery have taken to laughing while you preach."

"But Me—Mevrouw!" spluttered his Reverence. He was really disconcerted. "I can hardly believe—"

"Yes, Gertrude, you are surely mistaken," interposed the Baron, who had at last finished his computation of the day's deficit.

"I am not mistaken, and it must be put a stop to," said the Baroness.

"It is his Reverence's own fault," said the child.

There was a general outcry. "Wendela, you forget yourself," said the mother sharply. "Wendela, little maiden, how do you mean?" asked the Baron.

"Shall I tell?" said the child, out loud. She was looking at the pimple; and the pimple winked at her.

"There's a hole in the velvet cap his Reverence wears at sermon-time," she continued slowly, "and his Reverence's hairs stick out in tufts. Sometimes they stick out in two tufts and sometimes in three. And the boys—bet." The stress she laid upon the venerable title would have been unconscionably naughty, had the Baroness not believed it impossible.

"Gracious Heavens!" ejaculated the shepherd of the school-children's souls.

"Marbles, and—lollipops, and things," she went on hastily, now thoroughly frightened at her own audacity. "Last Sunday there was only one tuft, so none of the bets could count."

The Father rumpled his grey locks in manifest distress. They formed an untidy fringe round his bald red head, and he had long insulted and despised them. He now tried to pretend that they did not belong to him. With but partial success.

"But my dear little one," said the Baron mildly, "you cannot know these things. You must be making them up."

"Papa!"—she flushed scarlet—"Papa!" In the ensuing silence, she felt that any avowal would be preferable to the imputation of untruthfulness. "Piet Poster told me," she murmured.

"For shame, Wendela," said her mother. "Let us hear no more about it. Try a fig, Father. They are not as good as Veronica's, but even hers are not equal to the figs of my youth."

"Quite so," answered the Father, who was angry with his housekeeper, suspecting some spite in her neglect of his clothes. "I am grieved, Wanda, by your intimacy with these blasphemous—I say blasphemous—children. You might be led into imitating their wicked ways." He looked quite sadly at her. The pimple puckered up its little lips and appeared ready to weep.

"Figs," said the Baroness, "require exceptional care. They are so apt to run to seed."

"Tush, my dear Father, it is not as bad as that,"—the Baron stretched out his hand to his little daughter, moved by her distress—"you can hardly imagine my Wanda wagering her dolls against the village on the growth of your hair." And he laughed softly.

But this was dreadful. Without touching the outstretched fingers, Wendela started from her chair. "I—I am afraid," she explained in a great burst of tardy tears, "there was just one little bet, Papa, the Sunday before last, with—with Piet Poster."

"Leave the room immediately," cried her calm mother, with unwonted acerbity. "Consider yourself in disgrace! Piet Poster! I am deeply sorry to think it could be possible!"

"But I—I lost, mamma," sobbed the culprit.

"That is hardly an alleviation, though certainly better than your winning. You have lost, however, a good deal more than your sweets."

"It was plums, Mamma," cried Wanda, as she fled in a tempest of angry dismay.

"I hate priests," she said to herself, in the darkness of her own room. Somehow she laid the blame of the whole miserable business on Father Bulbius's round, innocent head.

CHAPTER V.

THE STRANGER COMES TO DEYNUM.

"A PRETTY amusement indeed," said the Baroness indignantly, as the door closed on the delinquent, "for the heiress of Deynum. Gambling with her peasant-boys."

"On the subject of their pastor's wig," added Bulbius despondently.

"Poor little heiress of Deynum," said the Baron.

"You are too indulgent, Reynout. I do not want to be harsh, but there are limits."

"Indulgent?" responded her husband. "Well, why not? I would have the heiress of Deynum enjoy what happiness she can. While she can." His voice sank over the words. And it seemed as if the dim light sank with the voice, and it grew still darker in the great, dark room.

The Father gazed down at his fingers, spread out upon the table-cloth.

"Mon ami, you are out of sorts to-night. Come let us have coffee, and then you and his Reverence can play your game of écarté."

"Yes," said the Baron, with an effort; "I will ring the bell."

And then, suddenly, with an awkward jerk of the arm, he snatched from his pocket the letter which had been burning a hole in it for the last three days. "There!" he said. He flung it on to the middle of the table, as if it were hot in his hand.

The priest made an involuntary movement to pass the

4

paper on, then drew back again. The Baroness sighed, and coughed to hide the sigh.

" Fresh troubles?" she said softly. " Poor husband."

" On the contrary," the Baron smiled somewhat fiercely. " A happy deliverance. Count Hilarius van Rexelaer—so the gentleman calls himself—once more offers to purchase Deynum, as he offered a couple of years ago."

The Baroness looked contemptuous. " Is that all?" she said.

" I suppose he has heard, somehow, of Borck's proposal about the farm."

The lady's pale eyes flashed. " Rather to Borck than to that man," she said. " Even almost rather to Borck."

In spite of his trouble an amused look came into her husband's eyes. " Really?" he queried incredulously.

" Yes, yes, yes," she iterated, with vehement passion. And then she grew pale and calm again.

" But we shall sell it to neither," she added presently. " God is good."

" Beyond human hope or prayer, amen," said the priest fervently. And as he meditatively sipped his wine, his hot countenance grew solemn with an unspoken prayer for Deynum.

A knock came to the door. " There's a man sent up from the station, Mynheer," said the baron's old servant. " Fokke Meinderts, your Worship remembers, old Mother Meinderts' son. The second one, that broke his leg last autumn—"

" What does he want? interrupted the Baroness. She always interrupted Gustave. Her husband never did. " You lose half an hour a day by his meanderings," she had once remarked.

" So I do, my dear. But I gain a good deal more."

" How so?"

" A good man's affection."

" Nonsense."

"And perhaps"—this a little slily—"ten years sooner of heaven?"

"Ah!" said the Baroness.

"I will go and find out what he wants," said the Master of Deynum. He stumbled wearily to his feet, and immediately his wife's spirit soared to one of her pinnacles of sacrifice.

"Let him come in here," she commanded. "J'espère qu'il ne sentira pas trop mauvais." Gustave understood French, but his mistress considered he had no business to. And as for poor people, she approved of them in their own homes, where she diligently visited them.

The individual who was now ushered in appeared at the first moment to be a mass of revolving arms and legs. In reality he was an ordinary peasant, confused, bodily as well as mentally, by the Presence in which he unexpectedly found himself. And it seemed as if a few right arms came jerking from his shoulders, as he began:

"An't please your Worship, and the Chief says (i. e., the station-master) and I was to say as there's a dead gentleman at the station that wants to come to Deynum." He paused.

"Even the dead," said the Father with a solemn twinkle, "desire Deynum."

"Leastways, when I say 'dead,' your Reverence, I mean, as good as, or more probably so than not. He wasn't, when I left, but he would be, the Chief said, before I got here. You understand?"

"And what of this dead man, who is alive?" asked the Baron. "Was he coming here? We expect no one."

The yokel looked down at his great, dirty boots.

"Oh no, he wasn't coming here, Mynheer the Baron. He wasn't coming anywhere, because he is a foreigner. Leastways was, if he is dead. 'Tis a sin I should say it. But he can't remain in the waiting-room, and his servant wants to get him to the inn, he says. But there's only a waggonette at the inn, you know. And the Chief said he thought—if you were acquainted with the gentleman—it might be better like that, you understand."

Fokke Meinderts looked round upon the company in triumph and executed a rapid revolution, like a Catherine wheel. He felt altogether unexpectedly successful.

The Baron started up eagerly. His weary look had entirely left him. Already he saw this foreigner—this gentleman—left to die in the miserable open shed which does duty in Holland for far larger stations than Deynum.

"Of course!" cried the Baron. "I am much obliged to the station-master. Gustave! Where is Gustave? Tell them to put to the horses! I will take the landau. At once!"

"But, my dear, you are tired!" ventured his wife.

"My own, there is nobody who can understand him. It is half an hour's drive. Amuse his Reverence, while I—" The door fell to behind him.

"Dear man," said the Baroness.

"Quite so, Madame," answered Father Bulbius absently. "So far I am altogether with you."

CHAPTER VI

THE Baroness and her Priest adjourned to the drawing-room, there to await the development of what in their un-eventful life was almost an adventure. The Baroness sat down to her nightly game of "Patience," and the Priest took his place beside her, as he invariably did, when not playing écarté with the Baron. For they played écarté. He knew that it ought to have been backgammon.

But the Baron, a mild man in his pleasures, had re-tained this weakness for games with a pecuniary risk. So he persuaded the good father to stake fivepence a game, and the results of a long evening's contest were practically nil. But the Baron would get irritable none the less over his luck, and many a time had the father confessor decided to speak the terrible words "No more cards." He never did so, for his kindly heart sent a telegram to arrest them on his lips. Still, he thought it hard lines, when a few days after his sermon (in a mended cap) on the iniquity of betting, Wanda innocently asked him, as if the idea had just occurred to her, whether écarté was a form of gam-bling or not.

Has he suspected for a moment that his patron's foible had led that unfortunate gentleman astray from the courtly society of the Kings and Queens of the Card-table among the bulls and bears of the stock-exchange, he would have found it easier to settle the conflict in his own mind. The Baron preferred this large winning from Nobody. He did not like to mulct Bulbius, even of fivepence, though Bulbius, as his patron was well aware, was possessed of (modest) private means of his own.

Neither did the Baroness know anything of her husband's futile hunting-excursions in the howling wilderness afore-mentioned. Had she known, she would not have understood, and that, in itself, was sufficient excuse for his not telling her. The Baroness was one of those women who cannot be made to grasp the difference between consols and coupons. All their ideas of "bonds" and of "shares" are connected with a husband and a home. They are none the stupider for that. You could not look Gertrude van Rexelaer in the face and write her down a fool.

Nearly forty years ago—through one crowded, self-concentrated season—she had been a Court beauty. Her father, one of the few great Catholic nobles, had brought her up to the Hague from his Castle in Limburg, a part of Holland which no Hollander has ever heard of. And immediately the lovely provincial had become, at all receptions and entertainments, not "a nice," but "that nice" little girl. She stood forth an object of attraction to the other sex, of detraction to her own. In one word, her social success was complete. And one evening, at the Palace, a chivalrous Monarch, stooping to hand her a fan she had dropped in her youthful trepidation, requested the favour of a dance for a beardless and awkward young officer, who had caught his Majesty's kindly eye, as he hung dangling, forlorn, against the wall.

So did Gertrude de Heerle receive her fate from the hand of her King. The young officer turned out to be a distant connection, Reinout van Rexelaer. And a few months later the Beauty exasperated everybody, especially her father, by deliberately spurning from her the well-filled hand of a notoriously profligate suitor and accepting the better-filled heart of her handsome "cousin" Reinout. The Rexelaers always married into the family if possible, so as to get as much of their own blood as the Rubric would permit.

The pair were very poor at first, to everybody's satisfaction; and they were visibly happy, to everybody's disgust. The "everybody" were a couple of hundred men and women in society, and as few of these were happy, and none of them were poor, they had a right to protest. Presently brighter seasons came to the young Rexelaers, across a period of honest tears and mourning, when first Reinout's elder brother died, and then his father, the young people shook the tinsel-dust of the "Residency" from their feet, and the poor regimental pay out of their pockets and went to live at Deynum. They carried away with them a healthful scorn of the gas-lit glitter of that bursting bubble, which you and I, dear Vicomte, call "our world."

A period of calm prosperity followed, overshadowed by a gradually descending cloud. They had no children.

The Baroness had always been a fervent Catholic. The unfulfilled yearning for an heir deepened her piety into devotion and, as the empty years sped on, into bigotry. She sank into the hands of the priests, as an invalid is gradually fascinated by doctors, resolved to climb up into heaven and wrench down the blessing withheld. She fasted and mortified herself, and even undertook such short pilgrimages as were within her reach. She would have gone jumping to Echternach but here, for the first time, her husband interfered. So she stayed at home and sent for miraculous waters to drink and to bathe in. And she thanked heaven, whether it heard her or not, and prayed yet once more for a hearing.

Her hair had turned white some ten years after her marriage. "From moping," her husband told her, with tender reproof, but that was not so, these white heads being peculiar to the de Heerles, as you can see from the famous "Jan de Heerle" in the National Museum at Amsterdam. Baron Reinout never alluded to their common trial, except to rally his wife on her grief for it. Besides the anxiety to spare her, there was hope against hope in his heart. A Rexelaerless world? He had faith in the indispensableness of the Rexelaers.

With the whitening of her hair the last bit of colour seemed to die away from the Baroness. Her beautiful complexion had always had the pallor of marble; her eyes had been the weak point; they were faint; they grew fainter still. When the pleasures of this world fell away from her, she had taken to dressing very much in white. Her husband liked it; to her it was a compromise between the rainbow-hues of vanity and the black of religious seclusion. The villagers looked at each other, with something akin to awe as the slender figure went flitting between the trees, a vision of pureness, with the basket of charity on one arm. People began to speak of "The White Baroness" in all the country round. Perhaps she liked it. Perhaps what had been at first a natural predilection developed into a parti pris. For years she was "The White Baroness," a pure and pallid apparition, very silent, very kind to the poor and suffering, very strong- and narrow-willed. She surrounded herself with white doves and white chickens, white cats and white roses. The latter hobby, in especial, took possession of her; she could never get blossoms enough for the little Chapel in the Park. "An infant's soul as white as these," she murmured in her prayers, over and over again, in the silence of the sanctuary, and all the dead Rexelaers lay still and listened. "O spotless Virgin, a little, little infant, with a soul as white as these!"

The head-gardener at Deynum—they had a better one in those days—even succeeded in producing a new white variety which he named in her honour. She was very proud of it. Is it not written down in all the rose-growers' catalogues as "The White Baroness" to this day?

As her piety increased, she would have had all men share it, her particular form of piety, of course. And that is a difficult matter in a world whose good and evil are variously shadowed by each good man's individual eclectic light. Besides, Deynum was officially split up into two colours, Roman Catholic and Protestant. "Catholic and Beggar," the Baroness would have said. For the Romanists of Holland still daily insult their old antagonists with that most honourable by-word of "Gueux."

The Baroness pitied all beggars and would have fed them. But when they refused the communion of any other table than their own, her pity, turning under the thunder of papal anathemas, soured rapidly to wrath. And she made war upon them to drive them forth, as the Rexelaers, having themselves felt the weight of persecution, had never done before. She boycotted them, a very common thing in Holland, although rather an unfair one, because the Protestants, whether more tolerant or more indifferent, do not retaliate in this manner. And as the years went on she perfected her system of repression, cruel only to be kind. "In the choice between a son of the church and an infidel, why choose an infidel?" she asked. The Baron could not deny that she was theoretically right. But he strove practically to minimise results. "Let us be faithful in little things, dearest," said the Baroness, "we who ask so great a thing of God."

And the hot breath of persecution opened up the blossoms in cold Calvinistic hearts, as is its mission, and there was a revival. There had never been a Protestant church at Deynum, the worshippers going to the neighboring parish of Rollingen, but now it became suddenly manifest that this state of affairs could not be allowed to continue. The difficulty was how to get it altered, for all the available land in the village belonged to the Baron. A movement was set on foot, but it proved unavailing, for, even had his wife not been there to instruct him, Reinout Rexelaer would hardly have consented to so startling an intrusion. "Let them worship as they have worshipped for ages," he de-

clared. " If worship it be," added Gertrude. The dispute
spread into the newspapers. And the powerful lord of the
adjoining parish, Baron Borck, took it up. He was a man
of easy indifference in matters of religion—the more modern name is " tolerance "—but some stories of Mevrouw
Rexelaer's rigour had reached him, and his wife and daughters had petty grievances against their neighbours, and
there had been a dispute about a ditch. Baron Borck was
a Member of the States Deputed, which are a small govern-
ing body elected out of the States Provincial. He was a
man of authority and he used it in endeavour to get a De-
cree of Expropriation on the ground of general utility. But
the Baroness fought him with dogged pertinacity. " Shall
we bring down a curse upon us?" she repeated incessantly.
" We who have such especial need of a blessing?" She
dragged up the chancel-steps on her naked knees. She sent
forth angry glances from her castle turret towards the impudent Protestant steeple of Rollingen. And she sent
forth also from that same elevation, into the stormy night,
her favourite snow-white carrier-pigeon, that he might lift
up the story of her sufferings for the faith to the very
bosom of the Queen of Heaven. But the pigeon was a
nineteenth-century bird, and went back to his dovecot.

She conquered, whether by these means or others. She
carried her cause up to the Privy Council, and there she
conquered. Not a single member of that august assembly
could see any connection between a Church and a matter of
general utility.

And then the gift, so strangely, so fearfully sweet to a
hope deferred, came upon her as a reward. She accepted
it, humbly before God, triumphantly before men. In those
days of calm expectancy, with the smile of Heaven upon
her, she felt as Hebrew Hannah must have felt when the
Lord took away his handmaid's reproach. She was more
than forty years old. She had been married more than
twenty. The child was born; and it was a girl.

When they told her, she said: "God's will be done."
She said it aloud. And when they offered to bring her the
babe, she answered: "Presently." Which shows what her
heart said.

A little later its wailing cry broke in upon her faintness.
She turned her head from the wall. "Is that the little
one?" she asked. And they laid it upon her breast.

She went through the ceremony of her churching, and
she regularly attended mass. But during six months she
did not go to pray in the loneliness of the chapel, and,
throughout all that period, its altar remained destitute of
flowers. One morning she walked into the library and went
straight up to the curtain which usually hung down over
the book-shelves of the eighteenth-century Rexelaer who
had explained away the lion-myth. She pushed it aside
with resolute hand, and took down a volume—of Voltaire!
She stood turning over the pages undecidedly for a few
moments, then she shut it up with a shudder, and went
away again. Her eyes were dry and hard.

She loved her baby girl; it was not against the child
that her anger was kindled. The miraculous answer which
need not have been, yet now was, and was not an answer,
struck her in the face like a personal taunt. And she was
as one in an open boat that drifts away from the friend he
loves, beyond all loving, because that friend has cut the rope
which held him moored.

"Reinout," she said one day, before her convalescence,
while her life yet hung in danger,—"Give Baron Borck
the bit of land he wants, near the mill."

"Hush," said her husband. "You mustn't talk." He
thought her mind was wandering.

"Somehow, I don't want you to sell it. Simply give it.
Throw it in his face."

She lifted her eyes and looked at him. "You think I'm
not, not conscious," she murmured in surprise. "Reinout,
I know I'm in danger. I may be dead to-morrow. Write

to-night. A scornful letter. Tell him it doesn't—matter—how—they—pray."

And he wrote, after some hesitation. It was her answer. A defiance to High Heaven, with Death at her chamber-door.

Father Bulbius, who had bravely seconded her during the battle, opened his eyes wide with disappointment. And then he half closed them, as was his habit, and watched.

" My daughter," he said one day, after he had listened—in the confessional—to her recital of various peccadilloes, " you have difficulties of which you do not speak. The sun of your contentment does not shine as it did before."

" I am as you have always known me, Father," she answered. And he saw that that door was closed.

He waited another couple of months, and slept nine hours at night, and an hour after his noonday dinner. And of evenings, when not engaged with the Baron, he watched the Baroness's game of Patience, and he played his own little game of Patience too.

He won it on the day when the distressed Baron confided to him, as the greatest of secrets, that the Baroness had tried to read Voltaire. That evening the Father discoursed eloquently on the infidel writer, of whom he had never read a word, repeatedly regretting the speciousness of his arguments, which only your *deep* thinker, he said, could resist. In the lady's ignorance the name only stood out, a recollection of earliest eschewment, synonymous with Luther or the Devil. But her curiosity was aroused, and when she slipped into the library next morning, the volume containing " La Pucelle " came most easily to her hand. She turned from that in horror, successfully biassed by a very few pages, and took down a controversial work. These, then, were the thoughts of an infidel. And as she read, carelessly at first, his attacks upon a faith which lay dead within her, that faith awoke in its grave and cried out. These things were false. Yonder accusation was absurd.

Against this statement it could be argued— She rose from her reading with a flame in her pale eyes. She must reason about these matters with someone. Why, even a woman like herself could see the sophistry of the argument on page 105. She was rather proud of seeing it so clearly. She must tell Father Bulbius about it.

And she did. He showed her, intellectually, the evil ways of infidelity. Her woman's heart rose up against the foolish pride of feeble sense. And under ideal persecution she revived, as surely as the materially oppressed Protestants of Deynum.

"For My thoughts are not your thoughts," said the poor lady. "When one learns to understand what a godless man's thoughts are like, it is not difficult to admit that God's thoughts must be better, even when not, or when mis-, understood." The old fervour did not return to her, but there were once more "White Baroness" roses on the chapel-altar. Her almsgiving had never changed.

"Who knows what may still happen?" said the Baron, sturdily. "All things are possible with the Almighty," he said. And once when she had turned upon him, in one of their most rare dissensions and had burst out with "Not the ridiculous!" he waited until one evening in the chapel they paused, before a window gorgeous with a crimson sacrifice of Isaac. "That also was a race," he said softly, "which Heaven, in its Providence, could not allow to die out."

But the Baroness van Rexelaer had nothing in common with Sarah. Not even a liking for the children of Abraham.

CHAPTER VII.

HEUREUX EN MARIAGE.

"SHOULD you not have moved your ten on to the knave?" inquired the Father mildly. "That would have enabled you to get at your ace."

"Yes, but I wanted to free my seventh line," said the Baroness.

The Baroness's game is a very complicated one. It has the true merit of a game of Patience: like its homonym, it hardly ever succeeds.

"How well your little Carlsbad cards wear, Mevrouw," said the Father, searching, in his restless loquacity, for a subject of conversation. "You have never, I believe, been to Carlsbad?"

"No, I have never been anywhere," replied the Baroness.

"Nor have I. But I knew a young clerical colleague, who went there two years ago, for a melancholy he could far better have cured by a religious retreat at the College."

"Perhaps it was dyspepsia," suggested the Baroness. You see, she had read Voltaire.

"If so, he could have cured it by fasting. Besides, it was not the slightest use his going to Carlsbad, for he died before he got there."

"Indeed!" said the Baroness, with that sudden interest which the final catastrophe always awakens. Then she added mechanically: "How sad!"

"He died in a railway accident," continued the Father. "And the most provoking thing of all was that, when the doctors opened the body, they were unanimous in declaring that Carlsbad could never have cured him, after all."

"But that did not matter to him then," objected the Baroness.

"Perhaps not," replied Father Bulbius, doubtfully. "But somehow, it has always seemed to me so like a case of suicide, without the ghost of a reason."

The Baroness looked at the clock. A couple of logs of wood lay smouldering and flickering on the open hearth. The soft glow of the fire and the softer lamplight played over the delicate lines of the lady's face and over her slender, blue-veined hands, as she sorted her game. There was a gentleness about the warm quiet little drawing-room with its subdued, old-fashioned colours and a glamour of something almost like romance over the stately figure in grey satin with white lace collar and wrist-bands, white hair and white cap. In spite of the grey apparel which time had led her to adopt, the Baroness was the white Baroness still.

There was nothing romantic, however, about Father Bulbius, who sat doubled up by the little green card-table, his broad forehead closely knotted over the puzzle of his colleague's *felo de se*.

"He will be coming back again soon," remarked the Baroness, thinking of her departed lord.

"Hardly that," replied the Father. "He was definitely dead."

"Not definitely, I fancy. I merely understood that the station-master expected him to die."

"Oh, but excuse me, my dear lady, I remember nothing of the station-master's opinion. Though there certainly was a station-master concerned, whom everybody considered to blame. As for me, I should prefer to censure the foolish ones who go hurrying through Europe to escape from themselves. I have one insuperable objection to medicines; they all make me unwell. Trust in God and put a cold water

compress where the pain is. That's my cure." The good
priest liked the Baroness to leave him master of the field;
the Baroness did not listen.

The Baron found them thus amiably consorted when he
returned. His face was very grave.

"Dear me, if the man was dying, perhaps I ought to
have gone to him!" cried the priest with tardy compunction.

"He is dying," replied the Baron; "but he need not do
so without your aid. It is a foreigner, taken with acute
spasms in the train, who finds himself stranded here. Undoubtedly he is very ill."

"Where is he now?" queried the Baroness. "Is he
better? Is he a gentleman? Or shall I send him some
soup?"

"He is a gentleman. He is very old. The servant told
me his name was M. Farjolle; he says he is a Frenchman.
They are at the inn."

"At that place?" cried Mevrouw. "Mon cher, you
should have asked him here."

"Mon amie, he steadfastly refused to come."

"Ah, pardon. Of course you would do what was right."

"I do not think he understood," said the Baron. "He
offered a napoleon for the use of the carriage."

"For shame," exclaimed the Baroness, who considered
that no suffering could excuse such an error.

"I told him that he was mistaken, but that I should be
glad to accept a florin for the coachman," said the Baron
coolly. "And then I left him in peace."

"Which means," cried his wife quickly, "that you came
back on the box. Oh, Reinout, how could you? At least
say that the weather was fine."

"It might be worse," replied the Baron, and he walked
away to fetch the newspaper, sitting down quietly, now, to
its Home and Foreign News.

"Aha," he said suddenly, in the tone of a man who

makes a discovery. "This explains Monsieur Rexelaer's move. 'Appointed to the post of Sub-Comptroller of the Royal Household, Count Hilarius Jan Reinout van Rexelaer.' At last."

"And what is that, Mynheer the Baron?" asked Bulbius, slowly hoisting himself off his chair.

"Oh, it's the man that looks after the larder and buttery," interposed the Baroness sharply.

"Well, he has edged himself into the enchanted circle," said the Baron, "and now he wants to cut a figure as a noble and a great landed proprietor."

"And a Rexelaer," added the Baroness.

In the thoughtful silence that followed, the Priest took his leave. "Have you got an umbrella?" asked the Baron, following him out of the room.

"No. Why so? It isn't raining."

"Hush. Yes, it is. But it might be raining a good deal harder at this time of year; might it not?"

Mynheer van Rexelaer went back to his wife. She had risen and was standing by the mantelpiece.

"Sub-Comptroller of the Royal Household," she said slowly, and with increasing bitterness—too scornful not to reveal a little touch of envy.—"In all things for the last twenty years has Fortune favoured this adventurer, baulking, according to her custom, the better man."

He took one of her hands in his. "Not in all things," he said.

"How so?"

He pointed to the cards now lying in a little stream across the table. "Heureux en mariage," he said, "malheureux au jeu. Let the Count take his share. I have mine. No man, it appears, may claim both."

As he spoke, his look fell on the crumpled newspaper lying against his deserted chair. And his own words struck home to him. "Malheureux au jeu."

She pressed his hand, and they stood silent, side by side
5

Then he broke away, with an exclamation of impatience, to wind up the oil-lamp.

She came after him. "But he has not got Deynum yet," she said, "this Count." Oh the contempt of the last word from her lips!

"No, he has not got Deynum yet."

"But, Reinout."

"What is it, Gertrude?"

"He has a son."

CHAPTER VIII.

A PRINCE OF THE BLOOD ROYAL.

"SHE has looked them out in the 'Annuaire de la No-blesse,'" thought the Baron. "Yet what could she care about these people? How inquisitive the best of women are."

The Baroness had done more, while angry with herself for doing it. Writing to an acquaintance at the Hague, she had casually inquired after those other Rexelaers: "Do you know anything of our namesakes, the Count's family, I mean? There is a boy—is there not?—called Reinout." The unknown Reinout Rexelaer incessantly tormented her unwilling thoughts. Yet she turned to the answer with a sort of irritable pleasure.

"You ask after the Rexelaers," wrote the Hague lady. "Him one meets everywhere. Her I have never seen. I know his brother's family better; the wife there, you know, is one of our own set, a Borck, and I like her very much. Since the Count brought back his nigger spouse and her millions from Brazil, where he was secretary or something, he has worked day and night to recover the position they had lost through their impecuniosity, but the black woman is an obstacle. She locks herself up in a hot-house, people say, and cries for the sun. It is a great pity they should be Protestants—How was that, by-the-bye?—still, now that you, my dear Gertrude, have only a daughter, it must be a source of real satisfaction to you to remember that this other branch is blessed with sons. The Rexelaer-Borcks have two, and there is one boy, one child, at the Count's.

Yes, his name is Reinout, like your husband's. I suppose it is a family name?

"The little that I know of the lad is rather interesting, I think. For some foolish reason they keep him altogether apart; perhaps that is a Brazilian idea. He is educated, it appears, into a premature little man of the world, and put to bed in a court wig and ruffles. I don't know particulars. But he comes to a gymnastic class with my children, attended by the queerest, courtliest little Louis Quinze chevalier that you ever saw off a snuff-box lid. I met him there once, and he stood aside to let me pass, lifting his cap with the air of a young prince, enough to break the heart of a mother of hobbledehoys. He is a very handsome youth, dark complexioned, with big, expressive eyes. Of course the other boys do not care for him. He had a violent quarrel with my own Louis, in which I cannot help thinking Louis was wrong. I have run on, but I fancy that is about all. How is Wendela?"

The Baroness slowly slowly tore the letter up and placed the fragments on the blazing fire.

It was unavoidable that the boys with whom he was brought into such unsatisfactory contact should look askance at young Reinout. "Unbeknown is unbeloved," says a Dutch proverb. Schoolboyhood whispered derision of the little gentleman with kid gloves.

And when schoolboyhood whispers derision, its next step is to shout it. His companions, as his father fondly called them, began to tease him at the various classes where they met. They would bow before him and address him as "Your Majesty," in never tiring allusion to the ancestral King Hilarius, with whom Reinout himself had unwarily made them acquainted. All of them had plenty of ancestors of their own, but the King was a delightfully fresh source of amusement. And thence sprang the quarrel with the Louis mentioned above.

This Louis, one afternoon, had made a highly successful joke about Reinout and his dog, whom he nicknamed "the two Princes." Carried away by his own wit, he aimed, just as the class was dispersing, a couple of blows with a fencing foil at the lad and the brute, missing the former, but drawing a yelp of protest from the veritable " Prince." Quick as thought Reinout turned, and, first checking himself with a chivalrous "On your guard!" flashed a retort full into his aggressor's left eye. He was carried off in a fume of indignation, by his faithful Mentor, who knew not whether to scold or approve, and, on reaching home, he ran straight to his father's study.

"Papa!" he began impetuously.

"Hush!" said the Count, who was looking over his cash-book. The Count was an admirable, and scrupulous, financier.

"Well?" he asked, presently, jotting down some figures.

"Papa, it is all true—is it not?—about Rex Hilarius, and the lion and Wendela, isn't it?"

"Of course it is true, René," replied the Count with a smile.

The boy gave a great gasp of relief. "I am so glad to hear you say that," he almost sobbed. "Then I may *kill* whoever says it is not?"

His father burst out laughing. "Certainly not," cried the Count. "You may kill nobody. On the contrary, you must be on very good terms with all your companions. There's not one of them but you may want him some day."

Reinout stood lost in reflection. "Life is very difficult," he said at last. "Do you know, Papa, I think it is almost impossible for a man always to know how to act as a gentleman."

"Certainly not," cried the Count again. "Nothing is easier. It becomes a habit, like all others. Like speaking French without mistakes."

"But I don't mean politeness," said Reinout vaguely. "I mean about doing right."

"Of course," replied the Count, turning to his books again. "So do I, Reinout. Ask Monsieur de Souza. He knows."

But Reinout did not immediately return to his tutor. He went to look for his mother in the conservatory, where she lay, on her lounge, enveloped in heat, a novel of Catulle Mendès in her hand.

"Shut the door, René," she said without lifting her eyes. Her attitude was ultra-languid, but her soul was palpitating with the heroine's infidelities. The Countess had literary tastes and aspirations, as will be amply proved in the future. She even composed poetry. Private poetry, of course, as befitted her rank.

Reinout stood gazing at his mother in silence, for one whole minute. He was searching, confusedly, for explanation and expression. But his heart seemed too full for speech.

With her eyes unalterably intent on her book, the beautiful Creole—she was still beautiful—slowly drew to light from the folds of her dressing-gown a pink-ribboned confectioner's bag, which she held out in the direction of her son. "Take some sweets," she said.

The boy required no second bidding, but plunged his fingers eagerly down. "Are there any of those chocolats with the green stuff inside?" he asked.

She nodded, a little impatiently, and he went away, with his hands full, to demonstrate to Monsieur de Souza's not unconvincible ears that he must fight Louis to-morrow, and lick him.

Never, surely, had child a stranger tutor. Monsieur de Souza-Calhao was an old Portuguese gentleman of shattered health and fortunes, but of irreproachable ancestry and experience. The Rexelaers had come across him just before they quitted Rio, and had brought him away with them. He talked incessantly, pumping up his words with an audible draw,—he was a great sufferer from asthma,—and his talk, a life's harvest of gentle cynicism, delighted the Count. "Teach my boy," said the latter, "whatever you remember yourself. All the rest, I feel sure, is unnecessary. Contact with the world and those who know the world is the only education. At school children but learn what life teaches them to forget. Make a man of him, like ourselves, that has seen men and cities. And furnish him with enough arithmetic to reckon for number one." The two men shook hands. Count Rexelaer so thoroughly believed in what he said, that, from the child's earliest youth, he had taken him about with him everywhere. Well, nearly everywhere. When he left M. de Souza, he went in to his wife, and explained his plan. The Countess demurred. She had aspirations, poor thing, in her own foolish way, and she suggested the addition of "The poets." Count Hilarius smiled. "Ma chère," he said, "Believe me; I know my own class. The Almanach de Gotha and the Paris Figaro are a liberal education."

Monsieur de Souza carried out his instructions and improved on them. He was a shrewd and kindly man, not soured by his misfortunes, which he bore with easy philosophy. He liked his pale little pupil—"the child is not strong, don't let him learn too much," had been the verdict of a great Paris physician. "Ah, you see," said the father. It was an education which many a more correctly educated man might have envied. The tutor, for instance, would take Bucharest for the morning's subject, and would then talk for a couple of hours, first about the city as he remembered it—he had been everywhere—and the places of interest near, the dress and habits and peculiarities of the Roumanian people. "All this," he would say, "you can go and see for yourself some day," but then he would proceed farther and tell about the great Roumanian families, their members, their possessions, their relations to the brand-new German-silver crown. He would repeat these stories from time to time and ask his pupil about them, and so, gradually travelling round the world, the boy learned all about the net-work of vulgarity and vanity which keeps it together, the little tangle of kings, ministers and mistresses in which it swings. But he also learned a variety of other things, a smattering of conversation about latter-day pictures and operas, for instance, nothing beyond the limits of elegant ignorance. And he was early taught dancing, riding, fencing, his mother's accomplishments. The Countess Margherita came in to fence with her son and mortified him into efficiency by her successes. "Never kill your man, unless you want to," she cried, as she leaped straight at the boy's heart. To see her lithe figure bounding to and fro in a quiver of excitement,—she fenced in the French manner —one would have imagined it impossible that this was the woman who for days could only loll on couches in conservatories and munch lollipops.

"And especially, Monsieur de Souza," said the poor Countess, "I beg of you to supplement your own vast experience by the reading of books with my son. Let him know how the great intellects saw life." "You mean novels, Madame?" suggested the old gentleman. "Novels, Poems, Le vrai, Le bon, Le beau. Whatever edifies a character." So Reinout read his tutor's two favourites, La Bruyère and Montaigne. The tutor did not take kindly to the Countess's suggestion. As for works of the imagination, he held them in abhorrence. "If you *must* read," he frequently said to Reinout, "although I see no reason for your doing so, then memoirs are best." Reinout waded through a certain number of Court memoirs of the 17th and 18th centuries, and very queer information he got out of them.

But M. de Souza did not only acquaint him with the evil side of the old régime. This cavalier of the old school had its virtues as well as its vices. He had its code of honour, not a perfect one, perhaps, but far better than anything the boy could have learnt from his father. "Never do anything mean to a woman"—he might have added: "except under the cloak of 'love,'" for that was what he meant. "Never be afraid of any man." "Never do anything you need be ashamed of "—that sounds well, but many an unworldly soul might be surprised to hear of what things the chevalier was not ashamed. Self-stricken of misfortune, he taught his generous-hearted pupil to respect, and, if possible, to relieve it. "A gentleman should not save, but spend," the old spendthrift was never tired of repeating, "wisely, if possible, and, if not possible, ill. Money must flow, or it freezes." And he would tell again the story of the Duc de Richelieu and his grandchild.

The result of this peculiar training was a little aristocrat, heart and soul, face and bearing, manners and speech, a boy of fourteen, with much of the profoundly ignorant "knowledge of the world," of a roué, and no less of that unasked, good-natured pity for the vague millions outside its circle, which is built up on unmerited contempt. He was profoundly ignorant of the real lights of life, standing, as he did, from childhood upwards, under the glare of its wax candles, but he was eager, intuitively, to love, to help, to be of use by word or deed. And he remembered the words of the old Belgian gentleman: A gentilhomme devoir fait loi. And in the far distance he caught the vague music of their meaning, like the roar of a slowly approaching tide.

CHAPTER IX.

DISEASE.

"ANTOINE!"

"At your orders, Monsieur le Marquis."

"Hist. You take a delight in disobeying me."

"But I had understood that, when we were alone—"

"You had understood nothing. You never understand."

"If Monsieur wishes to have his title ignored, what of these?" As he spoke, the man carelessly fingered one of the many gold-stoppered bottles which he was arranging on the shaky little side-table. Cool impudence and indifference were written in every line of his shaven face.

"True," said his master pensively. "Lock the things away, and have new ones from Amsterdam. How much can they cost? A thousand francs, at the utmost. Find out an address, and write to-day."

"As it will please Monsieur. But when Monsieur remembers that all his underclothing is dotted over with the sign of his exalted rank, I would ask myself—"

"Well, get other things."

"I would ask myself if Monsieur considers it worth while."

If the man had looked for a storm of abuse, he did not get it. "Push forward that table," said the Marquis; "Place the morphia-injector where I can reach it. And give me 'Les Mémoires de Cocodette.' So. Now go down into the village and find out all about it."

"But it is pouring with rain, Monsieur le Marquis."

"Can I not see? Go down into the village and find out all about it."

The valet slunk towards the door. His master called after him. "I desire to know, especially, the name of the seigneur of the village. In whose carriage was I brought here last night?"

"That I can tell already to—to Monsieur. The name is Rexelaer."

"Ah! Well, find out the rest." The Marquis remained alone.

It was a poor apartment enough, even for a village inn. Strangers did not stop at Deynum. The place was one to feed your horses at before you hurried on. And the chubby-faced peasant hostess had been far more put out than pleased by the arrival, in her Lord's own carriage, of the distinguished invalid and his still more terrible serving-man. She had hurriedly prepared her own sitting-room—a secret never to be divulged—while the Marquis lay gasping, amid fumes of cheap gin and cheaper tobacco—in the hurriedly deserted parlour below.

The whole bedroom was full of indefinable odours, not especially evil, but suggestive, generally, of old clothes, and hard labour, and mustiness. There were little windows everywhere, unfit for airing, that yet let in marvels of draught. The bright red beams of the ceiling lay heavy on your head. A great bedstead with faded green curtains (of quite a different shade from the green strip of carpet) stood against one side of the wall, opposite two bad prints from fine pictures of the Holy Family. So far there was nothing at which you could take offence. But in the middle of it all was suspended a truly painful object, the joy of its possessor's heart, a brand-new paraffin lamp of the commonest make of cuivre poli, highly wrought in flowers and faces, and surmounted by a pale-green globe with a pink paper border. It hung there crooked and greasy, odorous and two-and-sixpenny, unusable though filled to overflowing, an

insult to the honest deal tables and rush-bottomed chairs
upon which it looked down.

But the Marquis noticed none of these specifically; he
only realized an unendurable discomfort. He lay back in a
common but comfortable wicker chair, his tall and elegant
figure wrapped in a white plush dressing-gown faced with
silk. And he was as carefully oiled and brushed as ever.

He was thinking of himself. He had rarely thought of
anything else for more than seventy years. But never had
he had sadder subject for his cogitations than now. During
a few moments, certainly, his mind lingered over the name
which Antoine had flung to him in departing. There rose
up before him a memory of a dusty road in the glare of a
July sun, and a little fellow seated in the middle of it,
across his hoop, white and hot, shame-faced but triumphant. Of course it must be so. He had understood the
connection at once. That he should come to this place, of
all others, to die!

"That dog, Antoine, smelt death," he said aloud, "or
perhaps I should not have told him. Yet, I don't know.
Great God, I am all alone in the world."

His life had been a long one, crowded with incidents
which had interested him absorbingly at the time of their
occurrence. In the seventy-three years of its duration not
so much had happened as in the last twenty-four hours.
And this much he now understood of time and eternity,
that the longest period of the longest life is the moment in
which it ends.

He was a great noble. He had lived the little round of
his class: horses, women, shooting, cards, women, horses,
shooting, women, cards. He had been in the diplomatic
service for a certain period: that only meant larger experience in the women of various nationalities; and he had
graced during many years the presidential chair of the Society for the Improvement of the Breed of Horses; that
meant a certain amount of betting, but he was rich and

could afford it. In fact, he had done his duty to his King, his Country and himself. He had done more than his duty, for he need not have patiently suffered banishment to Madrid, where the cuisine did not agree with him, nor need he have kept so many race-horses in the interests of agriculture. Even had he confined himself to the round above-mentioned, he could still have proved himself—what he was —a great noble.

There was the incident of the Marquise. How small it looked now! For there had been a Marquise who had spread her existence through no less than twenty-seven years of his life. He had hated her, because she had borne him no children, to be great nobles like himself. He had never paused to question his hatred, he, the roué, who had married a young girl. He did not think she had much to complain of: he seldom objected to her doing what she chose. She had only been an incident. He forgot her.

And his life, as has been said, had been very full, crowded with the labour of each day's many pleasures. He looked down it now, and he could distinguish nothing. He could not even remember any point of especial interest. Ah, yes, there was that—when he was quite a young lad— that innocent little girl who—whom—. He took up the book of dirty stories from his lap and began to read.

And this is what he read. A dull weight always there. At first the thought that it must be fancy. The question: Do I really feel it? Then, with increasing iteration: Do I not feel it? There it is again. I never felt anything like it before. I wonder what causes it. Something indigestible I must have eaten. But I never knew things to be indigestible before. I never was ill before. I am not ill now.

Of course not. But why this deadly feeling of sickness which keeps creeping up without any apparent reason? Why that sudden fainting at the club, which proves my fancy not fancy but fact?

He laid down the book at the unturned page, and sat staring through the narrow, muslin-curtained window at the steady rain outside. The elms on the village-green swayed cheerlessly under the lowering sky.

When was it that the stern reality had first seized him by the throat? Ages ago. Life is long, after all, when we look back upon it. Immensely long The summer before last? Last summer.

How annoying it had all seemed at the time. But his doctor had promised to cure him in a month or two. He had always kept a doctor, like a chaplain, without requiring either.

Then had come that first attack of pain. How that had suddenly altered the whole face of the matter! How furious he had been with the numskull who had allowed his indisposition to spread so far. He had hurried to Brussels to consult a great authority,—a great name, at least! He had learnt that he was suffering from inflammation, possibly a tumour—a *what*, great God?—yes, probably a tumour. Oh, nothing to be alarmed at, Monsieur le Marquis.

"But my habits, my daily—ahem!—duties. How, with your ridiculous diet of slops, can I go out to dinner, as I am accustomed to do five days of the seven? And the little suppers which—enfin!—which occur in the existence of a man of the world? I should have to be very ill, indeed, and I am not, before I could submit to such a life as you propose."

"Monsieur le Marquis, you are not very ill, but you are ill enough to render my régime absolutely imperative. Absolutely imperative."

"Is my illness dangerous?"

"Not yet."

"Ah! But, professor, are you not mistaken about the tumour? The fool who prescribed for me has allowed a chill to settle down into a chronic catarrh. A friend of mine has much the same symptoms as myself, and he suffers from a chronic catarrh."

"Monsieur le Marquis, I am sorry to say, you must not treat this affection too lightly. I will not answer for the consequences if you do."

Of how little importance it all seemed to him now. A week ago it had come upon him as the greatest catastrophe of his life. To have something serious the matter with one—well, not exactly serious, but "requiring care." To have to change one's whole mode of life—for a time, of course, on one's body's account. How vexatious! And he was only seventy-three, while Prasly-Latour had celebrated his eighty-seventh birthday last August in perfect health. The fates were unjust.

All this was vague, and far-away. His whole previous existence was but a thin dash, as a prelude, leading up to yesterday, a blot, a full-stop.

After two more attacks of fierce spasms he had made up his mind to know what was really wrong. Why this constant giddiness? Was his brain diseased also? He would go into a foreign country, where he would be free to speak. Amsterdam was close by; some-one had recommended a professor at Amsterdam, who had cured somebody else of a swelling somewhere. He went to Amsterdam.

Why had he insisted upon this man's laying bare the whole truth? He did not really want to know it. He would much rather not have known it. Oh the blessed ignorance of yesterday morning! Oh the blessed cruel doubt of yesterday morning! Oh the happiness of that torturing: Is it? compared with this irrevocable: "It is."

He had come out from that chamber of judgment with but one idea: Escape. Anywhere, away from the truth, from himself. Not back to old acquaintances, familiar faces, how are you's—I hope you're better; come and dine. Anywhere, into some quiet corner, unknown, to hide his suffering in a hole, like a cat or a dog. It was chance that had prevented his going farther than Deynum. He had intended to push on—somewhere—into Germany, miscalculating his strength.

He knew little of illness, but of *this* illness he knew. He had seen it take its course in his wife. Yet, he now told himself, her symptoms had been so different. All the preliminaries of his own case had been omitted; only the final agony had come, sharp and swift. It never occurred to him what she might have endured in silence. He cursed his fate which dealt more hardly with him.

He shuddered. The horror of a continuous, hopeless agony was upon him. Nonsense, he was exaggerating. She had not really suffered so much. She seldom complained. He did not remember any very terrible paroxysms. And yet he had received a general impression, from doctors and nurses, from occasional sights and sounds—still, he may have exaggerated. He regretted that he had not asked her oftener about her sufferings. He would have known better now.

There were maladies in which you suffered more than in cancer. There must be. He tried to think of them. He might have been a life-long leper, like his friend, the Duke. He tried to feel thankful that he had not been a life-long leper.

He broke into a horrible laugh. And then again he took up the book. For *one* thing he was thankful, that last night had come to an end, and that it was day again, wet and miserable, but day.

CHAPTER X.

A SHEPHERD AND TWO SHEEP.

MEANWHILE Antoine wandered disconsolately to and fro in the solitary village-street, his trousers turned-up to an unnecessary degree, his shiny umbrella dripping low over his bended shoulders.

"Ah, your turn has come at last, has it, old ten per cent?" he murmured over and over again, with quiet glee. "Great lords kick everybody under them, and the greatest lord is Death," he chuckled. He had an unpleasant way of chuckling internally, with melancholy, long-drawn face. The idea of the impending catastrophe appeared to afford him distinct satisfaction. He gave it utterance, letting it linger on his tongue, like a lozenge, as an antidote against the damp.

He stopped to stare along the deserted road.

"A pretty name," he said, speaking of the village. "And, for the rest, beastly—like many a girl."

Meditating thus, in a manner worthy of his philosophic mind, he dribbled down a little lane, which seemed to lead nowhere. "In ten minutes more I shall go back," he resolved, "and shall tell the old fellow anything he may care to believe. What's the use of his stupid questions? To-morrow, at the latest, we move on."

At this moment an energetic tapping caused him to lift the umbrella off his ears. He had reached a low tenement which stands well-hid behind an over-crowded strip of garden, winking, as it were, with one eye over a tall box-

6

hedge. If you look at it closely, you will see that it is a little more pretentious than its—distant—neighbours in its simple unpretentiousness. It is larger and, if possible, neater, and one or two concessions have been made in erecting it to other considerations than those of the barest utility. " Erecting " is an incorrect word; it lies prone beneath the trees. And just now it was a thing of most wondrous beauty to gaze upon, for the whole irregular length of its mixed up apartments and out-houses was ablaze, like a magnificent sunset, with the all-luminous death of a great Virginia creeper. Antoine saw nothing of this, not even the glittering caves, till he had found a little gate to peep through.

" Presumably meant for me," he said. " Whoever she is, she must be hurting her hand. I hope she's young."

The knocking increased in energy.

" I fear not," sighed Antoine, still peering under his umbrella. " No woman under forty would knock as loud as that."

The knocking ceased and a portly figure in black appeared at the door, a low door, half-hidden under a porch. The figure was making signs with the pipe, across the mists of rain.

" An old one, of course; like my luck," grumbled Antoine, who was near-sighted (ocularly only). " Well, a glass of cognac will not come amiss this damp morning."

" Push it !" shouted Father Bulbius in Dutch, with violent gestures of both arms and the pipe. Then he cried: " Pussy !" which is French and means the same thing.

" Yes, you may yell, old lady," muttered Antoine, violently jerking the recalcitrant latch. " Hang this gate; it's as virtuous as a Mother Superior. Hi, you there, you must come and let me in, if you want me at all !"

He desisted. Whereupon Bulbius, with a mighty resolve, in which courtesy and curiosity triumphed over caution, hitched up his cassock as high as was permissible—a little higher—and, holding it resolutely out on both sides, with the pipe sticking crossways, commenced a gingerly zig-zag over the puddles.

"Black!" soliloquized Antoine. "A widow presumably. Well, widows take most trouble. Here she comes. It is the mountain, evidently, on its way to Mahomed. It is—Good Heavens, it is a curé. In this land of all others! But do not derange yourself, Monsieur le Curé!" Then he stood aside, bowing and scraping. "This is Veronica's doing!" gasped Father Bulbius, dropping the skirt he had tucked between his knees, as he rattled at the gate. "She has locked it again."

Even as he spoke, another figure, gaunt and terrible, appeared in the doorway, and a big bass voice came booming through the wet. "Is it possible, your Reverence, with your baldness! Is it permissible thus to risk one's health? Ah but return immediately! Immediately! Besides, it is useless, for *I* have got the key!" And Veronica, the Father's housekeeper (and body-guard) came stalking across with straight, upright jerks like a squirrel.

"Murder will out," snapped Veronica, "but I say: Murder will in. Leastways theft." She unlocked the little gate with the very big key which she held in one bony hand. "Is this—person to come in, your Reverence?"

"Certainly, unless you have left the table loaded with plate," replied the Father, with a timid attempt to banter her.

"There are other valuables besides plate," retorted the woman, with a toss of her head. You're nearest to your own skin, says the proverb, and I'm sure there's no one else to be near to in this loneliest of lanes."

The priest pushed her aside, a little impatiently for him.

"Enterrez-vous, Mesjeu?" he said with a polite wave of his hand. The movement drove his long pipe backwards, causing Veronica to start away with a snort and a splash.

"Shall I not derange you, Monsieur l'Abbé?" protested

Antoine, bowing bareheaded, but under his umbrella, where-in he distinctly had the advantage of Bulbius.

"Oh no; I am not at all deranged," replied the latter gentleman, and led the way into the house.

"My good Veronica," he said, pausing at the door of his den, "I should like a half-bottle of port."

"There is no more port, your Reverence, and it seems to me that for a man who has been out in the damp, a good cup of coffee—"

"Yes, yes," said the Father, gently closing the door of his sanctum upon her—and motioning his guest to a chair.

There was not, however, a vacant one in the whole little room. From top to bottom the Parsonage was a model of primness and cleanly discomfort, angular, empty, white and cold, with that eternal smell of polish and soap and ubiqui-tously slippery sloppery in which the soul of the Dutch housewife delights. But to the rule of this general un-habitability one exception had perforce been established. The priest had made a stand with regard to his own little study. On the first day of the month he permitted his housekeeper to enter and "clean" it, deserting it himself during twenty-four hours. When this compromise was pro-posed to her as the result of long weeks of battle, ruse and subterfuge, Veronica first resigned her post, and then, as the Father remained unexpectedly firm, herself. She found some consolation in ceaselessly ascribing all the ailments she invented for him to the unhealthy condition of his apartment. And, seeing that an indolent man always makes far more litter than a busy one, the sanctum, as in-spected from outside the window, must have caused agony to a swept and straightened mind like Veronica's. Father Bulbius never picked up anything,—and he had an apti-tude for letting things fall,—nor did he ever replace a book, or whatever else he had taken down, unless there was an opportunity for putting it sideways, or topsy-turvy.

He now hurried to an easy chair—all his chairs bore

that name, and deserved it—and, knocking off a dusty pile of newspapers with one hand, while he hastily passed a slip of his cassock across the seat with the other, he apologised in broken French for the delay. Then he waddled to a cupboard, from which he carefully extracted a quart bottle and two small glasses. These he held up to the window with a smile on his broad face which seemed to pour a sudden flood of sunshine over the rain-oppressed little room.

"You are doubtless," he said, "the stranger of yesterday. I was anxious to afford you, sir, a shelter from the wet. I regret that circumstances rendered this difficult." He stammered out his words under a hailstorm of mistakes, but we will not delay ourselves with the mistakes and stammerings of others.

"I am the servant," said Antoine humbly, "of Monsieur Farjolle."

"I know. That is what I meant," replied the Father hastily, filling the glasses. "I have some decent cognac here. In spite of my housekeeper's objections, I occasionally take a little as a remedy against the damp."

Loripont was amazed by the quality of the liquor. Trust a gentleman's gentleman to know. But the truth is, Father Bulbius loved good tobacco, good drinks, and good humour. For the rest, the world might wag as it listed. And the worst thing in it to wag was his housekeeper's tongue.

"Monsieur your master, he is better this morning, I hope?"

"He is very ill, Monsieur le Curé," said Antoine solemnly.

"So I hear. So I hear," murmured the Priest, mournfully shaking his fat chin over his elevated glass. "I hope, my dear friend, that—" he hesitated. He was going to say "that he is prepared," but he felt this to be still too early a stage of their interview—"that you approve of the brandy," he said.

"It is most excellent, Monsieur le Curé."

"We owe it, like most good wines, to your beautiful country, Monsieur," said the Father, lovingly rocking the golden liquid against the light.

Antoine was silent. His master had expressly commanded him to disguise their nationality. Belgium is so small and so close by.

"For you are a Frenchman, I presume?" added Bulbius.

"I am a Belgian, Monsieur le Curé," replied Antoine, who could lie to anybody on earth, excepting to a priest.

"A Belgian—ah!" The Father paused, apprehensive of a presence at the door.

"Here is the coffee," came from the passage in sepulchral tones. "Will your Reverence take it, as I am not permitted to intrude?" And a tray was propelled through the narrowest aperture imaginable, with a brusqueness which gave to the very cups an attitude of defiance, as they jumped to the jerk.

"Nice warm coffee," said Bulbius meekly, in closing the door.

Loripont dropped a scrutatory glance through the depths of the too transparent liquid, which glance went down deep into the Father's heart.

"But she cooks with great care," replied the Father apologetically, "the dishes she likes. She says her instinct advises her what is wholesome. My instinct"—his eyes twinkled—"is invariably wrong, she says. But this is ungracious," he cried suddenly, "and, to a stranger, offensive. It is right I should not care too much about eating, and Veronica's peculiarities, I trust, will be looked upon up yonder"—he pointed to the ceiling—"as something of an excuse for the quality of *this*"—he ticked his fat finger against his glass.

"But your Reverence is very comfortable here," replied

Antoine, a little ironically. "I see you have farm-buildings attached."

"Ah, that was unavoidable. I have to occupy my house-keeper. If you are married, you will know that a woman devotes at least all her spare time to her neighbour's affairs. A dangerous quality in the house of a parish priest. Veronica is always complaining that she has too much to do. So she has, although, by-the-bye, she insisted on getting the cows, when I was ordered fresh milk. It is necessary that she should have too much to do. And, besides, the griev-ance keeps her in a pleasantly bad temper. She would not, for the world, do less."

Antoine Loripont smiled. He had an immense venera-tion for the clergy which was altogether independent of their personal faults or peculiarities. It rested solely on the consideration that, if death should happen to be, not an *impasse*, but a passage (so he expressed it), the guards at the farther gate would wear the livery of the Pope. "Pour s'assurer une bonne place au spectacle," the fellow said bru-tally, "il faut avoir de bons amis dans les coulisses." And he was superstitious, with all the superstition of a weak cynic and evil-liver.

The guest's smile recalled Father Bulbius, already half ashamed of his garrulity. But oh the splendid opportunity for pouring out pent-up grievances into patient ears that, on the morrow, would bear them hundreds of miles away! He could not have ventured to speak thus fearlessly of his "house-cross" to the family at the Castle. The smaller our world is, the larger are its ears.

"I am breaking the ninth commandment," he now con-fessed with rueful countenance. "And worse. In those days a man's neighbour alone was protected: it was deemed incredible that one should speak evil of those of his own house."

And to himself he added: "You who are yearning to pump this stranger, who called him in on purpose, you ac-

cuse others of being busy-bodies. Oh, Bulbius, you hypo-
crite, I shall punish you as you deserve." He took out a
little much-faded pocket-book from beside his bulgy breast.
In this little book he carefully made a little note. It was
his record of penances, and whenever he realized that he
had wronged a fellow-creature, he wrote down a punishment for himself in it. Let it be hastily added, for the
benefit of those who feel an affection for the poor old
father, that the self-inflicted penances were not overwhelm-
ingly heavy. He did not scourge himself, for instance. He
had tried it once, gently, but found that it hurt.

Loripont's keen eye watched the little book with great
interest. It recalled to him his own daily dealings with the
Marquis. "You have other intercourse, however," he said.
"The carriage which so kindly brought my master from the
station—" And the Father's stream of chatter babbled
over into another channel, and he sang the praises of Deynum and the Baronial house of Rexelaer. "An oasis,"
remarked Antoine, "in this wilderness infested by the
Gueux."

"True," replied the Father demurely. "Yet I have
known Protestants who were good men." He was not going to allow a Belgian to abuse Hollanders in his presence.
"The pity is that they refuse to be converted; at least, so I
have often been told. Help yourself, my friend."

"I will take a drop more of this coffee, with your Reverence's permission," replied Antoine, reaching over for the
cognac-bottle and grinning in the Father's face.

Then he rose. "You will not be here for any time?"
queried Bulbius, who had really got nothing out of the
stranger, after all.

"Oh, no, we shall probably be leaving to-night."

"But your master! He is dying. Should he have any
need of spiritual comfort—"

"I grieve to say, Monsieur le Curé, that my master is an
atheist and an infidel."

Father Bulbius heaved a deep sigh, as he accompanied the faithful son of the Church to the door.

In the porch Antoine stood still.

"Infidels, Monsieur le Curé, when they die, go to hell, do they not?"

The priest wagged his head to and fro. "Undoubtedly," he said—with great hesitation.

"Then my master, when he dies, will go to hell?" persisted Antoine.

"Let us hope he will not die an infidel," said Bulbius gently. "Poor fellow, you must implore the Virgin for him. You are a good man. If you stay, come and see me again."

"Your Reverence—if your Reverence has not caught cold already—" cried a sonorous voice from the kitchen.

The Father fled back to his room.

CHAPTER XI.

"ENTRE L'ARBRE ET L'ECORCE."

For the twentieth time the Marquis laid down his book and glanced at the travelling-clock which stood ticking nervously beside him. "He does it on purpose," murmured the Marquis. "I cannot, I will not, be alone."

Even at that moment, had he known it, his solitude was coming to an end. For the landlady was stumbling up-stairs in a frantic hurry, tripped up by her loose slippers as they dropped away from under her feet.

"The Landheer!" she gasped, falling over her various belongings and snapping her apron-strings. "I hope he didn't see that my back-hair's come undone."

She thumped vigorously at the door, and then—for though foreign gentlemen might be terrible possibilities, the "Landheer" was a magnificent fact,—she "irrupted" recklessly into the bedroom, crying: "The compliments of Mynheer the Baron, and his Nobleness desires to know how the strange gentleman is!"

The Marquis moved one white hand in delicate protest. "Go away," he said softly, in broken Dutch. "Go away."

Hendrika, though delighted to hear her own language, stood "struck all of a heap," as she afterwards declared, by the strange gentleman's attire. Long white robes, in her simple mind, were connected with the least dressed of un-dress only. Doubtless, distinguished foreigners wore such night-garments as these. "Oh la!" she said. She was an apple-faced young woman without any figure to speak of.

She fell back a step or two. "Mynheer is waiting. Please give an answer. I'll shut my eyes," said Hendrika, and suited the action to the word.

The Marquis sat staring indignantly at the uncouth, crimson-cheeked figure, which stood untidy before him, with tight-screwed eyelids and pendent arms. The woman's talk was of course incomprehensible to him; her manner made him uncomfortable. "Perhaps some sort of an idiot," he thought. "But one cannot throw things at a woman. I wish she would take herself off." And he rang the hand-bell, as a last resource, for he was neither strong enough nor sufficiently attired to move from his chair. He hoped that that summons might bring up the landlady.

It caused that personage timidly to open one eye. Whereupon, beholding the stranger's horrible expression and the uplifted hand-bell, she fled behind the door, giving the Marquis an opportunity of which he immediately availed himself, to send half a dozen heavy articles crashing up against the panels, as the best means both of frightening her and shutting her out. Hendrika shot violently towards Antoine, and that gentleman, pitching her anyhow down the staircase, walked into his master's presence with a sneer of questioning surprise.

"You infernal miscreant!" shrieked the old man, threatening him with the last thing he had snatched up, a big paper-knife. "How dare you leave me to be insulted by every hussy that cares to come and stare at me? Are you showing me to the village for a penny? I—I believe you would do it."

"Monsieur will be heard," retorted Loripont calmly, "by the gentleman at the foot of the staircase."

"Gentleman! What gentleman?"

"The gentleman who brought us from the station. He is asking for Monsieur le Marquis. Monsieur de Rexelaer, I presume."

"I will see him," said the Marquis, after a moment's re-

flection.   "And you, with your everlasting clumsiness about·
my title, mind not to betray who I am."

But the insulted Hendrika had meanwhile conveyed to
the Baron the information that the old creature upstairs
was out of his mind.   He had abused her and thrown things
at her, and he had even refused to hear anything concerning his Nobleness the Baron.   "And I should never have
taken him in at all," argued the landlady, "but for your
Nobleness's commands.   My inn is intended for respectable
people from market, not for foreigners, no one knows why,
whither or whence."

"No, no, it is some misunderstanding.   You will see;
he will pay well," answered the Baron soothingly, as he
turned away.

But Antoine stopped him and ushered him into the
presence of "my master, Monsieur Farjolle."   And the
Angel who watches over the fortunes of Deynum looked
from one face to the other in tremulous doubt.   Perhaps
he realised, vaguely, that this was the beginning of the end.
For angels, whatever they may foresee—pure eyes are far-
seeing—cannot read the future plainly.   They know that
God's goodness, like man's evil, is boundless; they remember the Past.   But the problem, for them as for us, still remains an equation, in which the fourth quantity, the Future,
is eternally marked with a cross.

"I had not intended to intrude," said the Baron, bowing
stiffly.

"It were cruel to deprive me of a pleasure, Monsieur,"
replied the Marquis, all urbanity, motioning his visitor to
one of the rush-bottomed chairs.   "Have I the pleasure of
speaking to Monsieur de Rexelaer de Deynum?"

"Yes, that is my name," said the Baron, with a quiet
little glow of pride.   He was nearly sixty; he had never
learnt to suppress the feeling altogether.

"Mine is Farjolle, Monsieur le Comte."

"Ah no; pardon me," said the Baron promptly, but

with an awkward blush. "That is another family altogether; they spell their name differently. Count Rexelaer
is no connection of mine." He hesitated a moment. "I
am Baron Rexelaer of Deynum," he said.

A complicated look of confusion, vexation and incredu-
lity came over the Belgian's face. "Impossible," he
thought. "Some quarrel. But, evidently, it's the wrong
man." Aloud he said : "I have yet to thank you—" "It
is nothing, it is nothing!" from the Baron—"ah, but indeed, you cannot rob me of the pleasure of being indebted
to you, Monsieur le Baron."

"The old peacock will betray himself at once by his
strut," soliloquised Antoine, where he stood behind his
master's chair. "And why shouldn't he? It's only half
a masquerade at the best, this stupid joke about Farjolle."

The Marquis turned round, as if he had understood.

"Get you downstairs," he said. "And, if there's anything edible in the house, you may eat it."

"Then," said the simple-hearted Baron. "Why not
increase so trivial a pleasure by accepting the hospitality of
my house till you can proceed on your travels?"

The Marquis's face clouded with the painful memory of
the last word. "There will not be much more travelling,"
he said, "I thank you sincerely, Monsieur. But I am too
ill to be anyone's guest." An ashen pallor lay over his
sharp features. He had aged since yesterday. The chin
seemed lengthening out upwards, as if striving to come in
contact with the eagle-nose. Yet he had fixed in his teeth
as usual that morning, and they fitted as well as ever.

"On that very account—" began the Baron, "but I do
not press you, though our worst, simple people as we are,
would be better than this." He swept his arm round the
room. "Besides, it is hardly worth your while perhaps. I
hope you are feeling well enough to continue your journey."

"Excuse me; I am not going to continue my journey.
I am going to stay here."

The Baron stared in undisguised amazement. His frank eyes somewhat disconcerted the man of the world.

" I was not on my way to any place in particular," continued the Marquis hastily. " Mine was a journey of — pleasure. I was looking for a quiet spot in which to—rest. This seems a charming one."

" It is indeed," acquiesced the Baron emphatically.

" Just so. Do you know—perhaps—of some small furnished house I could hire in the village? Excuse my troubling you with my private affairs. For the moment I cannot travel. Nor can I remain in this room—" with an expression of extreme disgust.

The Baron sat thinking for a few moments, an earnest desire to be of use distinctly marked on his manly face. Then he looked up with an eager smile of satisfaction. " I have an idea," he said, " I must go and inquire." And he hurried away, without waiting for the other's premature gratitude. On the staircase he looked at his watch. " I mustn't keep Gertrude waiting lunch," he thought.

Two hours later he appeared at the Parsonage and, receiving no answer to his knock, walked straight through, into his Reverence's study.

" His Reverence is in bed," said a deep voice behind the intruder. It was the worst part of Veronica's tyranny that she showered verbal reverence upon the victim, out of season, and out of sense.

" Ill? Dear me, he was well enough last night."

" *And* came home in the rain," replied Veronica, impressively. There was reproach in her eye.

" But *with* an umbrella," expostulated the Baron.

" Umbrellas are no protection against the under-damp," retorted Veronica enigmatically. " The under-damp is especially dangerous to fat men. It rises alongside the thin ones, but it strikes against the fat men and upsets them."

" Humph!" said the Baron. " Well!" And he pushed deliberately past her. Veronica followed grumbling. She feared no one on earth where her priest was concerned, but, still, the Lord of Deynum was—the Lord of Deynum.

The Baron opened the bedroom door, and, as he did so, a scramble was heard and the thud of something heavy collapsing into something soft. Father Bulbius was discovered in bed, the clothes pulled up tight under his double chin, his face melting with heat and more purple than ever.

Veronica came stalking after the visitor. "Is it comfortable, your Reverence?" she inquired with solemn interest.

"No," replied the Father without looking up. "It hurts." There was resentment in his tone. He was actually sulky.

"So it ought to, if it's to draw out the cold"—but at this stage the Baron bundled out the handmaid—with his eyes—and closed the door behind her.

"Had you not better lock it, Mynheer the Baron?" suggested a faint voice from the bed.

No sooner had this hint found acceptance than Father Bulbius threw off the bed-clothes and sat erect. With an almost piteous "By your leave," he removed a sticky yellow mass from his ample breast and laid it beside him on the pillow. The Baron stood watching. "I cannot understand you," the latter burst out wrathfully. "It is indeed time that I renewed my oft-repeated proposal to deliver you. In fact I am here with that object. Send the woman away and come and live with us."

"But I *have* got a cold," protested the Father, turning in immediate self-defence. "I sneezed twice, I assure you, before I got into bed, of my own free will."

"Then put on your plaster again," replied the Baron grimly, "I sha'n't squeeze my hand twixt the beech and the bark. But my advice is: send the woman away." He hesitated a moment; then he said abruptly, "You give up this place, which you and she are always declaring unhealthy and declaiming against, and you come and live at the Castle, as you have often said you would like to do. It is a deliverance, my good Bulbius."

The parsonage, properly speaking, of Deynum was a poor little house near the church; the Chaplain who served the Castle-chapel had always lived with the family. The Protestant minister came across from the village of Rol-·lingen.

"And where would Veronica go to?" queried the Priest.

"To the—," the Baron checked himself. "To her relations. Isn't she always telling you that she ought really to leave you and attend to some old creature at home?"

"Ah yes, but she merely says that because she wants to have the old lady here. Veronica has a venerable great-aunt of ninety-three, so deaf she can hear nobody's voice but Veronica's. Veronica certainly has a splendid voice. And perhaps I am rather selfish"--this ruefully--"but "—with sudden triumph—"you see, I *don't* have her, Mynheer the Baron, which proves that I possess a will of my own."

"Then use it, and come to the Castle."

"It is most kind, but I could not expect it of Veronica."

"I have an opportunity now, such as will never occur again, to rid you of lease, furniture and all."

"You tempt me sorely, Mynheer the Baron, but just think of Veronica."

"Oh, I'll settle Veronica," cried the Baron, and ran from the room.

Father Bulbius sank back, smiling contentedly, on his pillow. But, almost simultaneously, he started up with a shriek. And his bald head, as he hastily removed the burning mess into which he had dropped it, shone like a lobster through its sauce.

"Veronica, I hear you are anxious to return to your

relations?" cried the Baron, suddenly appearing in the kitchen.

The old housekeeper was busy among her pots and pans. In fact, she was preparing another plaster. She turned round very slowly. "I never said so, Mynheer the Baron," she answered, more slowly still. "Did his Reverence?"

The Baron was a little taken aback by the solemnity of her manner. "Oh come," he protested. "And there's your aunt, you know, who is ninety-seven, and who can hear no voice but yours. You have undoubtedly a very fine voice, my good Veronica."

"Mynheer the Baron is very kind. My great-aunt is barely ninety-one. Has your Nobleness a candidate for my place with his Reverence?"

"His Reverence is coming to live at the Castle. This house, which is so unhealthy, is going to be let."

Veronica slowly put down the plaster which had lain steaming in her hands. "Not like that," she said, and her deep tones sounded like the distant roll of thunder. "Excuse me, Mynheer the Baron, but I can't believe it of his Reverence. Not this house. Not like that."

"And why not this house?" inquired the Baron impatiently. "You've grumbled enough at it for years."

She turned upon him almost fiercely. "And you, Mynheer the Baron, would you sell Deynum?"

He did not deign to answer her impudence directly. He only said: "And your aunt, whom it is your Christian duty to look after? And your master, whom the damp is killing, you say?"

She started, and, for a moment, a swift tremble shook her. "True," she said, and marched straight past the Baron into Bulbius's room. She entered so quickly that the invalid had not time to replace his cataplasm.

"It is true," she began abruptly, "that the damp is bad for your Reverence. It is especially bad for fat people be-

7

cause of the 'underdamp.' The 'wonder-doctor' told me who cured my aunt of her fidgets. So I know. And my grand-aunt wants me badly, and you'll be more comfortable at the Castle. And the Baron is right."

"Nonsense, Veronica," murmured Bulbius in a shrill whisper from among the bedclothes. "Shut the door. Do you mean to say you have told the Baron you are willing to go?"

"So be it. He is right."

"Fiddlesticks. And who will attend to my require- ments as you do? I love the people at the Castle, but I can't go and live with them. You're the only person in the world who can cook my porridge exactly as I like it, or who can mix my grog of nights. And there's my posset after service—and—and—"

"And Flora with that calf coming," burst in Veronica. "And the pigs that won't be fit to kill for another month, at least. And there never was anyone like your Reverence for wearing holes in your black stockings, and—"

"Go and tell him that you can't," cried his Reverence. "Go and tell him immediately that you won't. There's a jewel of a woman! Go and tell him that *you won't.*"

"But he'll think I'm grudging your Reverence a health- ier residence."

"But he'll misunderstand my refusal to enter his family."

"So be it," said Veronica again, and marched to the door.

Before she reached it, it was opened from the outside by the Baron van Rexelaer. That gentleman had tired of the saucepans. "So you see, Father, it's all settled," he said.

"No, I cannot, Mynheer the Baron," Veronica was be- ginning heroically; but Bulbius, brought face to face with the crisis, arose in his bed, and to the occasion.

"It is settled that we decline your kind offer," he said. "There are too many objections. And I do not think I could manage without Veronica."

"Your Reverence," exclaimed the Baron vehemently, "is a child and a slave. There, there; you may forgive me to-morrow. You won't think better of it? No, really? Then keep on your house for that woman. Good-bye."

He ran away in a rage. He was mightily offended. Veronica stood watching him from the porch. "And you might as well sell Deynum? Why don't you?" she said when she thought he was out of hearing. But she had miscalculated the strength of her splendid voice.

The poor Father, much perturbed by his patron's displeasure, drew his little book of penances from under his pillow and made a note in it. The plaster, endured from simple good-nature, was a point to the good. "It is true," he said to himself, "that I am ridiculously susceptible to wet feet. And Veronica really takes most excellent care of me. On Sundays, especially, she is altogether tractable, but it cannot always be Sunday." Then he yawned, and got out of bed, and wondered what Veronica would say to that.

But she said nothing, when she came in presently, with red eyes.

CHAPTER XII.

THE Baron's anger had cooled somewhat before he reached the little postern which leads from the bottom of the lane into his own park. He walked slower, having started with a run. And his footsteps suddenly died into stillness on the sodden leaves which filled up the narrow by-path, as he wound slowly forward into a wilderness of russet and gold. Evening was falling, with that tearful sadness which often heralds an autumn sunset, and the pale sky was visibly growing gray and blurred above the sharp outlines of the fading trees.

His own trees. He knew them, individually. You cannot understand, unless you have had trees yourself. They possessed faces with which they met his eyes, in every change of joy or sorrow. He knew them as the colonel of a regiment knows, or should know, his numerous men. He always had a ready approval for the fine fellows that did their work bravest, budding early and blooming late, but also a gentle thought of indulgence for the weak ones, the stragglers, and an understanding that their lesser beauties were not so much the result of evil intention as an accident of circumstance or place.

He stopped to-day before an old oak, far-spreading and stately, but dead at the top. He eyed it lovingly. It stood, sombre and lonely, in a little clearing, bordered by a curve of lighter trees. He remembered how it had begun to decay in his father's time, and what an outcry there had been when the fact was first discovered. He might have recalled annual conversations with his steward always in the same stereotype form. "It will do as it is for the present, Dievert." "Yes, Mynheer the Baron." "It is a pity that this particular tree should take to going." "So it is; so it is, Mynheer the Baron." From time immemorial—to the villagers—it had been called "Lady Bertha's Oak," because of the little daughter of the house who, climbing recklessly up into its bosom, had been caught, as she slipped, in the arms of a fair, sad lady that must have been the Blessed Virgin herself, and borne safely to the ground. The little Freule Bertha had seen and declared it; it was written in a fifteenth century parchment that lay emblazoned in the archives of the family, and a weather-beaten cross, with a faint 1474 marked upon it, still leans, crooked and moss-eaten, in this secluded corner of the park.

"It will last my time," said the Baron, turning away from the tree. He wandered along, sadly meditating that no blessed Virgin was likely to spread her arms out under his little Wendela's threatening fall. Ah, those were brave old days when the Saints were still especially interested in us gentry.

"But it's not as bad as that yet," said the Baron, shaking off his gloomy thoughts. "With Strum's help I shall find money for the mortgages. I dare say my primary object with Bulbius was selfish. I should have let the house at a far higher price to this Monsieur de Farjolle, or perhaps sold it. Dear me, I wonder now whether I had thought of that?"

Somebody was moving in the brushwood. He turned to the slight rustle, attentive, as country gentlemen are. You might find a stray pheasant here occasionally, but it was too early in the day for poachers. The man came slouching along, one of his own labourers. The Baron stopped, slowly remembering, as the rustic saluted him. "Your little boy better this evening, Sam?" "Yes, thank you, landheer.

He's but poorly, thank you. And we remain humbly thankful to Mynheer for the broth." The broth was his wife's doing. He met her, as he turned into a broader avenue, a basket on her arm and their little daughter by her side.

"Well, and have you succeeded, mon ami?" asked the Baroness, his confidante in this as in all other matters but one.

"No, indeed," cried the Baron, with a sudden rekindling of his wrath. "The man is a fool!" And he savagely struck at the lemon-colored leaves of a chestnut which hung drooping perpendicularly from their stem.

"Be silent," said the Baroness in English. Her pale eyes lighted with reproof. "How can you, Reinout, speak in that manner, and before the child, of a priest?"

The Baron was eloquent in no language, least of all in English. He walked on in silence, and presently held out his hand to his daughter, who took it gravely, without a change in her brown eyes. She drew it against her mother's white woolly shawl. "Isn't it nice and soft?" she said.

They came in sight of the house. The chill avenue widened out gradually to a clear tract of grass, on which the dark forms of browsing deer moved indistinct beneath the drooping twilight. Against the far horizon the park began afresh, a great half circle, black beneath the slaty sky, but illumined, at one point, by a steady crimson flare, where the weak sun had sunk away. In the distant foreground, beyond the meadow, spread the brown mass of the Castle, enclosed by a moat whose current, invisible here, shone dully a little farther off. The sombre brickwork rose naked from the water, a confused mass of buttresses and excrescences, with a great square tower and a couple of smaller round ones, all jumbled up together under a fanciful tracery of weather-cocks, peaks, and flourishes, and a-glitter in the shimmer of its countless dull-blue windows and its topmost ball of Atlas against the dying light.

"How cold it is getting!" said the Baroness. "We stayed too long with Mother Bosman. She is sinking fast."

Wendela had lagged behind to stare after a long-vanished squirrel.

"Are you sure," questioned the Baron, waveringly, "that it is quite advisable to take the child to see old women die?"

"Most decidedly. She cannot too soon learn the responsibilities of her future position. Besides, she is no longer so young. She will soon be admitted to the Communion at the same altar where one of her ancestresses stood up to be married at her age."

"Betrothed, my dear. Elizabeth van Rexelaer was fourteen when she married. And those were other days."

"We are never too young to become acquainted with suffering, if our lot be cast among the great in this world," said Mevrouw van Rexelaer. "When I was twelve, my dear mother lay dying of consumption, and I was her only nurse."

"But, then, you had always a most remarkable character," said the Baron from the bottom of his heart.

They had paused by the bridge which leads to the courtyard, a brick courtyard with a stone road down and round it, nasty for horses in slippery weather. Tubbed orange-trees stand here during the brief months of a northern summer, in stately lines across the square and up the wide stone steps. Some of these orange-trees are said to be two hundred years old. They are giants to move, twice a year, with much groaning and creaking. And successive Baronesses have worn a sprig of their blossom in bridal wreaths, and afterwards dutifully made preserve of their fruits every summer, until the Baronesses themselves, in their turn, were soldered into leaden cases, with their faded bit of orange-blossom, and all their hopes and fears, to be hidden away in the vault under the chapel. Ill-luck to

the bride who neglected the orange-trees; the White
Baroness's own marriage had been delayed till the flowers
came out.

"I have something still that I wish to see about," murmured the Baron, pausing on the bridge.

"But, mon ami, why do you always run out into the
sunset? Come within. It is the worst time of day."

"No, no; I have things of importance to attend to."
He turned away quickly, then, recollecting himself, came
back after his wife, and led her across the dusk of the courtyard and kissed her hand upon the steps.

"Why is it, Reinout?" she asked abruptly. "What?"

"One worries sometimes about the mortgages. It is
nothing."

"The lady sighed. "Wanda!" she cried. "Where is
Wanda?"

"She has lagged behind. I will send her to you." He
went back under the shadow of the great black walls. By
the bridge he met his daughter. "Go in to your mother,
Wanda," he said.

"But I want to come with you, Papa."

"Oh, no. Go in immediately." He disappeared into
the darkness of the trees. The Bourse was long over; the
day's quotations were in print and would presently reach
him. Nevertheless was he anxious to kneel at the altar before he went on to "The Mountain." He did not reason
about these things. Nor do you.

"I, when I am grown up, I shall do as I like," said
Wendela to herself in French. Not a child that was ever
born but has found comfort in those delightful words, since
little Cain first muttered them, when his mother ordered
him to put on his furs again. Even Abel must have
thought them.

"I, when I am grown up, I shall do as I like," said
Wendela. Then she added "without being naughty," and

ran away in the wake of her father. She did not, however, follow him into the chapel, a pardonable divergence when it is remembered how frequently she was obliged to accompany the Baroness thither. She branched down a lane which leads to the kitchen-garden and orchards, and, when she got close to the garden-wall, she gave a shrill whistle, a most unladylike thing to do.

The whistle was answered, and a small boy's form loomed out of the darkness, on the top of the wall.

"Are you there, Piet?"

"See I am, Freule."

"Why don't you say 'Wendela,' Piet?"

"'Cause you're twelve now. I told you I should never say 'Wendela' again."

"There! you've said it."

"Never. I told you so on your birthday. You know I did, when I brought you the peaches."

"You stole the peaches, Piet."

"I tell you I didn't. I worked for them with Father. I never stole anything in my life. It's mean of you to say that again."

"And I didn't eat them. I wouldn't 'cause you wouldn't say 'Wanda.' You remember, Piet, I threw them away."

"I know you did. It wasn't nice of you, Freule. I'd worked for them real hard, three half-holidays."

"Well, say 'good evening, Wanda,' now."

"I sha'n't. Don't worry, Freule. You're too big."

"Oh you rude boy. I wish I were bigger, and I'd hit you."

"You can hit me now if you like. I'll come down. I don't mind being hit by a girl."

"You don't mind 'cause you think I shouldn't hurt you. But I should. You're afraid of being hit by your father."

"That's not true, Freule. I don't care when Father hits me."

"Well, then, get me a pear. One of the French ones."

"I won't, Freule. I tell you, I don't steal."

Wendela blushed scarlet in the dark. "I don't want you to steal," she said hotly. "What a horrid boy you are! Ain't I the heiress of Deynum?"

"And don't I tell you this year's pears ain't next year's pears? When you're the lady of Deynum, you may kill yourself, eating pears."

"So I shall, if my husband's as bad as you are."

"Oh, stop that. We left off being husband and wife three years ago."

"But people *can't* leave off being husband and wife, unless they're 'Gueux.' Mamma says so. You wouldn't be a 'beggar,' Piet?"

"No," cried Piet Poster with great vehemence, kicking his feet against the wall.

"Well, if you leave off being my husband, you must be. You are. You are."

"Don't call me a 'beggar,' Freule. If you do, I'd almost—"

"Almost what—?"

Piet Poster clenched his fists behind his back. "I'm going away," he said.

But this was not what the little lady wanted. "I won't say it again," she cried. "Look here, Piet, when we're grown up, I shall really marry you, and then you'll be lord of Deynum. You'd like that, wouldn't you? And then you could scold your father."

"All right. What'll the Baron say?"

"Oh—oh—oh! I say, Piet, I didn't come to talk about that. I came to tell you about his Reverence."

"What about his Reverence?" asked Piet in a reverential tone.

"He knows."

"What about? The—the cats—the—!"

"No, about his cap."

"I say! Who told him? How did he find out?"

"I told. I couldn't help it."

"Oh you sneak."

"I tell you I couldn't help it. And it was such fun. You should have seen his face!"

"Well, I didn't see it, so it's no fun to me. I think it was rightdown mean of you, Freule. We sha'n't be able to have any more bets." He spoke in a very disgusted tone, and began slipping down from the wall.

"Piet! Listen Piet! I shouldn't have wagered again anyway. I think it's wrong"—this last rather hypocritically.

"You! I was thinking of the boys. Good-night, Freule."

"I say, Piet! you won't tell I told?"

"Tell! No. You'd better be going home. It's getting dark, and you'll be afraid."

"You need not be rude as well as unkind," replied Wendela, moving off in dignified displeasure. She turned back for a parting shot. "Telling lies is every bit as bad as stealing," she cried, and was gone without saying "Good-night."

CHAPTER XIII.

NEXT morning Nicholas Strum, the Deynum lawyer, was ushered into the Baron's private room—a lofty, empty chamber with bare Gothic windows, its wainscoted walls hung with trophies and implements of shooting and fishing. It opens out of the library. The Baron was not a reading man.

The Strums have always been the notaries of Deynum, from the beginning—that is to say, of the Strums. There has been a time, of course, when there were Rexelaers but no notaries. Ever since there were notaries at all, however, the Barons van Rexelaer have been married and buried under the legal surveillance of an Andrew or a Nicholas Strum. The present man was Nicholas. The Baron had preferred Andrew.

Andrew had been old, very old, from his earliest youth, and slow, ponderously slow—benignant, bare-headed, broad and bow-backed, absolutely reliable. Nicholas was tall and heavy, lanky, lumpy, and loutish. But Nicholas was clever. He had been born in a stand-up collar, and his mother had always admired whatever he said and did. His father had shaken a massive head over the boy's shrewdness. But that did not hurt Nicholas, who admired himself even more than his mother admired him. Andrew was dead. Nicholas was very much alive.

There were various reasons why the Baron should dislike Nicholas. One of these was what Mevrouw van Rexelaer styled the "lawyer's brazen infidelity." The Strums, of course, had always been zealous Roman Catholics, but, Andrew having sent his son to the University of Louvain, so as to keep him free from contamination, the young man's innate spirit of contradiction had there, under the influence of rampant ultramontanism, developed an indifference to matters religious which had branded him at home as a "liberal Catholic," a creature almost unknown in the Netherlands. Originally the man had only wanted to go his way in peace, but the conventional horror of impiety and liberalism all around him fast drove him towards radicalism and irreligion. He was sick of the cult of "the Powers that be," in spite of his personal respect for the Baron. And the Rexelaers, on their part, would have preferred to break with this un-Strum-like Strum, had they seen their way to doing so. "How can pence develop into pounds," asked the Baroness, "in the hands of a man who does not believe in miracles?" "How indeed?" said the Baron. "You may well put that question here." And he smiled, by himself, as he had always had to, at his sad little joke.

"Sit down, Strum," said the Baron.

Strum sat down and gathered his long legs about him. The Notary possessed, quite unconsciously, two manners which had but one quality in common. He was either voluble and insolent, as soon as he felt that he had got the upper hand, or silent and awkward, when in the presence of a stronger power. In both cases he was rude, often chiefly from shyness, for shyness lay at the core of this big, unemotional-looking lump. You required but to watch his timid, spectacled eyes to see that. He had been polite, according to his lights, to Count Rexelaer, a possible patron. He was always especially volubly insolent to the Baron, from a fear of becoming too servile, like his father, and also from a lawyer's natural contempt of financial embarrassment.

"Well?" said the Baron, after a moment's expectant silence. He coughed uncomfortably.

Strum coughed uncomfortably. Then he broke out suddenly, with the abruptness of a popgun.

"Your Nobleness has received my letter?" The Baron took up from his writing-table a paper, which he had been fingering all the while.

"Of course," he said, "It came up last night. But why write? Your father never wrote to me in his life, Nicholas. And, besides, the letter tells me nothing. Difficulties about renewing the mortgage! Why? Which? It is a couple of months yet before the question need arise." He was very agitated already. He was one of those men whom the very mention of "business" agitates. Not having grown up within its inner circle, they have learnt by experience that for outsiders all "business" practically comes to legalized spoliation. And the outsider never understands the trick till it's done.

"I wrote," said Strum, "immediately after my final interview with the Hague bankers. The stakes are too momentous; the sum is too large." He jerked forward his outlying foot with a great thump at nothing. "We can't wait till the latest moment which is often a moment too late, as my dead father used to say." He always quoted his dead father to—or rather against—the Baron van Rexelaer.

"I miss him every day of my life, Mynheer the Baron," he continued—a mere nervous overflow of talk—, "But most of all in these great transactions with regard to Deynum. I miss him very much."

"So do I," said the Baron, with very different conviction. "Come to the point, Strum, please. Surely four and a half is a sufficient rate of interest."

"The interest is high enough," began Strum, "they would probably renew for less—"

"Then why bother me?" cried the Baron with a gasp of relief.

The young Notary made a deprecatory movement with his left hand, ere he proceeded to crack its fingers with his right.

"Had they not made up their mind not to renew at all," he said. He drew away his broad lips to his ears as he spoke, revealing a set of irregular yellow teeth. The movement had nothing of a grin in it, it was a mere muscular twitch which gave his face an expression as if he were going to swallow you.

"The risk is immense," he went on hastily. "The estate, valuable as it is, cannot bear the continued depreciation of land. They will sell while they can and the sooner the better. For them and for everybody, I should say." He spoke blusteringly. He was every jot as ill at ease as the Baron.

"Your dear departed father used to say, Nicholas," remarked a low, grave voice behind him, "that the man who does business for gentlemen should always be a gentleman himself." The Baroness, smooth and colourless in her laces, had entered noiselessly through the library-door.

"Chère amie, chère amie," expostulated the Baron, "leave me and Strum "—yes; he said "me and Strum "—"to settle these matters between us."

The Notary was boiling internally, but he only boiled over in drops. "Mevrouw," he said, with a great crack of his curved thumb, "it would be a good thing for all parties, if there were no business to be transacted at Deynum. But the fact remains, Mynheer the Baron, that the mortgages will not be renewed, and that the whole immense sum of money must be found, which, of course, is impossible."

"How do you know what is possible or impossible?" asked the Baron haughtily.

"Only in so far as your man of business can judge."

"You are that, but not my confidant."

"I should be neither or both, Mynheer the Baron, as my father used to say."

"He never said it of you, Nicholas," interposed the Baroness. She had been standing watching his clumsy twitches with pallid contempt. She now moved away to a window-seat. Her vague eyes rested on the distant park. They drew her husband's in the same direction. He had not the strength to remonstrate again.

Nicholas bit his lips. He thought he could manage the Baron, but he was afraid of the lady, whom he cordially disliked.

"Of course, if the money will be forthcoming, so much the better," he said. "In that case I need not further trouble you with the object of my visit, which was an offer I received yesterday."

"What offer?" asked the Baron, a little shamefacedly. Strum closed his eyes behind his big round spectacles. "The bank informs me that an excellent opportunity occurs—of which it would be to the advantage of all parties to avail themselves—for transferring the whole of the mortgages into other hands, into private hands, as I understand."

A sudden tremor played over the Baron's face. The Baroness glanced round from the window, and then back again at the trees.

"I understand," said the Baron in a husky voice. "And that is why they refuse to renew. Who is the 'private person'?"

"No name is mentioned as yet."

"Were you aware, Strum, that I declined, a couple of days ago, the offer of a certain person at the Hague to purchase this place?"

"Yes, Mynheer the Baron."

"You were. Then you knew of the offer before it was made. Perhaps you suggested it during your stay at the Hague?" The Baron was not a good hand at irony; his voice grew louder: "It is a conspiracy," he cried, "and you are in it!"

"A conspiracy, if you like," replied Strum roughly. "I was asked my opinion as to the advisability of such a proposal, and I said: Make it, by all means. I thought it the best, the only solution of a gigantic difficulty. And I think so still. I should call this anxiety on the part of Count Rexelaer to purchase the place a most wonderful piece of good-fortune!"

"Count Rexelaer," repeated the Baron. "Just so. You are your father's son, Nicholas, and, although you do not know as much as he did, you probably know enough to understand that I would rather see this house a smouldering ruin than the property of Count Rexelaer." He turned upon the Notary: "You had no right," he said, "to take both my pay and Count Rexelaer's."

Nicholas Strum returned his patron's look, full in the face. Then he rose as majestically as his ungovernable limbs would allow. "It is your Nobleness's good pleasure as it is your prerogative," he said, "to insult your inferiors. But such insults, as my father used to say, hit back, like guns. I acted for the best." And he left the room.

The Baroness drew near to her husband. "If there is not money enough, we must live still more simply," she said, taking the woman's view. But her heart sank as she thought of her housekeeping-book.

The Baron lifted his face from his hands: "Perhaps I was hard on Strum," he said. "He cannot look at these matters from our point of view."

"But why does that man want to become sole mortgagee?"

"It is next best. At the first hitch he would sell, and —purchase."

"I do not understand exactly," she said. "Do you, dearest?"

"No, I do not understand exactly," he murmured humbly.

8

"But God will leave us Deynum," she said, and, as her cheek touched his, she burst into tears.

Nicholas Strum went tramping downstairs in a towering rage. He was very much wronged, and he had cause to be angry.

"Serve them right," he said, as he struck his umbrella viciously at the oaken banisters. "'Tis like this that the great folks make themselves hated, with their beggarly, haughty, ignorant ways! 'Tis a sin against God and them to come lowering their greatness, even when just debts have got to be paid. And my father was right, as that White Creature put it: 'Gentlemen should do business with each other and for themselves.' I wonder how they'd manage. For each of them expects to give all the kicks and to get all the half-pence."

Thus righteously grumbling, he went in search of Count Rexelaer, whom he had left in the park.

CHAPTER XIV.

Upon receiving, through his own Notary, the Baron's curt and absolute refusal to enter into negotiations, Count Hilarius immediately started for Deynum. Matters were coming to a crisis. He had succeeded, after months of waiting and intriguing, in getting himself nominated on the Board of Directors of the Bank which held by far the greater part of the Baron's enormous mortgages. Once there, he had prevented a renewal. And now the supreme moment had arrived. The place must either fall into his hands, almost immediately, or the Baron must dispose of it to others and probably lose it to the family for ever.

The Count took Reinout with him, Monsieur de Souza being laid up with one of his bad attacks of gout on the chest. And nothing delighted Reinout so much as a glimpse of the country. He was another creature there, away from the straight pavements of his daily life, rushing to and fro in reckless, aimless animal motion, bewildered and intoxicated by the sounds, the smells, the great sky overhead.

Father and son stood in a clearing in the woods, from whence they could get a vague view of the house. They had halted there, at a safe distance, leaving Strum to proceed on his errand. To Reinout the brisk autumnal walk had been a source of overwhelming amusement and interest. The Count, also, enjoyed this first sight of a place which had been the Mecca of his thoughts ever since he could think at all. It caused him an immense satisfaction to return the salutes of the rare peasants they came across. He felt a sort of proprietorship in them.

"Look, Reinout, there it is!" he cried. "The home of your ancestors!" He drew his son towards him, and they stood gazing side by side. The Count was deeply moved.

An indefinable thrill of pride and disappointment ran down Reinout's back. It was very grand, but, after all, it was earthly. He had dreamed, through long years, a dream of the intangible. And the October air lay chill and brown over all that dreary stretch of trees—and the shadowy distant building with its feeble film of ascending smoke.

"It isn't a bit like Brazil," he said.

The Count could not suppress a movement of impatience. Why did the child at every emergency, always say or do the stupidest thing? "Run away, and play," he said. And Reinout eagerly availed himself of the permission. He wandered off into the wood, attracted by one delight after another, and ultimately lost his way and came out into a country-lane where he met a carter who drove him back to the village.

The village he found almost as curious as the woodlands surrounding it. He inspected the Protestant Church, and took off his cap to Father Bulbins, who came out of the Parsonage to have a look at him. And a little troop of boys having collected on the green, he distributed his pennies among them. Just as he had disposed of the last, the baker's lame child, Tony, came limping up to find out what was going on. Reinout saw, and despairingly felt in his empty pockets. Then he said aloud: "Oh, I *can't*. Mamma won't mind," and unfastened a small gold stud which held his collar and slipped it into Tony's hand. After that he took refuge in the public-house, where his father had told him they would have some bread and meat before leaving, and asked Hendrika for a bit of string.

The Marquis had grumbled for forty-eight hours. He had not slept. He had only dozed, grumbling. He had eaten nothing, but he had drunken a few cups of bouillon which Antoine had concocted. He had grumbled over them.

The blow which had struck him down seemed to have paralysed all other life within him and to have concentrated his powers into one persistency of grumbling. It was an outlet for his rage against God and himself, a safety-valve of his despair. He lay back among his pillows grumbling. The sun was climbing the white sky. The sick man felt weak.

"I must get up," he burst out, infuriated by this feeling. "I never could stand lying down. You remember, Antoine, how weak I became after that fall with my horse."

Antoine said he remembered.

"True," said the old man eagerly. "Bed does not agree with me. I will get up." Antoine brought his dressing-things, the new ones. The Marquis had been eager for them to arrive, and had not looked at them when they came.

He now allowed himself to be dressed, with many outbursts of irritation and peevish complaints. And in the intervals of abuse he talked of the accident which had occurred a couple of years ago. "It was Belle-maman," he said. "You remember Belle-maman, Antoine? She was not a bad mare, and I never knew her to stumble before. She took fright at a rascally undertaker whose black bands fluttered in her face. Here, don't crumple my shirt, you. You don't even know how to fit in a stud."

"We all of us take fright at the sight of something ugly, Monsieur le Marquis," said the valet politely. He was having a bad time of it, and felt vindictive. The Marquis talked no more about his accident. He swore till his toilet was completed, and then he stood gazing for a moment by the window. His attention was attracted by the little group of village-children and the central figure, with its graceful bearing, distributing largesse, like a lord.

"It is the same boy," said the Marquis instantly. "Then the family is the same, after all. What did the old man mean?" He turned round to his valet. "Help me downstairs," he said.

"But yes, Monsieur le Marquis," replied Antoine with alacrity. By the time the pair had stumbled down, Reinout had entered the inn-parlour, and they found him confabulating with the landlady. He looked up as the door opened, and his eyes remained riveted on the sick man's face.

"You remember me?" said the Marquis abruptly, as he sank on to the settle.

This question put an end to the boy's doubts. "I do now," he answered honestly. "You are the gentleman who gave me the watch."

"And you are René de Rexelaer. I also, you perceive, have not forgotten. You live here?"

"No, Monsieur, I never was here before. I live at the Hague."

"And this Baron, up at the Castle, he is your uncle?"

"No, Monsieur, we are of the same family, but two separate branches. We do not know each other."

Reinout stood up and answered like a man, though a little embarrassed by the string in his collar. Hendrika had fled.

"Why not?"

"I do not know, Monsieur, unless it be because we are Protestants. Rovert van Rexelaer became a Protestant in 1673."

The Marquis smiled. Ah, that was the reason then. He could quite understand it. These country bumpkins are all alike, he thought.

"You have a mother?" he asked after a moment. "Yes? Describe her to me. What is her name?"

"Mamma is very beautiful, and dark," said Reinout, a

little wonderingly. "Her name is Margherita de Cachenard. She and I, we come from Brazil."

"Very well," said the Marquis. "After all, I am asking what is no business of mine. Now, listen to me, my child. You are going back to the Hague in an hour or two?"

"Yes, Monsieur, as soon as my father comes."

"Then you will never see me again. You remember the adage I taught you, half a dozen years ago?"

Reinout nodded, half a nod and half a little bow.

"A gentilhomme devoir fait loi," he said.

"That was it. I had forgotten, myself. Live up to it. Make it a truth. I have not." A silence fell on the gloomy inn-parlour. "I have not. Eh? What do you say to that?"

"I am sorry," said Reinout simply.

"So am I." The old man's voice sounded true. He staggered up and motioned to his impassive servant. "Adieu," he said holding out his hand. The boy touched the wasted fingers, and in the solemn stillness the old man went away.

When Count Hilarius reached the inn half an hour later he was in a very bad temper. Everything went against him, he said, and all on account of a pig-headed old fool that desired his own ruin. He was angry with Reinout for looking untidy, and annoyed at the discovery of Monsieur Farjolle. He hesitated about sending up his card to that gentleman. It would be absurd to return the watch after all this time. But Antoine came down and said his master was very ill and saw no one. He was a French wine-merchant; they were going on to Paris to-morrow. So the Rexelaers went away.

That evening the Baron sent off two letters. One was addressed to his Amsterdam brokers and contained a final order which was to bring him immense and almost certain success. The other went by hand to the village. Its contents were as follows:

The Baron van Rexelaer van Deynum presents his compliments to Mr. Nicholas Strum, and begs to apologise for any expression he may have made use of this morning which could give Mr. Strum just cause for offence.

CASTLE DEYNUM, Thursday evening.

"I don't care," said Mynheer Strum, ungraciously throwing down the piece of paper. That morning he had had to bear Count Rexelaer's silken ill-temper as well. "The fellow's afraid, that's all. I hate these aristocrats. There's nothing drives you wild like constant, compulsory cringing. I'm sick of the lot."

His old mother glanced timidly across the tea-table. She knew her lord and master was in a bad temper, but then, also, she was of an inquiring nature. "A letter from Mynheer the Baron," she said. "Are you commanded up to the Castle again to-morrow, Nicky?"

"No," he answered roughly, "it isn't any business of yours, mother. I wish you'd hold your tongue, always jab, jab, jabbering about the Castle."

"But I feel what a privilege it is for you, Nicky, to have all the great Baron van Rexelaer's business to do just as your father had."

"Hang the great Baron van Rexelaer!" cries Nicholas. "I wish I could send him about his business. I'm a socialist, I am, mother. There, hand me the newspaper. When the smash comes, there'll be no more Barons van Rexelaer."

"And no more notaries," said his mother quietly. She would not have been such a stupid woman, had she been a little less fond of her son.

CHAPTER XV

THE next couple of days were spent by the Marquis in a semi-lethargic condition, the result of the nervous torture he had undergone. At the twilight-hour on the second day he roused himself and announced his intention of going out for a walk.

"But at this moment," remonstrated Antoine. "And in this country, with the falling damps!"

"Am I to go out when you choose?" asked the invalid. "It rained all yesterday. I am sickening in this musty room. A walk will do me good."

The valet shrugged his shoulders. Why, after all, should he waste his breath?

"And I am anxious to find out," continued the Marquis, while allowing himself to be as carefully arrayed as if he were going to a garden-party at Laeken, "whether it is absolutely certain, as this Baron wrote me, that there is nothing to be got in the village. I cannot stay any longer in this miserable inn."

They had now been at Deynum nearly four days, and Antoine was fast losing all hope of getting his master away. "Indeed, Monsieur le Marquis has delayed here too long already. The smells alone must be injurious to health. If Monsieur le Marquis would but venture just a little journey farther—"

"Yes, I know," replied the Marquis. "You want girls to flirt with. I tell you again, nothing brings on these terrible spasms but railway-travelling. I have had them three times, and each time immediately after, or during, a railway-journey. I am dying, but I shall die in my own way, and I shall take my own time about it. You would like to have it over in six months. I am going to take a couple of years to do it in."

He said this but he did not think it. He would have acted quite differently otherwise. His whole strangeness of behaviour found its root in the fallacious conviction that disease had numbered, not his months, but his days.

"I shall die at Deynum, if I choose," he said. He stumbled along, leaning heavily forward. And constantly he would pause and pretend to be hunting for his pocket-handkerchief. "I have caught cold in those infamous draughts," he said. And he lifted the handkerchief to his face and gasped for breath behind it.

" The chillness of the evening air—" began Antoine.

"Silence. Ah, here is the park. It is really very good. But it is not as good as—home, eh ?"

Before the servant could answer, the master broke into a violent oath. His own word had stabbed him like a knife.

He shuffled on under the trees. And every now and then he righted himself and strove to walk straight, and then fell forward again on his servant's arm, and shuffled on.

Presently they were confronted by a view of the house. It lay asleep in the solemn water, dark and still. "Good," said the Marquis again. "Simple, but good," and shuffled on.

It was not till they had turned into the Long Walk, which leads to the village, that they came upon the figure of a man stretched prostrate across the path.

Antoine sprang forward with a cry of surprise. The Marquis, thus suddenly deprived of his prop, staggered back in the impatient effort to stand alone.

"It is Monsieur le Baron!" cried Antoine, lifting the insensible body.

"And what am I to do with Monsieur le Baron?" replied the Marquis querulously. "It is hardly presumable that he is drunk. He has probably had an attack. A sick man cannot carry a dead one."

They looked round helplessly. "Shout!" said the Marquis. "We are not far from the house."

Antoine obeyed and sang out lustily. The Marquis pointed to a white mass lying beneath a tree close by. An open letter, a couple of newspapers,—the evening post.

"Shout again," said the Marquis.

A child came running up. "What is wrong?" she asked fearlessly. "Tiens, des enfants maintenant!" mumbled the Marquis. "Ma petite, this gentleman has fallen, but he is not much hurt."

"It is Papa," cried Wendela. "Oh poor Papa!" She was struggling with her tears, to the Marquis's alarm. "We must carry him to the house," she said, having mastered them. "You, Monsieur, will you help?"

"Mademoiselle, I regret sincerely, but I cannot," replied the Marquis deeply humiliated. "Surely someone will come."

She flung him a look of incredulous contempt. "I can do it," she said, and vainly tried to lift the heavy foot. "Halloo!" cried Antoine again.

"Halloo," replied a bright voice. A milkmaid was coming along a side-path.

"Ah, Lise, is it you?" exclaimed the little Freule. "You must help carry Papa. He is ill. This gentleman is not—strong enough."

But, recalled perhaps by the shouting, the Baron now stirred and muttered and opened his eyes.

"I am quite well," he stammered. "I stumbled, that is all. Where are my papers? Where are my papers?" he repeated excitedly.

Antoine gathered them together and put them in his hand. The Baron rose to his feet, with the valet's assistance. "Ah pardon!" he said, "Monsieur—Farjolle." The Marquis was leaning against a tree in profound disgust. What a disgraceful thing was bodily weakness! The shadows were spreading wide and heavy. It was cold.

They formed into a little procession, the Baron leaning on Antoine Loripont's arm, the Marquis pretending not to press on Wendela's shoulder. The old gentleman broke the silence once. "My little one," he said, "some day you will understand the suffering of not being able." Wendela coloured in the dark, and set her teeth hard to bear the weight of his arm. Lize, with her clinking pails, brought up the rear, her cheerful step in continuous contrast with the slouch of the others.

"I keep in touch with your shoulder," said the Marquis presently to his companion, "because I am afraid of a false step on this unknown road. I hope I do not hinder you in any way?" "No," she gasped. But she did not ask why he still clung to her all the tighter after they had emerged into the open near the house. By that time the Baron had almost entirely recovered from his shock. "You will come in, Monsieur, and rest?" he said, turning round. "Gladly," replied the Marquis, whereby he meant that he was too utterly exhausted to decline.

Once in the house, he found himself compelled to remain. The two horses had been out for a long drive in the afternoon, but one of them must take him home after dinner. That meal would be served in half an hour. "I am all right again," said the Baron, "I really am all right." And he introduced Monsieur Farjolle to the Baroness.

That lady was charmed. A gloom hung over the household since the interview with the Notary. The stranger's presence would cause a diversion. A man of the world, a gentleman, and a Catholic!—not that you noticed anything of the religion; still it was a comfort to know it there. And the Marquis, who had locked himself up in his despair since first it closed around him, was astonished to discover that he could still laugh and talk—though with weary heart and body—in the courteous nothings of social intercourse.

Father Bulbius came in to dinner—not an unusual occurrence—and his bright face clouded over with importance at sight of the other guest. After having kissed the hand of the lady of the house, at imminent peril of apoplexy, he wandered away to the Baron, who was sitting wearily in the shade.

"Do not let me disturb your Nobleness," said the Father, slowly letting himself down on the low divan. He dropped his voice: "Have you any idea who that gentleman is who calls himself Monsieur Farjolle?"

"Yes," replied the Baron quickly. "He is a foreigner. He calls himself Monsieur Farjolle. That is enough."

"Ah, but his servant this morning let fall a title which aroused my curiosity. I questioned him, and I discovered—"

The Baron stopped him. "Hush," he said.

"But, my dear sir, of course I heard nothing in my official capacity," cried the Father bridling. "Surely you know me better than to imagine that the secrets of the confessional—"

"I know, I know, your Reverence. Come, let us talk of something else." The Baron slowly shut and reopened his eyes, that sure sign of exhaustion, whether of body or brain.

The Marquis, meanwhile, was praising the house to his hostess. He drawled out his words with an unconcerned ease of expression which seemed conscious that men would find leisure to listen as long as his Grandeur found inclination to speak.

"I have lived here; I shall die here," said the Baroness, bravely. "It is that, I suppose, which endears the place to me unspeakably. But, to you, Deynum must be terribly dull." She cast a commiserating glance at the old man's hollow face. She could feel for all the various moods of refinement. The stranger must be morbidly afraid of the society of his equals to put up with the accommodation of the village inn.

"Oh, no; I like the country," said the Marquis. He was greatly bored. He looked down at his smart patent-leather boots; there was a splash of mud across one of them, and it persistently drew his attention. With one carefully kept hand he smoothed his white moustache and curled over his ears the locks which were neatly drawn forward from the parting at the back of his head. He was not dressed for dining. The fact did not discomfort him; nothing could have done that. But he felt annoyed by it.

"I," said the child, who had drawn near to them, "I, too, should like to die at Deynum."

The Marquis winced. "You, Mademoiselle," he said lightly, holding out his hand to her. "A pretty child like you ought not to talk of death."

She did not take the hand. "Death!" she replied gravely. "That is purgatory; it is horrid. I meant 'dying.' I should like to die at Deynum and go and sleep with the others in the chapel. Afterwards—it is horrid, but one does not know!"

"But you are a little philosopher," said the Marquis with a ghastly grin.

"The child does not understand what she is talking about," interposed Mevrouw van Rexelaer rising. "Permit me to take your arm, Monsieur."

At table the little life left in the sick man seemed to flare up under congenial surroundings. He ate sparingly, but he drank a glass or two of his host's wine and warmly commended it. And he told a couple of amusing stories, cautiously, as if afraid of compromising himself. Father Bulbius sat admiring him open-mouthed.

Stimulated by the Marquis's example and especially flat-

tered by the praise his cellar was receiving from so manifest a connoisseur, the master of the house also somewhat
shook off the lethargy of his own sorrows, and even so far
conquered himself as to tell the story of the King's Wine.
How in the glorious year '15, the great year of deliverance,
he, being then about twelve years old, had lived with his
mother for a time at a small country house in Brabant near
the frontier, while his father was with the army in Belgium.
And how on one beautiful calm June evening news had
flown up from the village that a courier was come with the
tidings of a great victory to bear to the King. His horse
had broken down; he was clamouring for another—would
the Baroness give her best? And how he—little Reinout,
as he was then—had run away to the stables and saddled
his father's "Bruno," with only a cry to the groom that he
would be back again to-morrow, and had ridden out upon
the high-road he scarcely knew how or why. And then
how he had rushed onward all through the soft summer-
night, with but one thought in his heart of the great victory
and the joy of the King! and had crossed the mighty
waters of the Moerdyk and the Maas, while some took his
gold sleeve-links and buttons in payment and others helped
him on with God speed! for the glad news that he bore.
How a post-keeper had lent him a horse when Bruno could
bear even his light weight no further, and how, at last, in
the glory of the proud June morning, he had drawn rein,
fainting but triumphant, at the Palace gates. How he had
cried for his grandfather who was one of the Court cham-
berlains, and how, between tears and laughter, he had finally
poured out his story at the Sovereign's feet, half an hour
before the State courier came in with the Despatches. How
the King, when the truth was confirmed, had patted his
head, saying: "What must I do for you, my fine little fellow?" and how he had answered with his eyes on the table:
"A glass of wine, please, your Majesty and Grandpapa, though
it isn't my birthday—" and how the room had swum round,

as all the courtiers laughed. How the King had declared that he should never want *that* to drink the royal health in, and had sent his father a hogshead to lay aside for him, with the intimation that, when next he did his country good service, he must ask for some more. "I reminded him of his promise on a later occasion," said the Baron in conclusion, "and I got another, and larger, present of the same. It is good wine, as you say. I used to keep it, but now I drink it. In a few years there will be nobody left to do so."

"There's me, Papa," said the child.

"Women don't drink wine," replied her father. "They sip it, without tasting."

The Baroness had heard the story several hundred times before, but she had never heard it told to a Frenchman. She was the more surprised that her husband avoided specifying the "other occasion," which was merely the siege of Antwerp in the Belgian war.

"He is too modest to allude to his own military exploits," she thought.

"The King is dead," said the Baron, saluting as he emptied his glass, "Long live the King!"

Gustave, by the side-board, saluted too.

"I have not yet had an opportunity of telling you," said the Baron, when the two gentlemen were alone together, waiting for the carriage, "how much I regretted the failure of my attempt to find you a suitable lodging. I fear now that you will very soon be leaving us."

He felt how complimentary was the "us."

"You are too kind, my dear Baron," murmured the visitor, without regarding his own words. The old man sat staring vaguely before him; he was dead-tired, miserably oppressed by the weight which no companionship could cast off. He spoke a few sentences about the weather and the crops, and the other answered him.

"I am ill," said the Marquis suddenly. "I am dying. I can't travel any more. I won't travel. I can't stay in that filthy inn. Monsieur de Rexelaer, can you really not find me some place I could buy to die quietly in?" A hungry, hunted look came over his face; he was yearning to speak of his trouble to someone besides Antoine.

The Baron got up and walked across the room, away from his guest. "I know of one house," he said, "if you were willing to pay for it."

"I will pay anything," cried the other passionately, "I want rest. This stupid anxiety is killing me before my time. What is the house that you speak of?"

"It is this," said the Baron with his back turned. He clutched at a chair and sat down.

There was an awkward pause. Then the Marquis said stiffly, "You misapprehend me, Monsieur. I was very much in earnest. I am perfectly well aware that you cannot place this house at my disposal."

"Why not, Monsieur le Marquis?" said the other from his dark corner.

"What! You know me! That scoundrel has blabbed!"

"Forgive me. The fault is not your valet's. From the first moment I heard your name, I was aware that I had the honour of speaking to the Marquis de la Jolais."

"Ah!" cried the Marquis.

"There are not so many of us that we do not know about each other, at least in Holland and Belgium. Forgive my indiscretion, which I deeply regret. I was speaking under the influence of excitement. But I warn you, I fear that your name is known to others than myself."

The Marquis bowed, exaggeratedly vexed. He had clung to his sick man's whim. "But this—this—how shall I say?—about your castle?" he asked. "It is a pleasantry?"

"Monsieur, is it a subject I should joke upon, even did I desire to insult you? If you wish to buy the place—the whole thing—you can do so. The air does not agree with

9

my wife. You see how pale she looks. I am anxious to settle abroad."

"But I want a house, not an estate," said the Marquis. He rose as Antoine came forward with his wraps, and, motioning him back, tottered across to the dark spot in which the other was sitting. "I thank you, sir," he said, "for the signal honour you have done me. Believe me, I know how to appreciate it." They shook hands in silence, and then the Marquis was driven back to the inn.

CHAPTER XVI.

" J'OSAIS."

"Encore un de flambé," said the Marquis to himself. His class-feeling was honestly sorry for the Baron; none the less he could not entirely suppress a faint glow of satisfaction that another of the world's mighty ones should have come to grief, like himself. "Sold up!" he said, and smiled bitterly.

He could easily put two and two together and conclude that the Baron had speculated and lost. " If he has played away such a family estate, what a fool he must be!" thought Monsieur de la Jolais. In so far he partly wronged Baron Rexelaer, for that gentleman, unable to pay off the mortgages his ancestors had accumulated, had only taken to speculation as an ultimate possibility of escape. By his operations he had lost more than twice the original deficit. The news of the final crash had reached him through the last post. His brokers, refusing to hold out any longer, had sold.

There was no écarté that evening. Only the Baroness's Patience, with Father Bulbius watching it.

"Here, you, Antoine, listen," said the Marquis imperiously. He had had his evening injection of morphia, and the valet was about to withdraw. "I have something to say to you. My identity is out."

The valet's conscience smote him; on that account he smiled superciliously. " But what could Monsieur le Marquis expect?" he said. "And with an alias which is Monsieur le Marquis's own name?"

"Peace," interrupted his master. "You told. Whom?"

Antoine protested with vehemence. The Marquis listened carelessly, half-hidden by the faded green bed-curtains. Presently he said: "Let us understand each other. This person, will he tell others?"

"But nobody knows!" cried Antoine.

"I suppose that means he will not. You will go to him to-night—to-night, do you hear!—and offer him money to hold his tongue. If it is the priest, as I presume, so much the better. He will keep his promise as well as the money. Or, still cheaper, you might pass your words through the confessional?"

Loripont's countenance expressed his disapproval of such levity. He thought his master little better than a heathen.

"Your religion comes useful occasionally," the Marquis went on. "Where's that little Virgin of yours? Find it."

Loripont obeyed with a scowl. He drew from under his shirt a tiny silver image, fastened to a string, and kissed it reverently, and then stood dangling it, irreverently. Once before, upon their first coming together, his master had make him swear by it, swear never to steal or cheat. He had religiously kept his oath. The little image was his guardian-angel and every-day god. It was no good for the other world, but it looked after him in this. Fortunately the Marquis had not exacted a promise of absolute veracity. The wisdom of government lies in the regulation of liberty.

"I will give you," said Monsieur de la Jolais, toying with the trifles on his bed-table, "one thousand francs for every week I have to live. That is my offer. My demand is this:

"First. You will send for your wife, and you and she

will tend me with unmurmuring devotion. Secondly. You
will both preserve absolute silence about me and my doings,
now and ever afterwards. There is no mystery. I do not
intend to do anything extraordinary, but I will not have my
sufferings known to the world. As soon as I am dead, you
will convey my body back to Saint-Leu, and you will give
out that I died of some chest-complaint—Pneumonia. That
is all. Swear. I can trust your to frighten your wife into
her part. Swear for both."

"I will swear, Monsieur le Marquis, on one condition—"

"You have heard the condition," said the Marquis,
sitting up in bed. "The money shall be paid you. Swear."

He cowed the man with his keen eyes. Antoine mumbled "I swear," as he lifted the little image to his lips.

But immediately afterwards his manner changed. He
leant back against the roughly-painted door, slipped the
little doll out of sight behind his collar, and folded his
arms.

"Take a chair!" said the Marquis, with courteous scorn.
But the valet did not modify his pose. "I also have my
conditions, Monsieur le Marquis," he said. "Will Monsieur le Marquis have the goodness to listen to them for a
moment?"

Monsieur de la Jolais sank back and plaintively wondered where was the strength of those good old days when
he would have cursed the fellow out of the room. His head
was growing dizzy. He merely said : "You should not first
have taken your oath."

"I permit myself to differ from Monsieur le Marquis,"
retorted the valet. "I remembered that I was dealing with
a gentilhomme."

The Marquis felt the force of the rebuke. "What is
it you want?" he said. "Be brief. I stand in great need
of rest."

"Monsieur le Marquis de la Jolais-Farjolle," began Antoine, striving in vain to keep his voice quite steady, "when

I entered your service eight years ago, you bound me down never to appropriate any of those little advantages which a gentleman's service naturally brings with it. You paid me the usual wages. I therefore earned less than half of what is usual. I have kept faithfully to my promise; I have never appropriated a halfpenny. I believe that, on the whole, I have not given serious cause for dissatisfaction?"

"So be it," said the Marquis. "You could have left, if you wished."

"Not only did I not earn my due," continued the valet, "but I was obliged to spend part of my wages, on your behalf, to keep up the honour of our name. Permit me to say it, Monsieur le Marquis, but a man in my position who respects himself and his connections cannot expose himself to the charge of continuous underpayment of inferiors. Wherever, during all these years, you have instructed me—at home or abroad—to give a cabman or a porter a franc, I have been compelled by circumstances, Monsieur le Marquis, —excuse my mentioning it—to make the sum one franc fifty, and sometimes two."

"The more fool you," said the Marquis.

"So I have always thought, Monsieur le Marquis. But one attaches oneself, against one's will, to the great name one is connected with. Permit me to add, Monsieur le Marquis, that I have carefully kept account of all the sums I was thus compelled to advance in a little note-book, which I have here." He touched his breast.

"Anything more?" asked the Marquis.

"There is just one point which I am afraid I must still mention,"—he hesitated—"Taking into account the great risk of these advances, I have considered myself entitled to reckon ten per cent. interest on each payment from the day on which it was made. I can assure Monsieur le Marquis on the solemn oath by which I bound myself that the accounts I have handed in have always been rigidly accurate, and that in the extra charges I now bring forward I have never exceeded the limits of what I considered the unavoidable."

"*You* considered," said the Marquis.

"Monsieur will allow me to point out that Monsieur le Marquis de la Jolais-Farjolle has the reputation of being the most extravagant nobleman in Brussels. He has not the reputation of being the most generous. He would probably be known as the stingiest, were it not for his humble servant, Antoine Loripont."

He stared his master straight in the face, but not impertinently. Then he produced his little account-book and held it out. "The sum total," he said, "is three thousand, seven hundred and forty-three francs, nineteen centimes. The centimes sound unreal; they are the outcome of the interest-reckoning. I vouch for strictly honest accuracy, by the Mother of God—" and he pulled out his little image again, and kissed it.

"Go to the devil," said the Marquis.

"As Monsieur the Marquis pleases. But I mentioned this subject because I wished to forewarn Monsieur le Marquis that I shall consider myself entitled to refund myself this money—which I have always looked upon as a loan—from whatever moneys or articles of value I may happen to have in my keeping at the time of Monsieur the Marquis's possible demise—I have understood that much from the beginning."

"You shall make an inventory for me," said the Marquis. "I shall send it to the Notary's."

Their eyes met. "I was mistaken," said the valet coolly. "I should have delayed my oath after all."

The Marquis turned his face to the wall. "Take the money," he said. "Take it now. But, for Heaven's sake, let me sleep!"

The repose which he longed for did not, however, visit him as soon as he had expected. He, who had always been an excellent sleeper—it was natural to his tranquil good health—had yet to learn that there is an exhaustion which does not precede, but precludes, recuperative rest. Sleep, like the jilt she is, does not come when courted. She attracts, and casts her glamour all around her, and then laughs and runs away.

And she leaves behind her all the torment of that living night-watch which is so unlike the life of day.

All the hideous moonlight of a soul distorted, in which depths of unknown stillness wake and move beneath the shifting shadows, to a rush of restlessness that dies away and yet is never altogether gone, while the thousand shapeless spectres that rise and breathe and have no being come roaming to and fro in the chilly greyness—into unending distance, with a weary drawing of the brain, and then back again upon the burning eye-balls, with a blow as of a hammer, and once more down avenues of vagueness, never fully visible—far—far—never out of sight.

The Marquis sat up in bed. "Rest," he said aloud. And then he fell back again, and tossed from side to side.

And as he did so, there woke within him an indefinite consciousness of something—something wrong—at that point where the dead weight lay under his breast. For the moment only there was the vague expectancy—half curious, half.anxious—and then steadily, like the pressure of a borer, slowly piercing farther, there came deepening on his soul a persistency of pain. Then, the expectancy that it would pass over, that it was relenting, lessening—a sharp twinge, almost welcome, in the momentary diversion—a sudden hope!—and then again, slowly, steadily, the piercing, pressing pain.

He revolted against it in the fury of his impotence, tired no longer, no longer conscious of fatigue. He struck his hands wildly into the darkness, and threw back the bed-clothes, and pulled them up again. He lighted a candle, and stared at his haggard face in the glass, and fiercely dashed out the light. And at last, when he had pressed his fists against his pursed-up lips and told himself again and again: "I will not," he broke into a shriek of agony and thrust his head down into the pillows and tried to believe he had not heard his own voice.

It had rung out, nevertheless. Presently there came a knocking at the door. The landlady, aroused by the cry, had risen hastily to inquire if she could be of use. Should she call Mynheer's servant who slept on the other side of the house? Mynheer was taken bad again; did he want the doctor sent for? Her man could easily go if it was desired! With the simple logic of her sort, the landlady was all the more voluble because the Marquis did not understand her. But even in his necessity the latter resented the sympathetic tone of her voice, as it came pouring through the keyhole. He refused to be pitied by these creatures. He called for his servant, and cursed him when he came, and, at length, by the help of fresh morphia, was lulled into some kind of repose.

And thus we can comprehend one of the reasons why Monsieur de la Jolais, when shipwrecked at Deynum, had elected to remain there. Be it known, then, that Antoine, when he described his master as the most extravagant noble in Brussels, had but given one half of the characterisation as it was repeated in the salons and clubs of that city. It was true that the Marquis, wherever his own pleasures and comforts were concerned, indulged in that careless extravagance which is so often found in stingy men of wealth. He was notorious for having ordered an extra train to Paris upon missing the regular one, and then having quarrelled over his fare with the cabman who drove him from the station. It was he who had—ah, but that is a nasty story. The man is dead. Better let it alone.

He had another reputation, however, of which he was far vainer, the only thing, perhaps, of which he was really vain

—the reputation of having been, all his life, the bravest of a reckless set. From his youth upwards he had enjoyed the excitement of foolhardy feats, risking his life a hundred times, uselessly, for the laughter and the triumph of the thing. He had rejoiced to think that none of his comrades cared to take a particular ditch and hedge on his own estate; he liked to show them how to do it, as he said. It was he who had driven a horse in a chaise from the high box of a phaeton and pair behind it, holding the reins of all three, up the Montagne de la Cour, and round by the Royal Park. It was he also who had lain down between the rails —for a wager—and let a train pass over him, but that was very long ago. Moreover, he had fought at least a dozen duels in his day, and, on one occasion, when his adversary's bullet carried off the point of one of his moustaches, he had turned coolly to that gentleman with the punning words: " Vous me rasez, Monsieur." He had been a hero among his companions for the devil-may-care contempt of death which had never found a worthy occasion of displaying itself, and it was to this well-known trait that he owed his nickname of " J'ose," an abbreviation for Josephe. He had been intensely gratified by this public recognition of his valour. It was the one "greatness" which he had achieved for himself. Wealth, influence, position, he had been born to these; he was calmly proud of them, but when he forced his frightened horse along the parapet of the terrace of his family-seat of Saint-Leu, he felt that he was achieving a distinction which no ancestors could have power to bestow. He was vain of it therefore, in bright contrast to that entirely different feeling of hereditary pride which, in reality, is but a cumbrous thing to bear, at its best.

And this man who had so often tempted death as a possibility now recoiled from it in horror when it came to him, a certainty, under the form of disease. Somehow or other, it was all quite different. The light fell otherwise. Before, there had always been the energy of escape, straining every nerve into momentarily increasing sureness of victory; now there was nothing except the consciousness of powerless failure. It was no longer the old leap over a fence, but a slow, remorseless fall against a wall of adamant.

And, above all, there had not been this terrible actuality of pain—death through suffering; it was a new thought. Dangerless, inactive, stupid suffering, it was upon him already. He recoiled from it. Worse than that, he trembled at it. And in his own horror of the tremble, the dread, the cowardice, he fled he knew not whither, if only from those who would mark, and jest at, his fall. J'ose. He would die as he had lived. But he did not "dare." Some wag would alter his sobriquet into "José." None must know of this illness. He tried to get away into Germany; any little watering-place would do. And then, when he lay stranded at Deynum, it seemed to him that Deynum might be the very place he stood in need of. He could not venture to travel again, least of all in his own country. The shriek of this night decided him. None but Loripont or his wife must ever hear him shriek again. He could have killed the poor landlady for her looks of compassion, and the all-comprehensive waggle of her good-natured head.

"You will go," said the Marquis to Antoine in the early morning, "and fetch me the Baron van Rexelaer. My compliments, you understand, and all that sort of thing."

Antoine departed, and on his way he met Father Bulbius. The good Father was pottering about in the village, *his* village—more his than anybody else's, for, whoever owned the bodies, the souls were the priest's. He was enjoying the breezy freshness of that early hour, and he stopped before a little flaxen-haired mud-pie makester, and patted her on the head and said she was good. But he felt that he could not honestly have treated himself in the same manner. He was selfish. For when strangers ask us for our houses and chattels, we, if we be good Christians, should grant their request. Especially when the rent they offer is high.

Between fear of his conscience and dread of his house-keeper the Father had a bad time of it. He espied Antoine and went towards him, hoping by his aid to reconcile them both.

"Good morning, Monsieur Antoine," he said, nodding his benevolent countenance to and fro. "And how is the patient this fine morning? Better, I hope, and able to continue his journey?"

"No, your Reverence, he is not better," replied Antoine. "Seems to me he is near his journey's end."

"Dear me!" cried the priest nonplussed. "I hope he is prepared to depart!" To himself he said: "Anyhow, you see, it would not be worth while."

"By no means," replied Antoine decidedly. "I endeavour to do my duty, but it is very trying for a servant, your Reverence."

"Fortunately you have all the conveniences of an inn. It is very convenient, is an inn, Monsieur Antoine. Much more so than a house of one's own. If you want a thing, you simply ring for it."

"And simply do not get it," said Antoine.

"You are not—comfortable? I hope you are."

"Oh no—" began Loripont. Then he caught a glimpse of the Father's imploring face. "Not uncomfortable," he added, and smiled to think how good he was to the priests.

"Well, well, we all have our trials," sighed the Father. "Some of us have not what we want, others have what they would gladly be without. Au revoir, Monsieur Antoine."

"Serviteur, Monsieur le Curé."

But Antoine paused, and then retraced his steps.

"Monsieur le Curé," he cried, "a thousand pardons. There is just one question I would ask you if I dared."

Father Bulbius, who had been meditatively contemplating a still far more meditative pig—astray from the right path, like himself—started in anxious expectation. Should he venture—a second time—to refuse? And what would Veronica say, if he came back to her houseless after all?

"Monsieur le Curé," said Antoine, hesitatingly, "a little mass—eh?—just a little one for my—master; it might do much good, perhaps, but it couldn't—eh, do you think so? —do much harm?"

"Certainly not," replied the priest with an approbatory smile. "The idea is an extremely praiseworthy one. But Monsieur le Marquis is not yet deceased. And besides, would he spend money on masses?"

"It isn't possible, I presume," said Antoine, still feeling his way, "to smooth over some of the unpleasantnesses beforehand? Purgatory is a very awful thought, Monsieur le Curé."

"It is indeed," assented the priest, with true solemnity.

"There is a little sum I have set aside," hazarded Antoine. "It is not as large perhaps as might be considered desirable. But the Marquis has not been a good master to me, and I feel justified in leaving it—insufficient. He shall have five per cent. of the sum he refunded last night," reasoned Antoine. "And I hope," he added aloud, "that my action in this matter will be accounted to my credit when my own time comes."

"Our most meritorious acts," said the priest sententiously, "are not those, Monsieur Antoine, which impress us most vividly with the certitude of their meritoriousness."

Loripont winced under the rebuke. "Well, your Reverence," he said, "I am a poor man, but I can't bear the idea of even my master drifting away into—that! If you can do anything later on to make matters more comfortable, I should not wish it to be omitted."

"So be it," replied the Father. "May I ask: have you fixed on any sum?"

"Let us begin with a hundred francs," said Loripont loftily, suddenly rising from his reverential air into one of patronising importance. "One hundred francs, Monsieur le Curé." And he took his leave and went on his way to the Baron. "Religion is a very expensive item," he muttered to himself, "and supposing—supposing—it were none of it true in the end!"

You who laugh in your souls at reading of this man's thinkings, has the littleness of your life so dried up the tears within you that you have none left to weep over its majesty struck down in the dust? O God, all-loving, all-wise, all-terrible, this then is Thy service in the latter-day of Thy mercy, and we, Thy faithless, self-deceiving children, holding up our rags to shield us from Thy radiance, we call upon these, in their filthiness, and hail them as God! From the religious of our inheriting, our imbibing, our creating—from all religions but of Thine implanting—deliver us, O Lord!

CHAPTER XVII

NOT AS WE WILL, BUT AS WE WOULD, O LORD.

A COUPLE of hours later Mynheer van Rexelaer was ushered into the Marquis's presence. The ceremony of oiling, trimming and curling had been completed, and, in so far as the word is suggestive of worship, that ceremony might have been looked upon as a morning-orison to the Devil, who had been plentifully invoked with imprecations and prayers. The valet had smiled regretfully once or twice, as one who sees a child rushing heedlessly into punishment. After a double-weighted oath at his clumsiness in dropping the curling-iron—even valets will get nervous at times—he had ventured on a " Pourtant, Monsieur le Marquis—" to be immediately interrupted with : "Just so. Pour tant. For so much a month do you do me such service !"

The Baron found the invalid sitting discontentedly among the strange medley of his surroundings, a magnificent cloak of blue fox trailing on the sanded floor, a number of costly objects scattered about over the furniture, a soft luxury of toilet perfumes overpowering the paraffin.

" Do me the favour to take a seat," said the Marquis.

The Baron sat down.

" I am about to be impolite," continued the invalid. " I am an old man and the circumstances of the case must serve as my excuse. May I venture to ask, Monsieur de Rexelaer—forgive me—whether you still retain unaltered your intention of travelling abroad ? "

The Baron strove hard to steady his eyebrows.

"But yes," he said abruptly.

"And am I then to understand that you still do me the honour of proposing the possibility of my becoming the purchaser of your house in this place, which you no longer require?"

The Baron van Rexelaer got up and began to pace to and fro. He saw a look of fatigue and annoyance go flitting across the sick man's face. He remembered that he had been asked to sit, and so sat down again.

"Yes," he said.

"Then will you permit me to say that I have reconsidered your offer, which took me by surprise yesterday at an unfortunate moment. As I mentioned to you before, I want a quiet place to die in. That is all. You do not wish to let?"

"I could not," said the Baron. "I must sell—sell the whole estate—or nothing."

"So I understood," replied Monsieur de la Jolais. "Personally, of course, I should much have preferred a far smaller purchase. But I cannot help myself, and, when I am dead, it matters nothing what becomes of my money." This was true, yet even "the most extravagantly selfish nobleman in Belgium" would hardly have made up his mind to such vast gratification of his dying whim, had it not been for the thought of young Reinout, the other Rexelaer, over yonder at the Hague.

"You have no children?" said the Baron. "Still, it seemed to me that there is a young Monsieur de la Jolais in the regiment of the Guides."

"But, you know all about us, Monsieur," rejoined the Marquis with a faint smile. "It is my cousin. He is a young rogue who only this year neglected my Saint's Day for the races. I shall leave him Saint-Leu and its belongings. Nothing more. Saint-Leu is my home."

"I know," said the Baron sadly. "Who does not? One

knows of Chatsworth, of Dampierre. Even the vulgar. One knows of Saint-Leu."

The Marquis was gratified, whether dying or not. He nodded approval. "But I am taking up your time," he said. "If you will kindly direct me to the person whom you wish to act for you, provided he understands French, I will send my servant, who is entirely trustworthy, to settle the whole matter without delay."

"Monsieur," replied the Baron hastily, "if you will permit me, let us have no intermediaries. The various mortgages on Deynum amount to four hundred thousand florins. The net produce of the estate is about twelve thousand. We must not ask what thousands the building of the Castle has cost. I am told that, at the present moment, if sold by auction, it would hardly realize three hundred and twenty."

"I offer you three hundred and twenty," said the Marquis, "on certain conditions. One is that you allow me to take over all the furniture I require, exclusive of heirlooms, at a valuation."

"Take the heirlooms too!" burst out the Baron, losing his hold.

"Exclusive of heirlooms," repeated the Marquis softly. "These, if you wish, I will have properly catalogued and put aside. My second condition is that the secret of my identity be inviolably kept, by yourself, on your word of honour, by any official concerned in the matter, on oath."

The Baron bowed.

"I have a third condition which I hardly like to bring forward. My days are numbered. I am anxious—I should wish—"

"Monsieur," said the Baron. "In forty-eight hours." The other did not protest. In decency he could not.

"I," said the Baron, taking up his hat, "I also have a condition. One only. I should wish to have it inserted in the contract."

"And it is?"

10

"That you and your heirs and assignees after you solemnly bind yourselves never to sell the estate or any part of the estate to a person who calls himself Count Hilarius van Rexelaer or to any of his descendants, relations or connections."

The Marquis waited some considerable time before he answered. Then he asked wearily : "Say it again, please."

Baron van Rexelaer repeated the clause, slowly. "Sell the estate or part of the estate—*that* I will promise. Certainly. I have no objection," said M. de la Jolais with half-closed eyes.

"Or let," added the Baron, delighted at his own perspicacity.

"Or let. Undoubtedly. The clause to be binding in perpetuity. Au revoir."

The Baron van Rexelaer stumbled over the door-step, and crept down the steep stairs. He was not thinking very much of his loss; he realized it no more than a fond woman realizes her husband's sudden death at her side. He was debating how he should raise the money still wanting to complete the mortgage and yet manage to support his wife and child.

It was a very lovely morning in the park, brilliant with deep-golden sunshine, cheerfully warm and yet freshly invigorating—with no sound but the occasional rustle of a falling leaf through the quiet glow of the cool brown landscape.

He must go and tell his wife first of all. He stopped abruptly in the lane. There was a deeper depth, then, even to deepest sorrow.

Mevrouw was out in the grounds, they told him. Gustave, who spent the greater part of his time watching —or, as he called it, "watching over"—"his family," had seen Mevrouw go out with the Freule. The Baron wandered away, down one of the avenues, pondering over the deficit. And his unconscious footsteps led him naturally to the chapel, where he found his wife, alone.

He saw her through the open door, kneeling in the dimness by the chancel. He crept slowly into the building, and came close to her, and knelt by her side.

The Baroness was muttering paternosters. Her husband gently checked her. "Let us pray," he said, "for strength in tribulation, in deepest tribulation." And they prayed.

The little chapel was very silent, darkly shadowed, beneath its marble heroes and pictured saints.

"I sometimes wonder," said the Baron when they had concluded, "whether our petitions really reach His throne."

"Oh hush, hush," whispered the lady in a low voice of horror. She spoke as one who sees suddenly evoked before him visions of the dead.

"Are you so confident, dearest," said the Baron, in the same hushed accents, "that He would leave us Deynum, were we to ask it of Him?"

"He has left it us hitherto," replied his wife evasively.

"But were He to take it from us—supposing He had already taken it from us—would He, will He give us strength to bear the loss?"

The White Baroness rose slowly to her feet. "It is impossible," she said. "I will not believe it. Reinout, my husband, why do you speak of these things?"

Reinout van Rexelaer flung himself prone on the altar-steps.

"Oh God,' he cried with a sudden loudness that seemed to strike against the solemn hush around. "Oh God that hearest not petitions for this world's prosperity, hear now our cry for strength, to bear the weight of prayers unheard!"

He lay silent, with his hands before his face. And she stood beside him, white, and silent too.

Many minutes had passed, when she stooped forward and laid her hand upon his shoulder. She drew the fingers away from his face, and slowly lifted it upwards. Her own was set hard and strong as if carved in marble.

"Happy they," she said, "who suffer blameless for their fathers' sins. Yours, my darling, was a heritage of ruin, mortgaged acres and a noble name. And the name is nobler now in your unsullied keeping than ever knight has held in the days of yore. And the lands!—God gave them: man has taken. You and I, we have each other. Love is God's to give, not even His to take away!"

She pointed to the blazon over the chancel-window, as he still knelt staring at her with troubled eyes: "Ipsa glorior infamia," she said.

He rose to his feet and made as if he would have kissed her. But she put him away.

"Strong," she said. "Strong. We have struggled to retrieve the misdoings of our fathers. We have struggled our life long, and the end has been vain. And we are utterly ashamed. But ours is a glorious shame."

He had neither the courage nor the power at that moment to undeceive her in the midst of what, at best, was but a partial truth.

"Papa! Mamma!" cried the child's bright voice at the chapel door. It dropped as she came up the little aisle. "I have been looking everywhere for you, Mamma." There was a note of petulance in her words. It seemed to her young restlessness that her mother was perpetually praying.

"Shall we tell her?" asked her father aloud. The mother nodded Yes. "Child," he continued, turning full towards his daughter. "We are going to leave Deynum. We are going away."

She brought her hands swiftly together, as if to clap them, then checked herself, remembering where she was.

" Oh delicious ! " she said, with bated ecstasy. " Are we to stay with my uncle de Heerle? Or, Papa, will you take me to the Hague at last ? "

" Hush, Wendela, you must not—"

" But you have promised for the last three years."

" You must not misunderstand me, little daughter. We are going, never to return."

Wendela stamped her foot on the marble floor, an old, bad habit of her impetuous nature, which required a lot of breaking. " But no," she said, " I do not understand."

" It is going to be sold," interposed the Baron desperately.

As the words fell upon her, the child's face seemed for a moment to harden and lose all its youthfulness. It grew sharp and thin; it would have been wonderfully like her mother's, but for the flaming eyes.

" Sold," she repeated, as if thinking out the word—then fiercely :

" Papa, this is not *your* wickedness ! "

" Wanda? " cried her mother, but her father motioned back all protest. " Wickedness? " he said. " No, we are too poor to keep it, and therefore—"

" Then it is God's ! " she burst out and, leaping up the altar-steps, she suddenly struck down, in fierce passion, one of the great vases filled with white chrysanthemums, sending its beautiful weight in clattering fragments over the floor. And then she fled away, she knew not whither, in a loud tempest of weeping.

Piet Poster found her, half an hour later, curled up near Lady Bertha's Cross, under the trees, in a limp bundle of misery.

" What is it, Freule ? Are you asleep? " he asked of a lot of tumbled hair on two rounded arms. But no voice would answer. Nor any feature show itself.

Something told him however that the silent figure was not asleep, but animate, watchful, listening. We always feel that. He was alarmed, or perhaps a little curious. He gently touched, then shook, an irresponsive arm. Then, although he was only a little peasant-boy, he hit upon a powerful ruse.

"She is ill," he said aloud. "I must go for somebody."

And he ran off a few steps. She started to her feet immediately, hot and ruffled. "Can't you leave me alone?" she cried. "I want to be quiet."

He came back quite close. "I'm so sorry," he said. "You've been crying. What is it?"

"I'm not crying," she answered angrily.

He was too much of a gentleman to amend his words or to charge her with prevarication.

"I'm sorry," he said, "I didn't know." And he departed, with his hands pushed down tight into the pockets of his rusty small-clothes.

Upon which she, being a woman right down to the very bottom of her twelve-year-old development, called him back. "Piet," she said, "can you keep a secret?"

"Yes," he made answer stolidly, with a still lower push of his tightly-wedged arms.

"But I mean a real secret. Really truly. Never to tell nobody till somebody else tells you."

"Yes," said Piet, and lifted his blue eyes and looked at her.

"I am going away for good," said Wendela, with a catch in her throat, and then, giving way to the very luxury of grief: "We shall never see each other any more."

Piet stood some moments immovable, his round pink and white face very troubled. At last he said sturdily:

"Never is a long word, Freule."

She was piqued. "You don't care," she cried. "You've been saying all along that things weren't as they used to be. You've got another sweetheart. I know you have."

"No, I haven't," interrupted Piet.

"Yes, you have. And you'll want me less than ever now I can't make you Lord of Deynum. Though I should never have done that, for you're only a peasant-boy. You're a bad boy, besides, and it was only my fun."

"I know that, but I'm not a bad boy," replied Piet. "And you'll come back to Deynum when you've done."

"Done what? We're all going. Oh you stupid, the Castle is going to be sold."

"Sold," repeated the boy, just as his young mistress had done an hour ago. He gave such a dig with his fists that something cracked about his chubby, black-clothed body.

He was a slow-thinking boy: it took him a long time to work round to what he was in search of. Ultimately he said:

"I'll give you all my marbles. I'll give you the crystal one with the silver lamb inside."

"I don't want your marbles."

"Yes, you do, Freule. You've teased me about that silver one for weeks."

"I tell you I don't want 'em. I don't want anything. Never no more. You're a horrid boy. Go away. I thought you would have cried any amount about never seeing me again."

Piet Poster was utterly at a loss. "I am dreadfully sorry," he said. "More than about anything. More than if Nick had died."

"Thank you! To compare me to your goat!" cried Wendela in high indignation.

"But boys don't cry, Freule, when they're sorry. I never cry, never since I was a little boy."

"You're a little boy still. And you cried when Mamma scolded you for letting Nick get among her flowers."

"That's different. Your Mamma didn't scold me, and then something made me cry; I couldn't help it. But I didn't cry when father thrashed me for it."

Wendela walked off, without condescending to further

parley. She had seen Piet's father coming up along the lane. And she called back with sudden misgiving: "Remember, it's a fearful secret, Piet!"

The head-gardener heard the words. "What's this?" he said roughly to his son. "What mischief have you been up to again with the Freule?"

"It's no harm, father."

"Well, then, what is it?"

"It's a secret, father: I can't tell."

Poster was a brute. He struck the child a heavy blow on the head. "I'll teach you to answer me like that," he said. "Tell me this instant."

"I can't," said Piet, vainly trying to avoid a second blow. His father's curiosity was aroused. Piet Poster had a bad time of it that morning.

"They have no right to sell it," said Wendela to herself fiercely, again and again. "It is *mine!*"

CHAPTER XVIII.

AN ARISTOCRAT'S IDEA OF THE LAW.

THE news was all over the village in a couple of hours. The head-gardener felt the more angry with his son for having deprived him of the "primeur."

The Baron knew that everyone knew—had he not ordered his steward to publish the tidings?—and in each meeting with each of his vassals lay hidden a fresh discrowning.

He locked himself up in his room. That was a weakness, and so he told himself. The Baroness went among her poor as usual, encountered, at every step, by red eyes and looks of dull despair. One or two tried to speak, but she motioned them imperiously into silence, and then inquired after their ailments, or the baby.

The Baron, in the solitude of his private-room had enough to occupy him. Never, perhaps, was a home of many centuries so hurriedly shifted from hand to hand, and two days supervened of ceaseless packing and much confusion. All that the Baron wished to retain was rapidly inventoried by the steward and stowed away in the great drawing-room : the armour, the portraits, the safes with the plate and jewellery, and, above all, the archives. There was a great jumble of it, all huddled pell-mell, boxes and chests, and heavy oak-cupboards, "to be arranged hereafter"; with his own hand the Baron had locked them. The servants were active, but flurried, some of them deeply grieved and aggrieved, others interested and amused.

The Baron sat before his account-books. They are seldom pleasant reading to an honest man, for an honest man is usually a poor one. To him, who had been quite honest, but very imprudent, they were unpleasant reading indeed. His recent losses at the Stock-Exchange had, in spite of all his computations, exceeded anything he could have imagined possible, and the crash of the last day's sale had made them irretrievable. He had seen the ripe apple falling straight into Count Rexelaer's lap, and, with a sudden impulse, had dashed it away to the Belgian. And with the Baron there was no question of mere rivalry or malice in this solemn struggle to keep the dead lion's skin unsullied by the shoulders of the Pseudo-Rexelaer. It was the one duty he still owed to his dying race, that it should die.

The Count at the Hague would undoubtedly have paid more than any other living man—it was this which Strum had rightly taken into consideration; had the Count not been willing to assume the entire weight of the mortgages? And the Baron could well have used the money. To pay off the entire debt on the estate and to meet the demand from his brokers he must sell whatever funded property he possessed, and yet, count up his assets as often as he would, he still always found himself confronted by a deficit of fifty thousand florins. It is a small sum to have, but it is an immense sum to want. He must have it to save him from bankruptcy. Yet—be it noted at once—this does not mean that he was absolutely penniless. It means, unfortunately, that some thirty thousand florins of his wife's little property had been unexpectedly swallowed up in the vortex, but an income of four thousand (£330) still remained secure, this being derived from a fund not under his control, of which Strum, as the family-notary, was hereditary trustee. It was Rexelaer-money, the sum having been set aside by a head of the house in the seventeenth century, with the especial object of forming a small annual allowance to be paid, in perpetuity, to the wife of the reigning lord, under

the name of "The Lady's Dole." It had been so paid to
this day.

"The Notary Strum is waiting," announced Gustave in
a loud voice, after having twice vainly coughed. It was
Gustave's peculiarity to indicate everyone as far as possible
by his trade or profession. "There are too many masters
now-a-days," he said. "Look at me. I am plain Gustave
Gorgel." And he would throw out his chest and look very
big and splendid. The words were modest.

The Baron started and dropped his pen. "Just so," he
said. "Let him come in. You find me very busy, Strum.
It has come so unexpectedly, this decision to go abroad.
But I hope the change will do Mevrouw good. She is looking very white."

"Mevrouw has always looked white," said Strum. He
sat down, all of a piece, as if he were afraid of dropping
some part of himself and losing it. He was calmly contented. The sale would bring him in a large profit, and he
would probably become agent to an absentee owner. The
Baron was a fool not to have preferred the better buyer, but
that was the Baron's business. He, Strum, had done his duty.

"Still, I hope the climate of Germany will do her good,"
said Mynheer van Rexelaer.

"The climate of Germany is large, Mynheer. Which
part of it is to benefit the Baroness?"

"I—I am not certain as yet where we shall go."

"You are only certain, Mynheer, that you must be
gone." Strum dropped his eyes over his great gloved
hands, and spread out the hands on his knees. The shadow of the majesty of Deynum had lain over him ever since
his babyhood. In another day or two he would be rid of
these Rexelaers for ever. Ouf!

"Strum," said the Baron, roused to his duty by the
Notary's insolence. "We are ruined. You know it. It
would have broken your good father's heart, had he lived
to see this day."

"My good father's heart was continually breaking, but he managed to live very well on the fragments. 'Never mind a cracked heart,' I have heard him say, 'if only your head be sound.'"

For the moment the Baron felt agreeably cooled by this succession of douches. It was quite easy, he found, to confront his old dependents, if they remained indifferent to, or even secretly gloried in, his discomfiture.

"I have sent for you, sir," he said haughtily, "to transact business. There is one point especially which I must speak about. The fund under your administration, known as 'The Lady's Dole,' amounts at present, I believe, to a sum total of about one hundred thousand florins. I speak under correction?"

The Notary nodded, and blinked his eyes behind their spectacles.

"According to the terms of the settlement that money becomes the property of the last representative of the house, as soon as it is absolutely certain that there will be no more Baronesses van Rexelaer. That time has come. The certainty has existed for several years. There will be no more Baronesses van Rexelaer."

The Notary shrugged his shoulders.

"I require the money now to pay off the mortgages. That is to say: I require half of it. We must sell out."

"But your own private property, Mynheer?" began young Nicholas in—for him—an insinuating tone.

"I require the money," repeated the Baron in a louder voice. "And, according to the terms of the settlement, as I say, there is no reason for reserving it any longer."

The Notary took off his spectacles and commenced carefully rubbing them. And then a sly leer crept over his naked-looking face—we all know the suddenly undressed appearance of these short-sighted eyes—and he murmured:

"Except the fortunate fact that your lady is not yet deceased."

"What has that to do with it?" cried the Baron indignantly. "Do you expect Mevrouw to object? Shall we have her in?"

"No, no," cried the Notary hastily.

"I should think not," said Mynheer van Rexelaer, sinking back in scorn. "As I pointed out, Mevrouw is the last of those who could possibly be entitled to the interest, and she will be only too glad to forego it, if the capital can be used on my behalf and her own."

"But, unfortunately, trustees must be guided by their trust alone. Mine enjoins me to preserve the capital intact as long as there exists, or can exist, a consort of a Rexelaer van Deynum. It can therefore only be paid over to your widow or, if you survive the Baroness, to your daughter after your death. Surely you see that."

But he did not see it, simple-minded gentleman that he was. "Am I to believe," he cried nervously, "that you refuse me this money which belongs by rights to my wife and myself. Surely *you* can understand that she is the last Baroness."

Strum readjusted his spectacles and looked down.

"You refuse?" cried the Baron hotly, rising in his seat. "Yes or no?"

Strum pushed back his chair with a grating jerk along the floor. "And supposing the Baroness were to die," he said roughly. "Supposing you were to marry again. You are barely sixty. Supposing—'

"Hold," shouted the Baron, beside himself. "You insult me. I shall not marry again. I want this money. I must have it. *Must;* do you hear? It is the only possible means of avoiding disgrace. For centuries your ancestors have been the faithful servants of an illustrious house. I am an old man; you are a young one. For the last time I ask you: Will you rescue the name of Rexelaer?" He breathed hard. Oh, the humiliations of this pleading!

"I can't do it," burst out Nicholas with an oath. He

was moved, in spite of his common sense. " You want to make a dishonest man of me. I won't. And my dead father whom you always respected—"

" Go" thundered the Baron, pointing to the door.

" Why didn't you sell to Count Rexelaer, Mynheer the Baron?" Strum went on recklessly. " I had arranged it all for you, and there would have been money enough." He came nearer; a sudden idea had seized him. " The heirlooms," he suggested eagerly with the old smile of suppliant impertinence upon his speckled face. " The portraits and all the rest? Count Rexelaer would give a lot for those?"

And then, in the dimness and the whirlwind, the Baron struck him.

CHAPTER XIX

THE Baron was very, very sorry, as he sat alone, once more, among his litter of papers and account-books. That is the worst of a good man's forgetting himself, he is obliged to remember afterwards. While he still smiled at the other's threats of vengeance, the vengeance had already begun in his own awakening remorse. Yet he might well have dreaded Strum's seeming impotence, could he have read the future. We seldom can, but of one thing we may be certain. The revenge of the weakest cuts deepest, because most subtly planned.

"There is one thing I should like to know," said Gustave, standing, stiff and smart, by the Baron's elbow. That gentleman turned in annoyance.

"I believed Mynheer had answered my knock. I beg pardon," continued the servant, whose prevarications were always virtuous. He governed his master, to a certain extent, by alert apology.

"Well, what is it? Be quick."

"It is an impertinence, Mynheer the Baron." Generous natures, as Gustave well knew, condone a fault confessed.

"Then be impertinent. It would not be for the first time."

"Mynheer the Baron confuses me in his memory with the coachman. What I would venture to ask—begging pardon—is this." He stopped. "You remember, Mynheer, when we were children here together?"

" Yes. Is that what you intruded on me to ask ? "

" And you remember, Mynheer, when I got you your saddle after Waterloo—we were both twelve then—you remember ?—the King's Wine ! "

" Of course I remember. Things are bad enough, Gustave. Don't make them worse."

" And you remember," continued Gustave, speaking faster and faster, and louder and louder, " the war of 1830, you officer and I corporal. You remember Antwerp and the Hero Chassé and the great charge, and your wound, and how I found you, and the King's Wine again ? How we thrashed them, the blue blouses ! How they ran, the cowards ! You remember, Major ? And the Prince telling the army you were not only the noblest of his nobles, but the bravest of his soldiers, too ! "

The man's voice had risen to a cry of triumph. His master was scratching an envelope with a pen.

" And you remember, Mynheer," Gustave went on after a moment of sad silence, " our coming home to the Baroness, and later on the birth of the Freule, and all."

" Great Heaven," cried the Baron lifting up a haggard face. " Am I likely, in my grave, to forget ? "

" What I mean, Mynheer, is that we have always, so to say, borne everything—begging your pardon—together, from the cradle. Not that it has anything to do with my question which is just this, saving your Presence. Is there ready money enough for this sudden emergency, Mynheer, or is there not ? "

" There is not," cried the Baron, whose nerves were by this time altogether unstrung, " and if that scoundrel of a Notary has been chattering on his way downstairs—"

" No one has said anything, Mynheer. But I imagined it might be possible, in the unexpectedness of the change. And that brings me to what I wanted to say. It is only right, of course, that Mynheer should have secrets from me.

But I have long had a secret from Mynheer, and that was wrong."

The Baron looked up vaguely, waiting for more.

" I—I," stammered Gustave, quite at a loss, despite his martial bearing. " Mynheer has always had my savings in his keeping "—an expectant frown gathered on his master's face—" that is nothing. I mean the savings. But a number of years ago a cousin of mine left me fifteen thousand francs. I never told you, Mynheer. I was afraid you would want me to use the money, in a shop or something. And I left it with the rascally broker, to take care of it for me."

" And of course it is gone," said the Baron. " Well, you have fortunately still your savings, which are secure in my keeping, as you say."

Gustave smoothed his grey hair shamefacedly.

" I am afraid it is different, Mynheer," he replied with an apologetic smile. " The broker advised me to speculate with the money, as I didn't know what else to do with it. What was I to do with it, I that in my young time, when you never have enough, could not even pay the Vivandière? It came too late, that's the truth. I was here, and had all I wanted. The interest accumulated, and the speculations succeeded, and now, what with my savings and this money, I'm worth sixty thousand florins, the broker says."

" You are a singularly lucky man," said the Baron bitterly.

The other shook his head. " I don't know about that," he replied, " if I may make so bold as to differ. I didn't want the money, but I liked the speculating, after a time. It's amusing, Mynheer. But of late I've had scruples. Especially of nights, and they're dreadful, are scruples, worse than fleas, if I may be forgiven for saying so, for you can't catch them, and they go on biting, after they've had enough and you've said you were sorry. I don't think it's a nice way of earning money ; it's a better way of losing it."

" You think so, do you ? You speak from the winner's

11

point of view." The Baron's eyes went wandering away
over his open books.

"Well, you see, Mynheer, one man's winnings are another man's losings, aren't they? It's like cards. And what
I can't understand is that I who never would touch a card
in barracks should take to playing on 'Change in after life."
He shook his head over this enigma, an old tormentor.

"Well, don't grumble at your luck," said the Baron impatiently. He was disgusted with himself for being jealous
—of his servant.

"If I grumble at anything, it's my conscience, Mynheer.
I wish the abominable thing were dead. It don't do to have
a conscience and speculate. I don't feel happy about my
winnings. I never earned them. I've stolen them from
somebody, the somebody that lost, as at cards. I've stolen
them from you, Mynheer. Lord forgive me; the word's
out! And I wish you'd take the money back."

"And who told you I speculated? How dare you speak
to me like that?" cried the Baron fiercely. On any other
day he might have been affectionate, but on this he was
angry.

"I told you it was an impertinence, Mynheer. I can
only say: Forgive me. Mine was American railways too,
Mynheer, whatever they may be. It's always American railways. So you see, it's your own money I've got. I've taken
it from you and Mevrouw and the Freule. And I do wish,
for God's sake, and my own peace of soul, you'd take it back
again!'"

He actually held out a bundle which he had drawn from
his bulgy tail-pocket. His voice was passionate with hope.
He felt like a highwayman, making restitution.

"Take the things away," said the Baron testily, pushing
the outstretched arm aside. "You are indeed impertinent,
as you say. And what you propose is absurd, Gustave, as
well as improper. Be thankful that, now you must leave
me, you will be able to live in luxury." And then he drew

down his old comrade's face close to his own, and looked into his eyes. "I can't take the money, dear fellow," he said. "God bless you. It is you must forgive me. We shall think of some other way."

"I want no leave-takings," the Baron had said several times during that crowded morning. "I could not bear that." The Baroness had not answered at first; later on she had said: "There is nothing unbearable. Hell must be bearable, Reinout, or Satan would die. We must not count on incapacity for suffering."

The child was very silent, surprised that no one alluded to her sacrilege of the preceding day. They were to leave next morning early and go into temporary lodgings at Cleves, on the other side of the German frontier. "About one thing I am resolved," said the Baron. "I must never see this place again." The contract was to be signed that evening; the Marquis could take possession next day. A woman, Loripont's wife, had been telegraphed for, and the great mansion was to be abandoned to these three.

"Get a bottle of the wine, Gustave," said the Baron at dinner, sitting erect before his untouched plate, "and you shall have a glass of it too. I have had it moved to the drawing-room with the rest. No one else shall own it. Least of all a Belgian." They were a little dramatic in those terrible days. It was their salvation. To some lives there come moments when we cannot jog on in the midway of existence; we must either sink utterly, or soar. The child's thoughts were preoccupied with Piet Poster. She despised herself for eating her dinner.

The meal was drawing to a close, when Gustave slipped through a narrow opening between the heavy oak-doors. "The people are here, Mynheer," he said, "come to wish your Nobleness good-bye and God-speed."

"The people?" cried the Baron. "Who?"

"Everybody," replied Gustave, and threw wide the doors.

The far side of the hall was full of faces under the soft light of its stained glass, and with the glitter of the armour on both sides between grim portraits and masses of late flowers and greenery. The leaders were huddled together in front. Dievert the steward, and the head-gardener and the coachman, with the other in and out-door servants, and behind them the great farmers with their substantial wives, and the tradesmen from the village, and behind these again a medley of retainers and dependents, pressing the others forward, as the doors opened, till the whole vestibule was occupied. A flood of red-cheeked, awkward faces, the men in tight-fitting black, the wives in print jackets and far-stretching caps, belaced, befrilled, be-ribboned and be-starched. A crowd which had been anxious to put in an appearance, but which would feel far more comfortable when once again outside.

The Baron looked from one to another till his eyes rested on Bulbius in a corner by the door. "This is most kind," he stammered. "I am at a loss—" Then he stopped, seeing that the steward was about to make a speech. He rose and came forward, with his wife and child.

The steward, Dievert, was a supremely self-conscious man, corpulent, important, inclined to look warm. He looked very warm indeed as he began his carefully prepared oration:

"Mynheer the Baron, our highly respective—respected landheer, we, that is all those who are in any way connected with your property of Deynum, we have—we are—" He stuck.

"Dreadfully sorry you're going away," said a voice from the back.

The steward frowned, but this outrage suddenly restored him to the full command of his diminishing dignity. He launched safely into smooth floods of laudatory eloquence, praising the Baron, the Baroness, and all their ancestors and belongings, for all deeds done and undone, for their birth and their existence, for the death of such as had gone before. And as he heaped up his praises, his face grew warmer and warmer, and the Baron's heart froze cold as stone. Simple-minded as the latter was, he could see clearly enough in such matters as belonged to his competence. He was well aware that Dievert was an honest steward who had never cheated his master above, and never beneath, the legitimate limit of a steward's cheatery.

"And now that the sun is to set upon our village," perorated the spokesman of the peasantry, " now that—" (suddenly he began wondering to himself what the new lord would be like, and the thought distracted his attention. He stuck again). "Now that—now then—"

"Now then," said Wendela, too audibly, from her place by her mother's side. There was a general laugh, and in the reaction a woman's voice broke into shrill weeping. Others followed the tempting example. The speech was at an end.

"Thank you. Thank you," said the Baron, shaking hands with the wet-eyed and the dry-eyed, the simpering, the stolid, and the sorrowful. He stood in the entrance. In calmer moments he could have told you all about their sentiments and measured to an ounce (of groceries) the sympathy and sadness of every one of them.

"Come, Bulbius," he said, when it was over. "Come in and drink good luck to all of us."

"I can't, I can't," protested the Father in broken accents, and solemnly emptied the glass the Baron had poured out. Then, without more ado, he struck it against the side of the table, snapping it at the stem.

"Pray for us, reverend father," burst out the Baroness, " when we are gone. Pray for us night and day. You cannot pray enough. And peradventure—"

"Hush," he interrupted her. "Gracious lady, prayer

has no peradventure. Alas that sometimes, in God's wisdom, adversity should be its Amen."

He turned away, to leave them, but at the door he looked round. " I forgot to tell you," he said. " Veronica has been in a terrible temper all day. At one moment I feared she was going to beat me. She has such a tender heart."

CHAPTER XX.

THE MARQUIS'S HEIRS.

THE Marquis was restless. He walked up and down the room. For a moment a fictitious strength was upon him, and he rejoiced in it. The nun eyed him cautiously out of her little slits of eyes, under the solemn veil.

For there was a nun with him now, a Sister of Mercy. The Marquis wanted a hundred useless attentions in the constant changes of his whim. Nursing him was exhausting work, physically and mentally, for, in his continuous flight from himself, he could not be in repose, and he would not be alone.

And so every moment the sick man thought of something else he wanted, merely because it was something else. Loripont wearied under the perpetual strain, and showed it. "Then get somebody till your wife comes," said his master. "Not longer. Get a sister. They hold their tongues." The woman had come that morning, and had ministered to the Marquis's wants all day. She was a fat, middle-aged woman, mealy, expressionless, buttoned-eyed. She spoke in the shortest of sentences, and a sleepy voice.

"The house is exactly what I needed," said the Marquis for the twentieth time that day. He stopped and vaguely eyed the monstrous lamp in the middle of the ceiling. "I shall be absolute master of my surroundings there, alone with the Loriponts, in a wide expanse of park. I could not have found better, had I hunted for years. Of course it is enormously expensive, but what matters money to a man who may be dead in a month?"

He walked a few steps farther and halted in front of the nun.

"What matters money," he repeated, "to a man who will be dead in a month?"

"Nothing," replied the nun. They had sent him one who understood a little French.

"And besides, the value of the estate remains. I offered him the lowest figure; it may not be a bad bargain after all. Absolute seclusion! I should say luck had befriended me, were it not that I knew that everything is possible to him that pays."

He rambled on, to himself, not to her, though he liked to have a human creature listening. In an hour they would be coming with the deed of purchase. To-morrow he would hide himself, behind thick walls and wide woods, to shriek out his life if he chose. For the outside world, he would sink away into slow oblivion, and none of his whilom "friends" would ever apprehend that the unconquerable Marquis had, in his turn, been conquered by the great Conqueror, Pain.

"What would it matter," continued M. de la Jolais, "whether I left behind me ten francs or ten million? The Vicomte, my dear cousin, would not have a penny, could I deprive him of his share. I hate him. And as for my sister's child, whom I have never seen, why should I love her?"

"What do you say?" he asked, almost fiercely, turning on the Sister of Mercy. He did not much care what she said, as long as she talked.

"Nothing," replied Sister Constantia, smoothly, and went on watching him out of her half-closed eyes.

The Marquis sank into his large elbow-chair.

"A beautiful quality in a woman," he said half sneeringly, half smilingly. "Had Madame Cochonnard understood its value, I might now have had somebody worth leaving my money to. But she got into a habit of saying

'Yes!' the worst thing your sex can get into the habit of saying. Could you have loved a creature of the name of Cochonnard?"

The nun dropped her eyes. "We love no one, Monsieur," she said.

"A woman, I mean, of course," said the Marquis, testily. "I do not forget to whom I am speaking."

"Ah—," said the nun slowly. "We love everybody, Monsieur. Yes, I could have loved anyone, whatever their name."

"Then excuse my saying, ma sœur, that you have no discriminating taste. Why, the very name is unpronounceable in society, so naturally the woman that bore it was dead there."

He fell into a reverie. "To whom would you leave your money," he said presently, "if you were dying, and had no one to leave it to?"

He talked thus constantly of dying. He had gone through all the experiences of horror and indignation indicated above. Yet never for one moment had he realized the actuality of death. It was in him, yet outside him. He was present at the tragedy of himself.

But, for the moment, at any rate, he was alive.

"To my mother," replied Sister Constantia, "the common mother of us all. Lo, there are my mother and my brethren."

The Marquis made a grimace. "Yes, I know," he said, "It is a large family. But I have never felt attracted towards the Great Unwashed. That surely is pardonable in me, for I have always detested my relations."

"If I were dying," said the nun, roused from her placidity by his manner, "I would strive to make my peace with God."

"Hoity-toity," he answered. "I know what is meant by that. All of it to a lot of lazy priests, for masses they never say! No, ma sœur, I am an upholder of religion—it is invaluable—but I am not a fool."

They were silent for some time; she being too angry to reply.

"Waste is wickedness," added the Marquis spitefully. "I never spent a penny, but I got a penny's worth for it."

"Pennies become pounds in the heavenly exchequer," replied Sister Constantia.

He rested his face on his hands; the face was thin, the hands yet thinner, long, slender and white.

When at last he moved again, he said, without looking at her: "I wonder, would it be worth while?"

She waited.

"Not to give it to the priests, mind you. I won't give a penny to the priests. But to let the poor have it. Something must be done with it, and that way might have its advantages. Your convent, now, does it interest itself in the poor? I suppose so?"

"Indeed it does," said the sister. She opened her eyes wide, not that it made them any wider.

"Well, I must see. I have never thought it out before. I have never realized, nor wished to realize, the idea of having heirs. The old Baron here, I fancy, suggested the subject, and I daresay my 'poor relations' will do as well as anybody else. That means 'the monkeys,' doesn't it? I don't mean those; I mean the other set, the canaille. Peuah, it is an unpleasant subject. Oblige me by fetching Antoine."

Antoine, who had been lying down for too short a rest, appeared with sullen face. "I am too lonely," said the Marquis. "I must have something to amuse me. You, to-morrow you will have your wife. I do not know whether she amuses you, but she keeps you occupied. I think I should like to have some of the horses; there is sure to be plenty of room at that place. Write and tell them to send 'Jeanneton,' and 'Sooty Jack,' and 'Veuve Cliquot.' It will amuse me to look at them. And I might as well have the dogs—the house-dogs—from Brussels."

"But, if Monsieur le Marquis wishes it to remain unknown that he is here—"

"Tiens, that is true." How weak his head must be growing! "I fear I shall have to give up the idea. I am sorry. But tell them to send 'Jeanneton.' A groom can travel with her to the frontier, and you must fetch her there. I have been thinking, if there was anyone I should care to take leave of, and I have set my heart on seeing 'Jeanneton' again. She certainly is the one creature who loves me."

"Monsieur le Marquis forgets the dogs," said the valet calmly.

"She must be lonely, poor beast, among a lot of servants. She cannot abide servants, like myself. And perhaps, after all, I shall get better, and ride her. These doctors are constantly mistaken."

"They are," said Antoine.

The Marquis abandoned his listless attitude. "Do you know," he asked eagerly, "of their making a mistake in a case like mine?"

"Yes," replied Antoine, who had that morning heard the tale, through Bulbius, from Veronica. "I know of a case of a lady whom all the doctors had given up." And he launched into a wonderful account of some homœopathic cure. "I do not believe a word of it," interposed the sick man occasionally, as he sat drinking in the glad details. He was quite vexed when the arrival of the notary and his two clerks interrupted the story. A few minutes later the Baron appeared. He held out his hand to Strum, who ignored it.

The deed was read, the usual formalities were gone through, the necessary arrangements were made for the transfer of the purchase-money. The only "incident" of any importance occurred when the Baron van Rexelaer

passed across a slip of folded paper to M. de la Jolais. The
Marquis read " Will you permit the clause to be added, that
the chapel remain intact?"

"But certainly," said M. de la Jolais.

And then came the signing of the names. For the last
time the Baron, now signing away his manorial rights,
would call himself by the name which had been handed
down to him through five slow centuries. He laid down
the pen. Then, hurriedly seizing it, he sprawled the words
across the page. And he buried his hands deep in his
pockets, lest any should notice how they trembled.

Under this signature came the Marquis's in neat little
letters : Josephe Xavier Hippolyte de la Jolais-Farjolle de
Saint Leu."

" Et de Deynum," said the Baron aloud, in the bitter
scorn of his heart. And then he coloured scarlet, for regret
of the unheeding insult, as it seemed, to M. de la Jolais.
No one spoke.

When, all being over, the Baron van Rexelaer was pre-
paring to slip away, M. de la Jolais called him back. To
Strum the Marquis said : " Wait downstairs, if you please.
I may still have need of you." Strum bowed, with a grin.

The Baron put down his hat again, greatly flurried.
Had the Belgian perhaps heard—through that villain Strum
—of the impending bankruptcy? Was he going to offer
help? If so, it must be declined, but the offer would render easier and more acceptable the Baron's own proposal,
that terrible inevitable proposal, to which he had been
screwing up his courage all day long.

The Marquis waited till they were quite alone—in that
quite-alone-ness which does not come until a few moments
after the door has been closed. Then he said : " Do you
know any cases, Monsieur, in which doctors have been seriously mistaken in their diagnosis of diseases of the stom-
ach!"

"I know very little," replied Mynheer Rexelaer, "about any diseases at all." "He wants to lead up to something," he thought, "I wonder how."

"You will know some day," said the Marquis grimly, "about one disease—your own. Then you do not think you can answer my question affirmatively."

"I fear not."

The Marquis had been suddenly elated, he was now as unreasonably cast down. Dying men do not only catch at straws; they see them floating where there is merely a ripple on the water.

"Then forgive me for retaining you. Let me thank you once more, Monsieur, now we are alone, for your great kindness in abandoning to me your beautiful mansion so soon." He closed his eyes.

But the Baron stayed on. "Forgive *me*," he began, "if, before I leave you, I venture—"

But the Marquis, who never consciously interrupted his equals, had not even heard the other speak, so busy was he with his own thoughts. "My heirs must give the place its due," he said.

The Baron was much disconcerted. "I am deeply grateful, at any rate," he replied, "that it will remain in Catholic hands. The Vicomte de la Jolais, I have no doubt, when the effervescence of youth is past, will make an excellent lord of Deynum."

"The Vicomte will never make an excellent anything, Monsieur. There is one fault for which I know no pardon, it is disrespect and disobedience to the head of the house. For these I have disinherited nearer relations than the Vicomte."

"I do not believe in disinheriting," said the Baron gruffly. "Family-money is family property. For the chance possessor to divert it to strangers is a crime."

"The word is a strong one," protested the Marquis, nettled. "And a woman, then, who disgraces herself?"

"Her children are not to blame for that," answered the Baron obstinately. "And if the woman be the God-appointed heiress, then that woman in God's name. Never a stranger. Not as long as the blood-claim is there."

"Tiens, Madame Cochonnard!" said the Marquis. "Well, perhaps you are right, although it is you—permit me to say so, Monsieur—who have just resolutely excluded Count Rexelaer from Deynum."

The other's face grew purple. "There is no blood-claim *there*," he said vehemently. "Never now—thank Heaven —shall Count Rexelaer have any connection with Deynum."

Monsieur de la Jolais fixed his eyes upon the speaker's excited face. "I am in doubt what to do," he said slowly. "Advise me. The poor are one's relations, say the preachers. Why not leave one's money to them?"

"I am a good Catholic," replied the Baron, unhesitatingly, "but I would not rob those of my own house to buy a mansion for myself in heaven."

"Well, I daresay you are right, though it is strange that you should be the man to give me this advice. Under all circumstances you think the natural law should take its course? So be it. Making wills is a nuisance; I have always avoided it. I fancy it attracts death. Goodnight."

The Baron retained the door-handle in his hand, awkwardly. "There is still one thing," he stammered. "One moment, Monsieur de la Jolais. I—I find there are a number of articles—plate and so on—and—and pictures, excluded as private property, for which I should have no use on my travels. Some of the objects, and portraits are very valuable—" He hesitated.

"I am much obliged to you, mon cher Baron," said the Marquis stiffly. "I wish you had mentioned the subject sooner. Plate marked with your crest, or family-portraits,

I should hardly require. But we might see later on. Good-night, cher Baron; I am very tired."

He rang for his valet as soon as the Baron had departed. "Send that Notary away," he said, "I do not require him. I have changed my mind."

CHAPTER XXI.

J'OSE!

THE results of the unusual fatigue the Marquis had undergone soon made themselves felt. After a short and restless slumber he awoke in an agony of suffering. It was eleven o'clock. He called for Antoine and demanded morphia. The drug was given him, but, for the first time, it seemed entirely to miss its effect. A paroxysm of mingled passion and despair seized hold of him and shook him. Doubtless there was something wrong with the solution. He must have it seen to. He must have a different opiate. He must have a doctor. Till now he had resolutely refused to call in the little practitioner from Rollingen.

A messenger was immediately dispatched with a country-chaise. Then followed a horrible hour of anxiety and fruitless activity for the valet, the sister, all the people of the inn—a ceaseless hurrying to and fro, and whispering, and preparing of various things that were vainly passed from hand to hand. The patient lay among his pillows and moaned.

At last the doctor came. They had hoped everything from him; he could do nothing. The quality of his morphia was inferior to that of the Marquis's. He stood irresolute by the bedside. The sick man motioned him nearer. "Go out of the room, you others!" cried the Marquis. "Go!"

Then, turning to the doctor:

"This is cancer," he said.

The doctor nodded and replied in a low voice. "So I feared." He was a kind-hearted man.

"I have had these attacks of late. How long will they last?"

"Ah, Monsieur, it is impossible to say. They may—"

"Do not lie to me. The case is absolutely hopeless."

The doctor looked down at his boots.

"Absolutely hopeless," repeated the invalid, with a ring of hope and the faintest interrogation in his voice. He sat up, clutching at his breast. "Answer me. You need not answer. I see it in your face. I have known it for a week, for centuries. Absolutely hopeless." He fell back.

"But, my dear sir," began the doctor in that terrible, encouraging doctor's voice, "you have still many months before you. It is impossible to say what may occur."

"A year?" gasped the patient.

"Oh, most certainly a year, I should say. Very probably more."

"And this pain? It will increase?"

"You must not think too much of the future. For the moment—"

"Thank you," burst out the sick man, with sudden strength. "Go! Thank you! Antoine! Where is that scoundrel, Antoine?" He struck his hand-bell, till it broke under his hand. The servant came running in. "Get me paper and pen and ink. The quicker the better. Farewell, doctor; my servant will pay you. I am better. The pain is gone. I do not feel it. The paper, you block-head! In the dressing-case. Be quick." He lay back and wrote a few rapid words. "I have never done it before," he said to Antoine when he had finished, "but I daresay it is right like that. You can sign your name underneath: I suppose somebody must witness it. It is valid, I know it is valid. There, I have done my share of the business, and the good God must do His."

The thing was done. In the half-light of the shaded lamp the signatures were appended. The Marquis handed the paper to Antoine. "Take good care of it," he said.

"And now, remember, I died of pneumonia. Swear on the little image. Where is it? Swear."

In the stillness of that strange sick-chamber Antoine swore, trembling, the oath required of him.

"That is right," said the Marquis. "You can leave me. Go downstairs. I am going to sleep."

He closed his eyes but, as soon as he was alone, he again opened them wide. He stared vaguely, into the black distance.

"Peut-être," he said aloud.

Then he got up slowly, out of bed. It was true, as he had said, that he felt no pain for the moment. But he was so weak that he had to drag himself along the floor. He was old, and white-haired, and very weary. As he laboriously pushed along, he struck his arm against a shaky little table. The costly bouillon-cup upon it fell to the ground with a crash. "Aha," he said.

He dragged himself towards a black leather-bag which lay in a corner. This he opened and from its recesses he drew a small velvet case. Out of the case he extracted a toy revolver, ivory inlaid, and, placing the weapon against his left temple, he drew the trigger.

CHAPTER XXII.

THE HOME OF POESY.

A LARGE house on a grim canal—a number of flat, un-interesting windows in a flat, uninteresting façade. A low front-door, with a heavy greystone coping, and on each side, along the narrow " stoep," a row of stumpy stone posts, connected by iron chains. The rest of it a great daub of dirty orange plaster, without any excrescence or salient feature, except just one little rusty spy-glass sticking out on the basement floor—the whole building like a meaning-less, rich man's face, in its ugly and insolent self-con-tent, comfortably dull. Young Reinout's home at the Hague.

And opposite, and on both sides of it, similar dwellings, of darker colour, flat and grey, under the lowering sky and the general gloom and primness, with the foul canal asleep in the middle of the grass-grown street. A grand house in a grand neighbourhood.

Count Hilarius van Rexelaer drove up to his own door in the neatest of little broughams and entered hurriedly. His whole manner betrayed anxiety, but, then, as we have seen, he had an irritable way about him and a habitual nervous twitch of the eyes. He was a man harassed by many things, who took life restlessly.

He passed through the low entrance-hall with its damp marble floor and ran upstairs to a comparatively brighter part of the house. He looked into his wife's boudoir; it was empty, but sounds to which he was well accustomed were issuing from the conservatory beyond. A sweet voice was shakily crooning some French words:

> " D'un seul regard il m'a tuée
> Car ce regard resta le seul."

The singing stopped at the sound of the opening door. A copper-coloured mulatto woman, in iridescent drapery, rose up from the floor and made obeisance, as her master entered. The Countess Rexelaer lifted a slow head from her divan: " Ah, mon ami! Bonjour!" she said, and let it fall again.

" It is most vexatious," began the Count, spitting his words, as the French inelegantly but aptly put it. " There is nothing but worry. I can't stand the strain. I shall have to resign." He stopped, and scowled at the waiting-woman.

" Laïssa," said the Countess languidly, " fetch me a glass of Cape-wine and a biscuit—" and as soon as the mulatto had crept noiselessly away—" It is no use, my dear Rexelaer: I tell her everything you tell me."

The husband pushed aside a green parrot which had slipped from its perch on to a low chair by the couch, and having thus freed a seat for himself, he sat down, unheedful of the disturbed favourite's flutter and fuss. " Come here, Rollo. Poor Rollo. Pretty Rollo," interposed the lady. " Oh, bother, listen to me, Margot," said the Count. When he called her " Margot," she knew that he was either very much pleased or very much put out. She herself had officially decreed, on becoming a Countess, that her name should henceforth be Margherita. " Pearl, for you, if you like, Hilarius." He had long ago left off calling her " Pearl."

" Well, what is it?" she asked faintly. " You must not tire me to-day. The damp has given me my headache."

Said Count Hilarius solemnly: " The King had a bad egg for breakfast this morning."

The Countess laughed, but indolently, as one who has more serious things to occupy her thoughts.

"You laugh!" cried the Count in sudden wrath, "because you do not understand. By Heaven, it is no laughing matter. Who is responsible for the eggs? I. If it happens again, I shall resign."

"Nonsense," she said, sitting up, alert and sharp.

"Ah, that brings you round, does it? I tell you my nerves can't stand the strain. This is the third time since Tuesday week. The eggs are new-laid, of course, but some wretched little red mess gets inside them. I suppose it's the food. None of the under-people can explain, and his Majesty is furious—rightly—and says it never occurred before. And I only three weeks in office!"

"It must not occur again," said Margherita, "not if we have to lay the eggs ourselves."

"To have chickens here, you mean?"

"Of course, I mean that. I do not believe the poor animals are to blame. It is the result of a conspiracy. You say yourself that all the Court people are against you, because they wanted your place for the Chamberlain's cousin. Be sure that an enemy inserts into the eggs the unpleasantnesses which his Majesty finds there."

"You think so?" he said doubtfully.

"I am sure of it. We can keep the fowl here in the conservatory, if needs must, and Laïssa can feed them." She was sufficiently animated now.

"True," said the Count, rising, "you could easily add them to the menagerie. But, perhaps it were better to abandon the whole thing. These Court cliques are terrible in their dead-set against a new-comer. They are merciless."

"What?" cried the Countess, leaning on one brown, jeweled arm. Then she added in softest scorn: "Coward!"

"Oh yes, it is easy enough for you to speak. You haven't

got to face them! You simply stop at home and say: "Make a great lady of me!"

"Already?" she went on. "Three weeks of failure after six years of struggle. Coward, Coward, Coward!" She leaped to her feet with the last words, her eyes flashing. "Yes," she said, "I am going to be a great lady. I have paid for it. And I again say: Go and make a great lady of me. Go!" Then, suddenly, she laughed, and threw herself back on the sofa. "You should have studied poultry-fancying in your youth, my lord Comptroller," she said. "We must get Reinout some pigeons, pretty innocent things. My uncle de Cachenard—"

"Ah, spare me your uncle de Cachenard," he said angrily, and walked from the room.

The Countess, left alone, arranged the coils of her magnificent black hair and smiled to her Creole face in the glass. Then she looked round and said, "Coo-ee, Coo-ee," and the mulatto-woman came gliding back.

Count Hilarius had not been wrong in speaking of the menagerie. "Aviary" would perhaps have been a more accurate term, for the whole place was in a flutter of exotic birds. It was suffocatingly hot, an unavoidable concession to the animals in question, and not an unwilling one on the part of their mistress, whose natural tastes preferred the sun to any and every thing in creation except herself, but awarded the third place—a long way below—to a blazing hot fire. "A good stove," she used to say, "is like a husband—ça réchauffe. But the sun is like a lover—ça brûle."

She had built out this large glass house at the back of her dull little boudoir, and had stocked it with a store of greenery, feathery ferns and wide palms and a number of prickly tropical plants. She had orange-blossoms in it, and a mass of gardenias, and the strong perfume of these starry flowers mingled very perceptibly with the odour of the birds. As for these, a whole lot of them lived in open cages among the verdure, a bright-plumaged, twittering, unmusical rainbow of colours—"nature's jewels," said the Countess, toying with the diamonds she persistently wore on her arm. "If I am to be buried alive," she had said, when first brought to the house in the Hague, "at least, I will have a hole in my grave, through which to see the earth and the flowers." She lived in her conservatory. She was always cold, and she used to repeat with an unpleasing grin, that she never expected to be warm again—on earth.

The Countess sipped her wine. She was very sensitive and could only take nourishment at irregular hours. And her digestion was a weak one; wholesome food disagreed with it. She ate sweetmeats and cakes in indefinite quantities out of boxes and bonbonnières which were always left lying about. Often the various animals would get at these receptacles, and then would ensue much brief exultation and subsequent sorrow, and stains on the oriental carpets and silk hangings, not that anybody noticed the more recent ones among the many of earlier date.

The copper-coloured woman crouched down at a little distance from her mistress's divan, and one of the parrots, settling down on her shoulder, began screeching "Laïssa," which name, by-the-bye, was a corruption of Eliza. For the mulatto's mother, an exceedingly vain personage, had declared herself and her daughter, in a moment of presumption, to be of English extraction, and had stuck to the story ever after on account of its unreasonableness. Black? There were many Englishmen born black. Satan himself was an Englishman, as every good Catholic in Rio could have told you.

"You want to know, I suppose," said the Countess. "Eh?"

"I? But no, M'am Rita. Let me sing you your song again, and you can go to sleep." And once more Laïssa began rocking herself to and fro and moaning:

> " Sous les tilleuls j'étais couchée.
> Il a passé sous les tilleuls.
> D'un seul regard il m'a tuée,
> Car ce regard resta le seul."

The woman crooned the words over and over without paying any attention to their meaning, while her mistress—who was the author of their being—lay listening with half-closed eyes of content.

"The idea is beautiful," said the Countess at last, interrupting the endless chant, "but the execution might be better. Rhymes a, a, are all right, but not rhymes b, b. Do you think, Laïssa, that 'tilleuls' rhymes with 'seul'?"

"Very well indeed, M'am Rita," replied the mulatto.

"Ah, you always say 'very well indeed,' but that does not satisfy my literary aspirations. You are not a literary character, Laïssa."

"No, M'am Rita," said the woman submissively.

"Do you know, you stupid, what a literary character is?"

"No, my jewel. Is it something bad?"

"It is the grandest thing on earth; it is an angel. Especially when it is a genius. I often think that I should have been a genius, Laïssa, had I not been a woman."

"A woman is a very good thing too," said Laïssa. "I daresay men like the women best."

"Do not expose your boundless ignorance, even to me. Pass me the rhyme-dictionary; Rollo is scratching it. Naughty Rollo. I must look up another rhyme for 'seul.' Aïeul. How would that do?"

> "'Sous les tilleuls il m'a passée
> Sous les tilleuls de mon aïeul.'"

"I don't care for the repetition of the same sound, though some people might consider it musical. No, I have it. This is better, and has a delightfully aristocratic ring:

"'Dans le jardin il m'a trouvée
   Du beau château de mon aïeul,
   D'un seul regard il m'a tuée
   Car ce regard resta le seul.'"

"Sing it, Nursie; let me hear how it goes. Ah me, the words awaken painful memories. A castle of our fathers! I shall never forgive the Count that he has not been able to procure me one."

"The saints will help, dearie," said the mulatto soothingly.

"For shame, how often must I tell you not to talk of the saints! They are angry with me for turning Protestant. Let sleeping dogs lie."

"Well, then we must try the cards," said the mulatto. "Shall I lay them for you, my pet, while you eat some chocolate-creams?"

"Yes, do," replied the Countess cheerfully. "I must compose a second stanza this afternoon; my head is too tired. Give me the box, off the watering-pot. No, no, Rollo. Go away. Down, Flora! Ah, there is a capital conjunction—the aces!—the aces!—turn up the other ace —that's right! Oh you dear, good Laïssa!" She bent forward over the cards, a chocolate-cream in her hand. "Something fortunate is going to happen! Delightful!" And she unthinkingly clapped her hands and smashed the sweetie.

"Something fortunate is going to happen," repeated the mulatto gravely, as she continued to spread the cards on the Turkish carpet before her. "Great riches—but these you do not want, honey. You have enough."

"Never enough," dissented the Countess vehemently, pushing her hand in among the cards. "My uncle de Cachenard was a rich man; I hate him for not leaving me everything."

"In my country," said the mulatto, "a yard of cotton and a few figs. It is enough."

"Less than that," cried Margherita passionately. "No cotton at all, and one fig, and the blazing sunshine! For the animal it is enough. But for the soul within me a hundred millions, to buy splendor and power and greatness! I want rivers of diamonds, oceans of diamonds. And emeralds, and sapphires, and rubies!" She stopped for breath and bit off a fragment of chocolate.

"Yes, diamonds are pretty: I was not thinking of diamonds," replied the waiting woman, still continuing her combinations. "And other jewels; you shall have them, my pretty! See, here comes the Queen of Diamonds again. You shall have a beautiful castle. It is coming, just the kind that you like."

The Countess laughed. "An ancestral home," she said, "ordered in from the bazar! No, my good Laïssa, the old man at Deynum says 'no' to the Queen of Diamonds. It is impudent of him, for he has not the necessary money himself, and should make room for his betters. You may have my brooch with the turquoises; I shall not wear it again."

"Thank you, child," replied Laïssa. "But, for me, I believe in the cards."

CHAPTER XXIII.

AND OF STATECRAFT.

The master of the house meanwhile, in his library, stood disconsolately gazing at the imitation bindings behind which his cigar-cases reposed in security. They could afford him as little assistance as the long line of the "Taschenbuch der gräflichen Häuser," or even the encyclopædia. He had built his hopes upon the latter, and had vainly looked out a couple of words, winding up with "alimentation." And now he had sent round his man to the bookseller's.

Little things always troubled him largely, but this, as he well knew, was not a little thing. It is a merciful dispensation that, in the moment of achievement, we first begin to realize the difficulties which await success. Count Rexelaer, on his smiling entry into Paradise, found all Paradise smiling back hostility. You think his Paradise ridiculous! That is, because it is not yours. But in that case, once more, put down this book. You cannot understand it.

"All the world is against me," said Count Rexelaer bitterly. He was not exaggerating. He knew no other world than his little own. Nor does any of us, talk how we will. And if his world looks very small to you, that is, perhaps, because you stand so far below it.

From his youth upwards he had laid himself out to "serve his King," set aside for that service as much as was ever Levite in a worthier temple, and in the due perfection of that service he had found his glory and crown—coronet—

of rejoicing. His father, a nobleman of William the First's easy creation (1832: Hilarius, therefore, had not been born in the purple), had struggled and schemed and fought himself into the front rank only to fall out of it again into the background of discontent through some caprice of a monarch's disfavour. There had been several children and a small fortune. Hilarius, the eldest, had behaved admirably, as soon as he was old enough to understand. Excellent financier that he was, he had avoided the common fallacy that all expenditure must necessarily be regulated by actual assets, and had shown the good sense to keep up his position, like a European state, by borrowing money which a subsequent combination must pay. It would have been fatal, as he said, to "drop out," a mistake which so many have committed under the influence of temporary misfortune. "We are too recent to recede," he told his parents when they complained of his bills. "If people are saying that we are poor, mamma, you should order in a lot of fine new clothes." The old lady would certainly have liked to do so—for the sake of the fine new clothes—but she lacked her son's pluck. Her father had been a draper; she had bourgeois ideas of honesty.

It must be admitted, on the other hand, that Hilarius never wasted a penny on himself. What he spent he spent for his object. And he systematized both his expenditure and his debts.

When he left the University, where he had lived "correctly," Hilarius had obtained a small post in the diplomatic service—it was convenient to him, for various reasons, to remove himself from his surroundings at the Hague. He did his work well for a great many years, which means that he did nothing, decently, and with the necessary self-respect; in the meantime his brother married at home, fairly well, and his sister settled down into respectable old-maidism, and his mother (who had been a draper's daughter) died, and things began to look brighter for the family.

Then Count Hilarius's reward came at last. It was not a
First Prize, and he felt rather inclined to cavil at its second-
rateness; still it was better than the empty Certificate of
Merit, with which he had been hitherto obliged to content
his meritorious self. He was attached to the Dutch Legation at Rio—no more—he was getting on for five and thirty
already, and his light hair was beginning to thin at the top,
when little Rita de Cachenard—Margot Magot, as she was
called in the French colony—old Crœsus Cachenard's niece
and presumable heiress, fell franctically in love with him.
She was sixteen, and very handsome, not an easy character
to read, for, although she was naturally an object of interest, opinion remained divided about, not her charms (they
were indisputable), but her virtues. According to some she
was passionate but pure; according to others she was cold,
and cool, as marble. She wrote verses to the object of her
adoration, and blushed after having played them into his
hands. There seems no great harm in that. She was sixteen, and her eyes were large and black. Perhaps her soul
was as large, though not as black, as they. She wanted to
marry him; that was all. She had his willing consent, but
perhaps she would have tried to do it without.

Her uncle was delighted that his little Margot should be
a Countess. He was a fat old Frenchman and a republican.
It is perfectly impossible to set down here in what manner
he had amassed his very considerable fortune. Suffice it to
say that the blackest brand of blackguardism was indelibly
stamped upon every loathsome ducat which the young
Countess Rexelaer poured into the hollow exchequer of the
noble Dutch family. She poured in a good many. And
yet more followed when, shortly after, the old rascal oblig-
ingly retired from the scene of his compromising successes.
But he left his niece just one half of that whole she had expected; the other half he squandered and scattered among
a lot of obscure individuals whom nobody had ever heard of
before. Fortunately their name was in no case de Cache-

nard. Nor, for the matter of that, was the old man's; the disagreeable people who remember what they ought to have forgotten, could have given you an earlier and less elegant version. As for the "de," the "merchant," good patriot and republican though he was, had been obliged to forfeit his nationality and pay down no less than twenty pounds to obtain it.

Count van Rexelaer returned to Holland with his wife and her money-bags, and her tropical animals, habits, plants and waiting-woman. He made a point of remembering the money-bags—conscientiously—and they got on very well together. He also made a point of reminding his relations of these same money-bags, and the relations made a point of reminding everybody else and of doubling, in conversation, the number, size and weight of said money-bags. The subject was thus treated with mutual goodwill, and the family behaved admirably. Mevrouw van Rexelaer-Borck, Hilarius's brother's wife, smiled sweetly when one of "the black thing's" birds went messing over her new silk dress. But then, they were so intensely relieved to find that the new member of the family was "not actually black, you know, though we called her so in fun; she is dark, and really quite handsome. Like a Spaniard." This much Mevrouw Rexelaer confided to her mother, the old Baroness Borck, a connection of the lord of Rollingen. To her intimate friends she said: "My brother-in-law's young wife comes of a noble French family, ' de Cachenard.' He met her in diplomatic circles at Petropolis. Our *only* objection would be the great difference of age (he is double hers), but, after all, that is their look-out. She is a most charming thing. Just a little—how shall I call it?—exotic. Her parents have kept her out there too long, perhaps, as a queen among slaves, you know. Like the children of Steelenaar, our own Indian Governor-General."

"Was the father French minister there?" asked a friend.

"Yes—no," replied Mevrouw van Rexelaer quickly, re-membering, at the last moment, the inconvenience of printed lists. "Not minister, you know. But second-best. What is it they call it? A Councillor of the Embassy, I be-lieve."

"Ah yes. Like the Comte de Hautlieu."

"Exactly so," rejoined Mevrouw van Rexelaer, "like the Comte de Hautlieu."

In the meantime no one took the trouble to inquire what were the sentiments of the poor girl herself. The creature was now Countess van Rexelaer. What more could she want?

But, if the truth must be told, the creature had actually had the impudence to want more. She had wanted love—stormy, passionate adoration of the "kill-your-neighbour-and-kiss-your-neighbour's-wife" kind. Something grand, terrific, imposing—love with a capital L. Not affection; poor thing! she knew nothing of affection. That is a plant which must be trained in the home-garden, while love springs up in the wastes. Father she had never known; her mother she had lost at the age of five, which was a mis-fortune, the mother, with all her vagaries, having been born and bred a gentlewoman. Margherita had grown up at hap-hazard, in a lazy, sunlit mansion among a crowd of obsequious, villainous slaves and mongrels who pandered to her early faults, lest their own vices should be checked. She had been taught nothing, except French and Portuguese —and dancing and riding and fencing, and playing out of tune on the guitar. Even these accomplishments she had chiefly taught herself. She could fence splendidly, and that was about all.

It is to be appreciated in her, then, that she read such books as she could lay hold of—trashy novels. And one day, utterly bored by the emptiness of her existence, she had demanded a "professor of French literature." Old Cachenard, who held that woman's only mission was to be

fair, fond, foolish and, possibly, foul—there are many such
men : God forgive them !—had vainly tried to dissuade his
niece. Margherita liked her uncle (in all justice to her it
must be confessed that she had no inkling till after his
death how he had gotten his money), but she hated him
with a fierce hate when he contradicted her, which he very
rarely did. A Frenchman was procured who read Musset
with her—" Rolla "—and Victor Hugo—" Le Roi s'amuse,"
and she felt that she loved literature and took to devouring
more novels, with a preference for the days of chivalry, and
she wanted a knight to lift up her glove and kiss it (she
had very small hands) and make noble speeches to her,
beautiful, sentimental speeches—not crack disgusting jokes,
like uncle Cachenard.

So, when she was sixteen years old, she fell head over
ears in love with Count van Rexelaer. He was a noble of
exalted rank, a descendant of a long line of Knights and
Crusaders, a son of Kings. His very name declared it.
Rex Hilarius—she called it Rex Ilario—he had told her
about it (he was rather fond of telling) ; this King Hilarius,
his great grandfather, had ruled over a mighty people long
before South America existed ! He was greater than the
Emperor. He was stately and splendid (*i. e.* tight-buttoned
and thin) ; and his bearing was noble and knightly (*i. e.* he
bowed very low when he met her). She loved him, immensely, like an ocean. She would have liked him to die
for her, but not the other way, please. And she threw herself at his feet, and he picked her up, very politely, and
they were married. And not only had he no desire to die
for her, but he was not even anxious to live for her, nor
with her, more than necessary, after a time.

When the Countess realized that one cannot always have
what one wants—at least, not in our northern hemisphere—
she first had a bad time of it, violently bad but brief, and
then she felt fairly comfortable. She made up her mind to
want a lot more things, and to get them, so, resigning the

unattainable, she cultivated her caprices. She fortunately
took a liking to her little boy, who was handsome. Physically there were seventeen years between them; psychically
less. And she interested herself, from a lazy distance, in her
husband's climb to that starry canopy which shone forth as
his blue and vaulted heaven. Her position, unfortunately,
debarred her from the poetic greatness she had been born
to. Ah, what an artist was lost! But she cheered her
solitude with song, while waiting for her husband to make
a grande dame of her. It was very cold and bleak in Holland. But she had made up her mind to be a grande dame.
Mevrouw van Rexelaer-Borck kissed her.

And her husband worked for two. He was a quiet
faber suæ fortunæ, whose weak point was want of nerve at
a crisis, and whose strong point was want of feeling. He
plodded up slowly, but with an indomitable resolve never to
slide back. It was hard work for him at first. He was not
a favourite, his father's disgrace still clung about the family; he had none of those stilts and stays which are such a
help in climbing. His sister-in-law, Mevrouw Rexelaer-
Borck, however, was a host in herself. She had brought
excellent connections into the family, almost a costlier treasure than gold. And she had managed, by one of her wonderful strokes of luck, to acquire for her husband an extra
territorial title attached to a few acres of heath, dirt-cheap.
Frederik van Rexelaer was Rexelaer van Altena. Hilarius
—the head of the family, and, as such, the Count—was all
the more anxious to be Rexelaer of something.

Gradually he prospered. His great policy was never
to feel kicked. And by dint of this he sidled past better
people and even pushed in front of more powerful ones.
The High and Mighty began to remember that his father
had been one of them; for years they had only remembered
to forget. He was admitted into the Royal Household before he was fifty. There was not a part of his body which
was not blue from ill-treatment, there was not a corner of

13

his soul which was not black with lying and licking—un-
charitableness, unmanliness, and uncleanness,—but he was
a Great Man at last. Of course he was an exception; it is
said these are apt to prove the rule.

During three bright weeks he had borne his new-culled
honours, as a maiden bears her betrothal-wreath. Bright,
truly, but with flashes of lightning, amid the distant roll of
thunder. And often it wants a little climbing to realize
the unclimbed heights above.

He paced his study-floor with gloomy eyebrows. It was
almost a relief when a servant knocked, and brought the
news that a man was waiting to see him.

"What sort of a man?"

"A common man," replied the well-drilled domes-
tic, with thankful consciousness that he was not one of
these.

Count Rexelaer walked out into the hall.

"Who are you?" he asked sharply.

The individual thus addressed seemed to cower away
into the very ground. "I am a poor man," he said. "A
humble man, Heer Count. Have pity on a father of four
little children. I have been turned away from the service
of the palace. I was clerk there, for twenty years I have
kept the kitchen accounts. I earned nine florins a week.
It isn't much, but it was always something. And I
have always been honest, Highborn Heer Count. I
have—"

"I remember," interrupted Count Rexelaer impatiently. "You were discharged a fortnight ago. I forget
why."

"There was a story, Highborn Heer, about a kitch-
enmaid. There was not a word of truth in it, I swear
before God in Heaven!"—he lifted a lean hand on high
—he was a worn-looking creature, with a big nose,
the only big thing about him, and bright fever-fed
eyes.

"And what was the girl's name?" queried Count Rexelaer, staring at the ceiling.

"Dora Droste, Highly Nobly Born Heer Count."

"Of course," said the Count, still staring aloft. "I remember all about it perfectly." He brought his eyes down to the level of the man's face. "How dare you come here?" he said furiously. "You were turned away and you richly deserved it. We shall soon teach you, and such as you, what to expect."

"But I swear I am innocent," replied the man in earnest tones. "A father of four children, Heer Count."

"Just so. A father of four children."

"I was teaching her to read, in my free time, most noble Heer Count. She had begged me to teach her to read."

Count Rexelaer smiled. "I remember all about the case," he said. "You may feel thankful you were not prosecuted. Get out of the house this moment. Jan, show this person out."

"Is that final?" asked the fellow.

"Absolutely final." Count Rexelaer retreated to his study-door.

But the man intercepted him. "Count Rexelaer," he said, almost in a whisper, "you're playing a bold game. It won't do."

The Count drew back. "You are mad," he said. "Jan!"

"Unhand me," cried the fellow, bursting out violently. "No one dare to touch me! You—you! it is villains like you who make socialists, revolutionists, murderers! Oh you blackguard! But I swear that as sure as my name is Wouter Wonnema—"

Count Rexelaer closed his study door.

"Here, get out of this!" said the man-servant. "What do you mean by pitching into master like that? If he were to give me notice to-morrow, I should simply grin and go."

The other looked as if he were about to launch into a long explanation; then he thought better of it, and rapidly stumbled downstairs, cursing and threatening.

CHAPTER XXIV.

A WINDOW OPENS.

REINOUT, turning the far corner of the quiet street on his homeward way from a lonely walk, was astonished to perceive an individual stationed opposite the house and gesticulating at its smooth front of many panes. The man stood out solitary against one of the long line of trees, melancholy canal-trees, in little rounds among the stones, fresh from a German toy-box. His appearance was needy, but not untidy. His figure much shrunk, yet nowise abject in its indigence.

Reinout, as has been said already, knew nothing of the actual world. He understood that the poor were part of the divinely ordered plan, created to give the rich an opportunity of exercising the virtues, especially of charity towards their brethren and of gratitude towards God. And had he been told that the poor lacked bread—which he was not—he might easily have added his name to the list of those favoured ones who are credited with having answered: " Then why don't they buy cakes?"

There could be no mistaking the strange man's meaning. He shook his fist menacingly with fierce glances and mutterings, and then, after a final thrust of his lean arm, he turned and crept in the direction from which Reinout was coming.

As soon as they were close together: " Why did you do that?" asked Reinout, reproducing the other's threat.

The man started and stared. " Because a villain lives

there," he answered sullenly, "if it's any satisfaction to you to know," and he sought to continue his way.

But Reinout interposed, with flushed cheek and trembling lip. He had all his mother's impetuousness and much of his father's caution. He had the former's strength of passion, and none of the latter's nervousness. In his indignation he was going to burst out: "But that's my father!" when curiosity checked the words.

"Why a villain?" he questioned, a trifle imperiously. Wonnema stopped again. No one could look closely at Reinout and not recognize the Jonker's social status. "All rich men are villains," replied Wonnema evasively. Prudence fortunately kept him from particularising the Count's offences to the first boy that questioned him.

"But why are rich men villains?" persisted Reinout, greatly relieved, meanwhile, to find the charge so much extended.

"Why? Because they're born to 't. Because they suck it in with their mother's milk. Because God has given them the right, they think. Because a rich man's happiness is built up of a thousand poor men's sufferings. That's why."

Only the last "because" conveyed a definite meaning to the questioner. It struck straight with all its newness. Surely things were the other way round.

"That's why," continued the strange man, warming to his subject. "Because the rich can do no wrong, and if they *have* done wrong the poor must suffer for it. Here am I starving, because my innocence must cloak a rich man's guilt. Go your ways, boy, you'll be a villain some day, if you aren't one already. You're born to it." He passed into the road and walked a few paces farther. Then he turned for a final easement of his over-burdened heart. "And yon's the biggest villain of all," he said, once more lifting a thin finger of scorn in the direction of the orange-plaster wall.

"Hold your tongue," cried Reinout boldly. "My father lives in that house." But Wonnema had already resumed his trudge. The boy stood hesitating. Of the other's last speech he had again understood one sentence only, which reached his heart. "Here am I starving." The man was of course a beggar. What other connection could there be between rich and poor? He had been turned off at the door and was angry. People *were* turned off, as Reinout knew, for the Count disapproved of almsgiving. The boy had a whole florin in his pocket, half the month's pocket-money. "Starving?" He ran after the retreating figure. "Here, poor man!" he said. And to his utter amazement the beggar struck the coin to the ground. "My children are famished," said Wonnema thickly, trembling with emotion. "I would rather see them dead than take home one penny of yours!" The florin lay glittering in the mud.

Reinout retreated in dismay. He did not look round again, from a delicate instinct that the other was still staring hungrily at the silver-piece. But Wonnema let it lie.

The boy crept into the house, all his heart and head in confusion. For the first time in his life he had come into contact with the Spirit of Protest against things that are. He knew of course of the existence of wickedness and sorrow—vaguely—these were unavoidable and to be endured. He knew that wickedness incorporate—mad ambition—had slain blessed saints and martyrs such as Louis the Sixteenth. For there had always been thieves and murderers, big and small. But an honest, if mistaken, cry against Evil in High Places, an arraignment of divinely-instituted Order before the bar of God Himself, of this he could make nothing. Irresistibly he felt that the poor wretch had been sincere. "A rich man's happiness is built up of a thousand poor men's sorrows." "Some day you will be a villain; you are born to it." He sat down on a bench in the hall to think it out. And, his eye falling on some letters in the letter-box, he carried these in to his father, as was his custom, and

then went back to his seat. It was no use asking Papa
about the poor. Papa felt no interest in the subject. And
he differed from M. de Souza. "You should never give to
beggars," he had often said. "It encourages them to ask
for more."

Reinout lay back on the open bench and closed his eyes.
That refusal of money. What did it signify? There was
no room for it in the whole little system of his calm existence. And the more he thought of it the more bewildered
he grew.

While he still lingered there, he heard his father calling
his name in the library, in a strange "strangled" voice. As
he started up, the door flew open, and the Count came rushing out, his face distorted with excitement. "Reinout," he
stammered, "Reinout!" and catching the boy to his breast
he covered him with kisses, laughing and sobbing by turns.
Reinout kept quite still; a horrible fear traversed his brain
that his father had become insane; he set his teeth tight.

"My boy, my boy," said the Count at last more calmly,
holding his son at arms' length and looking into his eyes.
"Imagine, what wonder! What triumph! God has given
us Deynum. In the most wonderful of all manners, it is
ours!"

"Ours?" repeated the lad, bewildered.

"Ours, yes, ours. Mine, yours. Ever afterwards. Yours.
Yours, some day when your poor father has been laid to rest.
Yours, Reinout, Count Rexelaer van Deynum!" He once
more drew his heir towards him, and kissed him, solemnly
this time, between the eyes. "And now I must go tell your
mother," he said, and turned to the staircase. "Gracious
Heaven," he thought to himself, as he mounted it with
dancing step, "how queerly things work round!" Yet, he
was not one of those who feel that Heaven is gracious, even
when things work round—queerly.

Reinout, left to himself, repeated: "God has given us
Deynum." More money, then. More grandeur. Did that

mean more "villainy"? Nonsense. The man was crazy. God has given us Deynum. What is "God" to Reinout? An image set up at very rare intervals, special "points de vue," along the road of life. It is a double-visaged image, like Janus. One face has angry eyebrows: Fate; the other smiling glances: Luck.

CHAPTER XXV.

MISS PIGGIE.

ALTERNATELY slapping and stroking her lapdogs, Florizel and Amanda (abbreviations by Reinout, regardless of inverted gender, Flora and Ami), Madame van Rexelaer lay humming her second stanza, which, translated into English, would have run somewhat as follows:

> "Then let me sleep the sleep of death.
> And bear me where my fathers are.
> My dying sob was the final breath,
> Of the noble house of Cachenard."

She was purring over this poetical effusion when the Count suddenly burst in upon her.

"Prepare yourself," he said, "for the most extraordinary, the most incredible good news!"

"O Rex," she exclaimed, flushing with pleasure. "You don't mean to say I'm invited to stay at the Palace of Loo?"

"Rex" was the name she had given him in the earliest dawn of her enthusiasm. O Richard! O Hilaire! O mon Roy! She hardly ever made use of it now, but the moment was one of ecstatic abandonment; visions floated before her of delicious new dresses, three a day, and the intimate intercourse of an august home-circle for half a week, so different from the tumult of an omnium gatherum where you made your bow in the crowd and sank back like a wave on the sea. She screamed aloud with expectation.

"No, no, that another time!" said the Count. "How can you talk such nonsense, when you know the Court is here? Just listen to me, and put down those dogs for a minute."

"I thought it was an invitation," pouted the lady, "I don't care if it isn't an invitation. I don't want anything else."

"It appears," the Count continued, without taking any notice of the last remarks, "that your mother had connections of whom you never knew anything—very respectable relations, to say the least."

"My mother's name was Dupuys," replied the daughter of the noble house of Cachenard, removing her face from behind Florizel, whither she had retreated in her sulkiness. "It doesn't sound a very aristocratic name. My uncle once told me that she had come from the north of France. He never said anything about her relations."

Count Hilarius had always carefully avoided glancing down into the depths from whence his wife had ascended to his side. Not to know is the safest way of lying. It was enough to live in constant recollection of the uncle's career, without discovering what the parents had done. He had grumbled at the dishonour and he had also grumbled, the price being so heavy, that his wife had not brought him more at the price. Fortunately Rio was far; and the parents were still farther.

"I cannot make it out very clearly as yet," he now said, "but, as far as I can see, your mother was a very different person from what she pretended to be. The Belgian lawyer who writes presumes that I am acquainted with her antecedents and is therefore far from explicit. But it seems that she was neither more nor less than a Demoiselle de la Jolais-Farjolle, of the Belgian house of la Jolais de Saint-Leu. She seems to have run away with a—a—her husband." He stopped, and eyed his wife curiously.

"And what is that, la Jolais?" asked the Countess.

"It is one of the greatest families in Europe," replied the Count drily. "The head of the house is the Marquis de la Jolais-Farjolle."

Mademoiselle de Cachenard clapped her hands. "How delightful!" she cried with a bright little laugh. "How pretty! A Marquis! It is more than a Count. What a good thing I did not know when I married you, that my mother had been a Marchioness, Hilarius. I might not have been satisfied with a Count, after that."

"Your mother was not a Marchioness," answered Rexelaer irritably, "no more than your uncle Cachenard. Whatever she was, she seems to have had the good taste after her —adventure, to sink all her past down a well, henceforth to be known as Dupuys. But, now, as to results."

"No, no, you are jealous! How charming it sounds! De Cachenard, née de la Jolais-Guignol. Much nicer than Rexelaer. I wish I had known!" And she hugged Florizel to her face till he squeaked.

"De Farce rare, née de la jolie guinguette," cried the son of all the Rexelaers, exasperated by these taunts. "Your mother was a gentlewoman—more shame to her!— and she ran away with a groom out of her brother's stables, and his name was Cochonnard!"

"What?" shrieked the Creole, dropping Florizel with a thud on the floor. "It isn't true. Oh you horrid vulgar man to come and tell such stories!" And she burst into a tempest of screeches and (audible) wishes she was dead.

"Allons, allons, how can you behave so childishly!" interposed the Count, somewhat disturbed by this exceptional ebullition of feeling. "You have known all along how your uncle got his "de," and that you were not even legally entitled to use it."

"I was my uncle's heiress," wailed Margherita, "and I don't care. I won't be called Cochonnette."

"You are called at present," said her husband soothingly, "the Countess Van Rexelaer."

"I don't care," she interrupted him with a fresh burst of tears. "I wo-wo-won't be called Miss Piggie—Miss Piggie, indeed! I wo-wo-won't."

"But for goodness sake, listen to reason. There is the bright side yet to come, and it is almost incredibly fortunate. The Marquis de la Jolais, your mother's half-brother, is dead. He died, intestate, about a fortnight ago, and if, as they imagine, you are his only near relation, all his private property will come to you."

"I don't care," said Margherita, opening her eyes, nevertheless.

"Nonsense. They have been telegraphing to Rio, and the answer has come that they must apply to me. As indeed they must. There is quite a distant cousin, they tell me, who succeeds to the Belgian estate by a contract independent of wills, but you, being the niece, are the heiress who comes into the rest."

"All the other money was mine too," said Margherita.

She stung him. "Yes," he said, "it was, Mademoiselle Cochonnard."

Then Margherita screamed once more and fainted dead away.

Years ago, when this used to happen, the Count would pull down the bell-rope. Now he walked out of the room.

CHAPTER XXVI.

SPLENDIDE MENDAX.

A DAY or two later, further advices having been received meanwhile, the great news had obtained sufficient consistency to allow of its being communicated to the Rexelaers-Borck.

The facts as to Margherita's mother were briefly these. The Marquis de la Jolais,—the Marquis J'ose—himself his mother's only child, had had a step-sister many years younger than he, the late darling of the whole family. He had been as a father to her during many years, and just as he had arranged that she should be most desirably married to (not with) an old friend of his own, she had eloped with a stable-boy. The head of the house had immediately erased her name from its annals, and, having been apprised later on that she was living at Lyons with her spendthrift husband in absolute destitution, he paid her over the sum of ten thousand francs, on consideration of her sacredly binding herself to sink all her antecedents and to assume henceforth the name of Dupuys. The bargain was faithfully kept. The man Cochonnard died early from drink; his broken-hearted wife did not long survive him, and their little daughter Margaret was left with her rich bachelor-uncle. The Marquis remained unaware of all particulars. He had forbidden his lawyers to communicate with him on the subject, and he had caused it to be generally understood that his half-sister had died without a child. Nevertheless, one of those rumours that always come knocking at barricaded ears had vaguely informed him of some facts concerning the Cochonnards and their money-making. He had loved his sister as much as he was capable of loving anything; a hundred times he wished she had died in her bloom.

Once his eye had fallen on an announcement in the Paris *Figaro* of the marriage of a Count Rexelaer, of whom he knew nothing but the name, with a Mademoiselle Rita de Cachenard, of whom he knew nothing at all. He had glided on to the next paragraph. But a few weeks later he received a short letter from the old uncle. In the joy of his heart Cochonnard had thought the moment was come to reconcile his little Margot with her mother's noble relation. That gentleman tore up the letter, furious at having his uncertainty thus rudely broken into. As for the improvement in the young lady's original patronymic, it filled him with unfathomable contempt.

Nevertheless, he now knew what he knew. His sister had a daughter living, and that daughter was a Countess Rexelaer. Of the Rexelaers of Deynum. He was not as well up in Dutch families as the Baron was in Belgian. But even the Baron had known nothing of Mademoiselle de la Jolais except that she had run away, long ago, with some footman, and had died shortly afterwards, in Paris, he believed. The Marquis was not sorry to think the child should have done well. But he washed his hands—literally, laboriously—after having torn up the old man's letter.

One summer he had gone to spend a week with some friends at their seat near Blankenberghe, and fickle, foolish Fortune had cast the child Reinout straight across his path. He had fled from the association that night with both hands to his ears. But the memory clung to his dried-up old heart. He liked the look of the boy. He liked his manner. He had liked, above all, that bold dash into danger. The Marquis J'ose knew good blood when he saw it.

And on that terrible night of his flight from Amsterdam, the word "Deynum," as it crashed through the carriage-window, had struck comfort to his soul, in the midst of its agony. "This is nothing," the guard had cried, "this is Deynum." Truly, it was nothing to him; he had willed that it should be nothing, but it was the only name which, at that hour of supremest loneliness, had conveyed to the wretched sufferer a remote idea of relationship. He knew nothing more of the Rexelaers than that they had their home at Deynum. He could travel no farther. The place fascinated him. He would keep up, all the more strictly, the incognito he had already assumed. He would look out for himself. Perhaps—who knows?—he would find ultimate pleasure in this daughter of his race. He would see the boy again. He was dying. Death strangely alters our perspectives.

He remained, therefore, a day or two at the village-inn, whence he would in no case have been anxious to depart, and tried to feel his way. He soon perceived that there were complications which his ignorance was unable to unravel. He was too proud to write off now, for information, to his lawyers at Brussels. These were the wrong Rexelaers. Of course they were related. There were jealousies, evidently, and bickerings. The Marquis was too much occupied with himself to take any great interest in these. Then came the incident of the house. He wanted the lonely castle with all a rich man's sudden, irresistible want. And if later on it should, in the course of life's accidents, become young Reinout's property, well, that was no inducement, but it was certainly no objection to buying it. As for the clause about never "letting or selling to Count Hilarius van Rexelaer," he could easily subscribe to that. Count Hilarius would either inherit the property through his wife or never possess it at all. But the sick man had not as yet settled these things in his mind; perhaps, later on, he would make a will. He was bitterly irritated at the failure to discover his niece in the hour of need. Yet he wanted to die unknown. He wanted to be nursed. He wanted both extremes. He wanted neither. And in the midst of his uncertainty the catastrophe spread sudden silence over all.

Reinout went up to his room with the wonderful discovery that the mysterious old gentleman of his long boy fancies had now developed into a blood-relation, a fairy god-father, a great giver of gifts. The splendour of a powerful position, large landed proprietorship with all its responsibilities and advantages, the sudden uplifting into a "great family," this had come to his mother, and through his mother, to himself, direct from the dead hand of his secret friend. He understood the importance of the inheritance as few boys of his age could have done. Yet it was not so much an uplifting as a restoration. He knew all about the fief of Hohenthal-Sonnenborn, and the Countship of the Holy Roman Empire, and "I will make you Baron Butterworth." The hero of the latter story he revered as the founder of "our branch." At last, then, after the lapse of three centuries, a Count Rexelaer would again ascend the ancestral throne. He understood all that. You cannot help knowing thoroughly what your father tells you at least once a month.

He locked himself into his room with "Prince." He could not have told you why he liked to lock himself in, although nobody ever disturbed him. It was a fancy, a craving of the lonely child for absolute loneliness. Next door was the schoolroom, bare and tiresome; this was his own sanctum, dull and dark like the rest of the house, but bright to him with all a boy's accumulated treasure. He had a fine collection of seals, and a smaller one of postage stamps (neglected), and he was now busy in getting together, at the Chevalier's suggestion and under his superintendence, a set of engravings of "distinguished" person-

14

ages, native and foreign. Some good swords and rapiers hung against the wall, a present from his father; in one corner stood a turning-lathe, in another a complete suit of armour from a children's ball (William van Rexelaer, first Count Hohenfels) and an out-grown toy uniform of a Prussian Hussar, for in earlier days Reinout had loved to dress up. The place of honour, however, was occupied by a small glass cabinet, in which were carefully arranged a variety of old-fashioned gloves and mittens, half a dozen centuries of hand covering, big and little, silken, leathern, or velvet, embroidered, bejewelled and laced. The Chevalier's life-long hobby, gloves of celebrated women—(he had spent on the hands what the hearts had left him)—solemnly made over to his darling pupil on the latter's twelfth birthday, "the termination of childhood." "Collectionnez, mon enfant," said Monsieur de Souza. "It is good; it supplies a vocation. When next we are in Paris I will take you to see the fans of the Vicomtesse de Rovilly. They are worth several hundred thousand francs and she shows them to no one, but she and I are friends of the days gone by. That is the distinction of the collectionneur comme il faut. He does not show his collections." Nature was represented by a pair of gorgeous stuffed birds from Brazil, all glitter, and pricked-up-ness, and pride.

Reinout threw himself down on a magnificent tiger-skin, the present of an Indian Prince to Margherita, but neglected now and a little moth-eaten in places. The great black retriever fell over his young master, and they curled themselves into each other, warm and soft. Two things were troubling Reinout's thoughts, in spite of his eager desire to rejoice in his father's triumph: the lean finger of earnest protest upraised against the " villainy " of Greatness, and the strange Marquis's last, sad words : " Try to do your duty. I have not."

" I will," said Reinout, sitting up, with his arm round the dog's neck. " If only one always had somebody to tell one exactly what was right, it would be so easy. Why isn't there? I don't suppose anybody wants, purposely, to do anything wrong. Of course there's Monsieur de Souza. He always used to know, I think, but perhaps he doesn't always. I don't think he'd quite understand what this beggar-man meant, he knows so little about poor people. A gentilhomme devoir fait loi. That means to do your duty's always right. At any rate, it's always right to choose the disagreeable and be kind." And then he began to ponder the approaching St. Nicholas festivities and the presents he was going to buy for his cousins, the Rexelaers-Borck, especially for Topsy, his twelve year old favourite and playmate. He always received ten florins extra to purchase these presents with. He still hesitated, for Topsy, between a canary and a card-case (!). True, that was a subject on which he could ask his mother's advice. There were some subjects, you see, on which he could ask his mother's advice. He got up, and wandered downstairs to find her, the dog at his heels. Prince was not permitted to enter the winter-garden, because of his sweeping tail. He knew it, and the prohibition was a very sore point with him on account of Ami's and Flora's insolent manner of yapping against the glass-doors. He sneaked in to-day unperceived, and then turned with loud-voiced protest at Reinout's command to retire, backing and barking and bounding till, in another moment, he had upset a couple of pots by the entry. Margherita came into view from behind a great stand of chrysanthemums. Her eyes were still sulky; she looked down at the snapped stems with their helpless pink blossoms. They were her dear Brazilian lilies, just come back from the florist who had reared the seeds for her at much trouble and expense.

She did not say a word, but her face grew suddenly ugly, and she went back for a little whip which she kept to rule her own pets.

Reinout had seen his mother beat Prince once before, till she drew blood. He trembled from head to foot.

"Mamma," he cried, "it wasn't Prince's fault, it was me. I brought him in and I knocked him up against the flower-pots."

She hesitated, with uplifted whip. One moment he thought she was going to strike him; then she said, in a voice as ugly as her face, "Very well, René; your St. Nicholas money can pay for new ones," and turned her back on the boy and the cowed creature at his feet.

Reinout silently got his copy-books and went up to Monsieur de Souza. He felt that he had done his duty by his defenceless friend, whose entrance he should have fore-stalled.

His tutor and he were busy with Italy, which was by no means a united kingdom yet in those days. "And now re-peat to me, René," said Monsieur de Souza, "what I told you yesterday about Naples. How did there come to be a Bourbon reigning at Naples? Go on." And Reinout be-gan. "You are forgetting about the Casa Crocida's," inter-rupted the old gentleman presently. "I am coming to that, Monsieur," replied Reinout, colouring. "But the King, seeing the battle was hopelessly lost, turned and fled down a narrow ravine. After a long ride he reached the lonely house of a peasant by some cross-roads, and the peasant, recognising him, gave him a fresh horse. And the King said: 'Swear that you do not betray me,' and the old peas-ant swore on the cross of the King's sword. But just when the King was gone, flying to the left, a troop of the enemy rode up and they asked which way the King had passed. And the peasant said, 'To the right,' but they did not be-lieve him, and they made him swear on the cross again, and he told them that he hated the King because he had taken his only son for a soldier, and then he saw that the enemy had got his son with them as a prisoner! And the captain of the enemy said: 'We will turn to the right'—for they had to choose, you see, by the old peasant's cottage—'and if the King is not caught to-night, we shall slay your son.' And the peasant said : 'The King is gone to the right.'

"And when the war was over the King sent for the old man and made him a baron. And the son, who had escaped, became a great general. That was in the thirteenth century "—"Fifteenth," corrected M. de Souza—"and the King gave them as a motto 'Splendide Mendax,' and the present head of the house is Prince Paul Casa Crocida, who was ambassador at Paris under Louis Philippe, and arranged the treaty of Maisons-Douillette, and whose wife is a Pamphigliosi and an aunt of the Italian minister here."

Presently the Count came in. He liked to think he remained in touch with his son's education. "Well, my dear Chevalier," he said beamingly, "I hope we shall be able to move to Deynum in time for Christmas. We can hardly be ready as early as St. Nicholas (5th Dec.), but we must have a regular Christmastide with all my brother's family. They are so English, you know. The air is dry up at Deynum. It will do your rheumatics good."

"It will do good then unto the good and to the evil," said the old Chevalier, smiling. "Like the good God Himself."

"And you, René," continued the Count, turning to his staring son, "you must keep your presents till Christmas. We shall have a splendid time."

"There will be no presents," said Reinout, a little sullenly.

"Nonsense. Why not?"

"Mamma has taken away my money," replied the son of the house, with his elbows on the table.

"Have you been misbehaving? Oh, never mind. We can't have the whole thing spoiled just now. I'll let you have an extra gold piece for the sake of Deynum." And Count Hilarius fingered the money in his waistcoat-pocket. As a rule he, with his pecuniary preciseness, was a complete stranger to "tips."

Reinout did not move from his ungraceful pose.

"I'd rather not, Papa," he said, in his young pride of martyrdom. "Mamma wouldn't like it."

"Nonsense. Catch!"

And Reinout, not being a prig, caught.

CHAPTER XXVII.

LOW LIFE, FOR A CHANGE.

A few evenings before the memorable Christmas-tide of that memorable year, a group of heavy-browed peasants sat solemnly smoking their pipes round the stove in the tap-room at Deynum. The stove glowed red-hot in the centre, the room was ill-lighted and stuffy, amid its perfumes of gin and paraffin, and its slow-wreathing clouds of smoke. Could you have pierced beyond the lowering beams of the ceiling, you would have found in the chamber above a dark stain hid away under the square of carpet. They had scrubbed the boards repeatedly, but the stain remained.

The "memorable" year 18—. Surely, in all human language, there is no more ridiculous word than "memorable," the bellows with which we try to rekindle our little dead sparks. To the lookers-on at Deynum the year was memorable, because it brought events which interested and amused them, "pained" them also, but even pain, in a great catastrophe, is a form of amusement to the lookers-on. To you, who live in the centre of the Universe, my epithet looks extravagantly oversized, but to you the Christmas of that year is memorable because of Tenorelli's magnificent début at the Scricci, or because the festivities of the season brought your first attack of gout in their train. Or perhaps it is memorable to all the hundred millions of this rolling world of Koopstad, because of that great victory which "changed the course of history." So be it. It is memorable to Tante Suze, because peat was a halfpenny cheaper that winter than it has ever been before or since.

The peasants of our poor little village sat round the fire on that winter's evening, and smoked. But they always sat there, of winter evenings, and they always smoked. They sat motionless, in great, black hulking lumps, with their caps drawn over their eyelids, and their eyelids sunk over their immovable cheeks, enshrouded in lazy mists from each man's pendent pipe. And mine host tried to make them talk, as in duty bound, while he filled their little glasses with thick white gin, for was it not his duty to provide entertainment, and his profit to provoke thirst?

The remarkable circumstance on the particular evening here mentioned was this, that the guests talked of their own accord, and without any prompting. It were erroneous, however, to imagine a babel of conversation. In the silence of the heavily-shadowed bar-room some tight-coated, rusty creature—the only bright spot about whom was probably his vermilion face—would suddenly hazard a few slow sentences, frequently without removing the pipe which pulled down his lips. And then, after a brief pause, during which the clock against the wainscoted wall ticked with stimulating preciseness, a few solemn words of reply would ooze forth from another creature, exactly similar in features, and manner and accent, to the one who had spoken last. And, however insignificant the opinion emitted, each speaker wore an air, in emitting it, which would have done honour to a conclave of dignitaries of the Church.

"Yes, it's true enough," said Jaap Hakkert, the butcher. "I met Fokke Meinderts myself this afternoon driving a cart-load of boxes from the station. The family are coming next week."

"What do they want cart-loads of things for?" queried a voice from behind the peat-basket. "Wasn't there mountains in the Castle already? And didn't the old Baron leave them all?"

"Everything," broke in the landlady's fat voice, "excepting the plate and the pictures and the family papers and things. Those the Baron had removed to Father Bulbius's two days after the—the accident."

There was an especially long pause this time, heavy with thought. At last Job, the landlord, remarked, as he meditatively took down a bottle of spirits: "There's nothing coming but 'personal effects,' Dievert tells me. Whatever those may be, great folks require a good deal of them, it seems. They can't be clothes only, for nobody would want such boxes of *them*."

"Much you know about it," burst in Hendrika with a scornful slap of her red hand on the bar. "Great ladies have hundreds of dresses, a couple for every day in the year!" She cast aggressive glances at her cumbrous husband from her bright, bold eyes. Evidently an old subject.

"The Baroness hadn't dozens of different dresses, retorted Job, on the defensive. "One always saw her in the same black silk."

"The Baroness wasn't a fine town lady."

"She was a real fine lady!" cried the landlord.

"She was the greatest lady that ever was," said a feeble old man, who sat nearest the stove.

They all spoke of her in the past. To the villager one who has definitely quitted the village is dead.

"I mind me when you never came across her but in a white robe, like an angel," the "oldest inhabitant" went on. But at this several of them cried out. They all remembered that, they said. Uncle Peter must not give himself airs. The old man subsided querulously. "I mind the Baron's grandfather," he muttered, "with a bag to his hair, and buckle-shoes." But nobody heeded him. Their loss was too recent. And besides, they had heard all his stories before.

Everyone sat staring gloomily and smoking. Presently Jaap Hakkert "screeched" his chair along the sanded floor.

"There's one thing I can't understand," he said very

loud. "This old gentleman that—that *died* was a good Catholic—eh?" And he looked round fiercely, daring the whole circle to deny it. Not that he cared much, but that was his bullying way.

"He was a Catholic," replied Hendrika, "but not good. Now, his man was a pious, amiable gentleman, and so pleasant to speak to." She smirked a little, half frightened under the furious glances of her lord.

"And these people, his heirs, are nought but beggarly Protestants," Hakkert went on, ignoring the landlady. "And what I want to know is, how?"

Most of the peasants lifted up their eye-lids for a moment and gazed stolidly at each other; then they dropped them again. The butcher sat up, his whole bulky body a mass of indignant interrogation. "And Rexelaers too," said one man who had not spoken before.

"It doesn't seem in nature," said the voice from behind the peat-stove. There was a general murmur of approval. The old man spat on the ground. "God forgive them; perhaps they can't help it," muttered a gentle-faced personage, who sat a little outside the circle, the village-tailor.

But this sentiment did not find acceptance.

"Some people are born so," added the tailor, with a twinkle in his eye.

"Not Rexelaers," declared the butcher violently. And he struck the ashes out of his pipe on to his raw, fleshy palm.

"Well, whatever they may be," interposed the ever conciliatory landlord, "we shall have them among us in a week, and we shall see."

"And we shall hang out flags and put up a couple of triumphal arches," said the tailor. "It's a pity the season is too late for flowers."

"No arches!" burst out a young fellow, who now spoke for the first time. He spoke with great vehemence. And he came forward from a little side-table, by which he had been sprawling in the darkness, his hands in his pockets, a stumpy brown pipe between his lips—a big bright-looking young fellow, with a shock of yellow hair. The others all stared slowly round at him.

"I'd like to see the sneak would dare to hang out a bit of colour," he cried, slowly edging his way into the circle. He held up the little brown pipe in one huge brown hand, the other he clenched in a threatening lump in the pocket of his tight black breeches. "Who of you wants to rejoice at the old lord's downfall? Not I."

"Not I," said the man behind the peat-basket, and then most of the others said "Not I." "Ah, but what does the Commune do?" said the tailor. And he smiled.

The Commune, in Holland, has a Burgomaster, a couple of assessors and a village-council. The Burgomaster is almost always a man of birth and position, by preference a large landed proprietor. The Baron had been Burgomaster of Deynum; the post was vacant.

All eyes were turned—with a long, slow movement which left the heads unaltered—in the direction of a portly farmer whose rubicund full moon shone with the radiance of fifty years' prosperous butter-making. This was the Deputy Burgomaster. "We must see what Dievert says," this worthy made haste to declare. Dievert, the Baron's steward, was the other assessor, and had been, for many years, practical ruler of the Commune.

"If the village-council do anything in the way of an official welcome, they deserve to be hung," declared Thys, as he turned on one heel. "They won't," assented somebody. "No, that they won't, nor none of us," cried the landlady energetically. "Bravo, Thys; are you off to Lise up at the Chalkhouse-farm? He! He!" The landlady, like all her sex, dearly loved a bit of love-making; other people's was always second-best. Thys was Lise's sweet-

heart, you remember. They were to be married in
spring.

"No, they won't," affirmed Jaap Hakkert, who was a
member of the Council, "not for beggars of Protestants.
We don't want no d—— beggars of Protestants at Deynum."

"Hist," interrupted Job, who was another member. He
looked round anxiously. For Protestants, though they do
not thirst for the true religion, may still be made welcome
at a Catholic bar. At Deynum the Pharisees of both sects
visited the Publican's house with a beautiful readiness which
would have been deemed reprehensible eighteen hundred
years ago. But to-night, as it happened, the landlord's eye
beheld none of these men of false faith and honest pay, such
as his soul both scorned and cherished.

"No, that the Council won't," said Job, disgusted by
their absence. "Damn beggars, whether masters or servants."

"Best take your masters as they're sent," said the tailor.

Thys turned threateningly by the door, already half invisible, looming terrible through the darkness. "It's my
belief you're glad," he said illogically. "Boys, let's shame
him. Hurrah for the old Baron! The Holy Virgin help
him. Hurrah!"

Dutchmen are not easily moved to exhibit feeling. Nor
did these now spring to their feet with uplifted caps. But
most of them took up Thys's cry, with a clumsy grin on
their faces and a doubt, at their hearts, of young Thys's
foolish fuss. In those same wooden-walled hearts, however,
there was but one prayer of sympathy for the poor great
ones so suddenly driven from their midst. The Dutch
peasant, as a rule, thinks and feels true. The Baron had,
all his life, been a good lord to his people; the Baroness, a
very patron Saint. The new man was a fine city gentleman,
despicable for having been born in a street. And, besides,
as far as they understood, he had not even paid for, but had

stolen the property, which the Baron had expressly condi-
tioned should never be his. " We will insult him," said one
fellow aloud, giving voice to the general sentiment. The
tailor sat gazing immovably at the red eye of the stove.
Some ashes fell, and the red eye winked at him.

CHAPTER XXVIII.

REINOUT II.

A LIVERY servant of Count Rexelaer's, with heavy fur collar and orange cockade, stood in lonely grandeur on the little Deynum platform, under the glimmering oil-lamp. Two carriages were waiting beyond, their lights radiant across the snow of the starry December night.

The whole family came bundling out of their compartment, in an avalanche of winter wraps, the parrot, the yelping lap-dogs, a couple of attendants, a chaos of baggage, animate beings, and cold. "Oh, there's John," called out Reinout. "How's my pony, John?" For he had received the promised pony from his father a couple of weeks ago.

The station-master came sidling up, with awkward curiosity, which the lord of the manor suddenly felt and resented. He hurried his wife into the foremost of the conveyances and they drove rapidly off, along the bleak country-road. "The cold is unbearable," whispered the Countess, shuddering. "Oh, Mamma, how can you say so? Look at the lovely softness of the snow," the boy's eyes were dancing with excitement. "We are going to have oceans of fun. There is a lake, and when my cousins have taught me to skate, I will teach you." "Thank you," said Margherita. "Happy child, you have forgotten!"

They drove through the village presently in the soft snow-light; all was deserted and still. The Count looked towards his wife uncomfortably. The horses pattered briskly on, past the little square with its silent church, and round into the avenue of the park. "Ah!" gasped the Count.

They came out into the clearing and saw the dark mass of the Castle rise up on the other side of the water. Suddenly the bell in the tower began to ring, a pitiful call to meals, very unlike the triumphant harmony of church-bells. The horses' hoofs went clattering over the bridge and up the courtyard. The great doors were thrown open, and a flood of light poured down across two bending figures, Strum and Dievert, on the steps. Count Hilarius gave his wife a nervous hand and led her past the Steward's unnoticed " Welcome to your noble Countships " into the hall of his fathers. The place was full of people. " Ah, the tenants, of course, and the villagers! Very kind, very kind," murmured the fine gentleman. The Steward came hurrying up behind him: " Hurrah for my lord the Count and his lady!" A feeble shout responded in which Reinout's voice rang out above the rest. The lap-dogs sprang forward, barking irritably.

All eyes were fixed on the outlandish waiting-woman, with the parrot on her arm. And at her appearance the stupidest lout among the peasants realized, with terrible distinctness, that here were aliens indeed.

Margherita paused under the great stained-glass lamp. " This vestibule is terribly bare," she said, in French. Strum understood her and moved uncomfortably. And indeed the great panels showed only too plainly, to all but the owners of the house, where the portraits and suits of armour had been taken down. " In summer," interposed the Notary, " there are more flowers. The rest of the house is well furnished. Of course some personal—items—' The Count winced. The Countess, without heeding the speaker, had passed on into the dining-room.

" And these are all the tenants?" said Count Hilarius. He swept his hand along the crowd of staring, unemotional faces.

" As good as all, Heer Count," was the enigmatical answer.

"Ah! Well, my good people, we shall doubtless be excellent friends. This is my son, the Jonker* Reinout." The familiar name fell like a dead weight.

Reinout, not knowing what else to do, as his father pushed him forward, held out his hand to a couple of burly old farm-people opposite. "Good evening," he said.

The motherly farm-wife seized the hand and grasped it warmly. "Good evening, little Heer," she answered, "the saints preserve you!" A murmur of approval ran through the half-defiant ranks. Count Hilarius turned to go.

But Dievert detained him, dragging forward an unwilling personage, who had hitherto been trying to look invisible, Boterton, the loco-Burgomaster. "Now then, Boterton!" Boterton's face was purple. "The Commune bids your Nobleness welcome, Heer Count," he stuttered. "In the name of the village," he added, "and the Council." After the enunciation of which profound sentiment he lapsed into silence.

And the careless walls of Deynum looked down upon this scene also.

"Oh yes," said the Count. "Who is the Burgomaster? Eh?"

"There is none, Heer Count," replied the Notary. "Not at present."

Count Hilarius flushed. "Good-night," he said. And fled.

Somehow the whole thing reminded him of—of what? Suddenly he remembered. Of the return of the Bourbon to his capital, when the enemies of his country brought him back. It was not a bit like coming home to his own.

"Laïssa," said the Countess, "I am dead with fatigue— and emotion. This, then, is the château de mes pères. It

---

* Title for unmarried sons of noblemen. Pronounced Yonker.

is handsome, but 'faut qu'on s'y habitue.' Ugh, what a
country! Had Brazil not been discovered so late, M. le
Comte's ancestors might perhaps have been Brazilian!"

"The château has come true," replied the mulatto.
She did not love this marsh of her indwelling, "but the
cards had foretold, M'am Rita, that it would lie in a
land of *knaves*."

The departure from the Hague had indeed been fraught
with emotions. The birds, all but Rollo, the parrot, had
been left behind, their doctor refusing to sanction the journey. Margherita had wandered disconsolately from cage to
cage, and taken poetical leave of them. "Adieu, Fifi. Tu
dois rester ici. Et moi, je vais partir. Adieu, mon Casi-
mir." She herself would not have travelled, but for the
Count's threat to receive the Rexelaers of Altena just the
same, without her.

And then the terrible journey itself. At the station
she had been met by a refusal to admit her poor little
curled darlings into her compartment. They must be
thrown into a luggage-van, plush-baskets and all, there to
die! The authorities were inflexible. The Countess still
more so. There had been a scene on the platform, and a
crowd. Laïssa had pushed over, with impassive arm, an
official who happened to interpose, and the pets had been
ensconced upon the carrriage cushions, and Margherita,
as she lay back among her furs, had hissed "Canaille" in
the station-master's face. Procès-verbal had been drawn
up; the nervous, distinguished-looking gentleman had been
compelled to give his name: Count Rexelaer van Deynum,
a Lord of the Household!

"I will never travel with you again, Margot," Count
Hilarius had declared, as the train slowly glided into motion, the spaniels, at their mistress's instigation, barking triumph against the glass. "Had you been a man," Margherita had answered, panting, "you would have beaten that

15

cowardly dog-torturer within an inch of his life." "And a pity of the inch," she added, " mais il faut bien respecter les convenances."

"And the Court?" suggested the little-souled Count, touching, in his little-souled anxiety, the one point where she would wince. " In these Democratic times, such a row, with its possible consequences, may cost me my place."

" I don't care," replied the Countess, caring very much.

CHAPTER XXIX.

THE MESSAGE OF THE SILENCE.

THE boy, left to himself, as the crowd slowly melted
away from around him, stood staring, between the marble
columns, up into the darkness of the roof. He could dimly
discern, emblazoned high above, the well-known lions with
their shining swords. The familiar faces of the royal
beasts made him feel at home immediately. He nodded
to them. And then he ran to the glass front-doors, and
looked out.

The landscape lay before him, clear in the tremble of its
snow-smitten waiting for the moon—the white courtyard,
and the dull glitter of the trees beyond. Away, where the
bridge was, there must be water. He wanted to find out
about the skating he had promised his cousins; in another
moment he was racing through the pleasant snow-sheltered
air.

Reinout had never beheld the face of nature. He retained a vague, delicious recollection of the Paradise of his
infancy, glorified by Margherita's never-ending regrets.
The loveliness and the sensuousness of living, as felt by
every beetle and by every bud, had lapped him body and
soul; he had rioted in happiness, nothing to do but to
breathe where every breath was heavy — sometimes too
crushingly heavy—with enjoyment; his young existence
voluptuously prostrate beneath the splendour of its own
excess. That sun-sick dawn had left its flush upon his face
and heart; the child of the equator would never freeze into

a cool, white Dutchman; but there had been no intercourse with nature in the constant seclusion of awnings and shutters, the shrinking, the ceaseless protection from all that is pernicious in reptile, insect or flower. From these climates European children come away with the light of the sun in their eyes. That is all they remember.

He was still young when they brought him to the Hague. There was an apple-tree in the garden there. It never bore any apples, and Reinout's interest in it had always been Platonic.

But now!—oh the sudden revelation, the personal contact which lay in that one thought: this is home. The trees, the fields, the water, these were "ours," not with the sense of proprietorship, but with the power of enjoyment. Nature, henceforth, would stand ready as a playmate, and her abode, with its fathomless treasures, would be his. What matter, if at this their first embrace she hid behind her wintry coverlet? He could hear her laughing under it, and the gaunt trees whispered endlessly some wondrous mystery of her life.

He stood for a few moments gazing intently into the moat—he could not get down to its shining surface from here—and then he turned and ran in among the towering beeches, eager to have them on every side.

The very glamour of the scene brought it more impressively home to him. We never hear Nature breathe so close to us as in the luminous, listening silence of a wind-stilled night of snow. Reinout, suddenly, heard her.

O that fairy soul-seeing, into the unreal presence of the snow-scape! It is all so actual and yet so visionary; yesterday it was not, to-morrow it will have vanished for ever. We know that it is a beautiful illusion, both of shape and colour, a dream momentarily materialised, fading away from us even as we touch it, into the hard blacks and browns of daily life—but oh the virgin purity that tempts us and escapes us, that seems to breathe in death and bid us grasp it; surely this is not the world we live and suffer in, and the glamour melts away, and it is the naked, naked world after all. But perhaps it broke upon us as a dim foreshadowing—nay, fore-lightening—of that life in which the snow will lie upon our hearts and eyes for ever, white beneath the burning Light of God.

You smile at the thought of a boy of fourteen, with his head full of skating and the holidays, suddenly crushed beneath such an avalanche as this. It did not reach him. But he heard its voice afar off and stood vaguely listening for a moment, ere he bounded away in search of something new.

He was wild with the prospect of the ice-sports, the sleighing, the fun with his cousins, although all these, except Topsy, were too old to play with him. Poor little fellow! He was boy enough at heart, had he but known how to show it to other boys. There was not a manly sport which he did not take to, often with a zeal far beyond his slender frame. Several times before this wonderful acquisition of the pony, he had ridden away recklessly on anybody's horse. The Count was no equestrian.

He ran along the Holy Walk, by the merest chance, and presently was attracted to a faintly glimmering light in the distance. This drew him towards a little building, of which the door stood ajar. He stole into the Chapel. It was dark but for the lamp at the altar.

The boy stood spell-bound on the threshold. A Church, like those "at home"—Roman Catholic, therefore—but full of statues and tombs. A sudden awe came over him. Was this also a dream or a reality, this conclave of the dead, in the wood? He felt terrified, and started back.

Somebody moved at the noise. Somebody else, then, was in the building. Somebody rose from his knees by the chancel and came towards Reinout, a boy like himself.

"Who are you?" asked the boy.

"Reinout van Rexelaer," replied Reinout stoutly.

" Oh, *what* a lie ! "

" Say that again ! " cried Reinout furiously. " How dare you? Who are *you?* I *am* Reinout van Rexelaer, from the Hague."

They could hardly distinguish each other in the dusk of the building.

" N-o-o-o," said the other boy, in long-drawn wonder. " You don't mean to say so. Oh my eye, what luck. This comes of praying. I say, come outside. I want to ask you something. I can't ask it here."

They went out into the night together. Said the strange boy, as soon as they were outside : " Will you fight? "

" Fight? " echoed René in amazement. " No. Why? "

" I suppose you're about as old as I am. How old are you ? "

" Fourteen."

" That's all right. I'm thirteen; and I'm smaller. Now. Will you fight? "

" No," replied René, moving off.

" Ah, you're funking. Coward. And you won't fight because I'm not a jonker, like yourself."

" Won't I? Look out then ! " replied Reinout, and flew at his adversary.

They had a hard battle of it for a few moments under the shadow-shrouded trees. There was nobody to see fair play, but they managed honestly without. At the end of three minutes, however, Reinout had to give in; his antagonist had vanquished his superior sparring by brute force and by a vehemence which the taller boy was very far from feeling. The little noble was fairly licked.

" I've thrashed you," cried his antagonist triumphantly, " I'm glad I thrashed you." He left off pummelling René, and drew back, out of breath.

" Yes," said Reinout, wondering where his left eye was. " You have. I don't know why, I'm sure."

The other had run off. He stopped, and came back.

"Remember," he cried, "I said I was glad I'd thrashed you. Be sure and remember."

"You certainly are not a jonker," Reinout could not help retorting under this provocation. "That's not the way to end up. Here, give me your hand."

"I won't," replied Piet Poster, and scampered away.

CHAPTER XXX.

"JACK-SNAPS."

NEXT morning Father Bulbius drew on his stoutest boots—under Veronica's personal supervision—and marched away through the snow. "To draw on stout boots" in Dutch is to brace oneself for bold endeavour. Well, Father Bulbius drew them on and proceeded to the Castle, to pay due homage to the new Lord. The visit was not a very satisfactory one—how could it be?—in spite of Count Rexelaer's studied condescension; the good priest hung his head dejectedly, as he came away.

He had heard from Dievert that the Countess had been born a Catholic. Count Hilarius deeply regretted that this had not been the case with himself; "it would have looked so much more genuine." He would have gone over, but he dreaded inquiries into the reason, and discoveries by the Baron. Better talk about Rovert van Rexelaer. Who became a Protestant, you know.

Father Bulbius shook his head at intervals all the way home. "A renegade!" he said, thinking of the Countess, who had remained invisible. "You cannot help being born of the devil, but you *can* help asking him to adopt you." And he sighed.

"Well?" said Veronica, waiting in the porch, her arms a-kimbo.

"You were right," replied his Reverence, "the snow is melting. It is very wet."

"But the Chapel?"

"We shall see." The Father tried to edge past her: the entrance was narrow, Veronica bony: we all know that the good Father was stout. He stuck.

"But the contract? You told him the Baron has it all in the contract?" Veronica persisted excitedly.

"I dare say the Heer Count will do all that is right. My feet are damp, Veronica; I think that I ought to change my shoes."

"So you ought to, poor lamb," cried Veronica, and hurried to fetch the slippers she had kept toasting before the fire. "I shall have to look sharp after that Chapel," she said to herself, "or they'll take it away from him yet."

The Father's sanctum now presented a very different appearance from that under which we beheld it last. It was swept and cleaned—O triumph of the Broom!—but it contained more litter than ever. For the whole room was packed full of the treasures from the Castle, massed together under the guardianship of a number of fierce-looking knights, with closed visor, who stood ranged beneath their banners, strange sight in the dwelling of a soldier of Peace. The plate-chests were in the Father's adjoining bed-room; the pictures, lords and ladies, in all their bravery of ruffs and doublets, of wigs and powder, crowded the garret. The quiet cottage overflowed with the glory of the Rexelaers.

The Father said he slept with one eye open and dreamed of tramps. Through the door he could see the plumed knights nodding in the moonlight. He had borrowed a revolver from Dievert, but he had energetically refused to borrow the bullets as well. "Do you take me for a murderer?" he had demanded indignantly.

He had been very proud and pleased, nevertheless, when the Baron had sought admittance for his treasures on the day after the suicide. He would gladly have harboured the living Noblenesses as well as the dead ones. "Oh, not that," said the Baron. "We must never come back. We are going to live at Cleves and forget."

The deserted Castle had been bad enough; the Castle bright with unusual gaiety was worse. No longer did the Father venture to creep up the avenue, as he had done daily, before the arrival of the servants and carriages, to get a melancholy peep of the lines of closed shutters. "*Crows* they call us!" he sighed.

So he kept away, and grieved, and grew more indolent than ever. He discovered that he regretted his écarté of evenings, and this discovery involved another. It was for his own sake, then, and not for the Baron's, that he had continued to play. He did not stop to inquire what he regretted, the game or the partner. "What hypocrites we are!" he mused, and he eyed his little book of penances suspiciously, wondering how much of its contents would prove false. And one day he impatiently threw the whole catalogue into the fire. Decidedly, adversity was improving Father Bulbius. But he pulled it off again before it was burnt. Improvement is uphill-work.

The lonely Father turned in his easy chair—oh, but it was deliciously easy!—and thought how excellent had been Veronica's fish-cake. The day was a fast-day; he had had nothing else; and he had eaten too much of it. He nodded. The fierce warriors around him seemed to nod haughtily back. He stretched out his hand to a favourite book—it was a Horace—on the floor. He found that he could not reach it, and nodded again. And the whole room slowly went to sleep.

"There's a woman to see your Reverence," said Veronica, standing in the doorway. She considered his Reverence had slept long enough. On the whole, she was very gentle to him in these days, showing her angry sympathy, like the wise woman she was, by constant abuse of those that were gone. She had seen what she had seen in the Baronial kitchen, said this excellent housekeeper. "The Baroness was always liberal," Father Bulbius would plead. "Just so," replied Veronica, ostentatiously scraping the butter-knife.

"There's a woman to see you!" she repeated aggressively.

The Father started awake. "If it's a beggar," he said, with an apprehensive frown, "send her away with a hunch of bread."

"It's not a beggar, your Reverence; it's Vrouw Poster."

The Priest's face cleared. He disliked all petitioners, because of his incapacity for saying "No." But, good man that he was, he had a good man's weakness for a chat with the fair sex, if not too alarmingly fair. "Vrouw Poster," he echoed brightly. "I'll see her here."

"Very well," replied Veronica, accentuating each syllable. She introduced the visitor, still aggressively, and, as soon as the door had closed again—too soon, therefore, for prudence—that visitor, a comely peasant woman, burst into tears.

"Good Heavens!" cried the Father. "Is Poster dead?" Simple-hearted man! All wives are doomed to weep once for their husbands! some after the husband's death, some before. If not after, then all the more before.

"No, your Reverence," sobbed the gardener's spouse. "It is Piet!"

"How shocking!" cried the Father. "How dreadfully sudden!" He rose from his chair. "Well," he said reflectively. "The boy was a good boy—on the whole."

"It's not that, your Reverence. He's not dead—"

"You said he was," interrupted the Father, annoyed. It seemed that Vrouw Poster had taken a liberty with his feelings.

"Leastways not altogether. Not that I know to the contrary. But he's run away."

"Fetch him back," said Father Bulbius, and sat down again.

"That's just what I mayn't do, your Reverence. His father says, let him stay away till he comes back of his own accord."

"Well, his father, though harsh, is not a man without sense." Bulbius began leisurely to fill his pipe, messing the tobacco over his already snuffy cassock.

"Oh your Reverence, but he won't! I know Piet. He's that dogged. Often and often he's said to me : 'Mother,' he's said, 'if father don't treat me better, I shall run away to sea.' And I used to laugh at him ; the blessed Saints forgive me. But he's never been the same since the Baron went away; he was terribly partial to the Freule. And yesterday evening his father beat him for not having gone up with us to the Castle to see the new Lord come in. And this morning he's gone, and his bed's not been slept in, and he's left a paper with 'Good-bye to mother and Nicky' (that's his goat), and he's out in the snow—Oh Lord !" and the poor woman began to cry afresh.

"My dear creature," said Bulbius, considerably disturbed by these symptoms of distress, "he will doubtless return before nightfall, as soon as he has had enough of the cold. And if not, it will be easy to recapture him."

"He won't come back," sobbed Vrouw Poster. "He'd rather die on the heath. And his father's a harsh man, though I say it that shouldn't."

"No," said the Priest, gravely. "You shouldn't. Don't." He could think of nothing else to comfort her. Presently he added : "His father's lesson may do him a lot of good. He *is* an exceedingly mischievous boy, as we saw in that affair of the betting. Let him find out that there are worse places than home. He won't stay away long, and, meantime, you have seven other children to look after."

The woman stopped crying and stared at him. Suddenly she realized that he was childless. "Your Reverence does not understand," she said quietly, and quitted the

room so abruptly that Veronica had not time to get away
into the kitchen.

He called after her through the open door. His conscience smote him. "Come back," he said, "I want to
understand. Now, what can I do for you, Vrouw Poster?"

"I had hoped that your Reverence would reason with
my husband. The child *must* be fetched home immediately. It is wicked. It is cruel."

Just what Bulbius had dreaded, argument with a man
like Poster! He gave a long pull to his pipe.

"Well, I will go with you," he said.

The Head-gardener, like many men, had no objection to
pastoral exhortations, provided they were given from the
pulpit, when, if unfortunately not asleep, he could hear
without accepting them. Now, placed between assent and
dissent, he dissented. Father Bulbius was well acquainted
with his various parishioners, all the better, perhaps, for
keeping a little aloof. He disliked receiving a "No" from
others as much as uttering it himself. He had foreseen
this refusal, and therefore he had sought to preach resigna-
tion to the gardener's wife.

"In a day or two, when he has got tired of begging for
crusts, he will come back," said Piet's father, "to the best
beating he ever had in his life."

But obstinate people are often mistaken, and cruel people always. Piet Poster did not come back.

His mother, therefore, was compelled to seek comfort
in the care of her other children, as Bulbius had suggested,
and the Priest went occasionally to add his equally effectual
consolations, not sorry, in spite of his shrinking, to find
himself once more within the well-loved precincts. He
was returning late one afternoon from such a visit, in the
ashen-grey December air, when his path was crossed near
the vegetable garden by the new heir of the house, on his
all-glorious, all-delectable pony. Reinout quickly lifted his
cap. It was a little thing, but the frank grace with which

it was done, went straight to the good priest's heart, not a distant or a tortuous road. He was so afraid of these strangers, afraid of their inevitable dislike of himself. "A pretty pony," he said, timidly, with a ceremonious salute.

"Isn't it a beauty?" cried Reinout, only too delighted with this fresh opportunity of showing his "treasure." "I'm so glad that you like him, Mynheer. And you haven't even seen him gallop yet." "Mynheer" to the priest from a Rexelaer! Alas the day!

"Would you like to see him gallop?" suggested Reinout.

"Very much indeed, Jonker."

"Then would you mind holding this for a moment? Please keep the paper down tight, or they'll jump out. I lost one coming along, and had an awful hunt for him." And the Jonker extended a small paper-covered bowl to his new acquaintance.

Father Bulbius was preparing to take it, when a new thought struck the boy.

"Oh, perhaps, Mynheer," he said eagerly, "you could tell me what they are called." He edged up closer, driving the Father unconsciously against a tree. "Nobody knows at home. They all say 'bugs' of everything. One of the labourers gave me these; they were in the vinery. But he says they're just beetles. Look, this is one. Take care. They pinch awfully with those little pincers. Can you tell me? I should so like to know."

Bulbius had not been a peasant boy at Deynum and afterwards a seminarist for nothing. The two heads bent over the bowl in the dim light. "Those are not beetles you have got there," he said, "but, then, the common people call most insects beetles. These are called 'Jack-Snaps' in our parts. They have got a long Latin name, I daresay, but I should have to look that out for you."

"Oh, would you? How very kind of you, Mynheer. Have you got a book, then, with all the names inside? I want to find out immensely. I am so glad to know that these are 'Jack-Snaps.' I shall tell Sam; he gave them to me. There are lots of animals in the green-houses; what a quantity there will be everywhere in summer! I had no idea there were so many in the world. It is capital fun!"

"You like being here, Jonker?" said Bulbius, a little sadly.

"Oh don't I just! It's splendid. And to-morrow all my cousins are coming! And we are going to keep Christmas. And they are going to teach me to skate!"

As he talked thus excitedly, the brown pony, which had been standing beautifully still, gave a sudden and terrific leap, almost unseating its rider. Father Bulbius retreated with wonderful alacrity behind the tree, and peeping from thence was spectator of a struggle during which the pot and its contents were tossed away on the snow. At last, having probably freed itself from the pincers which had first caused its restlessness, the animal quieted down and Reinout triumphantly patted it, as the Father gingerly emerged.

"I *never* knew him do that before," said the young master reproachfully, and the pony unfortunately could not explain. "But oh the Jack-Snaps! I must find them!" And he leaped to the ground and began eagerly hunting in the snow.

It was almost dark. The Father struck match after match in the wind-still air, and bent his burly figure as best he could. They searched together, but vainly. "It can't be helped," gasped the Father at last. "You must get Sam to find you some more animals, Jonker, and if you come to my Parsonage, I'll tell you their names."

"I'm so sorry to have lost these," said Reinout, "and, besides, they will die in the cold." He rode off soberly. The Father watched his figure disappear into the evening mist. "No," said the Father aloud, "it could never be done. Besides, mixed marriages are a very great evil. But a nice boy, nevertheless. A really nice boy."

CHAPTER XXXI

REINOUT'S COUSINS.

NEXT afternoon Reinout went down to the little station with a couple of carriages, and all the Rexelaers van Altena were let loose out of the crowded Christmas train and came driving back with the young heir through the startled village. The village was very much interested. The former lords had lived in the silence of an approaching dissolution; the curtain had now risen for another and a brighter play. The village criticised the smart town carriages and the smart town ladies, and the liveries and the horseflesh, especially the horseflesh. It still said "Well!" but the tone was sinking from doubt to content. Jaap Hakkert, the butcher, agreed with the two bakers that a full table and a full purse at the table had their advantages. The tailor smiled. And the oldest inhabitant said that things reminded him of the Baron's father's father's time.

Thys looked into his Lise's eyes. "Do you remember," he asked, "how hard pressed the Baron was when he refused to sell the Chalkhouse Farm?"

"Of course, Thys; we all remember," said Lise. Thys was Lise's cousin, as well as her lover. He had lived all his life at the Chalkhouse Farm.

Count Rexelaer's younger brother Frederick, as everybody knows, had married a daughter of the great Gelderland family of Borck, a cousin of that powerful Baron Borck of Rollingen whose estate joined on to Deynum. The lady had brought her husband a little money and a number of influential connections. He was a quiet, insignificant, sat-upon little man, a member of the magistrature and an utter failure as a lawyer. But he played whist very well. And she was comfortable and florid, and managed everybody and everything. You got on excellently with her if you said "Yes" in the pauses of her talk. They made Frederick van Rexelaer a judge before he was forty. Her cousin R— was minister at the time.

"My dear Betsy," his Excellency had said, suddenly surrendering after a long tussle, "as you have got his name proposed—Heaven only knows how you managed it!—I will appoint him in spite of—"

"Thank you, Herman, that is like you—"

"Superior claims. But on one condition only. He must solemnly bind himself to me *never* on any account to express a separate opinion. He must always 'concur' with his colleagues.* You understand me. I can have no awkward questions cropping up."

"I understand perfectly," replied Mevrouw Rexelaer-Borck. "I promise."

"But I would rather have his own word bind him—"

"Really!" said Mevrouw with a peculiar smile. "Well, of course you know best. I am much obliged to you, Herman. You are the best friend we have."

But she had more best friends. The judge faithfully kept his promise, and he found it very easy to keep. And they knew the right people, whom to know renders utter misery impossible. Besides, they were anything but miserable, although they experienced some difficulty about always making both ends meet exactly in the manner they wanted. She liked children. She liked managing. And he liked whist.

And the five children, as they grew up, liked themselves,

---

* Verdicts, in Holland, are pronounced by juries of judges.

16

which is always a great advantage. And they liked their
mother's numerous relations—a rarer coincidence—and their
large circle of acquaintances. Of course they all believed,
heart and soul, in the Greatness of the Rexelaers, and tried
to forget that the brand-new title of this branch was not—
officially, at least—a revival of the Holy Roman one. Grandmamma Rexelaer (the haberdasher's daughter) had never
existed at all. Grandmamma Borck was alive, and a very
great lady indeed.

The chief event of these good people's life had been the
arrival from foreign parts of the head of the family with his
wife and his olive-coloured cherub and all their delicious,
if rather disquieting, paraphernalia of foreignness. And
the Rexelaer liveries once more shone in the streets of a
city of flunkies, and the lion's-paws stretched forth their
swords from the panels of the Creole Countess's brand-new
carriages—ipsa glorior infamia—and her family arose and
called her blessed. The children were rather disappointed
about her colour. Rolline, the younger girl, had long identified her aunt with her nigger-doll Jumbo; Jane, the elder,
avowed a preference for café au lait. Margherita was not
a bit like Jumbo. She was very handsome, and the whole
family talked, in public, of her beauty alone.

" My dear," said the venerable Baroness Borck to her
daughter, " I asked Madame de Jercelyn about the Cachenard family. She said she had never heard the name. And
there, I think, we had better stop."

There were five young Rexelaers van Altena—where is
Altena?—two sons, Guy and George, the younger just out
of his teens, and after these three daughters, Jane, Rolline
and Antoinette. They were all golden-haired and good-
looking and stupid, except Jane, who was sharp of features
and of soul. Guy was at Leyden preparing to follow his
father's career with all his father's chances of success;
George, the beauty, foolish, good-natured, Apollo-faced
George, was nowhere, everlastingly plucked in the A B C.

"George will have to marry," said Grandmamma Borck. The girls, too, would have to marry, though what could anyone make of plain-featured, plain-spoken Jane? They were always well-dressed, and they were "altogether English," which means that they spoke Dutch with an English accent and English with a Dutch one. That was the proper thing among their "set" at the Hague, and you must on no account make use of any language but English in public places and conveyances, and very nice it would be if the Nemesis of Pronunciation did not infallibly rise and mock you. And the Freules van Rexelaer never wrote other than English notes to their intimates, and, if they wanted to be particularly affectionate and undyingly faithful, they signed them—"yours truly"! Yes, they were very English, indeed.

Reinout's especial friend, twelve-year old Antoinette, therefore felt much aggrieved at the French name she bore. She had been called after the wife of the minister who had given her father the judgeship, and she went about as a living monument of gratitude. To comfort her the others had dubbed her Topsy, and the nickname suited her; she was a shock-headed tomboy in those days. She had been wild to get to all the glories which Reinout had graphically foretold. Almost before the train had stopped, she plumped, past her cousin's extended hand, down on the platform, flinging her arms round the retriever's neck. "Prince first," she said, looking up, with all a child's precocious coquetry, at her "preux chevalier."

Mevrouw Elizabeth ascended the castle-steps with stately smile. She never worried her children, leaving all these things to governesses and to time. Her heart, at this moment, was full of the bitter sweet of the first visit to Deynum. The whole family rejoiced and envied. "The home of our fathers!" Up till now the only real sorrow in the life of this daughter of the Borcks had been the harrowing conviction that the entire city of the Hague was coustantly conscious of the distinction between real Rexelaers and false. Most people in the Hague, had she but known it, were thinking, as she did, of themselves.

There had been some trouble about getting away, at this time of the year, from Grandmamma Borck. That wonderful old lady had originally taken but very little interest in her daughter's common husband's still more common sister-in-law. She took no great interest in anything nowadays, excepting the dual contentment—culinary and conversational—of that active member, her tongue. She lived to eat (little, but well), and to talk (well, but much). And she had managed to preserve her figure. And she liked tyrannizing over a rich orphan grandchild, whose money ported them both.

She woke up to a firework of questions, however, when the great news of the inheritance suddenly fell with a hiss on a hundred spluttering tongues. Mevrouw Elizabeth, who faithfully visited her mother at least three times a week, now had to go daily, and tell all she knew. A little more, under the pressure of much questioning and progressive irritability.

"Of course I remember the Marquis la Jolais at Brussels," coughed the Dowager over her laced handkerchief and scent-bottle by the blazing fire. "He was handsome, though a little bit of a dandy. They used to call him the Marquis J'ose. He was very courteous to women, but then everybody was that in those days. Don't ring, Cécile. Put on the coals yourself. And to think that this little no-one-knows-who should be his niece! I remember all about the affair with the groom and the business at Rio. Leave the room, Cécile, and your aunt and I can talk it over again."

"Yes, grandmamma," answered Cécile demurely, where she knelt, tongs in hand, a pretty figure, before the fire. "Grandmamma and you are quits," Topsy Rexelaer used to say. "Each makes life as hot as she can for the other."

Grandmamma was cold-blooded and exceedingly " frileuse ";
Cécile was warm-hearted and chilled.

"They are wanting us to go and spend Christmas with
them," Mevrouw Elizabeth began a little hesitatingly. "It
would be good fun for the children, in spite of Margherita's
affectation of grief. She has gone into mourning, Mamma,
preposterous mourning, an extra inch for each additional
nought of the legacy. She makes a fool of herself. You
remember how everybody laughed at Clara van Weylert's
crape."

"I do," said the Dowager grimly, " and I remember the
joke about the additional inch ; it was Dolly Weylert made
it. You ought to bring me some new jokes, instead of
spoiling old ones in the telling. I go out so little ; I hear
nothing. I often wish I was dead."

Mevrouw van Rexelaer knew what this meant. " We
won't go to Deynum, unless you like," she said. And then
she added with her ready tact : "The children will feel it's
their duty to stay and cheer up grandmamma. You always
get miserable at this time of the year."

The Dowager angrily shook off her daughter's arm.
" Cécile can dress me a tree," she said, " with bonbons and
a doll ! Wait till you are my age and Jane tells you to feel
young. I shall be thankful to know you are all revelling
at Deynum without any trouble to me. To a woman, after
seventy, life is a humiliation and a disgrace. There, there,
I am tired."

Mevrouw Elizabeth rose with a sensation of relief. Poor
Mamma! Her gout, you know! And the festive season.
"It is a great responsibility for Hilarius," she said, " this
large property. And Margherita is hardly the woman—"

" Fiddlesticks. I daresay she will give away soup tickets.
Tell Cécile, as you go out, to bring me up my bouillon."

CHAPTER XXXII.

MARGHERITA DISCOVERS THAT YOU CAN MAKE EVEN A COLD COUNTRY TOO HOT TO HOLD YOU.

"Yes, it is very beautiful, Hilarius," said Mevrouw Elizabeth at dinner. "But it is an immense responsibility."

The Count jumped at the idea. He, who had always been known in his own family as "The Grumbler," was rather embarrassed in the presence of his relatives by his great good fortune. "It is indeed," he answered, pulling down his face. "I have no end of worry already, in connection with the repairs and accounts, and things."

"I was thinking of the souls," said Mevrouw Elizabeth.

"Oh; ah, yes, of course. Will you have some claret?" He smiled across the table nervously to his brother, who, on his part, was praising everything, as in duty bound, to Margherita.

"Yes," said Margherita. "And for me, of course, there are many touching memories. But we are going back as soon as possible. Immediately after Christmas. I do not like the country. At least not one which is all white blanket. In my home the country was all flowers." She turned to Guy. "How I envy you at Leyden," she said. "They tell me that the students have a magnificent library there. You can get all the new books. Have you already read—I am reading it—'Les Maitresses à Papa'?"

"N—n—no," stammered her nephew. "I've asked for it several times. But some professor's always got it, don't you know."

" Well, you can read it here. I have brought it with
me. And anything else you like. There is a large library."

" I should like some of your own poems best, aunt," replied Guy with a bow. He was a fool, but his career at the
University had taught him, as he called it, " how to manage women." None but a fool ever thinks he has learnt
that.

" Flatterer! Do you fancy I believe you? I reserve
them for Laïssa. It is the bane of my sex and my rank
combined that I cannot aspire to literary fame."

This was a favourite illusion of Margherita. She had
even embodied it in the following lines :

> " Vous me donnez, o dieux, bien plus que je réclame
> Vous m'écrasez, o dieux. Quel bonheur est le mien !
> Je suis poète—assez !—et noble—assez !—et *femme*.
> C'est trop—car ce n'est rien."

The idea left an unlimited margin for dumb-poet-ship.

Young Reinout was telling his neighbour Topsy all
about the glories and discoveries of his new abode. He
had barely stopped talking to her ever since her arrival,
and still there was so much to tell ! Already had he shown
her his " favourite " nooks and crannies and taken her up
to the little oriel window in the west turret, from which,
" if you squeeze your neck round *so* " (" Oh don't, Rein ! I
can squeeze my own neck, please !") " you can see (what
milksops girls are !) the little spire there—don't you see ?—
of the church. And, oh, Topsy, that reminds me ; there's a
delightful old priest, who is going to tell me the names of
all the animals in existence. You and I must go and see
him together." And he had taken them all to admire the
great stained-glass window in the upper hall. " It is very
nicely done," said Jane, who painted a little. The cousins
had wondered whose were the roses argent that blended
with the other shield. But the owners were dead as the

roses, and their glory had certainly nothing in common with these upstarts of to-day.

And now, at dinner, Reinout was full of the coming festivities, an English Christmas with holly all over the house (alas, mistletoe is unattainable) and a genuine flaming plum-pudding.—"As long as I needn't touch it," said the Countess Margherita. He was so excited that he was behaving badly—he who never had an opportunity of behaving badly; the opportunity and the use he made of it were things to be thankful for! Monsieur de Souza was away for a holiday in Paris, "to look up old friends," he had said ("de vieilles amies"). "Allez, my dear Chevalier, I understand you; to make young ones." "Monsieur, what do you think of? These things, in a few years, they will be for your son." Well educated, well cared for, of boundlessly magnificent future, happy René!

So thought Mevronw Elizabeth. "What a charming pair they make," she said complacently to her brother-in-law.

Before Count Hilarius could answer, Reinout, wheeling round to whisper in Topsy's ear what he had bought for his mother, threw out his arm and upset his wine-glass with a great smashing splash over the dessert-dishes. A sudden flame leaped up in the Countess's dark eyes. "René," she cried in a voice hot with passion, "leave the table immediately. You are not fit to sit down with your aunt!" He got up unwillingly: "Mamma!" he began. "Silence. Your manners are like a pig's. It makes me sick to see how you behave." He walked out of the door, and first longed to slam it and then closed it carefully. And as he crept heavily upstairs, he muttered: "She has a right to send me away, but not to insult me. And who is she to talk of cochonneries?" For he had heard a whisper—somehow; who shall say how in a house of many servants?—of Mademoiselle de Cochonnard.

Well, he only knew that the name of his mother's noble

family had originally been spelt and pronounced as above. Probably there was some interesting story connected with its old-time origin. When he was older, he would find out what the legend was. Some stirring tale like that of the maiden Wendela and the grand old lion—oh how he loved him!—who had come with his flaming sword to set the maiden free.

He locked himself in with his dog; he felt sore, for his mother had publicly humiliated him. And he got together his few beetles and bugs and sulked over the boxes and bottles. It was a new mania. And then he leaned out on the stone parapet, over the water, with his nose against Prince's, and wondered who lived in the moon.

Frederik van Rexelaer found time for a few words of quiet chat with his brother, as they stood side by side in the smoking-room over their coffee—the two young men were playing billiards a few paces off.

"What is this that I hear about an unpleasantness at the railway-station?" he began. "Nothing really important, I hope?"

"Nothing," replied Hilarius, tapping the parquet with his foot. "I wonder Margherita was so foolish as to mention it. She does not take kindly to our rules of implicit obedience. That is all."

"It was not Margherita that I heard it from, Hilarius. Simmans told me of it, the young Clerk of the Police Court. One of his officials drew his attention to the names."

"Good Heavens!" cried the Count, standing horror-struck, cigar in hand. "You don't mean to say they are going to follow it up?"

"They evidently are. She will be summoned for resisting the constituted authorities."

"And locked up! Or set to oakum-picking! The idiots who manage these things in this country are capable of anything. She is right. We should have stopped in Brazil!"

The Count stamped up and down the room. The billiard-players looked wonderingly across.

"I would thank you, Hilarius, to speak more advisedly of the organisation of which I form a part." The meek little man was nettled. This prospect of a coming scandal was anything but pleasing to him in his official position. "It is not the fine," he added, "but the—the social complications. The whole thing should never have occurred."

"Then keep it from going farther." The Count irritably chewed his sandy moustache.

"How can I? We do not live under Louis XIV. The whole scandal will be in all the papers to-morrow. It comes as a Godsend to the Ministry, who at this moment, as you know better than I, are at war with the Court-party. They will make much of it. 'Scene at a Railway-Station!' 'A great Court Lady resists the Authorities!' Under ordinary circumstances the affair would be too insignificant to mention. At this moment it is almost a Political Event!"

Hilarius beat a tattoo on the border of the billiard-table. He listened but abstractedly to the rest of his brother's small-talk. He was anxious for an opportunity to be alone with his wife, and as soon as this presented itself—in her dressing-room, late that evening—all his pent-up vexation burst forth.

"And if the thing really becomes a weapon in the hand of the Radicals," he added, after repeating the information which Frederik had brought him, "I shall never hold up my head at Court again."

"Then stop it," said the Countess, toying with her bracelet. She spoke with seeming indifference, her eyes on her arm, but a flush played over her sullen cheek.

"Frederik says that is not within his power."

"He wants to make himself important by magnifying the difficulty. I shall not ask him myself, but please tell

him that I *expect* him to stop it.   What else is one a judge
for, even so stupid a judge as he?"

"Margherita!"

"Is he a genius, your brother?   I had not perceived it."

"No, he is not a genius.   Would that some other people were not."   He ground his heel into the hearthrug.
"Heaven only knows to what this preposterous business
may lead."

"If you mean me," she answered quietly, lazily lifting
her handsome head, "I am not a genius.   I am a fool.
This is your good fortune.   And mine.   I cannot understand the little ways of your little country.   I know nothing of your party-intrigues.   But I am going to be a great
Court Lady, Hilarius.   That was agreed when we married."

"You are setting about it in a rational manner!" he
cried, and flung himself back against the mantelpiece.

She took no notice.   "Who is the person responsible?"
she asked.

"A man called Simmans, I understood Frederik to say."

"Ask him here."   She shut her bracelet with a snap.

CHAPTER XXXIII.

A COUNTY-MAGNATE.

"And now," said Count van Rexelaer to himself, as he slowly drew his chair towards the writing-table and made himself comfortable, "pleasure "—he pulled a face—" being over, I may give my mind to business at last."

It was true that pleasure was, for the moment, a thing of the past. The house had grown quiet again. The Calendar between the windows marked an early day in January. It was one of those calendars with a text for every day in the year, and his sister had given it him. Occasionally Count Hilarius's eyes would thoughtfully linger over the text.

The Freule van Rexelaer, the two brothers' only sister, was a timid maiden lady, living in a small provincial town on a small income and doing a great deal of unnoted good with it. She had come to Deynum to see the old year out, having declined to share the Christmas gaieties, for the simple reason, which she wisely kept to herself, that to her mind the commemoration of the Nativity should be a religious festival. The great house and its splendours flurried her.

"Oh, how thankful I am," she said to Mevrouw Elizabeth, "that I have not these servants to look after."

"Not *these* servants. No," replied Mevrouw Rexelaer-Borck with due emphasis. "But people with one servant are always afraid of them. I am not." She rested her crochet on one knee, looking over her nose at her thin little sister-in-law.

" Ah, but then you are such an excellent manager," said
the old maid timidly.

" I certainly see a few things which escape Margherita's
attention. No fear of her being worried, poor thing !
Thank Heaven, *I* have eyes." Mevrouw van Rexelaer-
Borck was always thanking Heaven, not so much for blessings received by herself, as for blessings withheld from
her friends.

" Yes, my dear," replied the Freule quickly. " And I
was telling you about the Coffee-stall Mission to Paris Cab-
men ; " and so she led the conversation on to safer ground.
Mevrouw Elizabeth, who liked the philanthropy of circulars
and Lady Patronesses and paragraphs in the press, was
anxious to introduce the coffee stalls into the Hague, the
only difficulty being the absence of cabstands. Perhaps
these could be created.

Utterly dissimilar as the two ladies were, they had in
common that sympathy of lifelong surroundings which no
later intercourse can replace. They understood each other
when they differed. Neither ever quite understood the
foreign sister-in-law, even when they most appreciated her
intentions. Fortunately the Countess did not court their
friendship ; she lay in the old Baroness's simple boudoir,
and Laïssa read her frequent bulletins from the Hague,
sent by the maid who had charge of the pets. And sometimes they would consult the cards to find out when Mevrouw Rexelaer-Borck was going away. That lady once surprised them at such a moment and denounced the heathen
superstition in no measured terms. " The wicked folly,
Margherita ! " she said. " Why, *I* could tell you as much
about the future as these senseless bits of card." " I
wish you would then," replied the Countess meaningly. Mevrouw van Rexelaer turned away in lofty scorn.
" Does this creature understand English ? " she asked.
She especially disliked Laïssa as being more " exotic "
even than the parrot. The mulatto looked up from the

floor, with her great white grin. "Laïssa no understand," she said.

Reinout introduced everybody to the Chapel, in which he already took an especial pride. "I hope you will alter this, Hilarius," said the Freule van Rexelaer earnestly, after a silent survey of the chancel. And then she drew on her galoches again, because the floor felt damp.

Mevrouw Elizabeth had expressed herself with more commendable distinctness. "This popish mummery," she had said, bringing down a heavy hand on the altar, "of course must *go*. I wonder, girls, at your uncle having left it so long. And, good gracious, the flowers are—fresh!" Not even Mevrouw van Rexelaer's indignant stare could dim the pure sweetness of the chrysanthemums. Vrouw Poster had renewed them, according to custom. With an extra prayer for vanished Piet.

"Hilarius," said Mevrouw Elizabeth in the course of the evening, "our dear Margherita has surely abjured the errors of her youth."

Hilarius colored painfully. "What do you mean, Elizabeth?" he cried. "If your mother has been talking shameful slander—"

"I was alluding to the Scarlet Woman," interposed Mevrouw van Rexelaer hastily. "To the Beast," and then, in answer to his astonished stare: "Hilarius, how can you be so ignorant? I mean that your wife is no longer a Papist, but we must not underrate early influences, and there is positive danger in these popish surroundings. Unless you take care you will have her going back to her bead-telling and bone-kissing, or whatever the people do. I should not speak, if it were not for the risk to René. You know very well that the Jesuits have an eye exclusively to rich men's sons. Already the old priest here has made friends with the boy. He took Topsy to see the man, but I forbade her going again. He gave them sweets, Hilarius. Mark my words. He gave them sweets." Deep down in her heart she had an honest, though not clearly explicable, fear that the sweets—for the new heir of Deynum—might be poisoned!

Count Hilarius had been startled by her evident good faith. He had lived too long in a clime where all men acknowledged the same form of religion without practising any to take note of the flowers and frippery in a sacred edifice; he was too indifferent to understand much of the fierce yet tremulous distrust which still lingers, on the field of Alva's achievements, in the hearts of the degenerate children of a nation of martyrs. He had no large experience of pious women; and yet he felt that Mevrouw van Rexelaer was not like his sister the Freule. But it does not require any very active piety to dread the idea of being burned alive.

As he now sat in the Baron's room, his eyes vaguely fixed on that old gentleman's guns, Hilarius reverted to Mevrouw Elizabeth's words. He wanted no complications, religious or otherwise. What he dreaded above all things was unpleasantness. It hampers one so.

His steward appeared before him, smooth and serene.

"I have been looking at the list of the tenants," said the Count, taking up a paper from the table before him. "Most of them I remember seeing at the New Year's Congratulation. A pleasing custom. Is it general in these parts?"

"At your service, Mynheer the Count," replied the steward. "It was always so in the old—time of your ancestors."

"But there are some names I cannot recall. Here, for instance, is a man called Hummel. Who is he?"

"He is old and bedridden," replied the steward. The man was a neighbour of his own, who often did him good service.

"Well. But here is a large farm, the Chalkhouse. I

do not remember the people at all. 'Driest' the name is. What of them?"

The steward, who had long been expecting this question, coughed gently. "As Mynheer the Count pleases," he said.

"What do you mean? Why don't they come to pay their respects?"

"Because they are—Ah, I wish Mynheer would ask them himself—they have not the proper feeling of the other tenantry."

"You mean that they are dissatisfied with the new order of things?"

"If Mynheer the Count pleases to put it so."

"I understand. They pose as champions of the old régime. And the opposition—about our reception—ah, you see I know—had they a hand in that?"

"Mynheer the Count knows so much, it is improbable that he should not know all."

The Count made a mark on his register. "Why were not the church-bells rung?" he asked suddenly.

The steward smiled a peculiar smile. "I am a good Catholic, Mynheer," he said. "The affairs of the church are not mine to control."

And then they discussed various matters pertaining to the estate. On these occasions Dievert found sufficient reason to regret the past, for the new master went into every item and never paid a penny without knowing what for. He even had no ready perception of the steward's all-conclusive argument that "it had always been so in the old Baron's time." Dievert understood that Count Hilarius was no gentleman.

They were still busy when Strum was announced. And the one man of business bowed himself out, as the other bowed himself in.

The Count liked the bowing. This was pleasanter than dancing attendance on his Majesty's representative at the

Court of the Sultan of Tierra del Fuego. Even pleasanter than living, as an officer of the Royal Household, in a dull house on the Orange-Canal, with a dark-visaged wife. There is no real greatness without the territorial element, the rent-roll, its votes and all its complicated influence. "In the same family, you know, for nearly a thousand years. Quite unique." Count Rexelaer felt kindly concerning his spouse.

"Sit down, Strum," he said with comfortable graciousness. The Notary considered that his new patron had dropped the "Mynheer" unconscionably soon. He recalled the time when the Baron was wont to say "Sit down, Strum," and when he had waited thus, on the edge of his chair, and cracking his fingers. He would still flush up to the roots of his red hair, by day or night, the great clumsy booby, when his thoughts reverted to the last visit here, and the insult he had received. He hated the Baron with relentless hate.

"I have been looking through the deed of purchase,' said the Count, rousing himself, as Strum gave an awkward little cough. "It is plain enough. In his dying hours the thoughts of the Countess's venerable uncle were evidently all of her and her child. He was deeply attached to my little boy. That prohibitory clause,—how he must have chuckled over it!—well, it was a legitimate stratagem, the only means he had of eluding the Baron's vindictive opposition to myself."

Strum acquiesced, thinking to himself what bores these rich people were.

"The contract says the Chapel must remain as it is. Now what do you take that to mean, my good Notary?"

"A Catholic place of worship, Mynheer the Count."

"Ah, it strikes you in that light because you are a Romanist yourself."—"A Romanist, if you will, but no bigot," began Strum—the Count waved his hand benignantly; he did not approve of being interrupted by his
17

Notary—"to me it means 'a burying-place of the Rexe-laers,'" he said.

Strum gave one of his sudden, sprawling kicks, causing the Count to start aside. The Notary understood perfectly what the other was driving at. "My father used to say," he answered slowly, "that in law every interpretation, how-ever absurd, must be considered as if it might be correct."

"I do not consider this interpretation absurd," inter-rupted the Count. *He* might interrupt. "On the con-trary, it is the only rational one."

"That is what I mean," answered Strum. He took off his spectacles and wiped them. And he blinked his eyes before the rising sun. Never mind, he might be as insolent as he chose to the Baron, in the shade.

"I sent for you," continued the Count, "to speak chiefly about another matter. Where is my cousin at present? Do you happen to know?"

"I believe the Baron is at Cleves," said Strum.

"I have an inventory here of the things he has taken with him. It is a great pity. They should have gone with the house. He must want money. You could not sound him on the subject?"

"I could write to him directly in your name, Mynheer the Count." A great leap of gratification crossed the Notary's face.

"I did not mean that. All these things are at present, I am told, at the parish priest's?"

"Yes, Mynheer the Count." Strum hated the Baron too much to willingly concede him so advantageous a market. The Baron's views on the matter he could not bring himself to understand.

"That is all," said Count Rexelaer. "Good-day." And to himself he added: "A very useless Notary."

Strum went home in a bad temper. But, then, inter-views with the great always put him out of sorts. He was the worst kind of person for a Notary; other people's business bored him. "I am as good," he thought ceaselessly, "as any of these." At his core, therefore, he was dumbly overbearing, as many shy people are.

"Your father used to tell me everything," said his mother a little complainingly (a fond illusion on her part), "and he would bring me such sweet messages from the Baroness, and pots of her own orange-preserve."

"It must taste very bitter in her mouth, if she's got any left," said Strum.

"She was an Angel," protested his mother warmly. "I wonder if this new lady is also good."

"Good? Of course she is good. All great ladies are good, mother, without pro's or con's. It's only the honest, hard-working ones that have to prove their goodness."

"Nicholas, Nicholas," said Mrs. Strum, gently shaking her old head, "you are very different from your father."

Now these words from a mother—even from Mrs. Strum —bear a tacit reproach in them. Nicholas was not accustomed to reproach from his mother. But the "White Baroness" was that lady's patron saint.

"We can't all be like each other," he grumbled roughly. "I'm as good a man of business as father was."

"Oh, yes, Nicholas. I know you are much cleverer," said Mrs. Strum, as she took up her stocking again.

CHAPTER XXXIV

THE TWO REINOUTS MEET.

Count Hilarius found Reinout enjoying a series of lonely tumbles on the ice. The boy had reached that stage of skating when the tumbles are a dozen yards apart. His father called him to the side of the pond.

"René, I don't want you to go and see this priest any more."

"Father Bulbius? Oh, papa, he is a dear old man. He has given me a live salamander. And he knows all about the Castle, and the people that used to live here. And he tells such beautiful stories. There was a little girl here once. Have you heard about Lady Bertha's oak?"

"No. But I don't want you to go and see him again. By the bye, did he ever speak to you about the Chapel in the Grounds?"

"Yes, Papa, the day after Christmas. He told me it was the first time in five-and-twenty years that he hadn't said mass there on Christmas day. He looked very sorry; I thought he was going to cry."

"Just so. Now, Reinout, you will promise me never to go and talk to this man again. And there is another thing. I don't like your skating about in this manner all alone. You must always have one of the men with you. Now promise about the priest."

Such a sullen look spread over the boy's dark face that his father noticed it. "My dearest child," said Count Hilarius, drawing his son towards him, "cannot you believe that I am acting for your best? You are the sole hope and pride of my life, René, the one thing I love with all my heart. If anything happened to you—" his voice shook, "there would be nothing left worth living for."

Reinout stood silently looking down at his skates. Presently something drew up his eyes—rather against his will—to his father's bended face. And he said, illogically, but with great earnestness: "I will, Papa." Nevertheless, he was angry. Only the rare display of the Count's affection always melted his heart as sunshine tinges the snow. He loved his father, perhaps not quite as energetically as he loved Prince, because Prince and he understood each other so much better. But, then, Prince was a dog; the comparison was absurd. Reinout did not make it.

He called after Count Hilarius's retreating figure. "I must go and say goodbye, Papa," he said, "and explain."

The Count had a habit of considering his son's entire existence, in its pleasure and profit, from the parental point of view. "No," he called back, "it would be better not. Explanations, Reinout, are usually a mistake!"

"Oh, but I shall," said Reinout to himself. Obedience has its limits, and the child's education, if it had taught him anything, had taught him that courtesy transcends it. He ran off in the direction of the village.

Already he had many friends in the village, where he had fraternised with the lame child first, and then, through him, with the other boys. These country lads had a delightful acquaintance with the wondrous world around them, on whose threshold he stood entranced. And, although his intercourse with them might seem somewhat awkward, yet he was always splendid in his own queer way and certainly far preferred his new companions to the genteel children at the Hague who mocked "his gracious Majesty." The transfer to Deynum had given him a glimpse of reality: the Life of Nature, the Life Unmasked. He liked the face.

He threw a smile to Tony, behind the narrow cottage-panes, as he ran on towards the Parsonage. He had promised the boy an old box of soldiers of his own; he must bring it to-morrow. It was a beautiful thing to be rich and great and patronise. The threatening beggar had been quite wrong. The great lord shone at the Castle and the world beneath his feet lay flourishing in his smile. Monsieur de Souza had explained it all.

He ran through the Parsonage garden, round by the stables to the good Priest's study. He knew the way well by this time. But in the door he suddenly checked himself. An old gentleman was sitting thoughtfully by the fire. The old gentleman looked up at the intruder, frowned, hesitated, and recovered himself.

"Father Bulbius is out," said the old gentleman shortly.

Reinout bowed and apologised, with that ready courtesy which young people found so exasperating, but which old ones were unable to resist in this our latter-day of ill-breeding.

As he was going, said the old gentleman with an effort: "I suppose they call you Reinout van Rexelaer?"

"Yes, Mynheer," replied Reinout.

"Father Bulbius has told me a great deal about you," said the Baron. And then he added, as if talking to himself, "But I pity the child!" and Reinout crept away bewildered.

The evening before, the good Father had sat, in all the cosiness of drawn curtains and howling winds, warming his feet against the stove and his hands around his glass of steaming grog. The kettle was singing its agreeable promise of more. Father Bulbius felt comfortable though lonely. For Veronica was away on her yearly visit to her friends in town.

"A holiday for me," Veronica used to say with some truth, "means two days of extra hard work." Undeniably, the catastrophe of the year in the Father's small household whatever it might happen to be, would always choose the thirty-six hours of Veronica's absence to occur in. Nevertheless did she amply enjoy her excursion on account of the manifold occasions for grumbling it was bound to afford. And the Father enjoyed his brief liberty in the pleasant prospect of her return.

He was sitting now luxuriating in the tranquil sadness of his reflections. There was much to grieve him in his present circumstances, and it pleased him to dwell thereon. The new master of Deynum, though indifference itself in all matters religious, had yet given encouragement, by the very fact of his Protestantism, to the persecuted heretics of the village. They were beginning to hold up their heads, and even—distinctly—to crow. And it was reported that the Baroness Borck of Rollingen—that Jezebel—had, during a state-visit at the Castle, succeeded in arousing its owner's interest by a terrible account of the poor "Beggars'" sufferings and the bad impression these sufferings had created in the neighbourhood. The Baroness Borck had been anxious for years to get a Protestant pastor appointed to Deynum, her own minister finding the double duty too heavy. Count Rexelaer, in his eagerness to conciliate the great people around him, would probably accede to her request, and a rival parsonage-house would arise on the village green. Meanwhile the Count had closed, and double-locked, the small chapel in the grounds.

Father Bulbius sighed, and gently sipped his grog. To-morrow evening Veronica would mix it. There would be less rum, but boiling water.

He was roused from his slumbrous regrets by a gentle knock at the front-door. It was ten o'clock, and an ugly, windy, snow-tormented night. He started to his feet, hastily swallowing the too darkly coloured mixture; his one thought was that something must have happened to bring

Veronica back. Only she seemed to him strangely patient, as he slowly stumbled to the door.

He opened it, and there stood the Baron van Rexelaer.

"How do you do, Bulbius?" said the Baron. "Anybody with you besides Veronica?"

Father Bulbius burst into tears.

"Tut, tut," said the Baron, and hastily walked into the Sanctum.

When Father Bulbius joined him there a moment later, he was standing in the middle of the room. He had taken the shade from the lamp and its full glare fell on all the piled-up lumber from the castle. He looked much the same as ever, excepting that perhaps his bearing was a trifle more erect than in those last slow months of his suspense. As the priest stole in, he turned and replaced the lamp-shade. "Well, and how are you getting on?" he said. "Anything new in the village?" Oh yes, there were several things new in the village. Father Bulbius only muttered the name of some old creature recently dead.

"Dead," repeated the Baron meditatively. He walked up the room once, and down it again, and then, stopping abruptly: "May I take off my cloak?" he asked. Father Bulbius fell forward in the eagerness of his response. He hung up the Baron's hat, without knowing it, on one knight's protruding visor, and over another's mailed shoulders he carefully and awkwardly spread his patron's well-remembered queer-fashioned Inverness. The dead soldier looked worse than grotesque under his plaid-lined mantle; he looked dumbly insulted. The Baron went over and removed it.

"The damp, you know," he said apologetically, and began softly polishing the shining metal. Father Bulbius's soul burned with sudden shame.

He plied his guest with a number of questions, while pressing upon him the slippers he had just taken from his own feet. "I have others," he said, and went into his bedroom, and came back with a pair of galoches. And then, in sudden alarm at his overflow of curiosity, he excused it with the necessity of finding out the Baron's requirements. "And when has your Nobleness eaten last?" he said. "Ah, but I dread that the house contains nothing but bread."

"I want nothing, my friend," said Mynheer Rexelaer. "Mevronw and the child are well, like myself. But how about Veronica? I miss her."

"Your Nobleness does her too much honour. She has gone to see her relations. Her usual visit, you remember."

"Oh certainly," replied the Baron. "I hope she will find her aunt in health. It is fortunate, perhaps, that she should not be here. Ah no, I forgot; it is unfortunate," he added, rising hastily, and making for the door.

Father Bulbius intercepted him with wonderful plump alacrity. "The room upstairs is ready," he said, "or will be in a minute. As for supper, I will run over and see if Hendrika—"

"No, no, my good Father. To tell you the truth I had not intended to disturb you. The last train having brought me to Deynum, I found myself unexpectedly in your porch. But it is quite time I left you in peace, and so I am going away again." He got his cloak and hat, overhearing the Father's anxious "Whither?" and stumbled along the passage. The Father followed in desperation. "But shall I not see your Nobleness again?" he almost sobbed. Suddenly the other turned and caught both his hands. "I am behaving like a brute and a fool," he said thickly. "It is a great, true happinesss to see your face again. May I stay, in spite of Veronica's absence? In spite of all the trouble I shall give?"

"Don't," replied the Father, vainly trying to steady the workings of his gutta-percha cheeks.

"But one thing you promise me. It is already past your bedtime. You go now, as if Veronica were here, and

you leave me to sit up as long as I like—among these."
He pointed to his re-found treasures.

"But there is so much to speak of," pleaded Bulbius.

"There is not," repeated the Baron, wearily reseating
himself. "To tell truth, I feel nowise inclined for sleep.
I may take a short turn presently; I like the snow. Never
mind me. I shall not set the house on fire."

"The whole house is at your Nobleness's service," said
Bulbius. He could say that, freely, for the next four-and-
twenty hours. "But see, Mynheer the Baron, it is not yet
eleven?"

The Baron looked into his face and actually laughed:
"And when was Father Bulbius ever known to resume his
game—" he asked—"when once the Castle-clock"—the
laugh died from his voice—"had struck the hour of ten?"

"To-day," said the Father boldly, spreading his fat fingers on the table, "to-day, if your Nobleness pleases, he will
play as long as you like."

"Nonsense, Bulbius, you never had a card in your
house."

For only answer the priest went to his cupboard. "I
have been obliged of late," he said apologetically, "to play
a little écarté by myself of nights. But I find it very dull
work."

"So I can understand," replied the Baron quite seriously,
as he shuffled the cards. The old antagonists had settled
down to their game, almost before they realized what they
were doing. It came as a relief from a well-nigh unendurable strain.

The wind struck against the casement, as they bent
by the lamp. Father Bulbius looked up apprehensively.
"Only bluster," said the Baron, "I mark the King." And
in another moment the player's ambition had got hold of
them and both were anxious to win. The Baron became so
increasingly successful, that Father Bulbius could hardly
resist feeling a little annoyed. But no interest in his cards

could keep his sleepy head from nodding, and at one time
he had six cards in his hand, and about midnight he re-
voked. Then the Baron got up. " Just a whiff of air !"
he said. " It will do me good. Give me your key, Bulbius, and if I find you up when I come back, I depart for
good and all, as, perhaps, I ought to have done at first.
Good-night."

The Father let him go and then set about preparing the
guest-chamber. A couple of the most richly framed lords
and ladies which had been deposited here, he dragged away,
with much labour and some damage to gilding, into Veronica's chamber. " Let the poor gentleman sleep, if he
can," he said ; he knew well enough where the Baron was
gone. He came down, wiping his hot face. There was oil
in the lamp; the fire would smoulder on indefinitely. He
sent up a little petition to his patron Saint to remind the
hens of their duty for the morrow, and then—at last !—he
sank on the bed to await his guest's return, and in another
moment was fast asleep.

CHAPTER XXXV.

A STRANGE LIGHT AND NEW DARKNESS.

MEANWHILE the Baron van Rexelaer walked rapidly through the wind and dark. He had waited for the dark. "I shall take the last train," he had said to the Baroness, "and go to the inn. So doing, I shall see nobody till to-morrow."

"Why?" asked the Baroness. She could not understand this postponement of the inevitable. The quiet lady had steeled her heart in reposeful pride.

But the Baron, although unable to explain himself, felt that between to-day and to-morrow, if we live by emotions, would lie a long period of time. He must first see the place again, alone; he must fight his fight. When he had hurried away, three months ago, he had hoped never to return. Which of us, having buried our dead out of our sight, would bid love lift the coffin-lid?

"I *must* consult with Bulbius, but I shall not go up to the Castle." This thought had repeatedly risen to his lips; he had checked it; he did not want his courageous wife to consider him a coward. He crossed over to her and kissed her on the forehead where she sat in her high-backed chair by the poor little Pension-window.

That was not much more than half-a-dozen hours ago. He had promised his wife to eat something on his arrival; he did not like breaking even a trivial promise to his wife. He ought not to have minded giving Bulbius a little trouble. "I *am* a coward," thought the good gentleman, as he walked

on through the silence. After midnight all Deynum, except its watchman, was asleep. Sometimes the watchman
also.

In another moment he passed under the shadow of his
own trees. Here the night lay pitchy dark, in spite of the
driving snow, which melted as it fell. The Baron, hastening unhesitatingly on, emerged into the avenue. Then,
suddenly, he became aware of a light approaching at the
farther end and stopped, disconcerted. Should he go back?
As he stood staring stupidly at this twinkle in the distance,
he became aware that it was stationary, and then he understood. An innovation. A lantern by the bridge. And in
that small discovery the hopelessness of his loss fell upon
him as it had never fallen before.

"They need not have broken their necks any sooner
than we did," he muttered, bitterly. And presently he
stood beside the water, shrinking from the tell-tale bright-
ness of a varnished street-lamp of Margherita's erecting.
Another glimmered half-way down the "Cour d'honneur."
Right opposite towered the black mass of the Castle, with
the wind howling round it, a melancholy wail.

The snow, which had been falling all night in fitful
sweeps, now slowly checked itself, and, among lifting clouds,
the outlines of the stately building stood dimly forth in a
changeful play of light and shade. And instantaneously
the whole of it, each nook and angle and curl of tracery,
shone out into the darkness, illumined by his love. We are
but sensuous creatures; talk as we will of visions of the
mind, we see with our poor physical sight and with very
little else. He stood staring, staring, as if his eyes could
never drink their fill, and then a veil crept over them.
When he looked again, the vision was newly shrouded in
darkness; only a dull broad shaft still fell, from where the
clouds were closing, across old Atlas, on the topmost pin-
nacle, bending beneath his world of cares. Another moment, and this ray also had sunk from sight; the snow be-

gan to thicken upon the lessening wind. With a shuddering sigh the Baron turned to go. Ever afterwards he remembered that parting glimpse of the patient hero, beneath the drooping sky.

" Away," he said softly.

He crossed the sward, not without anxious glances towards the windows, behind which Hilarius and Margherita were peacefully slumbering, and crept towards the Holy Walk. Before returning to the Parsonage he must stand for one brief moment—and one brief prayer—among the dead in their unbroken rest. That alone would calm him. " I am a vainglorious old fool to have come," he told himself. And he thought of that repose which no agony of wounded pride can ruffle, and which comes so soon to all.

No light was burning in the chancel. He tried the door ; it was locked. Never had the lamp hung thus extinguished during all the years the Baron could recall. " They light up their own yard !" he said aloud, " God help me ; I am becoming the bitterest of men !"

Half an hour later he was back in Father Bulbius's sanctum. Walking on tip-toe, he softly stirred the dying embers and drew forward a chair. The lamp burned low. The clock on the mantelpiece struck half-past one. And the sound suddenly told him that the stable-clock at Deynum had not struck while he was out. He rose in some perturbation, wondering if anything could be wrong with it. And then he laughed ; what was Count Rexelaer's stable-clock to this stranger and sojourner?

No, he was more than that. Come what might, he was still the last of Deynum's historic lords. He strengthened himself in his seat, and then, drawing a bunch of keys out of his pocket, opened an oak chest which stood near. The keys of the Castle he could lose and had lost, but not these.

Presently Father Bulbius, awakening in dismay and discomfort, saw a light streaming through the chinks, and seized his unloaded revolver. And then he remembered that he himself had left the lamp on the table. "Dear me," he said, " I must have had a few minutes' nap," and he rolled off the bed, and was making for the door when his attention was arrested by the rustle of paper. Letting himself down somewhat laboriously to the keyhole, he saw in the gathering gloom of the silent study the Baron van Rexelaer, with parchments and papers heaped untidily around him, a yellow charter upon his knee. The Father crept back softly into bed.

CHAPTER XXXVI

THE HEAD OF THE HOUSE.

NEXT morning, over their frugal breakfast, the Baron explained to Bulbius the object of his coming. On leaving Deynum he had still lacked fifty thousand florins to pay off his debts. This money, not being able to touch the "Lady's Dole," he had found himself obliged to borrow at ruinous interest, for six months. Not to have done so would have meant bankruptcy, disgrace.

"Bankruptcy is not always disgrace," interposed the Father, who prided himself on his knowledge of the world. "Yours would not have been."

"This loan, in any case, must be paid off," said the Baron, "before it reduces us to beggary. So I have made up my mind to sell whatever trumpery I still possess. I can't help it. It's no use fighting any longer against fate."

What could the Father reply? Three months ago he had advocated this sale. And the Baron had answered: Never to the one man who would buy. Father Bulbius regretted the Baron was so bad a man of business.

Confessor though he was, he knew nothing of his patron's money-transactions. Do we ever confess? Even to ourselves?

"No use fighting against fate," repeated the Baron thoughtfully, and then suddenly he burst out: "Observe my strange experience with the Marquis de la Jolais! I cannot make him out at all. It looks as if he did it on purpose. And if so, he acted a lie."

" I fear that is the only explanation, Mynheer," assented Father Bulbius mournfully.

" So the Baroness tells me, and the Baroness is always right. But I cannot understand it! A la Jolais! Surely gentlemen do not lie ! "

The Baron held a view—not a theory, for he did not consciously theorise—that men were turned out in groups, like machine-made statuettes. A soldier was a soldier; a sailor a sailor, and so on. Each group had its inevitable virtues—and vices, but the Baron noticed the virtues most.

He was agitated now; all references to Count Rexelaer's vile stratagem or marvellous good fortune upset him. Father Bulbius stole away on the plea of ordering some dinner from Hendrika, the landlady. It was during his absence that Reinout unexpectedly appeared before the Baron, Reinout, whose praises the Father had discreetly brought forward by an occasional word in a letter, a word that said little and left much to be divined. " I pity the child," said the Baron. He did not allude to the subject when the Father came back. Together they began looking over the scattered heirlooms and appraising them. Some of the pictures were valuable; the costliest plate had already been disposed of before. Both realized, with growing distinctness, that fifty thousand florins is a very large sum.

They were so occupied that a loud ring at the front door came upon them with a start of alarm. " Possibly a tramp," said the Father. The villagers usually went round to the back, there to be barked at by the now absent Veronica. Nobody ever rang.

With rumpled hair and dusty cassock Father Bulbius went to open the door. His grumble changed to an uncomfortable smile of recognition in the presence of Count Hilarius van Rexelaer. That gentleman had never called at the Parsonage before.

" This way, if you please. This is my ' state '-room,
18

Heer Count," cried the Father in a flurry, shutting one door and opening another. The visitor entered an apartment whose chill glories—the pride of Veronica's cleansing —froze the marrow in his bones. Count Hilarius was a Southernized Hollander. He looked round in dismay.

"Take a seat, Mynheer the Count," said the Father, benignly.

The Count's teeth chattered. He had intended to be circumspect, but the cold made him forget his diplomacy. "I came to ask you, Mynheer," he said brusquely, "about the articles which have been removed from the Castle and which you have in your keeping."

"They were excluded by the contract, Mynheer," cried Bulbius in a flutter.

The Count arched his sandy eyebrows. "I should hardly have waited so long," he said, "had that not been the case. But I am anxious, if possible, to acquire them. Strum says all the cupboards are locked, but I should like to see the other things." He paused inquiringly.

"That is quite impossible," replied Father Bulbius with a vehemence born of agitation. "I may show them to no one."

Count Hilarius felt the cold settling on his bald head. He put on his hat, and he also rose from the red velvet sofa.

"You misapprehend me," he said stiffly. "I wish only to see the pictures, the armour, etcetera. All these things are heirlooms which should remain with the family, and should never have left the Castle. I am going to offer my cousin, Baron Rexelaer, to re-purchase them."

"I can show you nothing, Mynheer the Count," repeated Bulbius in a tremble. "I am very sorry. It is quite out of the question." Would his visitor never go?

But the visitor, who had only been one moment in the house, already felt quite willing to leave it. He was furious at this behaviour from his parish priest, and he hurried out into the hall, drawing his fur-coat around him.

In his haste—or was it done intentionally?—he threw open the wrong door and walked straight into the Sanctum. The Baron was not there—Bulbius gave a gasp of relief—but the whole room was littered with his treasures.

Count van Rexelaer's eyes travelled slowly over the open cupboards and boxes and their scattered contents. At last they arrested their pale gaze on the Father's burning face, and Bulbius read an accusation in them which was simply monstrous.

"I had understood that these receptacles were locked," said Count Rexelaer at last. "If their owner left them in this peculiar condition, he cannot have attached much importance to their contents."

Father Bulbius felt utterly annihilated.

"If," repeated the Count with unmistakable stress. Meanwhile his eyes literally danced and gloated over all these glories of his house. He had never beheld any of them before.

"The Baron begged me to arrange them," stammered Bulbius.

"Indeed? And do you do so every day?" Count Hilarius was furious to think of these inestimable splendours abandoned to an ignorant and unscrupulous priest. He had brought away with him from Rio the conviction that all priests were unscrupulous. He stamped his foot in his agitation. "I distinctly understood from Strum," he continued, "that these cases were locked."

"You accuse me of neglecting my trust, Mynheer?" cried the Father, losing patience.

"I said no such thing. Had I wished to do so, I should not have used the word 'neglecting.'"

"Violating, perhaps?" screamed the Father, bounding like a fiery ball. He cast prudence to the winds. O this Protestant upstart! All the wrongs of the flock flared up in the shepherd's heart, like tallow round a wick.

"You forget yourself," said the Count stiffly. "I came

here because I am anxious Baron Rexelaer should be informed of my offer to purchase these articles for which he can have no further accommodation. If that be part of your duty as a caretaker "—he had all a little soul's spite, and was now intentionally insulting—"have the goodness to transmit my message immediately. I should certainly have preferred, if possible, his answering me himself." He leant against the same inlaid gentleman who, the night before, had resented the Baron's Inverness, and his eyes rested scornfully on the Father.

"He will do so at once," said a cold voice behind him. "Would you have the kindness to lean less heavily, Mynheer?" A gray gentleman,—gray of hair, not only, but of face and eyes—stood in a door which had suddenly opened in the wall. Count Rexelaer knew immediately who the strange gentleman was. "I—I," he stammered, altogether disconcerted, "I was not aware—I am Count Rexelaer."

"I could not help hearing you, Mynheer, from the adjoining room. I am the owner of this lumber. It seems simpler to tell you at once that I shall never sell any of it to *you*."

All the words were calmly polite, excepting that final, over-emphasized "you." "But why?" pleaded the other, somewhat recovering his sangfroid. "The things are wanted at Deynum. They have left horrible, noticeable gaps "—a flash of satisfaction died across the Baron's eyes—"and as head of the family—"

"Stop," interrupted Baron Rexelaer in a voice of thunder. "God knows I do not wish to be discourteous, but never shall I allow you to use those words to my face!"

"The higher title—" burst in Count Hilarius fiercely, while Father Bulbius shrank aside.

"Pooh!" said the Baron more calmly. "Money, even such money as yours, Mynheer, can buy almost all things nowadays. But it cannot buy—and you know it cannot—one drop of the blood of these." He laid his hand quite gently on the shoulder of the knight beside him. To him, at that moment, the empty armour was a living presence. "There, there," he continued softly. "I have no wish to insult you. I cannot give you these things, because you would make them live a daily lie. Surely you can understand that. If you like, you may have the silver; your father, wrongly enough, was permitted to assume our arms, and you may buy the forks and spoons."

"And the archives?" cried the Count.

Mynheer van Rexelaer looked at him and smiled.

"I will take nothing!" screamed Hilarius. "Mind you, you"—he turned to Bulbius—"and you! I came here in all charity to see what could be done. It is unwise to anger me. Rexelaer or not, I still am Lord of Deynum." He ran out into the passage. This time he found the front-door.

"Of course he is not of the family," said Bulbius, wiping his face. "How could I ever think he was?"

"I am sorry," said the Baron.

Count Hilarius ran home in a rage, and, as misfortunes never come singly, he was stopped in his own park by a man who had evidently been waiting for him there.

"A word with you," said the man.

The Count drew back. He was no craven.

"Let me pass," he said haughtily.

"One moment. This girl. The child lives."

"What girl?" cried the Count impatiently.

"Villain, have you such wealth of choice? Dora Droste."

"I know nothing of what you mean," replied the Count, endeavouring to push past. "Who are you? You have no business in this park."

"You know who I am. I have told you before. Not that it matters. I have nothing in common with the girl

but her misfortune." The fellow, a miserable-looking creature, held one lean arm across the path.

"If you want to extort money, you won't get it," said
the Count, pressing forward.

"You will do nothing for the girl?"

"No." Count Rexelaer lifted his cane.

The fellow struck it aside and, in doing so, knocked over
his puny antagonist, saw him topple back into the slush, and
ran off and out of sight.

CHAPTER XXXVII.

THAT night the Baron went back to Cleves.

An hour or two before his arrival Wendela sat strumming wearily on the boarding-house piano. It was a very bad piano, but this, to Wendela, was no additional affliction.

"One, two, three," counted the Baroness. "Wendela, you are not keeping time."

"Oh, what does it matter, Mamma? The tune comes right all the same."

"Not to those who distinguish properly. I thought it was my daughter's ambition to do everything well?"

"So it is, Mamma. Oh dear; one, two, three!" And Wendela paddled on.

Presently a nervous little Swiss body thrust her head through the door, then drew back with a couple of openings and shuttings, and finally entered and sat down. Many people cannot enter a public sitting-room in any other way. "Shall we be disturbing you, Mademoiselle?" asked the Baroness. "Not in the least," replied the little lady, in much trepidation, certainly saying the reverse of what she meant. Fräulein Drix was "exceedingly musical," and as Wendela's ten fingers went staggering over immovable stumbling-blocks, the poor creature vibrated behind the Review she was endeavouring to read.

The clock struck, and the musician dropped the piano-lid with a bang, which covered her mother's sigh of relief. The piece Wendela had been playing was Haydn's "Surprise." Very surprised would he have been to hear it was his.

"Do you consider it advisable, Madame," said Fräulein Drix, in a flutter of sudden resolve, "that *all* children should be taught the piano?" Wendela, who was gathering her books together, paused to listen. The Fräulein gasped at her own temerity, as she met the stare of the Baroness's pale eyes. Pale eyes can look haughtier than dark ones, and it was the one lady's look which answered the other. Aloud Mevronw van Rexelaer merely said: "I like my daughter to learn it," in leaving the room. The doctor remarked next morning that Fräulein Drix was not so well.

The Baroness was white to the lips as she took her usual seat by the window. She was a woman of immeasurable pride; she had always been accustomed to a tranquil supremacy of gentle patronage, unassuming, doubtless, where only condescension was required. Seclusion—intermediary servility,—it is the one great blessing which rank and wealth bestow. The Baroness knew little of the world outside her, till she differed with "Auguste" about the cleanness of the dinner-plates. Nor did she know too much of the world within her—what stronghold still lay there unconquered—till intercourse with the ladies of Frau Schultze's second-rate Pension came unpleasantly to her assistance. She loathed the little, squalid, quarrelsome life.

"But Mamma," began Wendela abruptly. "Perhaps she is right. I hate playing. And you said yourself I had an excellent voice."

"Your ear must be trained first, Wendela; it is far too imperfect. Allow your mother to judge. And do you remember: Seedtime is my time: Harvest-time is God's."

Wendela threw her arms round her mother's neck with a warmth of embrace which would have astonished Fräulein Drix: "I wonder whether it ever really happened," she said, "Guido van Rexelaer casting his seed on the submerged fields in the Spanish troubles, and the harvest coming up just the same. Tell me about it again, Mother. When you tell me, it sounds true."

"Of course it is true. How often have I not told you before ? "

"Yes, I know. But it all seems too beautiful to be real. Beautiful things never really happen, I think. It's only the ugly, and nasty and wicked that come true." The girl spoke with passionate conviction, shaking back the brown locks from her honest brow. Then, suddenly, she embraced her mother again with vehement hugs and kisses. "You tell me, mother," she repeated, "about good things, and God, and the Saints. When you tell me it sounds true, and I think I understand."

"Hush, hush," answered the Baroness, gently disengaging herself. "My little daughter must not wish to understand too much. Go and wash your hands, dear child; it is nearly time for supper."

Wendela ran off to her own room, a pale-cheeked, earnest-eyed child, impetuous of thought and movement, yet dreamy withal. In the hideousness of the present, the dream-life had deepened around her as a sheltering cloud. Nurturing her beauty-sick soul upon the splendours of fairy tales, she had escaped into regions of blissful unreality, where she delighted to wander, in endless imaginings, with a fairy hero of her own creating, to whom she did homage as her lord. Of course he was handsome, though she had never distinguished his features, virtuous as one of her mother's saints, and as a lion strong.

She would not have been a daughter of her race had she not identified this fairy-prince with one of her own great ancestors; he was Pilgrim van Rexelaer, the "Knight Pilgrim," whose marble effigy sleeps in the Chapel (its visor closed in its saintly humility), the Crusader to whom the modern version of the family legend ascribes the deliverance of the maiden Wendela. Not for one moment did the girl's

strong brain confuse the actual and the unreal. All
things existent, as she had said to her mother, were
ugly and evil; she deliberately turned her back upon
them and roved away into the mystic forest, where a
Saracen Chieftain pounced forth from behind the pine-
trees and Knight-Pilgrim came riding up on a milk-white
steed.

"For shame, Wanda!" said her mother, entering.
"The supper-bell has rung!"

Wendela tumbled off the bed: "Oh, Mamma," she said,
"I wish you need never have disturbed me. I was so happy,
over yonder, in the wood. In the dear wood."

The Baroness knew nothing of her daughter's dream-
ings, except that she was too often dreamy, but it did
not require any such knowledge to understand the allusion to Deynum. "God sends us the present to live
in, not the past," she said. "Get ready, child, and come
down."

They went into the supper-room together, and there
they found the meal and its appendages awaiting them:—
tea, made from hay, fat liver-sausage and frizzling potato-
pancake, and, furthermore, half a dozen superfluous-looking
personages who talked, dismally, at intervals, about the
weather and about themselves. "Superfluous-looking,"
because there really seemed no reason why any of these
creatures should exist, excepting the fact that each of them
probably possessed a pittance to spend upon herself and
thus to keep herself carefully, grumblingly and uselessly
alive. Before the repast was concluded, Mynheer van
Rexelaer joined the party and was greeted with a little
cackle of interest. Most of the ladies felt a certain tenderness for the good "Heer Baron"; true, he was married.—
My dear, if you will shut the door, we will have a talk
about that wife of his—he was married, undeniably, but he
was the only gentleman in the house. As a rule, he gave
them very little satisfaction. To-day, again, after lengthen-

ing periods of silence, they picked themselves up one by one, and carried themselves away, for thus only can the manner be described in which they departed from the table with their various shawls, work-bags and other weaknesses.

Even when left alone with his wife and child, the Baron did not break through his reserve. He confined his brief utterances to the incidents of the journey, and answered all questions with reluctance. " But I want to know everything about everything," said Wendela. He told her that her pets at the Castle had been disposed of : " Then I want to hear nothing about nothing any more," said the girl. A year ago she would have burst into a passion of crying; now she sat gazing silently, until, with an especially affectionate farewell to the Baroness, she wished her parents goodnight. There was a barrier between her and her father, unrealized, though not altogether unfelt, by him, unacknowledged by her.

The Baron took up the little German " Tageblatt." Presently he said, without lifting his eyes from it : " I hope you have been comfortable during my absence ? "

" Oh yes, we are comfortable. How can you ruin your eyes, mon ami "—the Baroness did not read German—" by this wretched light ? The lamp smells again ; the woman refuses to clean it."

The Baron laid down the newspaper. He sat shading his face with his hand, and presently he said, as one who thinks aloud : " The old home."

Madame van Rexelaer dropped her cards. " Tell me," she said, " I am longing to know. It is that still."

He drew back his hand quickly and looked full at her. " Is it ? " he said eagerly. " To you ? "

" I envy you, dearest, for having seen it again."

He started to his feet. " Would you," he said in a trembling voice. " Could you—" He remained looking dumbly at his wife, unable to proceed.

She stretched out both her arms to him. "Come here to me," she said. "It is the one thing I have been longing for, but not daring to ask."

And thus it was that the old Rexelaers came back to live at Deynum.

CHAPTER XXXVIII.

THE BORCKS.

THE village meanwhile had got accustomed to the new ones.

As, day after day, the green shutters were flung open, to the slow rising of the winter-sun, all round the weather-beaten sides of the Castle, those villagers whose errands brought them up to the offices gazed in pleasant approval of the fact that these numerous eyes still smiled down upon them and their merchandise. The saying had been that the family was only coming for Christmas. They were still here, and Joost Hakkert's monthly bill alone exceeded a hundred and fifty florins. Joost Hakkert was delighted. The Baron had left no debts, it is true, but he had always paid slowly while buying little ; Count Rexelaer's ready money came pouring into the village, and the village, as it felt, smelt, jingled and crackled it, hurrah'd for Count Rexelaer. One morning the tailor met Hakkert's youngest son in the Castle-courtyard bending beneath his basket-load of meat. "And does your father still insult the strangers?" he asked in passing. The foolish, beefsteak-faced lad stopped and stared.

One class there was which had full cause to regret the White Baroness. It is a large one, and at Deynum that lady had perhaps unnecessarily enlarged it. Margherita, on her part, had no wish not to be charitable, but that very common attitude is of little practical avail. The Count entrusted his systematised charities to Dievert, and every gentleman who has found out his steward (some, alas, have not yet done so) will understand what that meant. Dievert now often deplored that he had not had the management of the old Baron's largesse.

Meanwhile the whole regiment of workmen were busy all over the Castle, and herein he could find sufficient cause for rejoicing. Margherita, who possessed genuine taste and considerable knowledge of the lower forms of art, had thrown herself, with fitful energy, into the work of renovation and redecoration, and her husband did not check her capricious expenditure, although, unfortunately for Dievert, he checked the resultant bills. He was glad to afford some relief to the melancholy which would settle on the Creole's face as she stood looking forth on the ice-bound moat, and the snow and the scraggy trees. Much as she had complained at the Hague, she had never yet understood how wintry winter is. Would she go back? Ah no; she had a nervous dread, at this moment, of the city's tittle-tattle about the "Scene at the Railway Station," which was being diligently worked by the "Rads." Margherita had plenty of passion at her command for a fine burst of emotion, but she could not stand the wear of a lagging, nagging annoyance.

After a few weeks Mevrouw Elizabeth van Rexelaer returned to her relations at the Castle. She brought Jane with her, and also Cécile Borck, her dead brother's child, a shy, simple-hearted girl. Grandmamma Borck had her dear friend, the Countess de Bercy, staying with her, and Cécile's presence hampered their talk. In spite of her orphanhood and modesty, Cécile was not a nobody in the Borck family; her father had misallied himself to one of the Koopstad Lossells and had left her fifty thousand pounds in the funds. Grandmamma looked after her and them.

She came, therefore, to see, and be seen of, her cousins, the Borcks of Rollington, and Mevrouw Elizabeth, her aunt (who had missed the dear people at Christmas), ostensibly did the same. The new owners of Deynum were glad of this bridge of communication with their powerful neighbour, but they would hardly have tolerated Mevrouw Elizabeth's early reappearance, had not other considerations come to the fore. Young Simmans, the functionary charged with the Countess's "procès-verbal," was very intimate at the house of Judge Rexelaer; he was even credited with aspiring to the hand of the Freule Jane. Had Jane been less plain, this presumption would have been resented, for Simmans was nobody's son but his father's.

"When you are down there," said the Dowager to her daughter, "you can write to Henry Simmans to come and see you and find out the facts from Margherita. She is a fool. I barely know her, but you can tell her so from me. In my youth the populace took pleasure in the noble arrogance of their superiors; the times have changed, and the best thing for us to do is to keep as quiet as we can. Like the rich Jews of the Middle Ages that used to wear the filthier rags. From the height of my eighty years' experience I say: Society scandals to-day are society suicides, and should be punished by society as such." She struck her cane on the floor, and sat angrily twitching her poor old mouth, which was fallen in over her peaked chin. She was seventy-three, but her daughter knew better than to contradict her. She had been thirty till she was fifty, and had then leaped into precipitate old age.

"Live as badly or as madly as you will," she added, after a moment, "but build your park-walls high."

"Quite so," said Mevrouw Elizabeth, who was nothing if not practical. "And I shall take down Jane, Mamma, and I might also take Antoinette. Dear René is so attached to Antoinette."

"They are children," replied the Dowager. "I have never paid much attention to the attachments of children. But, by all means, take Jane. It will be dull enough for Simmans."

"We shall have him proposing from ennui," laughed Mevrouw Elizabeth, with an attempt at playfulness which did not at all "suit her style."

"As most men do," retorted the Dowager.

So Mevrouw van Rexelaer departed for Deynum with Jane and Cécile, the Countess having declined the pleasure of Topsy's company, "because Reinout was once more occupied with his lessons." "As if *I* could not have brought Miss Wilson," said Reinout's disappointed aunt. Jane had pulled a face at the prospect of more Deynum in winter. "You can draw, you know," suggested her plump sister Rolline. "Yes; that's what I'm taken for," said plain-spoken Jane.

The Borcks of Rollingen called the day after their cousin's arrival, most unfortunately missing the Count, who had left for a period of "duty" at the palace. They were almost cordial to Mevrouw Elizabeth, and gracious to Margherita. "And was that dark, olive-complexioned boy, the Countess's son?"—the lady from Rollingen put up her eye-glass. "He is very handsome; do you not think so, John? He understands French? Oh, never mind; plenty of people will tell him that." "I am glad we are co-re-ligionists," she said to Margherita in parting, not knowing, or forgetting, the Countess's change of creed. She promised to call again.

Margherita "did not care," as long as she knew people to bow to. Just now she was entirely engrossed by the construction of a glass excrescence to her sitting-room, which would hang like a huge balcony over the moat. She took her visitors to see this. "It does not match a bit with the rest of the fortress-like building," said Elizabeth. "It does not," admitted the lady of Rollingen, frankly. Margherita knew that better than her visitors, but she must have a corner for her plants and her pets. "Did Mevrouw Borck like pets?" Mevrouw Borck detested them, and had fortunately not observed the recumbent Florizel, who had soiled the train of her dress during the visit. It was Cécile who timidly hinted, in her desire to say something kind, that houses built out of the water were known to be less damp than houses beside it. The Baroness Borck, tactless as she herself was, lifted her perpetual eye-glass and looked kindly at this young bearer of her name. "You must come and stay with us some day, my dear," she said. "We ought to know you better." Cécile blushed crimson: "I should be delighted, Mevrouw, but I am always with grand-mamma Borck." The Baron of Rollingen said little about the visit on the way home. Once only he opened his eyes, in the midst of his wife's chatter. "A tragedy in six words," he said. "I am always with grandmamma Borck."

And Harry Simmans came down to the Castle, to visit Mevrouw Elizabeth, and the Count asked him, after dinner, to stay for a day or two. Margherita took no notice. The weather being milder, the transfer of the tropical birds had been sanctioned by their medical attendant. They travelled down in glass cases, heated by spirits of wine.

"They are all that is left me of home," said the Count-ess. She cried as she let them loose in the "excrescence."

The Countess's only son, meanwhile, released from his early solitude, made friends with all the animate and inani-mate world around him. As long as his tutor remained away, he multiplied unpleasant pets and fraternized with village urchins; Monsieur de Souza, on his return, repre-sented this terrible state of affairs in no measured terms to the Count. "René s'encanaille." The words fell like a thunderbolt. It was the one thing which his whole educa-tion had been destined to avoid. The poor boy, who had been debarred from the friendship of his equals, found pleasure in the society of such children as could not dis-tinguish his peculiarities. The Count listened horror-struck. "René s'encanaille."

"He never reads," said the Countess. "Intercourse

19

with great minds is the sole education. I have always said so. Go into the library, René." And Reinout, who felt bored, wandered away, with his hands in his pockets, along the endless lines of books.

"Ma chère, I regretfully disagree with you," said the Count, following his wife into her boudoir. "The boy will get no good from all the rubbish in there. I never read through half a dozen books in my life, except when I was working for my degree. Reinout is to enter the diplomatic service. And for that he is being fitted as few men have been. He is learning by De Souza's experience what others have to learn by their own."

"Of course he will become a diplomatist," replied Margherita, languidly arranging some striped camellias. "But that is only the background. My son is to be more than that—a prophet, a teacher, an immortal!"

"Eh?" said the Count. "Oh, you mean: verses. Don't put foolish ideas into his head, Margot. Literature wouldn't keep you in bonbons, and, besides, it isn't work for a gentleman."

"And Hugo, then, who is a Count? And Musset? and Châteaubriand? And Lamartine?"

"Châteaubriand?" repeated the Count. "He is a beef-steak—or he invented one, or something. What has he to do with René?"

"Go back to your—diplomatic avocations," replied the Countess quietly. "And leave me to build up the future glory of my child."

"But why not?" said Van Rexelaer carelessly, looking at his watch. "As long as you make a gentleman of him first."

The Countess Margherita dashed her flowers violently to the ground. "Gentleman! Gentleman!" she repeated, "I am sick of the refrain, and you, Monsieur le Comte, I suppose *you* are a type of a gentleman?"

"But—Margherita—"

She came close to him. Involuntarily he shrank back. "A gentleman," she said, "is a man who breaks all the commandments—genteelly, and who keeps his—linen scrupulously clean." And she quitted the room.

Hilarius was left standing opposite his own rather stupid face in the glass. "Follies!" he said, and went to keep his appointment with—never mind.

Surely no woman was ever wholly bad. Surely not even the best of men was ever entirely worthy of a good woman.

Reinout loitered to and fro along the great, dim library. The weather was dreary outside, in the drip of a wide-spread thaw. There had been no books at the Hague, except his mother's boxes of novels. Novels were not books. These latter were for schoolmasters, professors and such-like. He now pulled out one or two from curiosity, philosophical works of eighteenth-century Frenchmen.

"Merci, Maman," he said, with a yawn, as he replaced them. He knew, disastrously, that his father thought his poetastic mother a fool.

He knew also that they differed about himself. Even now, as he left their presence, he had heard the Count begin: "Ma chère, I regretfully disagree with you—" A moment before he had had to endure the most vehement reproaches on account of his intercourse with the village-lads. Count Hilarius had been irritably violent, seeking offence where Reinout felt there was none. The boy considered himself aggrieved by the thought that his father was constantly stopping him somewhere.

Still with his hands in his pockets, he wandered into a little nondescript turret-chamber, where he found Cécile engaged at an old piano. His was not a deeply musical nature, but at this moment the melodious majesty of Beethoven swept solemnly upon his sullen mood.

He stood listening, and when she paused and looked at him—with those kind gray eyes of hers:

"What do you do, Freule," he asked suddenly, "when you don't understand?"

"How so, René?" This, evidently, was a case in point.

"About what people want you to do, I mean. And what you ought to."

"I ask God," said Cécile softly.

"Dear me! I thought you were too old to say your prayers!"

The young Freule's eyes grew troubled, and she looked as if she were anxiously searching for fit expression. But she only blushed, and murmured "Poor René."

Reinout wandered off into the hall. Why did all good people pity him? Ever since he could remember, Monsieur de Souza had called him "Fortune's Favourite."

He went up to his afternoon lessons. Tutor and pupil were reading together the memoirs of a Gentilhomme de la Chambre of Louis le Bien-aimé. Reinout thought it dull work. He was blasé at fourteen. But that was what the Count had always wanted: "There is no strength in the world," said Count Rexelaer, "equivalent to beginning life blasé."

But it had never struck him that Reinout, weary of his great world's littleness, might look out for another. Count Rexelaer did not know there was another world.

CHAPTER XXXIX.

HONEST HEARTS.

THE Chalk-house Farm was sinking to sleep under the dying day. Across its low brown roof the massive shadows broadened, seeming to pull down the heavy thatch, like a nightcap, over little windows, that blinked drowsily, black against the fading light. The few gaunt beeches which overtop the prostrate building stretched out their straggling arms to Heaven, in appeal for a covering too long withheld. Heaven answered by dropping its clouds among them and gradually wiping them out of sight. In the red-brick court-yard, between the bake-house and the living-house, a belated chicken was nervously over-doing its supper, if meals can be distinguished in a chicken's twelve hours' uninterrupted feed. A brown mongrel lay by the door and, occasionally opening one eye, stared vaguely at the four poles of the empty hay-stack. Over the whole landscape hung a gloomy calm. The gloom, not the calm, hung over Lise, who stood waiting by the long white fence which separates the farm-yard from the high-road.

Her mother came out into the twilight with a bright blue milk-pail. "He'll know soon enough, child," she said. "You needn't be in a hurry to tell him."

"Don't, mother," said the girl. Young people have no taste for irony. Lovers least of all.

"But of course your father knows best," continued Vrouw Driest, and disappeared through the low door, muttering. Hardly an hour went by but Lise heard those words from her mother's lips. They were the farm-wife's all-sufficient solace among the misfortunes and failures of life. She forgot them when anything turned out well.

There had been a time when Lise had occasionally answered: "But, mother, it was you that said—" "Hush, child, how can you be so headstrong! Of course your father knows, though *I* should not have sold that cow."

"She is over-anxious to tell him," repeated Vrouw Driest as she returned to the farm-kitchen. Peasants always communicate a thought to a number of people in succession. "I tell her he will hear it soon enough," she added, bending over the pot which simmered on the fire. The husband, a ponderous, slow-smoking man, whose very arm, where it lay inert on the table, was heavy with depression, never even moved in reply.

"I always thought it would come to this," said the wife, bustling about the kitchen. How often had she not declared that no power on earth would drag her to the Castle? But Driest, who had earned a quiet life by playing scapegoat, could not refuse the rôle to-day, when on the point of being hunted into the wilderness.

"There's the chaise," said the wife presently, and went to the door. "He's sold the filly," she added, and turned away again. "Let them do their kissing and nonsense alone," she thought, and cast a sad smile across at her husband's bent head.

"Thys," said the girl, at the gate, in the twilight. "It has come. Dievert told father this morning. The lease is not going to be renewed."

The young man checked his horse with a jerk, and, falling back, from the shock, in the light wooden chaise, he swore aloud at Count Rexelaer.

The girl said no more, walking beside the horse, as her lover slowly guided him into the stable. He also spoke very little, unharnessing, while she helped him, and beginning to whistle meditatively as he shook out the straw.

Presently she caught up a pitcher and, perhaps as an apology for her ill-tidings, went to fill it at the well. Without a word of thanks to interrupt his whistling, he took it from her, but as they crossed the courtyard together he said: " This will put off our marriage, Lise, till the Lord knows when." " Mother doesn't understand about my wanting to tell you," answered Lise, " but it didn't seem like knowing till both of us knew." He did not ask her to explain her meaning, though perhaps he hardly understood it. " Poor mother," he said, and they passed into the kitchen, where the meal lay spread beneath the dismal lamp.

" Well, Thys?" said the farmer, moving at last from his stolid despair. " I've done well," replied Thys, and, even at this moment, a note of triumph penetrated his voice. He had been away for three days, to the great Easter horse-fair at Utrecht. " There were French traders. These Frenchmen pay well." His uncle—he called him "father" —nodded solemn approval, and said " Good." That is a great deal for a farmer.

Then they sat down to supper in silence, till the mother began : " The family are back, Thys. They arrived on the day you left."

" Did they?" said Thys. His heart was heavy, but he cut himself an enormous chunk of bread.

" Yes, and I think the old Heer might have come to see us. But no doubt your father knows."

The old man looked straight across into his foster-son's eyes. " Lise has told you," he said. Thys nodded, with his mouth full.

" It's worse for you, boy. Mother and I are old."

" Speak for yourself, father," broke in his spouse. " I hope to make butter yet for twenty years, please God."

" And where'll you make it?" said the farmer.

After that a thoughtful silence fell upon the little company, not even broken when the Baron van Rexelaer suddenly stood in their midst. They shuffled awkwardly to their feet, in a movement of general embarrassment, around the half-finished meal.

"Can you let me have a cup of coffee, Vrouw Driest?" said the Baron, with extended hand.

The woman was a sour-visaged woman, but, at this mark of condescension, her expression grew positively fierce with emotion. She had lived all her life at Deynum; the Baron, to her, was still sovereignty personified. She hurried into her parlour to get one of her grandmother's eleven Japanese cups. Alas that there should be eleven! Had not Vrouw Driest's sister-in-law, on the occasion of Lise's birth, in dusting—There is an old saying, by one who knew, about "renovare dolorem." The sister-in-law is still ashamed.

There was a moment's interruption of washing and wiping. "No one that we know of has ever used this cup before, Mynheer," said the farmer's wife with pardonable pride, as she placed the bit of blue china before the Baron. "You and I, Driest," began that gentleman, abruptly, "are companions in misfortune. But I want to think that yours is preventable. Can nothing be done?"

"Ah, that's what I say," remarked the wife.

"You should have said it sooner then," retorted the farmer, turning angrily upon her. "If the Count says 'Go,' landheer, go we must."

"But need he say it? Don't think I don't love you for what you've done." He held out his hand, which the slow farmer took deferentially. "There, now that's settled, I want you to do me another favour, the next best. I want you to go up to the Castle and see the Count yourself."

"Never. We need no Counts here," burst in the wife. Then she pursed up her lips and fixed her eyes on the Baron's cup. Thys had moved his long legs under the table. Lise signed to him to keep still.

"It's no use," continued the Baron. "We poor people must bend or break. I'm broken. You'd better bend."

"We did it for the best," said Driest, a little sore.

It was this very soreness the Baron dreaded. He was not a diplomatist, but he was resolved to save these poor people.

"Look here," he said. "If the Count renews, you'll go up and thank him. Eh?" He turned to the wife.

"The farmer knows best, landheer," replied that lady promptly. *She* was a diplomatist.

"He's a thief," said the farmer slowly. "He's no Rexelaer. D—— him."

"Father!" cried Lise.

"Ay, 'father'! What's the likes of him to come among the likes of us? As soon have some false stock of my grand-uncle's breeding—he was a wild chap and went to Town for a hair-dresser—setting up at the Chalk-house Farm as a Driest!"

Music as all this might be to the Baron's ears, he saw the danger of it. "And who knows what *will* happen at the Chalk-house Farm," he said, coming round quickly to the practical side, "when you are no longer master here?" Vrouw Driest heaved a notable sigh.

"I don't care to be," replied the farmer, doggedly, "not under the new lord. Deynum isn't Deynum with a Gueux at the Castle. The Rexelaers have gone, and they were here longer than we by a matter of many hundred years. We can go where Mynheer the Baron's gone. It isn't so far as America, I suppose. Eh, Vrouw?"

"We've come back to remain," said the Baron huskily, moved to the very bottom of his heart. "I can't live anywhere else, Driest, nor can the Baroness. Now, how about you? Don't deceive yourself, my good, faithful friend. Old clodhoppers can't breathe on any clod but their own." He waved his hand to them all, and hurried away. The farmer brought down his enormous fist on the table with a crash that set all the dishes dancing. Thys smiled savagely. Vrouw Driest caught up her grandmother's cup, and laid it in her lap.

The Baron, slowly returning homewards, halted for a moment upon the little village-green. At this hour the place was quite deserted, but in the darkness you could trace the shapes of the Church and School, and other few buildings scattered around. That light yonder was Job Henniks'! There the cronies of the village were doubtless assembled, discussing the old lord and the new.

"Mynheer van Rexelaer, might I speak to you for a moment?" said a polite voice, which he did not recognise, at his side. He turned. "They told me at the priest's you would be coming this way. I am John Borck. It is, unfortunately, many years since we met."

"It is," said the Baron, stiffly, to his wife's old antagonist. They walked along the road, side by side, the Baron painfully expectant.

"The matter is purely one of business," began the Lord of Rollingen, stammering out the central thought of his previously prepared speeches, "and it is always best, I think, to transact business personally. I—I—if I understand rightly, there are some objects from the Castle you wish to do away with. If I am mistaken, I beg pardon."

"I have decided nothing as yet," said Baron Rexelaer, not in a pleasant tone of voice.

"Still, supposing you should resolve to—I understood from Cécile Borck, who is staying—look here, Rexelaer, we used to know each other well enough once. I don't want to do you a favour. Not I; I want you to do me one. You know I'm a great man for antiquities and family-histories"—Baron Rexelaer knew nothing of the kind—"now what's the use of selling portraits, for instance, to brokers? The Rexelaers and the Borcks have been closely connected in the centuries when nobody differed about religion, and a lot of your belongings must be of especial value to us. Now, why shouldn't you sell them to me, as I want them? If you like, we could easily make out an agreement, that, in the next twenty years, you or your daughter could take them back—at the same price. I think that would be fair. Or the same price and four per cent. interest. Yes, that would be fairer." This last inspiration came to John Borck in the moment of speaking and hugely delighted him.

"It can't be, Borck," said the Baron, in an unsteady voice, now. "For one thing, my wife wouldn't like it."

"Nor would mine," rose to honest John Borck's lips, but he checked the words. "It is merely a business transaction," he repeated.

"Nevertheless, I am most deeply grateful for your generous offer"—Baron Borck would have interrupted— "No, no, do not think I cannot comprehend. Your kindness even emboldens me, while refusing one service, to ask for another. Will you let me?"

"What is it?" queried cautious John Borck.

"There is a man here, one of my old farmers, who cannot get on under the new régime. He is a good man; the question is a—a personal one, regarding myself. It is Driest, of the Chalk-house, which you have long wanted to buy. If you had a farm for him, on the other side of Rollingen, I—I should look upon it as a great kindness to myself."

"I shall bear it in mind," said Borck. They had reached the Parsonage. "Permit me one question in parting," continued the Lord of Rollingen. "If you sell these things to strangers, how will you prevent Count Rexelaer's ultimately acquiring them?"

And now it will seem incredible to those who live in Koopstad and are wide-awake that this sleepy, single-thoughted country-gentleman had never even caught a glimpse of his danger.

"Remember what happened about the Castle. That was a dirty trick, I thought. I know a good deal about the

Rexelaers, more than you think. I was in no hurry to call on the people. But my cousin, you remember, married the brother."

"There is a good deal to know," said the Baron.

"Perhaps I know it. I know about the 'k' in their name, for instance. Ah, you didn't expect that, did you? I told you I was a bit of an antiquary. Now, to a great many people, that 'k' wouldn't matter a brass cent; it does to you and me, because we are old fogies. The old fogies ought to stick together in this brand-new day. You can take time to consider my proposal. I am in no hurry. Good night."

"Good night and God bless you, John Borck," said the Baron van Rexelaer. Here was a kind word from one of his own class at last.

The Lord of Rollingen was one of the richest and most powerful nobles in the country. He was a strange quiet man, of strong idiosyncrasy, who allowed his wife to do whatever she chose, except on the rare occasions when he did not want her to do it. When his young cousin Cécile, who scarcely knew her mighty kinsman, had penetrated into his room that morning with much fear and trembling, he had first been taken by surprise, then interested, then greatly pleased. He was an aristocrat down to the bottom, and therefore a just man as well as a proud. It is only your nine-tenths aristocrat who is prejudiced beyond the limits of justice.

"You are right, Cécile," had said Baron John Borck.

CHAPTER XL

OF SOME THAT RETURNED TO DEYNUM AND SOME THAT DEPARTED THENCE.

As spring went slowly deepening into summer—the process takes a long time in our Northern region!—the Countess Margherita's heart began to soften a little towards Deynum. It was by no means a cold heart; it was a warm heart benumbed. From her new conservatory—the excrescence—she would sadly watch the sun in his daily struggles to climb higher behind the gaunt rampart of distant trees, and when suddenly, one pale morning, the grim wall stood coloured over with a faint shimmer of silver-green promise, she screamed aloud to Laïssa, and went dancing away among her plants, like a butterfly, with all the parrots yelling and all the dogs wildly capering around her. Count Hilarius, who seldom took any notice of her "extravagances," looked in at the door. "What now?" he inquired, as she whirled past him, holding the furiously barking Florizel triumphantly aloft. "It is spring!" she cried back at him. "Summer is coming, *your* summer, the pale one, the second-best! Houp-là, Amarinda, ma belle!" "Oh Printemps, ô mon roi, que j'adore! Oh Printemps qui—qui—qui—ô Flore! Go away, Ilario; I cannot compose while you are by!" Count Hilarius most willingly went away.

"Laïssa," said the Countess, stopping out of breath, "I have often thought during the last long months that purgatory must be like this, all black. If only it gets a little greener,—a little greener!"

"You did not like it any better when it was white," replied Laïssa.

"And you then?" cried Margherita impatiently.

"Ah, M'am Rita,"—the mulatto shivered—"You speak of purgatory; it is hell. Paradise is flaming-hot. Hell is, like Holland, *cold*."

At the Hague things had been different. In a city the seasons do not change; only the temperature changes. And the Countess Rexelaer's temperature had been regulated by the heating-apparatus.

The great event of the season had been the return of the old family. It was reported in the village that Count Rexelaer, when told, had grown white with rage, and had sworn by high and low that such a thing should never be. Yet he could not prevent it, albeit all Deynum was his. In bygone days Father Bulbius had obtained from the Baron a life-long lease, at a nominal rent, of the house he still occupied, with the right to under-let. The Father now immediately availed himself of this privilege, and the Baroness reaped the reward of her early bounties to the Church. The old man appeared before Veronica one Sunday morning, after mass, in the full pomp of his sacerdotal robes. "We are going to occupy the house by the Church," he said. "The long walk is too much for me." Veronica bent her head, with a snort.

When Dievert brought the Count the few florins of the house-rent, that great personage screamed out that it was a conspiracy and he would have the law of the lot. But he left his new tenants in peace, nevertheless; his sister-in-law had dropped him a hint.

He scowled fiercely, with averted face, the first time he met the Baroness and Wendela in the village. But Margherita, venturing out in a close-carriage, passed an old-fashioned gentleman who made her an old-fashioned bow. She was charmed by his manner and said so at dinner, and re-

gretted that circumstances prevented their knowing their
cousins. " What do you think, chevalier? " " Madame,"
responded the gallant de Souza, " I never disagree with your
excellent judgment," and Count Rexelaer understood that
his son's tutor had just given him a lesson in manners.

The various grandees of the neighbourhood hastened to
call at the quondam Parsonage, and showed themselves
anxious to imply all permissible admiration of the comfort
the Baroness had conjured up around her. It was impossible for a room to look poor which the Baroness van Rexelaer
inhabited, and everyone declared that the Villa—" Villa," if
you like, but the Baroness preferred " Farmhouse "—was
really a delightful old place. As indeed it was; numberless
souvenirs and personal treasures lay scattered over the half-
furnished rooms, and Gustave looked after these relics of
the past, Gustave, who had returned to the family from an
enforced retirement, during their Pension-life, in the house
of a sister, whose many shiftless children had worried his
neat mind into despair. Such of the heirlooms as still possessed any market value had been sold; the rest Mynheer
van Rexelaer had ultimately ceded to Baron Borck. The
latter gentleman would have brought his recalcitrant wife
to visit the Baroness but that he dreaded to patronize in
misfortune. Everyone else came, however, except the rich
Amsterdam bankers, who forgot.

There was money enough now for simple wants, and
freedom from anxiety. The family subsisted on the annual
payment from " the Lady's Dole," and a remnant of the
Baroness's little fortune. Wendela resumed her lessons with
the village-schoolmaster. They could not make out whether
she was glad to be back or not. " I like the lessons," she
said.

Baron Borck intimated to Mynheer van Rexelaer that
the Count " would have no objection " to the family's occasionally walking in the park. He had asked him. Baron
Borck was a very influential man. Mynheer van Rexelaer

received the intimation with thanks, but did not avail himself of the permission. He walked out among the villagers, who stood aloof, deferential, but awkward ; his sole pleasures were a game with the Father or a chat at the Chalk-house Farm.

For the Driests were still at the Chalk-house Farm, and likely to remain there. It had happened on this wise. One evening Thys had returned home from the village with the news that there were to be flags and fireworks next week on the occasion of Count Rexelaer's birthday, and a state-visit of congratulation from the Commune.

"We shall soon be quit of all that," said the Farmer roughly. "I'm well-nigh through with Baron Borck's steward."

Thys went and drew off his heavy boots in the passage. Then, returning to the great blue-tiled fire-place which takes up one whole side of the kitchen, he stationed himself behind his foster-father's chair. "Well, I'll say it," he began aloud, " I've talked it over with Lise, and she says I'd better· Look here, father, now the Baron's back in Deynum, how about Joost Hakkert and Job Henniks and the rest ? "

" What are you driving at ? " replied old Driest. " Speak out, Thys. And come round from behind my chair."

But this latter command Thys—the great, long lout—preferred to ignore. " He'll be lonely here, will the Baron," said Thys boldly, " and he'll want someone to speak up for him, now. Father, I'm thinking : as the Baron's come back, it won't do for us to run away."

" You should have thought that six months sooner, then," cried the exasperated farmer, bounding in his ample arm-chair. " Get to your work, Thys, and leave thinking to clearer heads than yours."

The young fellow was slinking away obediently, but his uncle still called after him : " And you say that Lise's thoughts are as wise as yours ? "

" Lise fancied I might be right, Father."

"'Fancied.' Is that the way you young ones love each other? Hey, there she is—the hussy!"—for Lise appeared in the doorway, bearing a steaming tub—"and how about your mother? Does she also 'fancy you might be right'?"

"Oh, mother knows *you are*, father," said the girl demurely, and she added, when her lover had left the room : "So you see we are all four agreed."

Thus it came about that Farmer Driest went up to the Castle and had an interview with the Count. He came back and said he would rather not speak of the Count, nor of the interview. He did not understand the new Squire, he said. Being only a farmer, he could not know that even a great noble has sometimes, in little things, to do as his neighbours want him to. "You have behaved most disgracefully," Count Rexelaer had said. "You can stay on at the farm. Good-day."

"They are winning their way to the widest popularity," Mevrouw Rexelaer-Borck informed her mother. "Mina Borck says so, and she is the best person to know. Hilarius' pays for a Protestant parson, who is to be inducted next autumn, though I fear he is somewhat lukewarm in the face of papistical presumption. As for poor Margherita, with her painful antecedents, dear Mina lends her excellent books, but I warn her it will prove not the slightest use."

"Mina Borck is a fool, and so you may tell her," replied the irascible Dowager.—"If!" thought Mevrouw Elizabeth. —"If Hilarius intends to stand for the States Provincial in the Conservative interest, he cannot afford to make trouble with the Catholics."

"But, Mamma, ought that thought to deter him?"

The old Baroness grinned at her daughter with a full display of her pearly teeth.

"Especially, Mamma, as the Liberal Majority is overwhelming, in any case. John Borck sees to that."

"Majority or not, Rexelaer has his way to make at Court, and he must avoid all complications. He is a very

20

clever man; I admire him exceedingly, in spite of his nervous ways. I should not wonder if he died an 'Excellency.' He is worth two of your husband, Eliza, as far as
brains go."

"He cannot hold a candle to my husband!" cried Mevrouw Elizabeth indignantly, forgetting, for a moment, her
awe of the hooked nose and chin, "neither in looks, nor in
temper, nor in manners, nor in anything! His brains are
just merely his wife's money that was scraped together out
yonder, selling—"

"Well, I only said he had enough," interrupted the
Dowager impatiently. "And how about the police-sum-
mons? Is that little difficulty not yet out of the world?"

"No, indeed. Simmans purposely keeps the thing
going. I am certain he does it on purpose. He has been
down there three several times to examine her, as he says.
It is absurd."

"Is that your word?" said the fierce old Dowager. "I
should have selected another." ·

It was quite true that Simmans, the young functionary
with the sleepy stare, had been very often to Deynum. He
lounged about the Castle and grounds, and sometimes was
momentarily amiable to Jane, if she happened to be staying in the house. That young lady ignored him, or, suddenly awakened to his presence, endeavoured to make him
conversationally ridiculous. With poor success, for he had
a habit of lazily falling on his feet.

Mevrouw Rexelaer-Borck was much pained by her
daughter's behaviour, more by the young man's, and most by
her sister-in-law's. On no account would she have brought
Simmans to the house, could she have guessed that he sang
nigger songs to the banjo. In her respectable drawing-
room he had never even hinted at this unpleasing accomplishment.

She quarrelled with Margherita about more things than

these musical performances which formed the delight of the whole menagerie, with the exception of the howling dogs. She had quietly arranged, for instance, to have the idolatrous emblems removed from the closed chapel. Suddenly the Countess intervened—"with disgraceful vehemence," Elizabeth afterwards complained to her husband—"and language! You would have said a Scheveningen fish-wife!" "They are *my* ancestors," cried Margherita, who had really taught herself to believe this, and she stamped her foot. "And it is my religion!" "Pooh," replied the indignant daughter of the Borcks. "Your ancestors and your religion! They are both equally genuine. I would not give two-pence for either, or both!" After that, she departed from the Castle, which was a pity, for she took Jane with her, and Jane's hesitating lover ungallantly remained behind. He explained that he must "complete his inquiry."

And this is how he completed it. With a rapidity which astounded him.

> "Ah, pooty Miss Jemima, why-y-y
> You make dis han'some niggah cry-y-y?"

—"chorus, Laïssa, chorus!" Margherita clapped her hands. Laïssa and the parrots shrieked undistinguishable sounds. Florizel, seated at his mistress's feet, protested dismally, with uplifted head, in spite of slaps. The singing-birds all sang their loudest, increasing, as the hubbub rose higher, in their efforts to overpower it. Margherita laughed and shouted for glee.

> "'You'll be sorry nuf, when han'some niggah die!'"

Simmans stopped, out of breath, and laid aside his instrument. "I like it," began Margherita presently, and her voice had entirely changed its tone. "Almost, if one closes one's eyes, it were possible to imagine oneself out in the soft warm moonlight, away yonder, beneath the veranda. Of course the words are very different, but the sing-song is just the same. Laïssa does the crooning far better than you, Monsieur Simmans; still, you do it quite well enough for a poor ignorant European." Laïssa grinned. "The gentleman's songs are good, are they not, Laïssa?"

"Ours are better," said the waiting-woman mechanically.

"You are rude. I feel thirsty with laughing. Go, get me something to drink. Something cool, and very sweet, and that quenches one's thirst." The mulatto slipped away.

"Oh the loveliness of that moonlight!" began Margherita, left alone with her "judge," as she was pleased to call him. "You Northerners have no idea of 'living.' It is not worth one's while to *be*."

"I can see loveliness," he replied, fingering his banjo, "everywhere. It is a thing of environment. Never, before I came here, had I an idea how lovely this country can be."

"Indeed?" she said. "Deynum? But you must have a most extraordinary taste."

"The dead earth," he continued, "is not beautiful till the sun rises upon it. I have seen the sun rise on Deynum, Comtesse."

"At this time of the year? Do you expect me to believe that? Since when do young gentlemen from the Hague get up to enjoy a November sunrise?"

True, it was November. How long was this kind of thing to continue? Was she only a beautiful clod, or as sly as she was beautiful? No matter; this long-drawn sentimentalism led nowhere.

"I'm so sorry about the annoyance you have endured," he said briskly, "but, of course, the affair will be hushed up. I hear it has created much ill-feeling at the Palace. Your husband's official position, you know. Never mind; I have the whole thing in my hands, and you shall not hear of it again."

"At last?" said Margherita, "and when, Monsieur, will you take that final step?"

"Immediately." He struck a few notes on his banjo. "Shall I sing to you again?" he said.

"Yes, do. It is rather fun. Rollo, Jocko, attention, mes amis! We are going to begin!"

"Ah, but what I sing is for you alone!"

"I could not possibly be so selfish. Flora enjoys it too much."

"You will not be offended?"

"No. Why?"

And with an expression of tenderest feeling pouring from his half-shut eyes he sang in a rollicking, joking, devil-may-care voice:

> ' "Oh, pootiest M'am Rita, why-y-y
> You make dis wretched niggah cry-y-y?
> Will you nevah hear him sigh-igh-igh?" '

The countenance of the lady on the sofa suddenly clouded over. She flung herself forward, with a flash like a snake's, and struck the instrument, in the vehemence of her lithe brown arm, out of the singer's hands, across the brick floor of the conservatory.

"Encore une contravention!" she said, and looked him fiercely in the face. "Dressez procès-verbal, Monsieur le Substitut." And then, as Laïssa entered with a tray, "Tell the Jonker Reinout, Laïssa, that I should like to look at his sketches, now."

That evening the family at the Castle sat down to dinner alone.

A fortnight later "the Countess R——, wife of an Officer connected with the Royal Household," was sentenced to a fine in one of the petty courts. And shortly before Christmas the engagement was announced of the Freule Jane van Rexelaer with Simmans, "the son of Simmans, the Secre-

tary-General, you know." Presently the young lady received
a parcel from her kind aunt at Deynum, containing a guitar-
player, one of those beautiful "étrennes" which overflow
the Paris confectioners' windows at that season of the year.
The doll's head was empty, but the next post brought a box
of the perishable sweets called "fondants."

"Insert them from the outside, my dear Jane," wrote
the Countess, "in this mannikin I send you from Deynum."

"Is there a joke?" asked Mevrouw Elizabeth, who, at
that moment, forgave even Margherita.

"No, indeed," replied Jane gravely.

"The 'Fondants' are delicious," said sweet-toothed
Rolline.

CHAPTER XLI

"COUSINS."

So summer faded into winter, and winter blossomed into summer at Deynum, and "the Family" went away to the Hague before Christmas and did not return till quite late in the spring. Count Hilarius was now an important personage in Court circles. Everybody liked him; he was so obliging and unpretending, and he had plenty of money. "And that magnificent place in the country, you know, which had fallen into the hands of the younger branch of the family, till it came back to the Count through his wife. An extraordinary story. Yes, he is a very great man, is van Rexelaer van Deynum."

Margherita went to several balls and looked splendid in her diamonds. She began to like society, pleased with her success, once she had picked herself off the sofa and admired her figure in the glass. "I shall be ugly soon enough," she said. People declared that she had "du chic," and stopped to stare with sudden interest at the heiress of the house of "La Jolais-Farjolle—one of the greatest families in Europe! You can see it by the way she carries her head." Nothing is more amazing than the ignorance, in these matters, of "the few who know."

And the Countess even gave a couple of great receptions, one towards the end of the season, a second-best one, in honour of the marriage of the Freule Jane. "Rolline must do better," Count Hilarius remarked pointedly to his sister-in-law. When she repeated the words—two

hours later—to her husband, " He is mad with ambition,"
said the tranquil judge.

A week or two after the house at Deynum had been
definitely shut up, the Baron one morning stole timidly
into the park. This day he did not get farther than the
sight of the shuttered windows. Twenty-four hours later
he was trying to pat one of the deer. It was a mistake.
His wiser daughter curtly refused to accompany him.

And their life flowed on smoothly, monotonously, not
unhappily withal. The Baroness went among her poor
more diligently than ever ; the Baron pottered about in the
village, surrounded by a halo of pitiful respect. He was
too gentle-natured to resent the pity. And of evenings
Father Bulbius would drop in for his game and a glass of
" King's Wine."

" The Count has not got *this*," said Mynheer van Rexe-
laer, tapping his glass. " Hush, mon ami," interposed the
Baroness with a smile. " You are right, my dear," said the
Baron.

Wendela alone found no strength in her heart for rec-
oncilement with life. Perhaps because to her that loss
was an anticipation which for her parents was only a regret. She had resolved, from the first, to remain pitiless
to her own sorrow, and they who have the metal to make
such a resolution seldom lack the grip to maintain it. Between her parents and herself it had built up a barrier
which she hated and resented without the power, or the
wish, to remove it. She lived an emotional existence, not
outside but inside her even life with them, in an inner
chamber of which her firm hand kept the key. Silent almost to moroseness, she would occasionally break out into
demonstrative affection towards her mother, but always
with a perceptible jerk, as if recalling how much she loved
her. To her father she was dutiful and reserved, with a
conscious check on her thoughts of him. For she felt
herself, unadmittedly, to possess one of those strong-willed

yet impulsive characters which are habitually rendered wretched by the consciousness of having spoken—and thought—not at all, or too much. A faithful, truthful woman's nature, strong-hearted and clear-brained, one of those women the superficial write down "disagreeable," because of their straight lips and solemn eyes.

Considering all things, she was receiving a fair education, from the schoolmaster and her mother combined, an education which would prove absolutely useless in these days of diplomas and examinations, but of such things the Baroness knew nothing, excepting that they were a sin against Genesis iii.

One evening Wendela looking up from "Ta douleur, Duperrier," which she was committing to memory, abruptly apostrophized her father, in his arm-chair by the fire. "Papa, when I am grown up, shall I be obliged to earn my own living?" "No, Wendela; girls like you cannot earn their own living. What makes you ask?" "I wanted to know," replied Wendela. The Baron smiled contentedly in the shade. Wendela, on her parents' death, would be entitled to the entire capital of "The Lady's Dole." For, then, at any rate, Strum must rest convinced that there would never again be a Baroness Rexelaer.

If the girl had a pleasure, it was her hidden dream-life, to which she clung, even while conscious of having long outgrown it. She still loved to weave brave fancies around her Pilgrim Knight, not pretty little fairy idylls, but strong, bright tales of chivalry; wrong redressed and innocence upheld. Life was dark and thunder-threatened,—devil-haunted, as her mother said; through it rode her Hero of the Closèd Visor, in a trail of light.

"There is a boy," she said once to her mother, breaking one of the long periods of silence, so common between them.

"What do you mean, child?"

"At the Castle. There is a boy?"

" Yes, certainly; you know there is."

" I hate him."

" Wendela, you are now fifteen. You are too old for such childish sayings."

Wendela bit her lips.

There was no reason for anyone to hate Reinout. Certainly the reason could never be envy. He was now sixteen, and the least enviable of youths.

When first the boredom of Monsieur de Souza's stories settled heavy on his powdered and periwigged young head, Reinout had turned right and left, as has been shown, in vain hope of escape. The dry books of the Deynum library disgusted him; if he dashed away into the wide liberty of the woods and fields, he saw a scornful smile go wreathing his father's bloodless lips. And as he grew in years, he understood more clearly that his bringing-up was not like that of other boys. Old people thought him charming—a dangerous sign. He told the Countess de Bercy at dinner a long story about the late Empress of Russia's strange passion for bananas which were brought over direct from the West Indies, and " after her death no one ever rescinded the order, and recently the Emperor came on a cellar piled up with baskets of rotting fruit." He kissed the Countess's hand as he bowed her from her chair, and he caught the scowl of disgust at his " confounded priggishness" in her student-nephew Ivo's eyes.

" Papa," said Reinout next morning to his father, " I should like to learn about everything, like other boys."

" You can have masters, when we get back to the Hague, as you had last winter, René," replied the Count. " What is it you want particularly to learn ? "

" All about everything," burst out Reinout, and then he felt what a stupid answer that was for a lad of his age. " I mean," he added hastily, " I want to know why things are like this and what is going to change them. And about right and wrong, and suffering, and the end of it all."

" You will attend a confirmation class in a year or two," said Count Rexelaer coldly. "As for the rest, you are rather vague. If you mean political economy, you will have enough of that for your diplomatic examination. You will find it is all empty talk." And Count Rexelaer walked out of the room, leaving his son considerably nonplussed.

In sheer despair Reinout precipitately leaped into independent thought at an age when most boys still allow their teachers to think for them. He became a source of constant vexation to M. de Souza. " Why," he said one morning to that estimable " Court Circular," " do the villagers live in little houses and we in a Castle ? "

" You know very well that such is God's Ordinance," replied the Chevalier impatiently.

" But all men are equal," persisted Reinout mischievously. "And there seems to be no reason why all men should not be gentlemen, too."

" All men are not equal, and you know it. That was a lie of the French revolution. But if you mean that money has nothing to do with being a gentleman, you are right."

" I like the French revolution," retorted René, knowing nothing about it. " I wish it had succeeded."

After this, Monsieur de Souza felt that his mission was ended. He continued to live with the family, but, shortly before Reinout's sixteenth birthday, the boy received another tutor, a very clever scholar although not a cultured one. Reinout preferred Monsieur de Souza, with his old-world ideas of honour, yet he could not complain, having asked for the change. Besides, he now studied the Dutch Constitutional System and Political Economy, and International Law and a number of other sciences, useful and ornamental.

Count Rexelaer warmly thanked the Chevalier for the complete success of his plan. Undoubtedly it had worked well in many ways. Informed in a pleasantly cynical manner, of the littleness of all the world's greatnesses and the insipidity of its pleasures, Reinout never even experienced that delightful curiosity of naughtiness which leads so many boys astray. He did not want to lift a veil which had already been lifted for him with a neat arrangement of draperies. He had "seen the world." That is, he had been shown, as in a peepshow, one little corner of it, tastefully laid out in flower-beds, an Eden, whose Adams and Eves have long ago lost all that made a Paradise, except, perhaps, their naked shamelessness.

He did not like the city, at least not that stuccoed part of it in which he lived. He was eager to get back to Deynum and glad of the Count's permission to start a day or two before the others, with his tutor. "And see the fires are lighted," said Margherita. "I feel sure we ought to have waited till June."

Reinout, immediately on arriving, went out into the full beauty of the May afternoon. The place looked glorious, he thought, so fresh and green and quiet. He drew a deep breath of healthful air, air strong with the awakening of springtide, amid the rustle of the mighty oaks. "Oh, delicious," he said.

The great park lay peaceful around him, in its own majestic loneliness. Here and there the sober deer moved vaguely behind the trees. A dragon-fly went sailing past, and suddenly Reinout felt how spacious God is. Only Man is cramped.

Presently the chapel came in sight, in its tangle of sheltering ferns. He smiled as he remembered a recent difference of opinion between his mother and aunt Elizabeth. Mevrouw Rexelaer-Borck had suggested utilizing the little spire as a dove-cot; Margherita had objected, strenuously, and there had been a scene.

Reinout stepped off the path and went round by the

chancel, where a sight met him for which he was certainly not prepared. High up, on the broad ledge outside one of the arched windows, a tall girl was perched, her feet hanging down ungracefully, her face pressed against the glass. Of course he recognised her at once, though he had never seen her before but from a distance. And she, hearing the soft swish of his approaching steps, turned round hastily, in a whirlwind of long, dark hair, lost her balance, gave a cry of impatience, and came down with a rush. He ran forward and caught her.

"Not hurt, I hope?" he said, steadying himself, and her, under the shock.

"You needn't have stopped me, thank you," she answered roughly, and stood panting, not only from the fall. "I was coming down," she said.

The twinkle which came into his eyes said plainly: "Is that your usual way of doing it?" But that kind of courageous fib was not one which Reinout, "splendide mendax," would take exception at.

If Wendela had a good quality, however, it was straightforwardness. "Of course I lost my hold," she added hastily. "But that was your fault." She felt furious with him for having caught her dangling there.

"I am so sorry," he said meekly. "I hadn't an idea. Nobody ever comes near this place, you know."

"They used to come," she answered quickly. "And *that* didn't use to be there then." She pointed to an ugly stain of orange damp. "But they were our people," she added. "It is different."

"They are my people too," said the youth, smiling. "I am Reinout van Rexelaer."

She flushed. "They are not everybody's people," she replied recklessly. She felt very high and mighty, though conscious of discovering the very weaknesses she would fain have hid. Being fifteen, and a woman, she was tremulously scornful of male children of seventeen. "I suppose I must apologise for intruding," she said magnificently, and gathered her scant skirts about her and departed.

Reinout asked his father, as soon as that gentleman arrived, to have the chapel cleaned.

"Why not?" said the Count, who always said "Why not?" when careless what he said.

A month or two later the young fellow met his ungracious "cousin" again. He was riding down a quiet lane in the full white flame of a July noon. The dusty trees and half-hid wayside-flowers slept, still but dreamy, beneath the blazing splendours of the sky. Reinout's horse heaved its moist and fragrant flanks to the creak of the saddle, in all the deliciously strong reserve of a walking-pace. Reinout himself was moodily thinking of nothing, and he came upon Wendela where she dozed against a hawthorn-hedge, a book and a basket of wild roses in her lap.

She stopped him with a gesture, as he took off his cap. She had been dreaming of her dear "Knight Pilgrim," and she looked up,—out of the dulness of her daily life, at this courtly cavalier with the checked knickerbockers and olive cheeks. "Thank you," she said, "about the Chapel." She blushed, and suddenly he saw that she was charming.

"Oh, my father ordered that to be done," he answered lightly.

"No, it was you," insisted Wendela. "When Papa came home and told Mamma, I knew it was you." She hesitated. "I want you to do me one more favour. You couldn't let me into the Chapel, I suppose, just once?" His answer did not follow immediately, and, as the seconds slowly fell upon her waiting heart, she turned and fled. In a moment he had caught her up. "Freule, Freule," he cried piteously, "you are losing all your flowers!" She stood still, gasping, in the broiling July sun. "Of course you can go to the Chapel," he added. "I will ask my father for the key."

"Pooh!" she said, so vigorously that his horse shied.

She lifted her firm eyes to his, and suddenly he saw that she was also beautiful. "Nobody must know that I asked you," she continued. "I want to go in the dead of night. Just once."

"Nonsense. And the watchman?"

"I knew the watchman's hours, before ever you had heard of him," she retorted. "Do you think *I* am afraid of the night in Deynum?"

"Freule," he made answer in "a still, small voice," "I shall be outside the Chapel to-night, at twelve o'clock, with the key. At the risk of my life I shall abstract it from my father's desk! Till then the Holy Saints have you in their keeping; fair maiden, Good day."

She thought he was laughing at her religion, but what can you expect of a Gueux? With nervous hand she drew a little book from under her tumbled flowers. "Take this," she said. "Don't tell anybody I had it. The schoolmaster gave it me a year ago."

"But why should I take it?"

"Because it's the dearest thing I have. There!" And, dropping the book on his knee, she left him. This time he did not follow her.

"Rather a disagreeable child," he thought, as he sat looking after her retreating figure, twisted in the saddle, her book in his careless hand.

Said she to herself on her way homeward: "We are quits. I've paid him, for what I wanted most, with the dearest thing I had. I hate him. And, as Papa says, pay your enemy, however you may treat your friend. Mamma doesn't know; she hates nobody. As if it were right to love thieves."

CHAPTER XLII

THE DAWN OF THE HIGHER LIFE.

Reinout, walking his horse in the blazing sunshine, peeped curiously into the cheaply-bound little volume which was her "dearest thing on earth."

"Verses!" he said with ready scorn. "All women are alike."

He knew enough about verses. Sometimes he read the books his mother brought him and sometimes he praised them unread. "Always say 'yes' to a woman," the Chevalier was wont to remark, "if you feel it would hurt her to hear you say: No."

> "O mon âme.
> "O ma flamme.
> "O que je t'aime.

That is poetry.

> "Toujours du même."

"None of my talent has descended to my child," sighed Margherita. "And yet I feel sure he will be some sort of a genius. Perhaps a Prime Minister." "A what?" asked the Count, and walked away to dissemble his laughter. He rejoiced, however, to think that his wife had come round to his view, whatever her road.

"Well, she begins young with her love-ditties," thought Reinout, but, nevertheless, on his return, he settled himself in a window-seat with the book. It was a Belgian edition of Victor Hugo's "Les Voix Intérieures."

He glanced at the first page. The opening words struck him.

"This Age is great and strong . . ."

The quietly impressive words, so unlike much of Victor Hugo's later redundancy, sank slowly into his soul. Here was a gospel of the time, which met him half-way on his hap-hazard path. "Are you looking for me?" It said. "I am here."

When he had finished, he turned back and began again. He had never read other poetry before than love-songs and bouts-rimés.

And then he plunged headlong into the piece which follows, that magnificent poem on the death of the exiled Charles X. Here the novice soon floundered out of his depth, but he still held on, borne irresistibly forward by the rush of the rhythm, as all must understand who appreciate the sublimest of spouters. It is impossible to stop; the very bewilderment of the reader twists him helplessly onwards amid those whirlpools of eloquence. And in all the Titan's endless volumes Reinout could not have lighted on a poem more calculated to impress him than this one. Aristocrat as he must ever remain in all the prejudices of his bringing-up, lover as he had been destined to become, from childhood, of that lowly human greatness which your mere aristocrat ignores, this song of tenderest reconciliation struck chords within his being of whose existence his incompleteness had never been aware. And when he reached, with palpitating heart and eager breath, the great finale:

"Oh Poesy, to heaven on frighted wing thou fliest!"

he started to his feet, and stood staring before him, into a new gulf yawning ahead—or was it a visionary ladder, whose top is hid in Heaven? A world of illusion, Idea—the soul-world of beautiful hopes and fancies—the world in which all men are brothers, great and strong and greatly

21

worthy—a world at which the cynic laughs, with tears for laughter—; at last he beheld it; uplifted on the pinions of his ignorance, into cloudland,—and beyond that,—to the sun! He will never forget that moment, although to this day he cannot tell you, in intelligible prose, what took place in his soul. O the sweetness of it! The sadness of it! The beautiful, sorrowful hope! He did not know what he was saying, as he stumbled on through a wilderness of magnificent words. But gradually a single thought stood out clear among all this confusion of greatnesses, the majesty—not of your highnesses and excellencies and eminences—but of the naked Soul of man. He had been yearning for it, searching for it, unwittingly; at last he could grasp it, and read the riddle of life.

All that afternoon he hurried upwards, a breathless explorer on Alpine heights. Like an Indian Prince from his father's palace, he had escaped out of the gilded cage where the neat canaries warbled, away into the regions of the angels' song, "Peace on earth, good-will among men. Hallelujah!" His soul was drunken with poesy. He tore off the kid glove from his heart.

He was utterly unreasonable and nonsensical, full of clap-trap and tall-talk and foolishness. Yes, thank God; he was all that at last.

"What is it? What is the matter, René?" asked the Countess at dinner. "Oh nothing." Of course. She wearied of asking him. But she found him in the library, late that evening, poring over a large volume, half a dozen others scattered around. He looked up impatiently, as she came closer, and tenderly laid her hand on his shoulder. "What have you got there?" she asked. "Ah, that is right. He is pretty; is he not?"

"Oh yes," he replied savagely, but he went and opened the door very courteously for her and touched her brow with his lips. Then he returned to his Prophet, his Priest of the Most High!

A couple of hours later he was standing, in the soft summer darkness, before the empty altar of the hushed little chapel, by Wendela's side.

"It is desecrated," said the girl in a low voice. "You have desecrated it. I am glad to have seen it once more. From the window up there I could just reach the tip of the Pilgrim's helmet. Do you know which is the Pilgrim? No, poor boy, you know nothing. I will show you."

The chapel was very softly lighted by the radiance of the moon-filled night; busts and tablets stood out gently in a glamour of silvered gloom.

Mechanically Reinout followed the daughter of the real Rexelaers as she led him from monument to monument, telling in an awe-struck whisper, stories of the men and women whose passion-laden existences had sunk to rest beneath these effigies and urns. "Perhaps they are listening now," she said, "to hear if I tell you right?" The heavy night-air breathed warm about the pair. A little rustle awoke in the aisle. She caught hold of his arm.

"Isn't it a strange thought," whispered Reinout, "that all the lives of these dead men and women are concentrated, as it were, in you and me? You and me, come to visit them together in the dead of night."

"Papa says—," she began, and then she turned passionately upon him: "These are mine," she said, "mine only. Do you understand, you—Reinout Rexelaer? All the rest was mine once too, and these are still."

"But, Freule—" he stammered.

"Oh don't pity me; I won't have your pity. I am proud of our shame. Some day, perhaps, my dead, who are not really dead, might recover me the rights of which your father robbed us. And then what would be left to you?"

"Only myself," he replied, with a sorry, half-amused smile.

This answer impressed her, but she fought against the sensation. "And what is yourself?" she asked, her delicate little nose high in air. "With us it is different. Rich or beggared, high or humble, as Papa says, what need we care? For, ours is the greater glory, even in disgrace."

"I envy you that conviction," he answered thoughtfully, and with no suspicion of a sneer.

She held out her hand on the Chapel-steps.

"Good-bye, Knight Pilgrim."

CHAPTER XLIII

THE DAWN PROVES CLOUDY.

" WELL, I shall say it," declared Veronica. " Why not ? "

" What ? " asked the Father.

" Does your Reverence not know ? Then I shall keep my own counsel. But *my* opinion is : why should anyone be afraid of their betters ? If really our betters, the less reason to be afraid. And if not—" Veronica whisked a dish off the table and herself from the room.

Father Bulbius bent over the tattered volume on his knees, leisurely filling his pipe with the finest of Turkish tobaccos. He was no longer the happy possessor of an untidy snuggery ; the new house contained but two rooms on the ground floor, and Veronica had refused to abandon the " parlour." Occasionally the latter uncomfortable apartment would be honoured with a state visit from the Chevalier de Souza, who was both a freethinker at heart and a Catholic in etiquette, and confessed and communicated at Easter. Other intercourse with the Castle there was none. The brief enjoyment of Reinout's friendship had ended in a ceremonious salute.

Veronica, on her part, had no proper appreciation of ceremony. Having made up her mind to bestow a piece of it on the gentlefolks, she called out one day from the door of " our hovel," as she chose to designate the Parsonage, " Hey, Mynheer ! You are the Jonker from the Castle ? "

" Of course I am," replied the young man, standing still.

" I know you are. There's something I want to say to

you, Jonker. I've no more reason to love the Baron's family than you have. They've turned us out of our house as you've turned them out of theirs, and without paying, which is worse. But when it comes to keeping a woman away from the place she is used to pray in, twice a day for years, and all her ancestors lying round awaiting her, I say that it's a cruel thing. And I'd say the same to the Count your father, if I thought he'd listen to the likes of me. But I think he looks prouder than you, in spite of your haughty face that God gave you to go and be a Count with, as Counts there must be in this world below, though not in the hereafter." And she retreated into the house, leaving Reinout very much troubled in mind.

He did not willingly ask favours of a father who never conceded anything unless it was not a favour; after consultation with the Chevalier, he broached the subject to Margherita. To his surprise the countess immediately sat up, said, "Quite right. I understand," and went in to her husband; but that gentleman, immersed in his buttery-books, and annoyed by the interruption, contented himself with answering: "The question, like the people, is buried. What is buried had best lie still." Margherita came out to her son in the hall: "He won't," she said with flashing eyes. "And yet the whole place is mine." She went back to her occupation, which was teasing Florizel.

Reinout shrugged his shoulders and returned to his books. He had favourite authors nowadays, and they were fast molding his opinions: Byron, Shelley, De Lamartine, the aristocrat singers of freedom, and that incomparable Seer who had first flashed the light o'er his path. Of the "Revolt of Islam," for instance, he could reel off whole passages, though never quite clear as to who revolted or against what. He had not spoken to Wendela again; sometimes, when happening to awake at night, he would erroneously imagine her standing alone by the chancel window—as if Wendela ever broke promises, good or bad. But as a rule, he slept excellently well, and awoke in the morning, from a dreamless slumber, to dream.

"My dear Count," said M. de Souza one day, the quiet old gentleman who did nothing but dance attendance on the Countess and complain of the weather. "Things are going wrong with René. He is nearly nineteen, and he reads in the woods. Your system was wise, but you are prolonging it—excuse me—unwisely. He is farouche."

The Count tapped the ground nervously with his foot. "The other man says he is doing excellently," he replied, "and hopes to get him ready for his diplomatic examination in eighteen months more." The "other man" was one of those silent haters of the rich who fawn upon them. A republican himself, he tried imperceptibly to influence his pupil. The pupil distrusted him.

Count Rexelaer, while rejecting advice, set himself quietly to watch his son. And these observations soon culminated abruptly in the question: "Why do you never go and see so-and-so, Reinout? And so-and-so? Or what's-his-name?"

"Oh, bother what's-his-name!" said René.

"Still, it seems to me, that, as young men of your own rank—"

"I hate young men of my own rank."

The following academical year found Reinout at Leyden. A Dutch university is not a nice place. To enjoy its life you must be both exceedingly childish and exceedingly dissolute. The pupil of M. de Souza found himself utterly at sea, and retired into his shell, which he beautified by all the means in his power. To say that at this period he resembled his hero Shelley would be to create an erroneous impression, yet, with his far greater (hearsay) knowledge of "society," he had much of that poet's splendidly ignorant scorn of the conventionalities which galled him. He was full of a passive yearning for the Millennium, the Apotheosis of the Human by itself which Victor Hugo believes to be an approaching fact. He had no clear notion how the thing was to be started, but, meanwhile, he bought statuettes and engravings, and studied a little art, and disliked dirt and beggars (always giving to the latter), and loved the poor. The young men at the University did not share his horror of dirt (some kinds), and they loved the poor in a less platonic manner than he. They said he was queer. That was the greatest of sins in their eyes, for they were all exactly alike.

CHAPTER XLIV.

THE IRON HAND.

"I SHOULD like to speak to you a moment, Father, if you please," said Reinout one memorable autumn evening, as the family rose from table. He was now twenty-two, and had spent four lazy, luxurious years at Leyden. He was handsome and well dressed, and outwardly pleasingly proper.

"Certainly, my boy," responded Count Rexelaer, graciously. "Come and have a cigar." Inwardly he said: "Debts?" Few fathers of undergraduates would have required the interrogation.

Reinout placed himself leisurely in front of the mantelpiece, and deliberately lighted his pipe. He had come down unexpectedly to Deynum.

"I took my degree to-day," he said, ·quietly pressing down the burning tobacco with his fusee.

"What?" cried the Count, in a tone of genuine indignation. "And how about your farewell banquet? Reinout, you are joking."

Inviolable custom requires that the Dutch student shall leave the University in a blaze of prescriptive festivity. In justice to Reinout it must be added that the whole thing, like all Dutch student-festivals except "Masquerade," means merely: drink.

"There wasn't any farewell party," replied the young man. "I'm not going to have one. I think it's a bore."

Then he took his eyes off his pipe and looked anxiously across at his father.

Count Rexelaer did not return the look. He sat gazing moodily into the fire; the autumn night was chilly. At length he said, in quite a sad voice, "I was poor, and I had eleven four-in-hands." *

A moment afterwards he added: "You must have gone to a lot of other men's parties, and it seems very shabby to make no return. Perhaps the matter doesn't strike you in that light? I'm sure I don't know how it strikes you."

"On that score you may make yourself easy," replied his son. "I never went to anybody's parties. I joined some of the better societies, of course, but when I discovered the men were always getting drunk, I stopped away. Besides, I'm the first of my year to leave."

"You must have done nothing but work!" cried the Count.

"No, indeed; or I should have gone a year sooner."

"I rejoice that I have so clever a son." Count Hilarius rose and walked to the door. "You must have understood, Reinout," he said, with one of his irritable glances, "that I did not send you to the University to rush through it. Your news has taken me disagreeably by surprise. You must allow me a little time to digest it."

"I have no debts," began Reinout.

"I wish you had," said his father, bitterly, and closed the door.

Reinout remained standing, a meditative, graceful, regretful figure, with drooping pipe. He had expected some pleasure from the announcement of his sudden and successful termination of a career he had loathed from the first. "The Chevalier and Victor Hugo," he was wont to aver, "surely that is enough education for any man. The Chevalier for the fictions and Hugo for the realities." He was

---

* Dutch University custom.

shocked by the sincerity of the Count's disappointment. Unfortunately, he could never understand how clear, to the man himself, were the Court Comtproller's lights.

"Ah well!" he said, listlessly, and opened the door because the room was so hot. Then he took up a number of the Bibliothèque Universelle; the smoking-room table was covered with reviews—his doing; "As long as you leave me my Figaro," his father had said.

Laïssa's voice sounded across the vestibule, singing softly to her mistress:

"O rose, ô fleur, ô jeune fille!"

With an exclamation of impatience, the son of the house crossed over to the door again and shut it.

Next morning the Count did not put in an appearance, but M. de Souza dawdled over his coffee cup, with hands as transparent as the porcelain, humming and hawing and gently coughing as he sopped his roll. Margherita always breakfasted in her room. "I can take nothing before noon," she protested, "but chocolate." So she had a big bowl of that, with an abundance of cream and half a dozen French almond cakes.

For a long time the Chevalier said nothing. He was too perfect a gentleman to "make conversation," unless it was wanted. Besides, he was growing old, and the difficulty of disguising this fact at table sufficiently engrossed him. At length he began flicking a crumb or two from his sleeve.

"Your father has told me, René," he said, gently. "Of course he is grieved; so am I. You disappoint all our hopes. They were many."

Reinout listened humbly. He might despise the old nobleman's teachings; the teacher he could never otherwise than love.

"That, perhaps, might appear of but little account to you—"

"No, indeed," interrupted Reinout, eagerly.

The Chevalier waved his hand. "So I willingly believe. Disregard of the feelings of others, that most vulgar of faults, has never been yours. But I was desirous to add: You disappoint your own hopes as well. Your father says he does not know *what* you want. Nor do I. But of one thing I am sure; you want to be a good man, and a great. Good, certainly; great, probably. Is it not so?"

"I am much obliged for your kind opinion of me," murmured Reinout.

"Not a bit. We know each other, we two. Well, you insist upon going your own way to your object. You refuse all advice; you reject all precedent; you are eccentric, *new*. It is an immense responsibility. If you fail, it is you, personally, that bear the blame. Most men prefer that their faults should be those of the system they live in. And there is every chance of your failing. Whatever may be permissible at the end of a great career, nothing, at the beginning, is so fatal as eccentricity."

Reinout sat chipping a crust on his plate, with a vigour which scattered the crumbs.

"And, my dear boy"—the Chevalier bent forward, kindly confidential—"I think you have hardly realized how great that career is likely to be. You are placed, by an Almighty Providence, on a summit, destined to influence the history of your country, and benefit your compatriots. You turn and, in quest of the sunlight above you, you deliberately walk down hill. Once more, the responsibility you assume single-handed is immense."

"My God!" cried the pupil, with suddenly uplifted eyes. "I assume no responsibility! I only want to leave off being a gilded gentleman and to become a manly man at last."

M. de Souza paused in the act of rising, his keen eye filling with affection. "Be thankful," he said, "that your chains are gilded. We all have to wear them. I had not half your chances, René. I threw them away. And I am

—here." He wheezed a little—his asthma was very bad of late—and then tottered, with his failing dance-step, from the room.

Reinout remained alone, twisting the seal-ring upon his little finger. "The velvet glove," he muttered.

A few minutes later he met his father in the hall. The Count held a newspaper in his hand.

"It is true, then," said the Count, and pointed to the paper. "Do you know, Reinout, to the last I half hoped you were joking."

"I should not have ventured."

"The reality is worse than the joke could have been. And your academic dissertation? Am I to be permitted to see that?"

"I have a copy for you in my portmanteau," replied Reinout. He had meant to give it to his father the night before. "Hang it all!" he thought, "I ought to have let him have the thing before he asked for it." "Father," he continued aloud, "I am sorry to have vexed you. I—I daresay I am a bit of a fool at times. I will do whatever you desire."

"My good child!" cried Hilarius, jerking round at the foot of the great staircase, among the oleanders, and facing his stalwart son, "you talk as if *I* were your enemy! I desire nothing but that, while you are preparing for your appointment as 'attaché,' you 'go out,' this winter, like other young men! And, look here, René, I'll give you a phaeton and pair of your own."

Reinout clasped his father's proffered hand and wrung it silently. And his heart was soft with love and shame.

CHAPTER XLV.

COUNT REXELAER was, at heart, a melancholy man. But he was also constitutionally a grumbler, whose ever-anxious ambition no good fortune could appease. And to his honour be it said that he confined all his grumbling to his family-circle, while heroically smiling all day at Court.

And every man has his troubles; at least, so every man says. At Court the Count's sun was still in the ascendant, but at Deynum it had never fought its way out of the clouds. Truth to tell, Count Hilarius was not born to country-squiredom. His neighbours laughed when he stuck in the mud with his varnished boots, and shot a setter. He bullied his farmers in the wrong way, and patronized indiscreetly, and whatever he did "different" was writ down to the good of his predecessor. A vacancy having occurred in the States Provincial, the Count and the Baron were pitted against each other, much to the latter's initial dismay. And the Lord of the Manor actually found himself beaten by eight votes, chiefly through Baron Borck's remaining neutral at the eleventh hour. "It is not a Parliament-election; let the poor old man have this small compensation," the Baron of Rollingen had obstinately replied to all his wife's appeals. She did not argue with him. She had tried that during the first year of their marriage.

The defeated Candidate, in his fury, talked of shutting

up the Castle, to avoid contact with his rival. And this unfortunate election only accentuated the religious squabble which had so long agitated the village ; trust an election in Holland to do that. The Protestant minister, Count Rexelaer's protégé, who had zealously visited the voters, found but one word of counsel for his patron in defeat. " You must strengthen the Protestant element," he said. Count Rexelaer reflected that eight votes are not much. He did all in his power to strengthen the Protestant element. Father Bulbius wept tears of indignation, and then he girded on his sword. Meanwhile the tragi-comedy of birth and death played through its little scenes beneath the shadow of the cross.

The Countess Margherita also commenced, about this time, to cause her noble consort—" O Hilaire ! O mon roy "—some considerable anxiety. As she grew older and her charms began to wane—she was not yet forty and still sufficiently handsome—her extravagances deepened beyond the bounds of risibility, and a coquetry revealed itself of which her younger beauty had perhaps not felt the need. From indifference concerning society she had passed to fondness for it, and from fondness to an incessant craving after gaiety. " I must make the most of my sunset," said the passionate Creole, who borrowed her metaphors from the god she adored. She laced tightly of evenings, after the morning's sweets and sofas, and she powdered her yellowing complexion while mercilessly displaying it. The " abandon " of her manners was charming, so delightfully un-Dutch. " Oh, yes, she is a La Jolais, but—well, her mother died early. She was educated out in South America where her father was Ambassador."

The Rexelaers van Altena had not, on their part, pleased the Head of the House as much as wise Duty required of them. Jane had had any number of children and was obliged to rent a large house in a bad part of the town. Her rich father-in-law, who had suffered, at the time of the

engagement, from a cough warranted to kill in a year, was
now coughing his way up into the eighties. He was horribly stingy and had behaved outrageously to his son, whose
allowance he diminished proportionately at the birth of
every child.

Then, Rolline had married a poor Jonker for love.
" You ! " her grandmother had snapped at her, " who are
so fond of nice things ! " " I think being in love is a very
nice thing," Rolline had answered, undaunted. " I saw
Jane's marriage work round." Her mother had resisted her
as long as was practicable. The worst of it was, they had
to forgive her afterwards; her husband was so very well
connected.

Antoinette was still at home; she had grown up pretty,
if a little pert in expression. She was to capture her cousin
Reinout.

Guy also was to capture a cousin. His mother had long
ago explained to him that he must marry Cécile Borck's
sixty thousand pounds; he was weary of hearing her explain. Perhaps, although nearly thirty, he was bent upon
previously increasing his debts, his " persuaders," as he
openly called them. " My dear mother," he said, " I am
not yet sufficiently persuaded." Mevrouw Rexelaer did not
comprehend.

As for George, " He is the stupid one," said the Dowager.
" It's the stupid ones that most surely look after their own.
Some day, with that quiet way of his, George will make, or
take a fortune."

" Meanwhile," protested the placid Judge, " let Hilarius
go driving in his carriages, and leave us to our cabs. I am
sure we are comfortable enough." In which view the
whole family, though eager for the carriages, concurred,
excepting Jane, who was soured by her irrationally unfortunate circumstances. " I should not have minded a
reasonable contretemps," said Jane. " And what do you call
a reasonable contretemps ? " queried her husband, who was

somewhat afraid of her. "Your father's living to be seventy, not eighty," replied plain-spoken Jane. So clearly had this couple got to understand one another.

As soon as the great people remained away from the village, the village began to miss them, and one half of it railed at the other half. Therefore, when they returned after eighteen months' absence, Joost Hakkert was hot to propose floral arches of welcome, which the Baron's faction as vehemently denounced. None regretted these dissensions as much as that gentleman himself. His bitterness had melted away from him, notably after his election to the States.

"My good Thys," he said one day to that prosperous husband and father, whom he met on returning from what had now become his daily walk in the park, "you are acting ungraciously and unwisely. I tell you so frankly, for I know you mean well. And what you are doing is *not* done on my behalf." Thys scowled. We do not like Herod, of all men, to bring under our notice the fact that we are busy out-Heroding him.

But the Baron, having eased his conscience, continued his way content. He found Bulbius and the Baroness comfortably engaged in alternate monologue of reminiscence, Wendela bravely enduring the talk about Deynum. The Baron's entrance stopped it.

The Baroness Gertrude was aging rapidly. She had always been in advance of her years, and the last decade might surely count for two. She would look for her words, till her daughter tapped the floor with impatient, self-reproachful foot.

"I disapprove of all opposition to constituted authorities," said the Baron, walking into the room. "I wish these good people would listen to me. We ought to have no point of contact with the Castle. As it cannot be love, it should never be hate."

22

Wendela looked up quickly. "Why not a little hate?" rose to her lips, but she was grown up now and sometimes suppressed her rashest thoughts.

"You are too charitable, Mynheer," burst forth Father Bulbius. "As for me, I have no patience with persecutors. For I call it persecution to compel this poor lady, in her infirmity, to drag all the way to the other end of the village."

"Stay to dinner," said the Baron, to whom this subject was especially obnoxious. "I will tell Gustave." And he rang the bell.

"Nonsense, Father; you speak as if I were losing the use of my limbs," interposed Mevrouw van Rexelaer nervously. "Like Joost Hakkert's old mother."

"No, no," replied the priest pettishly, "I did not mean that. By the by, I was telling Mevrouw, when your Worship came in, that I had been to see Lise of the Chalk-house Farm, who has just had twins."

"Tiens, and he never told me!" exclaimed the Baron, vexed that Thys should have been so much vexed.

"Did your Reverence kiss the babies?" questioned Wendela.

She liked to provoke Father Bulbius, having retained her aversion to priests. "It all comes," she would say, "of that unconscionable catechism."

"I? No," cried his Reverence in alarm. "Besides, they were girls."

"But then, old Vrouw Hakkert is twenty years older than I," continued the Baroness. "At that age people cannot complain, if their strength begins to give way."

The Baron went over to her chair and gently stroked her white forehead. "You are still young," he said.

When Count Rexelaer's carriage, shortly after, passed under a red-lettered "Welcome," he was not particularly gratified to learn from his steward that he owed its erection to the Baron's forbearance. Besides, "unusual demonstrations have exceptional causes," declared the ex-diplomat. He felt that the old lord was much in his way. What would he have said, had he known how that gentleman was steadfastly schooling himself to play the rôle of a humble petitioner? Yet, so it was. For, when duties became plain to the simple-hearted Baron, he did them. And one morning the White Baroness returned from her daily pilgrimage to the distant parish-church, leaning heavily on Wendela's arm, even more than usually exhausted.

"I cannot," the proud, silent woman had gasped as she tottered to her bed-chamber. Presently Wendela came back to the sitting-room where her father was tramping stolidly to and fro. Had he noticed? she wondered, as she seated herself, with a book, in the window-seat. She had long understood that her mother's ailment was some sort of rheumatic or chalky gout, a gradual stiffening of the joints.

"This must end," exclaimed the Baron without checking his walk. He seemed to have forgotten his daughter's presence. Five minutes' more tramp were got through, before he spoke again. "I'll go this afternoon," he said. "There's a reason for it now." He walked out at the open door, and locked himself in his room.

Left alone, Wendela slipped off the window-sill and out of the house. She hurried up the lane, and into the coppice which leads to Lady Bertha's oak.

"He shall not so humiliate himself," she repeated. "He shall not so humiliate himself." She passed the oak without daring to look at it. Here, eight years ago, she had parted from Piet Poster, the boy-sweetheart whose name still hung motionless in the prayers she repeated by rote. Unlike her father, she had never beheld the oak, nor the house, nor the gardens since that day when she had bidden them Good-bye. How long ago was it, that she had crept up the avenue to catch one last glimpse of "Knight-Pilgrim"? Five years. Often she had wondered if Reinout

still retained the dear volume she had given him. "I had
done better to keep it," she thought.

Was it fancy that told her she remembered each stone of
the building as soon as it came into view? She sped onward, with beating heart, across the courtyard, between
the orange-trees, and rang the loud door-bell with a
crash.

"You must be mistaken again. I wish you would pay
more attention," said the ever-cautious Count Rexelaer to
the servant who announced her. Then he went into the
vestibule and found himself confronted by a lithe, hazel-eyed
damsel in a light muslin dress.

"I am the Freule van Rexelaer," said the damsel with a
quiver in her earnest voice. "No, thank you, I would rather
remain here."

"And what can I do for you, Freule?"

She told him.

Count Rexelaer fretted indignantly under his efforts at
self-control. He believed in a ruse of the enemy invented
to render refusal impossible. "Will you allow me," he demanded, "to consider the matter and communicate my
reply?"

"No," said Wendela quickly. "I mean, I hope not. I
am longing to surprise them. It was that made me
come."

"My dear young lady," said the Count, "who could resist so fair a petitioner?"

"You consent then, Mynheer?" cried Wendela with
sparkling eyes.

"If your father really wishes it, yes," he replied pointedly, and then, in obedience to a motion of her hand, he
drew back the glass door.

She ran all the way home. In the garden she met the
Baron. "I have been to Deynum," she panted.

"To Deynum?" Her father did not understand what
she meant.

" I have been calling on the Count. He is an amiable gentleman, too amiable, Papa."   .

But that evening came a letter from Count Hilarius van Rexelaer. He had consented, of course, where refusal had been rendered impossible, and if the Baron was really content to extort a concession, well, Count Rexelaer, having once passed his word, must admit himself bound.

" Oh, but this is infamous ! " cried Wendela with burning cheeks.

" My dear," replied the Baron mildly, " the gentleman is true to our motto. Perhaps he enjoys disgrace. Never mind ; I shall accept."

" Oh, you dear, dear Father," she said, and threw both arms round his neck.

CHAPTER XLVI.

TRUE to his promise, the Jonker Reinout returned with his parents to the Hague. And, decked out with ribands and flowers—white ties and gardenias—he was led, like a lamb, to the slaughter.

In the morning hours he worked resolutely at the Foreign Office, helping to wind and unwind the red tape with which international knots are tied and untied. At the University he had early discovered that the study of civil law means the study of casuistry to avoid it; these pains were superfluous, diplomacy soon told him, with regard to the professor's elaborate jus gentium. "Let the professor look after the law," said the Minister, his father's friend, Count L——, "and we will take care of the profits." Reinout's virgin acquaintance with statecraft befell in those days when the affluent doctrine of "might is right" was leisurely overspreading the sand-centred tower of the Holy Alliance. The ante-Alexandrian teaching that right is one thing and a good, might another and a better, was dead past revival; Bismarckian effrontery had not yet persuaded a hyper-civilised, hyper-covetous community that a man may serve God well by serving his neighbour right. Europe was waiting for a compromise between her popularised politics and her increasing morality, and meanwhile "the two have nothing in common" was the catchword with which she strove to content herself. "Oh my God, help me to understand!" prayed Reinout van Rexelaer.

In the afternoon and evening, and night-time, when the slow hours tolled for making merry, he dragged about from place to place after either parent, or more rarely after both. The Countess was now become an indefatigable pleasure-hunter, gobbling gaiety like a lap-dog which foresees the withdrawal of its mess. " René, mon petit, es-tu prêt? "— night after night he would see his mother standing in the doorway, with fan or opera-glass, and he would lay down his book and follow her.

Of course he knew everyone, willy-nilly. His father had secured his election to those clubs from which nobody is excluded, as well as those clubs to which nobody, unless not a nobody, gains admittance. This latter emprise had called for a little manœuvring. There were plenty of young men who remembered that Rexelaer, at College, had deemed himself too good to get drunk. But people fought shy of offending the Count, high at Court and soon destined to be higher.

With the ladies of the Residency, as the Dutch call the Hague, Reinout was far more successful, and also more at his ease. In the first place, women openly loved him for one of the chief causes of masculine dislike : he was by far the best " parti " in society. He might have been endowed with round shoulders, or even with a wooden leg. As for a wooden head, that " goes without saying." And yet he was as good-looking and generous-hearted as if these things had been worth his while. Besides, while he had long since abandoned the graceful, obsolete forms which the Chevalier had taught him, he had unconsciously preserved much of the manner of that gentleman's courtlier day. He could still think, and even speak, of a woman with reverence.

In many ways, otherwise, his education had been a gigantic failure. He had fingered the gilt clay-ball his father had laid in his boyish palm till all the gilding came off. That was not what the Count, himself so successfully worldly, had bargained for. He had wished his son to despise men,

that he might freely employ them as means to an end.
He had not expected him to despise the end as well as the
means.

Meanwhile the young man rode round in the whirligig
of pleasure, and got his fair share of enjoyment out of it.
He was by no means above dancing and flirting, or racing
and riding. But at bed-time especially, like Titus, he would
feel that he had lost a day. "I have never done anything
for anybody. I am twenty-three, and if I were to die before
sunrise, my life would have been a blank!" It would
always remain so. There is no more futile occupation con-
ceivable on earth than the diplomatic representation of a
state with no international influence. But it could not be
helped. For there is also no prison like "position."

One morning the young aspirant-ambassador, upon
reaching the Office, was struck by a look of unusual red-
ness about the eyes of the old door-keeper there. The discovery startled him: he did not remember having ever seen
the symptoms of sorrow on the face of a grown-up man.
He would have spoken; but the sacredness of sorrow sealed
his lips.

He spent the morning in hard work. They had put
him into the passport-department, and there, amid the
muddle of international births, marriages and deaths, he
might watch the woof of History. A delightful squabble
had recently arisen like a ripple upon stagnancy, because a
tourist's auburn locks had been written down red. The
gentleman was exceedingly abusive, from the safe side of
the frontier, and actually offered personal violence to his
Excellency. Whereupon Reinout most humbly submitted
his willingness to go out to Italy as proxy. His Excellency
frowned. He had two frowns at his service: a shrewdly
puzzled one and a solemnly determined. The two had made
him minister.

By noon the usher's eyes had lost their border, but it

was he who broached his trouble, as he swung back the
door.

"This'll be the last day, Jonker," he said.

"How so?" questioned Reinout in surprise.

Then the man told him. An order misunderstood; a
door left unlocked with important papers behind it; the
peace of the nation in danger; more than twenty years'
service and dismissal at the end.

"It's a great pity you did it," said Reinout severely.
"I suppose there's no hope?"

The man shook his white head pathetically. "Ah, if
you only knew," he said, "I misunderstood the order,
Jonker, because I was intended to misunderstand. There,
there; it's no use talking."

Nothing more could be extracted from him. He muttered something about "a candidate before there was a
vacancy" and "a man's servants are nearer to his hand
than the state's." The Jonker turned helplessly away. He
felt himself again in the presence of one of those immense
little abuses which seem to be society's daily bread. He
was fast learning to believe that all human flocks are tended
by wolves in shepherd's clothing. No need any longer to
speculate what the lean wretch had meant with whom he
had parleyed as a lad. "A thousand poor men's tortures
go to make a single rich man's comfort." What can one
do? Solve the riddle? Are not all the world's best and
wisest, at this moment, floundering in the marshes of solution, lured by every Jack o' Lantern that shines bright?

"I shall tell my father about this," reflected Reinout.
His father was to him an upright pillar of power. Not a
lamp-post of futurity, but an Atlas that bore the existent
world. According to a father's fallible lights, the Count
could be trusted to do present-day right. Reinout believed
in his father.

There was to be a small dinner-party at home that evening in honour of Margherita's birthday. A family party,

the Rexelaers van Altena, and a couple of intimates, sixteen in all. Count Rexelaer had frowned over one name. "It is absurd," he had said, "to ask that man on such an occasion as this." Margherita had laughed in his face. But an hour or two later she had invited her husband into her menagerie. "Mon cher," she had commenced, "I should like to recount you a little anecdote."

"Well?" said Hilarius, nervously snatching at Amarinda's tail.

"Don't hurt more creatures than you can help. You remember, Hilarius, how desperately melancholy I was when you first brought me to your land of everlasting twilight. You knew at the time; but I don't think it ever interfered with your digestion. Well, one evening I had been crying and said something to Laïssa about feeling I was going to die. The poor foolish creature, in extravagant anguish, appealed to the Chevalier, and the Chevalier came and mingled his tears with mine and confessed that he too was dying for want of a ray of sunshine. You need not scowl; he is a better man than you. You, by the by, were in Amsterdam 'on business.' I have noticed that your business more commonly calls you to Brussels now. I was desperate with home-sickness; I resolved to start by the night-train and take ship at Hâvre; I promised the Chevalier to let him accompany me. Everything was arranged, and when the time came, I woke the boy. He looked up at me, drunk with early sleep. 'Are we going to Papa?' he asked. Suddenly I seemed to realize"—the Countess's harsh voice faltered—"the disgrace which, innocent though I was, an esclandre would bring upon the child. I sent for the Chevalier and told him he must go alone. I still see him bend over my hand. 'An old sinner can live where an angel can,' he said. Ridiculous logic, was it not? Besides, I have never been an angel. Far from it. And two days later you returned from Amsterdam."

"I do not understand——" began the Count, hurriedly.

"To-day I am forty. Somehow we have drifted astray from our only child, or he from us. But a woman of forty will certainly consider the position of her son, even sooner than a woman of twenty. Ay, and her own."

"And her husband's!" cried the Count, rising as if to escape.

"And her husband's. The money is mine, and it pays for your trips to Brussels."

"Have you anything else?" asked Hilarius at the door.

"Just one word. You will have the grace, I feel sure, not to refer to this very old story in the presence of the Chevalier."

"The Chevalier has behaved very badly," exclaimed Hilarius. "I thought he was a trusty friend."

"He behaved like a true cavalier to a woman in distress. Nothing more. Understand me, Hilarius; this matter ends here. And also, I am now a woman of forty. I have wasted my whole life in your horrible country. I have shown that I, like yourself, can be trusted to keep up appearances. As for the rest, it is no business of yours. You will allow me, if you please, to do what I choose with the remnant of my youth and my happiness." She threw herself back on the sofa and waved both her hands to her birds. The whole chorus of them responded to the signal, and Count Rexelaer retired from the scene in a burst of joyous song.

CHAPTER XLVII.

A MYSTERIOUS POET.

A COUPLE of hours later Margherita, in amber velvet, was receiving the congratulations of her husband's kin. Reinout had bought her a brooch, with the florins obtained by brief betting at a Club écarté-table. Rolline stood admiring it wistfully under one of the huge lace lamp-shades.

Mevrouw Elizabeth Rexelaer came sailing in with her judge among her skirts. When Mevrouw Elizabeth entered a room, there was no vacancy in it during the first few moments for anyone else; to-day, by the time she had settled down, it became apparent that the master of the house had slipped in after her. He was in excellent spirits. " I have got some splendid news ! " he said.

" Splendid for us ? " asked Jane.

" Splendid for all, my dear, in so far as we all hang together."

" Ah, but we don't," murmured Jane, in a spiteful aside to her brother George. " Thank Heaven, we are not yet *all* dependent on Uncle Hil.

" Oh, shut up," replied handsome George. He had recently succeeded in extracting a loan from his uncle, to the envious admiration of the rest. The latter gentleman was offering his arm to his sister-in-law. The company rustled into pairs. And as they did so, the fond mother pointed to Reinout and Antoinette: " How charming they look," she whispered. " Yes, don't they ? " responded Count Rexelaer hastily. The heir-apparent of Deynum, restricted like Royalty, must choose from among half a dozen high-born maidens that humbly awaited his pleasure. He might be gracious to Topsy meanwhile, if he chose.

Everybody should be gracious to everybody. Mevrouw Elizabeth was delighted with Hilarius's expansive complaisance. "It is that low-born Margaret who spoils him," she reflected. "And now, my dear brother, tell us your news!"

Hilarius was eager to do so. A silence fell upon all the nephews and nieces as he told. "It has pleased his most gracious Majesty"—the Courtier's face assumed a fold of half ironical humility—"to confer the exalted post left vacant by Count Frank de Bercy's death upon his Majesty's faithful servant—*me!*"

Of course there was an outburst of perfunctory congratulation. But if anybody really cared, it was the old Chevalier. "The blessed saints be with him!" mumbled that perfumed relic in his immaculate shirt-front. And mentally he added, "If blessed saints there be."

The judge rose and toasted "His Excellency!" and the yellow-robed Creole beside him looked up with a vainglorious smile. Yes, it was nice. They all felt it was nice. "Admit that it is," said Topsy, turning her pretty, plucky little head towards her neighbour. "Oh, nice enough," replied Reinout, "Pharaoh's footman promoted to the place of Pharoah's butler deceased." But the girl only laughed at him. "You are very young," she declared. "You may always say those things to me."

In the smoking-room Count Rexelaer had to listen to the lisped congratulations of the gentleman whose presence he had striven to prevent, an attaché at the French Legation, "my compatriot," averred Margherita, "model yourself, my dear child, on the manners of Monsieur de Bonnaventure." Reinout had slipped away from an endless tale of his eldest cousin's gambling losses and taken refuge with the ladies, two of whom were differing politely on every subject they approached, while Jane sat buried in a pile of much coveted reviews and Rolline lay back dreaming of her dear little peach of a baby, all sweet and soft and good to eat. It was a relief when the gentlemen came upstairs, Count Rexelaer with a bundle of newly-arrived letters in his hand. His excellency halted in the middle of the room. "Margherita," he said, while avoiding his wife's eyes, "I am very much annoyed. I have just heard from Dievert that the people I so unwisely re-admitted to the chapel have kept some sort of religious anniversary there. A Catholic service, in fact."

" This is truly shocking," said Mevrouw Elizabeth, from among the perplexed audience, in her most impressive tones.

" Oh, I daresay they only celebrated mass," interposed Margherita lightly. She was angry about the reopening of the chapel, because it had been refused to herself. " Do not let us quarrel about religion, pray."

" It is not a question of religion, but a question of decency!" fumed the Count. "The old Barebones does nothing but tease me with his tranquil impertinence. I would give a good sum, could I drive him from Deynum!"

He squeaked out the words in his irritation. Margherita caught a smile of careless contempt beneath the French diplomat's waxed moustache. She appealed to him to create a diversion. "C'est bête," she said, "has nobody anything amusing?"

Jane wheeled round from her table. "Here are these verses," she interposed, "that people are talking about, in the 'Revue Parisienne.' Have you seen them, Aunt Margaret, you who are such a lover of poetry?"

" No. Read them to us," replied Margherita, glad of any escape.

" Oh, poetry!" murmured Guy, and, winking at Reinout, he wandered away to pause vacantly in front of a female statuette. Reinout at the first mention of the review and the poem, had fallen back hastily into impenetrable shade.

The poem was a short one in honour of an incident much discussed at the time. In a South American republic—of all places!—a murderer's execution had been twice interrupted by the breaking of the rope; whereupon the mob had invaded the scaffold and rescued the criminal, actuated, said the poet, by an impulse of heaven-born pity. "Brotherly sympathy," though perhaps a shade more accurate, would hardly have rhymed so well with—the sentiments of the singer.

Hitherto, said the poet, all light had arisen in the East, and he appealed to the nations of Europe to be foremost in heralding the daybreak of mercy. Else would its morning be not sunlight but storm.

> " Car c'est dans l'occident que l'ouragan s'élève
> Dont la grande marée effacera la Grève!"

Jane read well, and therefore enjoyed reading whether people listened or not. She had rung out the last lines with real spirit. Why did Reinout, in the silence which followed, shrink still farther back?

" It ends in a pun," said the diplomat. " That is bad."

"A pun! No; where?" cried Mevrouw Elizabeth. Her daughter hastily intervened. " The whole thing is modelled on Victor Hugo," she said. " Capital punishment is his hobby. But it is attracting a great deal of notice, and I think it is distinctly good."

" It isn't poetry at all," complained Margherita. " It is merely rhymed talk about politics. Poetry deals with the nobler affections."

The diplomatist beside her bowed low over her fan. " You have expressed it exactly," he said.

" The sentiments are French," declared Mevrouw Elizabeth, " and would meet with no sympathy here."

" You think not?" asked Reinout's voice from the

depths of a bay window. He came slowly back into the light. "As it happens," he said, "I can favour you, if you like, with a translation of Jane's poem. I bought it, by the merest chance, on my way home this afternoon." And, drawing a newspaper from his pocket, with a word of apology to the Frenchman, he gave them the whole thing over again.

"That is how it sounds in Dutch," he said.

"And very ugly too," said Margherita.

"The translation is not half bad," protested sententious Jane; "whom is it by?" George yawned audibly. Simmans had taken the paper from Reinout's hand. "Queer literature," he said, "for the Jonker van Rexelaer," and passed it on to the Count. That gentleman glanced at the title, and dropt the red-hot, revolutionary coal.

Reinout laughed. Mevrouw Elizabeth smilingly shook a substantial finger. "René, René!" she said. "You are an enfant terrible. But we know it is only your fun."

"What is it all about?" inquired the judge, pulling himself together and definitely waking up. "What has Reinout got there? I suppose it is the 'Cry of the People.' Well, Simmans, we have it at the Law Courts and the Ministries. I agree with him; it is far better to know what these foolish people say."

"Oh, the socialists, you know!" remarked Rolline's Jonker, screwing his eye-glass tight.

His fond young wife stretched forth her fan to playfully tap his arm. "Don't," she said, "you horrid boy."

But Simmans was resolved to have his say. "It is different for us," he declaimed, "who stand forth to protect society. But Reinout is one of life's favoured butterflies. We, on the ramparts, must accustom ourselves to the smell of the powder."

"Yes, that is what I always feel," interposed Margherita, turning from her earnest conversation with her attaché.

" The smell of poor people is so very disagreeable. It prevents one from being as kind as one might."

" But who is this Dutch revolutionary poet ? " persisted Jane.

Simmans picked up the paper. " An anonymous hero," he answered, " who signs with a P. P stands for Peter or Paul."

" Probably Paul," put in Reinout. " A prince of revolutionaries, if men had but obeyed him ! "

Half an hour later the Rexelaers van Altena were driving home. " A dull evening," opined Mevrouw Elizabeth. " Jane was stupid with her poem. And Reinout pushes his jokes too far."

" The salmi was good," replied the judge.

" Do you know, Mamma, I believe Reinout is in earnest ? " said Antoinette.

" In earnest ! " cried her mother, much flurried. " How ? What do you mean ? What did he say ? "

Antoinette shrieked with laughter. " In earnest, I mean, as regards the poor," she said as soon as she could speak.

" He knows nothing about the poor," retorted Mevrouw, turning away from her irritating daughter.

Guy and George, walking home together, discussed their relations with far greater freedom. They both agreed that the evening would have been most insufferably dull, but for the amusement of watching Margherita's " exotic vivacity."

" A flirt of forty ! " remarked Guy. " I don't think Uncle Hil half likes it. The more fool he. Besides, he's got more than his share of luck already."

" Uncle Hil's not half a bad fellow," said George.

" I don't wonder you think so. I wish you'd tell me how you managed to extract all that money out of him."

" Ah, wouldn't you like to know," said George.

" Yes, I should. Truth to tell, I don't think there was

23

any ruse about it. You're too stupid. You just asked him, and he said Yes."

"Perhaps so," replied George. "You might try it."

Reinout was putting on his overcoat in the hall, when his father came out to him.

"My dear boy," began the Count, "I have been wanting to say a few words to you for many days past. Of course you are quite welcome to spend your nights at the Club or wherever else you prefer to spend them. Only don't overdo it. Sometimes we see nothing of you for forty-eight consecutive hours. There, I am sure we understand each other. Exaggeration in all things is an evil. Good-night."

My Lord High Seneschal glided up to his bedroom, humming a bright little tune. Before extinguishing the light he nodded complacently to His Excellency in the glass, a mealy-faced, wiry-haired Excellency in a night-shirt. And although he had forgotten the quotation which, ten years ago, had spurred him on to scorn the lowest rung of his Jacob's Ladder, yet the thought was in his mind to-night. "So doth the greater glory dim the less." Nothing —absolutely nothing—was left him to desire. He sank into the blissful repose of an unshadowed success.

The Baron, at Deynum, laid down the Provincial Gazette with a smile.

CHAPTER XLVIII

STAINS.

GEORGE REXELAER had always been Grandmamma Borck's favourite. "He was so delightfully stupid," she said; she did not add that she had retained a quondam beauty's weakness for good looks. Grandmamma Borck would have married George to Cécile,—George, not Guy—could she have afforded to let Cécile marry at all. "Come and tell me everything, George," she would say. "You're too weak to stand alone."

She even helped him with a little, carefully counted, money. It was Cécile's. And she resigned herself to his being "a man about town," in these days when the turnstile of "examination" guards the old paths of honour and glory. "There are other heiresses," she said, "besides Cécile."

But the heiresses held aloof—honest Dutch maidens—God bless them! any one of them is worth six of the men. Once, indeed, the old woman succeeded in concocting an engagement, but in a month it was broken off. "I could marry a beautiful statue," said the damsel frankly, "for a statue would not open its mouth now and then to say a foolish thing."

George was content not to care. Even in his salad days he had been as cool as a cucumber. "I want," he admitted, "to have a great deal of money; it's the sole thing I care for, and some day I shall manage it. I know I could get it now, if they would but let me alone." "How?" the Dowager once asked him. "In business," said stupid George. The old lady laughed herself purple.

But a couple of months later he came to her with an important face and a tiny parcel. He had a habit of conversing with everyone on his slow life's journey—in trains, on steamers, in places of amusement—"for want," Jane used to tell him, "of something to say." Well, that morning he had been to Delft, in the barge, and had come across a sailor just returned from the Indies, and that sailor had proved the happy possessor of a magnificent secret which he was desirous to share, for a consideration, with somebody else. He had told George all about it, except, of course, the secret itself. Having strayed from his ship, it appears, on the coast of New Guinea, this man had fallen into the hands of a tribe of Papuans—the genuine Tatua-Papuas—and the Tatuas had tattooed him all over, in their own peculiar manner, and he had lived among them and done duty as a medicine-man. The tattooing of the Tatuas is of course ineradicable, but they paint themselves also with paints, greases and gums, and these paintings the sailor perceived they could easily remove by means of a plant called Papú. In fact, each lady used to be done up fresh from time to time, said the sailor, when the spring fashions came in; his own wife had shown him the trick. He had escaped from the tribe, and had got back to Europe, bringing the secret away with him, though not the wife, and here that secret was. He had extracted a dirty green lump from his pocket and shown it to George. "Warranted," he said, "to remove all stains, spots, blots, and blemishes on the human complexion or any other soft material, silks, velvets, woollens, genuine kids, etc., etc. Will not clean pots and pans. Willing to dispose of it for three thousand florins down, and dirt cheap."

"I like the reservation," said the Dowager, after listening to this ridiculous story. "I always think it looks so well in the advertisements. Throw away that dirty little ball, George. You know I have a horror of infection."

But foolish George had taken the matter seriously. Only three thousand florins, and a fortune to be made! "I assure you, grandma, there is something in it," he entreated, "I only wish you would let me shew you—" he bent forward, uplifting the little green ball between finger and thumb. "If you only had a grease-stain somewhere about you——" said George with scrutinising glances. But the Baroness's glossy black silk lay serene and spotless about her meagre limbs. "Nonsense," she said sharply. "Throw it away at once. And talk about something else."

But fools rush in——exactly. "No, no, I *must* show you. It's too wonderful!" cried George. He caught up a pen from an inkstand at his grandmother's elbow and, before she could stop him, he had dropped a small blot on the crimson plush tablecloth. The dowager screamed with indignation. She, who considered the smallest visible blemish the greatest of sins. "Only wait till it dries, Ma'am," expostulated George, "and I'll shew you——" She refused to be shewn. She ordered her grandson out of her presence. And he departed, leaving behind him, in his flurry, the little green ball.

The Dowager remained in her chair, gasping with indignation before the black speck on the cloth and the antidote which the criminal had left lying beside it. She sat thus a long time, in utter disgust, and watched the ink dry; then, partly from curiosity, partly from inability to endure the sight of the stain any longer, she took up the little strong-smelling pea, in the most gingerly manner, with her skinny, slender fingers, and began slowly rubbing the spot beneath the fading light. Presently she got up to fetch a candle from her bureau, and Cécile, when she came in half an hour later, found her grandmother mopping ink all over the tablecloth.

Next morning George received an invitation to come

and see his forgiving Granny. He found her in a most amiable mood, and they discussed pro's and con's in a businesslike manner. "I am sure I could work it," reiterated George. But the far-seeing Dowager had doubts. "Why, you would have to spend a hundred thousand florins the first twelvemonth in advertisements alone!" she said. The great thing was to possess oneself of the secret. That done, the rest would "develop itself" by means of a company or, still better, a syndicate. But how raise, within twenty-four hours, the preliminary three thousand? "Unfortunately," said the cautious old lady, "I have barely a penny of my own."

"Uncle Hilarius?" suggested George, very doubtfully.

"I have been thinking of that"; she sat and pondered. "That little story you told me a month ago," she said presently, "about going to call on your aunt and running upstairs unannounced into her sitting-room. You remember, eh?"

"Of course I remember, Granny," said George with downcast eyes.

"I told you to lay it by and speak to nobody about it. Put it in the bank, so to say. Perhaps the time has come to take it out. But, mind you, only in case of extremest necessity, for of course it will cause unpleasantness. So use all your other arguments first. You understand? And now go and speak to your uncle."

"No, I don't quite understand," said George.

"Dear, dear, how stupid you are. I feel convinced you will die a Crœsus. Well, I must tell you more plainly." And she did.

When Count Rexelaer had listened to his nephew for fifteen seconds, he said: "No, he never lent anybody anything; it was against his principles. He only gave." Even George was not simple enough to suggest: "Then give." But he pushed his appeal nearly five minutes longer, till the Count said " No " again, so exceedingly irritably and with such ungracious additions that George felt the moment was come to expose this particular nephew's discreet claims to more consideration. " I think you owe me a good turn, Uncle Hil," he began, as his grandmother had instructed him, " if only because——" And then the unhappy Comptroller of another and a more august household than his own found himself treated to that little story which had so much diverted the Dowager five weeks ago. How Nephew George had come to the house to call on Aunt Margherita, and how he had run up unannounced to the back drawing-room, and how——

When the enterprise was launched, in due time, it " took " almost immediately. The money had been found by a couple of wealthy contractors, of the name of Kops, Abraham and Benjamin, who had become partners in the business of which George and one of the young Kopses were managing directors. " Papuum ! Papuum !" (as the new product was called) spread all over the country, with a placard exhibiting a bright-coloured Tatua-Papua washing the paint off one side of his face. They first advertised " Will not clean Metals ! " again and again ; nothing else. That was an idea of the Dowager's, who entered into the fun of the thing and was responsible for two thirds of her grandson's success. " Papuum ! Papuum ! Will not clean Metals !" Everybody wanted to find out what it *would* clean. There was a young lady at the offices, always in attendance, most willing to shew you. You might spill whatever you wished to—in reason—on herself or her white satin dress. George was going to be an extremely wealthy man. He was as good as engaged to the daughter and heiress of Benjamin Kops (no Jewish blood traceable), whose empty little heart went bumping up and down at the idea of a handsome husband and a coronet. And it must be confessed he worked hard at the business. The delight of watching money breed seemed to have sharpened all his faculties. He sent round to every house in the Hague, a pea of the wonderful mixture with accompanying verses (which, bad as they were, he had *not* composed). The wooden-seats in the public gardens and all the tramcar cushions everywhere were renovated—once—with Papuum. A cake of it was given away to any orphan-child that could prove its parent's demise to have preceded "the greatest discovery of the age." Thrice over an attempt was made to import genuine Tatuas to parade the streets and sit in the offices; they all died on the voyage, but even that was an advertisement. The chief difficulty consisted in breeding the plant fast enough in enormous conservatories. The supply gave out once, and that was by far the best advertisement of all. There was a perfect battery at the doors, and a clamour for Papuum!

And the noble, the illustrious Rexelaers, they were petrified by this disgrace to their immaculate name? They were, till they found that this Papuum produced not thousands but tens of thousands of florins, and then even Margherita remembered that the money, unlike its producer, "did not smell." Besides, now-a-days, there are but a couple of countries remaining in Europe—Austria, for instance—where it is still possible to associate any earning of money with disgrace. Holland is not one of them. In the twentieth century there will be none at all.

The Rexelaers of Altena, the brother and sisters, chaffed George a little at first. They were always finding specks on his clothes and crying out for " Papoosel!" Once Topsy even dabbed him with paint from her colour-box, but he soon frightened them, by his rages, into letting him alone. He permitted no allusion, out of business hours, to his business side. This rule the old lady had especially impressed upon him. He went out into society just the same, but only after four, and in the office he wore coronets on his

cuff-studs. Many people compared him most favourably
with his elder brother, Guy. But he could not prevent the
roar of laughter which went up on all sides, when he acci-
dentally sat down on a freshly painted seat, in the German
minister's garden.

His father and mother were even pleased to sanction his
engagement to Miss Kops. Of course she must be considered "faute de mieux," but the match would consolidate
the business. Unfortunately the Kopses happened to be—
of all things!— Roman Catholics. Mevrouw Elizabeth
hesitated.

"They could not possibly be anything better," said her
mother, whom she consulted. "It looks less Jewish than
anything else. The girl's name, I hear, is Maria Christina,
a very judicious selection. I should at once make a rule
that she be known as Christina. You can say that there
are Maries in the family already."

"But there are not, mamma?" remarked Mevrouw van
Rexelaer.

"How tiresome you can be, Elizabeth," said the Dowager
peevishly, "and so rude."

CHAPTER XLIX.

THE LADY'S DOLE.

"I'LL do it," said Count Rexelaer aloud. "I ought to have done it before. But I was always too good-natured."

A couple of hours later Notary Strum, at work in his office, received a telegraphic message summoning him to My Lord of Deynum's presence by eleven on the morrow morning.

He rose from his desk with a growl and lumbered across the little entrance-hall, to the room where his mother sat knitting, as ever.

"Here's a telegram," said Nicholas. "Order from Pacha to come up to town to-morrow. Never mind rain, hail, wind or snow. Pacha says: 'Come. I whistled.'"

"Oh, Nicholas, with your chill!" said the old woman, and laid down her work.

"Yes, *with* my chill!" retorted Nicholas. "I couldn't well go without."

"I suppose you must," said the widow thoughtfully. "You see his Excellency doesn't know you are indisposed. And it is a great privilege for you to act as the confidential adviser of so magnificent a patron, Nicky."

"'Magnificent' is the word," replied Nicky, and went back to his office, banging the door.

All these years mother and son had jogged on side by side, or rather son a-top. "A wife and children would cost me a second servant," reasoned the notary. "Mother looks after me and the maid." But her company was not only convenience and complacency; for she had a maddening way of ignoring—from incompetency to comprehend them—all the dear fellow's favourite fads of thought and expression, and having lived her whole life in submission to God, the priest and the gentlefolks, she could not remember that Nicholas believed, or said he believed, in the Almighty but vaguely, in her other divinities not at all. She would gladly have sacrificed her life for her son—in fact, she did so, in a long-drawn daily sacrifice—but she was incapable of sparing him her old-fashioned utterances, from which he vainly fled. If he grew ironical, she took him in earnest. If he flew out at her, she would meekly cite his father. Nicholas quoted his father at the clients, not to himself.

When Nicholas started next morning at daybreak, he was safely wrapped up and galoshed and comfortered, and his mother came running after him, in the cold, with pocket-handkerchiefs and lozenges, of which he had already procured a supply. He sent her back with a growl.

He had the pleasure of travelling all the way to the Hague with a man who lamented " the decrease of deference in social relations." He bore this with the fierce silence on which he had long nourished his spites and discontents. "No use quarrelling," he would tell himself, " with one's bread and butter, because the butter's bad."

His " magnificent patron " received him with unusual friendliness, even thanking him for coming. " I wonder what he wants," thought Strum.

Count Rexelaer immediately proceeded to enlighten him. " Strum, I am going to do it," said his Excellency in his hasty way. " I mean, about ' the Lady's Dole.' You were quite right. I ought never to have allowed them to settle again in Deynum."

The Notary's heart leapt within him. He forgot all about the cold or the discomfort of coming. For years he had vainly been endeavouring to convince Count Rexelaer, and now that fine gentleman, just like a fine gentleman, sent for him, in the middle of winter, to say: "I am convinced!" No matter; he would be avenged on his enemy at last.

"I am greatly relieved," he said, blinking cheerfully behind his glasses. "Your Excellency knows with what increasing compunction I have paid the annual instalments where they were no longer due." In his heart he wondered: What has happened to set his Excellency still more against the Baron?

"Of course I knew that your view was the only correct one," replied Count Rexelaer coldly. "But from charity— pure charity—I declined to enforce it. Had the Baron seen fit to show that reserve which I had a right to expect from a gentleman, instead of assuming from the first an attitude which I may well call aggressive——" He paused and looked at Strum.

"Just so," said the Notary in sullen obedience, cracking his huge finger-joints.

"Just so," repeated his Excellency. "He has developed among the villagers the spirit of faction; he has openly opposed me on every occasion. I have borne it all in a magnanimous spirit, for I cannot bear striking a man when he's down. But at last our position has become quite untenable. One of us must go. Write him a letter to say that the money will no longer be paid."

Strum drew himself up eagerly, with one of his uncouth jerks; his speckled face was bright with exultation. "I could write it here," he said, and let your Excellency see it."

"There is no such hurry. But you will find pen and ink on yonder table."

The Notary availed himself of the permission. "I wonder what has done it," he repeated. "Surely not that mass on the anniversary of the death of the Baron's mother which they say he was so angry about."

It was but a straw which had caused Count Rexelaer's

long-gathering resentment to brim over. True, the Baron's
majority at a re-election had been over a hundred ; Father
Bulbius, embittered by Veronica's increasing perversity, had
taken to preaching distinctly polemical sermons, and such
of the country gentry as remained still untouched by the
corruption of the Hague had increased, since his Excellency's appointment, in invidious cordiality to his rival.
For all these things Count Rexelaer hated—secretly, nervously, deeply, according to his character—Deynum, its
Baron and its surroundings. Now that he had, not one
foot in the stirrup, but both hands on the bridle, he resolved
to hit back. O the delightful feeling ! Not even life-long
cringing can teach the worm not to turn.

Still, he waited for the last little something. It took
the shape of a letter from the Baroness Borck of Rollingen
to her cousin Elizabeth, containing the information that a
wide-spread conviction was obtaining in the neighbourhood,
that all difficulties would be ultimately set right by a marriage between Wendela and Reinout. Ridiculous as the idea
might be, it had commended itself to the country people
as a definite " restitution " ; " No need to inquire who first
started it," wrote the Baroness of Rollingen. " This is just
like their scheming Jesuitical ways "—the lady here thought
fit to ignore the engagement to Christina Kops, " a disgusting affair altogether "—" but I should be curious to know,
though we shall never do that, in how far your nephew, by
his conduct, may have given to the story a semblance of
foundation."

It was this last sentence which had set Count Rexelaer
thinking, for of course Mevrouw Elizabeth had shown him
the letter. He himself had been struck by the appearance
of that tall, dark girl the day she came up to the Castle.
He believed his son to be a great admirer of the weaker
sex ; why else these prolonged disappearances from home ?
Well, he had taken him behind the scenes himself, and was
the last man to object to a measure of dissipation.

But Wendela?—that was another matter. Dull as Deynum undoubtedly was, notwithstanding the numerous guests at the Castle, young twenty must be taught to distinguish. That was why fathers were created older than their sons.

The Baron van Rexelaer had been to see Lise and her three sturdy children. The old Squire enjoyed sitting of evenings with Farmer Driest by the kitchen-hearth or on the bench outside the Farmhouse; they were contemporaries and had in common a long life of insignificant little all-important country-experiences. They could talk of these for hours, in the quiet gloaming, over their solemn pipes, while the dear music of the lowing cattle fell soft upon the Farmer's ears from the winter stables or the summer fields.

The Baron would talk on, in leisurely accents, about Deynum, Deynum, Deynum. The farmers and their children and their morals and their cows and their difficulties, and their quarrels, and all their financial ins and outs, and a further infinity of "ands." His whole little universe of Deynum. Driest, on his side, would carry on the conversation with that mixture of deference and independence in which the Dutch peasant excels.

But perhaps the Baron liked playing with the children even better. He was foolishly fond of "babies," and grandchildren of his own he had none. The wee bits of humanity at the Farm adored him. Yes, he had many compensations.

He kept thinking of these during his trudge along the frost-broken lanes. Like many men whose troubles are very real, he loved to look upon the brighter side. He was far better off than he had any right to be. For his conscience reproached him still.

Some children were trying to slide in the slush. They nudged each other and jerked their caps. For "Mynheer" was the tangible Presence; the other, up at the Castle, could only be an August Name.

Veronica came round from behind the wall of the Parsonage, dragging a basket of peat.

"Good-day, Veronica. How is his Reverence?" said the Baron amiably.

"Poorly," replied Veronica. "He can't stand the draughts of this house."

"Dear me, I am sorry to hear that."—"Ah, I should think so," muttered Veronica—"I wonder whether I could go in to him for a moment?"

"I suppose you may," replied the housekeeper ungraciously. "He won't keep as quiet as I want him to."

"Ah, you let him have quiet?" said the Baron; even the mildest of men like their morsel of malice at times. Baron Rexelaer was perfectly aware that Veronica proclaimed him, whenever she dared, a spoiler of other men's goods. He had turned her meek priest out of house and home; worse than that, he had appropriated the small square of oilcloth she had left in her kitchen, a square bought with her own earnings some twenty years ago. That unconscionable, and unconscious, confiscation of oilcloth formed a grievance still greater than the loss of the whole of the former Parsonage.

The Baron knocked briskly at the living-room door. "I don't want anything," cried Bulbius in querulous reply. He turned a slow head in his arm-chair by the fire, and pushed back the bowl at his side which had evidently contained some unpalatable form of slop. Veronica had half-a-dozen mildewed health-dicta, which she reverenced like Gospel-truths. "Starve a cold," was one of them. The Father would sometimes buy biscuits, but these grew terribly stale in their paper bag. And he rejoiced that Veronica had not as yet discovered the bottle in the cupboard, nor the two glasses, which he *never washed*.

"You coddle yourself, Bulbius," said the Baron bluntly.

He had barely felt illness himself, and could not comprehend it unless, as in his wife's case, it assumed a visible form.

" I am not robust like your Nobleness," pleaded Bulbius. " You see, I am too stout."

" I do," said the Baron.

" But what is a poor creature to do."

" Gymnastics," said the Baron.

Father Bulbius spread out his vast body, which looked still more mountainous under his shawl.

" The rope would break," he said helplessly.

" There are other things besides the trapèze. You might try a ten-mile walk. But there; when a man has once made up his mind to die of apoplexy, no one can stop him. He must just have his way."

" But I don't want to die," protested the Father piteously. " Neither of heat in the head, as you now predict, nor of cold in the feet, as Veronica prophesies. There's the postman, Baron. Shall we have him in ? " And he rapped his fat forefinger against the windowpane.

Yes, there was a letter for Mynheer the Baron. It was Strum's letter. The old gentleman looked down at it, as it lay in his hand, with a quick presentiment of coming ill. Yet it was eight years now since he had been in the habit of watching for misfortune per post. He opened the envelope leisurely and took out the enclosure. And having read it carefully through, he laid it down on the table.

" God is strong," he said aloud, and nothing else. His voice was unbroken.

Yet its calm, deep passion frightened the priest. " What is it, dear Baron ? " he queried anxiously. " Nothing amiss, I hope ? "

" Oh no, nothing amiss," replied the Baron van Rexelaer. He talked for a few moments of other things—the weather, the village-school—and then he rose and departed. But his steps trembled under him, as he vainly tried to steady them.

The Lady's Dole, it will be remembered, was a fund which a seventeenth-century Baron van Rexelaer had instituted by settlements assigning the annual interest to "the Spouse of the Lord of the Manor, as long as the Lord of the Manor shall be a van Rexelaer." The words of the deed did not stipulate descent from the donor; the money was to revert to the last lady of Deynum or her heirs. The notary of the place was perpetual trustee.

Immediately on the acquisition of the estate by Count Rexelaer, Strum, his intellect sharpened by hate, had pointed out to that gentleman that henceforth the Countess Margherita alone was entitled to the annual payment of the appanage, she being "the spouse of the Rexelaer van Deynum." But the Count had repudiated this suggestion with disgust, even after the return of the other had so seriously disconcerted him. Gently, though vainly, the Notary persisted. Times change and opinions work round. One evening his Excellency telegraphed.

The Baron, walking home with Strum's letter in his pocket, refused to believe the incredible. He knew well enough, none better, that there was not a drop of his ancestors' blood in the veins of the Rexelaers van Deynum. "It is mere intimidation for some object of their own," he thought, and, without mentioning the matter to wife or daughter, he, next morning early, sought out the Notary.

The office-door was still closed when he arrived, but as he stood knocking and scraping, it was opened by old Mrs. Strum, who immediately dropped into a succession of curtsies. "Walk in, Mynheer the Baron," she began in awestruck tones, "I hasten to inform my son. It is long since your Nobleness accorded us the honour of a visit." And pushing forward her own easy chair—the room was manifestly a niggard's—she bustled away to find Nicholas.

"Shew him into the waiting-room," said Nicholas.

24

" Nicky! The Baron!"

" Shew him in, do you hear? Say I am engaged."

" Nicholas, your father would never have approved of that."

" Why didn't you go with my father, then, if you can't manage without him? Do as I say." And this hater of tyrants, who called Count Rexelaer "the Pacha," pointed with the tip of his quill to the door.

The old lady turned away with a sigh. " Your Nobleness will be more comfortable here," she said, leading the way. " It is so hot in the sitting-room." The Baron, utterly indifferent, sat down.

Twenty minutes' wait ensued, during which two peasants came in who, seeing their former lord, remained standing. One was an old man. " Sit down, sit down," said the Baron. Strum's clerk bent scribbling by the window, his fingers blue with cold.

At last a bell rang in the inner room. As the clerk put his head through the door, Strum's voice was heard saying: " Mynheer Rexelaer."

" Please to walk in, Mynheer the Baron," said the clerk, standing deferentially aside. A faint flush of colour crept over the old gentleman's wan cheeks.

" Good morning, Mynheer; take a seat," said Strum, and continued his writing for the tenth of a minute. Then he looked up. " Well," he said.

" I have received a letter from you, Strum," said the Baron, " I should wish to know what it means."

" What it says," replied Strum.

" I should like to know what is the object of the threat it contains."

" No other object than the threat itself, which is not a threat, but a notification."

" In other words, I am to understand, that it is your unalterable resolve to substitute the Countess Rexelaer for my wife as recipient of the Lady's Dole?"

"My unalterable resolve. What else can I do? My movements in this matter are dependent on the Count's generosity. Excuse my saying, Mynheer the Baron, that you have been living all these years upon his bounty."

"I—on his bounty," stammered the Baron.

"Undeniably." Strum cracked his thumbs for pleasure. Yet he could not quite overcome the tendency to lapse into civility. He brought himself to with a jerk.

"A Notary's duty is seldom doubtful," he added, "as my dead father used to say."

"Ah, leave me in peace with your dead father," burst out the Baron, "God grant he rest quiet in his grave!"

Strum passed his great hand through his untidy hair. He looked like a beaten school-boy as he joined his splay feet. "I am very busy this morning," he murmured, "and if there is nothing else——"

"Once more, the money will not be paid next month?" queried the Baron anxiously, despite his efforts at self-control. "It will never be paid again?"

"No, for it cannot be. It is claimed by the owner."

"You know perfectly well that only the testator's own family is meant. You, the descendant of the Notary who drew up the deed."

"The deed does not say so. I have no opportunity of consulting my ancestor."

"It is starvation," groaned the Baron, breaking down for one moment. "What object have you in taking the bread from our mouths?"

A suppressed gleam of triumph played behind the Notary's spectacles. "I am only doing my duty," he said. "Once before, when I was doing my duty, you struck me, Baron Rexelaer."

"I know it," replied the Baron, "I was not sorrier then than now."

Strum got up and faced his former patron. "I also regret it," he said. He opened the door into the waiting-room. "No, Mynheer the Baron," he continued, raising his voice, "I cannot give you that money, because it is not mine to give."

The old gentleman eyed the big lout before him with gentle scorn: "I will not tell my friends," he said in a low voice. "It would ruin you."

The Notary's mottled face twitched nervously, and though his attitude remained the same, yet his whole personality seemed to collapse. "I—I am nowise afraid, Mynheer," he stuttered. "I feel that, whatever my duty——"

"Did you not hear me say I would not tell?" asked the Baron, and he passed out through the well-filled ante-room, under a cross-fire of curious eyes.

Mother Strum stood curtsying at her window. For a moment the wild impulse shook him to claim her help. Then he recognised the hopelessness of such humiliation and smilingly took off his hat.

As he passed the Parsonage, he heard Veronica's voice intoning her only song—lame of rhyme and of reason:

> "A fair, a merry maid was I,
> With dancing step and laughing eye!"

"She may be back sooner in the old place than she expects," he thought.

Suddenly he found himself in his own sitting-room. "Wherever have you been so early?" asked Wendela. He tried to answer her. To his astonishment he could not. The room was clouding over and twisting round. He reeled forward to steady himself, and fell with a dull thud on the floor.

The Baroness, unable to assist him, shrieked once and then sat still, with trembling lips. Wendela had sprung forward. "It is only a fainting fit," she said. "Only the sudden coming into the heat!" and she strove to restore her father to consciousness. "Oh mon Dieu, mon Dieu!" repeated the Baroness, folding her useless hands. With her the words were no vain ejaculation, but a prayer.

CHAPTER L

NEW SCENES AND OLD FACES.

WHEN the Baron was "fully recovered" from his stroke, even the Baroness noticed the change in him. She herself, poor lady, was now become a constant sufferer, with little to do but to watch the slow ascent of her gout. Her head was growing feeble; she could be utterly broken-down at times, and querulous. And Wendela, the headstrong, the impatient, "born to conquer her fate," sat humbled in this school of suffering. The actual physical sickness commanded and obtained her helpful sympathy. She could speak of it, readily, for here was no one's fault but God's. " If anyone has blundered," said the sceptical girl, " it must be mother's Saints."

To her father also she was good; almost happy, in his weakness, to show him a tenderness free from reproach. But the Baron rebelled against himself. " Face the enemy!" he repeated, and he tried to do it with his stiffened leg. This seizure was nothing, he said. Had he not had a similar, if slighter, one many years ago on the evening when the Marquis had found him? He was well, for he had no time to be ill.

It was true that he had no time. The three weeks sped on rapidly to the first of March; on that day the " Dole " fell due. As the hours wore on without bringing the accustomed packet, the Baron, still very partially recovered, grew more and more restless; he shut himself up, foodless, in his room and sat staring at the inevitable end. Yet at night-fall his very desperation roused him. He wrote a hurried note, after lengthy inspection of that part of the newspaper which he had not glanced at for years, and sent Gustave to the post with it. The old servant shook his head over the superscription. And the Baron lay awake all night, alternately building up dreams of daily bread (no longer of prosperity) and debating with himself whether he should not telegraph a recall at dawn. Why should he? Failure could not make matters much worse, and success was become a necessity.

He trusted to his wife's now almost ceaseless orisons and bead-countings, although these were never for temporal salvation. The Baroness, stiffening in her chair, in a little alcove of crucifixes, images, and invocations, was rapidly becoming "dévote," dead already, but for her physical pains and her still active charity, a white, worn shadow. She would ask for her poor to come and see her—hers by the mastery of hearts; she knew them well: the respectable, the disreputable, the professional, the needy that are ashamed, and she sent Wendela among them with creature comforts; the spiritual fared but ill at that young lady's hands. Once the daughter, after long impatience, interrupted her mother's monotonous mumbling. "Are *you* happy, Mamma?" she asked abruptly. "No," whispered the Baroness, her pale eyes uplifted, as ever, to the solemn dying Christ. The girl went up to her room and threw herself down in a passion of weeping, her eyes averted, long after, in dull, rebellious thought, from that great Sufferer who had watched her slumbers ever since she was a cradled babe.

She rose at last to get her father his beaten-up egg. Wendela Rexelaer was a thoroughly incompetent housekeeper, and naturally hated both her incompetency and its object. She stopped to inquire at the Baron's door, almost hoping that he would refuse; the mess was such a weariness to make. "Oh no, I don't want it," called the Baron's feeble voice. She went into the kitchen and dutifully prepared it. And he swallowed it without complaint.

In a few days the Baron knew the worst. The last few thousand florins of his wife's small fortune had been swept away. He looked up from the letter at Gustave, who had brought it and who, in his tutored indiscretion, was lingering with averted eyes over a distant rearrangement of chairs.

"Gustave," said the Baron, "come here. Ten years ago you told me you were a rich man. Are you still?"

"Richer, Mynheer," replied Gustave promptly. "I can't leave off; for nobody can. It's like sliding down a hill-side into the valley of perdition. I'm winning your Nobleness's money still."

"I give you my word I had not speculated all these years," said the Baron hastily. "But you're right. It's gone. We are penniless. And "—his eyelids trembled; he stammered painfully—"I want you to lend me a little money—*now*."

For only reply the servant ran to the door. "Listen. Let me explain!" cried the Baron after him, desirous to tell about the Lady's Dole.

"Just one moment while I fetch it, sir," said Gustave, on the threshold.

"God forgive me," cried the Baron. "There are good men yet!" and his voice failed him. Gustave, meanwhile, who knew all about the Lady's Dole, had evidently made up his mind that the whole of his little fortune would just do to replace it. But he would not have presumed a second time to offer any suggestions thereanent.

"I only want a little at first, a very little," said the Baron presently, "just at first. When I get stronger I can do something, I dare say, and the Freule has a very fine voice. I should prefer to go to a large city. Your sister in Amsterdam who takes lodgers, perhaps we might go to her?"

The servant had the delicacy to keep back the rush of imploring protest which rose to his lips. "Amsterdam will be brighter for your Nobleness than Deynum," he said, "and for the Freule also. My sister will be proud. And you can always return later on."

"Never," replied the Baron. "Not even to be buried here!" And he broke down utterly and buried his face in his hands.

After a moment of hesitation Gustave slipped away without leave. "I wonder whether I did right," he debated with himself in the hall. "It looked almost more like a liberty to stay."

On the evening of their departure the Baron handed over to Gustave a correct I.O.U. for a fraction of the latter's savings, promising, with restless reiteration, punctually to repay. The valet carefully buttoned up the precious paper in his pocket-book, and subsequently, emboldened by a couple of parting glasses at Job Hennik's, he as cautiously tore it up, lest his heirs should at any time discover and enforce it.

So the family arrived in Amsterdam on a windy March night, and drove to Juffrouw Donders's lodging-house. This house stands—or stood—on a narrow canal in one of the humbler, middle-class parts of the city; the frowning houses look very forbidding; on both sides the stagnant water froths with garbage and weeds. But Wendela could see nothing of this, as she found herself blown, amid a whirl of sleet and general rawness, into a low, white-tiled passage, illumined by a far-away paraffin-lamp. The others were still busy with the Baroness; stout Juffrouw Donders came rolling forward and immediately overflowed. She was all abundancy and redundancy, all double-chin and shaking jaw. You fled away with the impression that there was too much of her, bodily, mentally, and especially orally. But, once out of reach of her shapeless good-nature, you looked back with regret.

"And this is the Freule van Rexelaer!" she began, with perceptible promise of very much more. "Oh, Freule, I seem to have known you from a child, so much have I heard of you, and your dear honoured parents! Everyone in this household knows everything about them! It will not be like coming among strangers to find yourselves in our midst!"

"They are bringing in my mother," said Wendela. "We should like to go to our own rooms at once, if you please."

"And so you shall, my dear Freule," replied the landlady with prominent sympathy, lumbering slowly to the front-door, meanwhile. She was not to be cheated of her welcome to the Baroness. She knew what was due to gentlefolks, as well as Gustave did.

Fortunately for the family from Deynum, she stood greatly in awe of her brother, who had often afforded her substantial support. During the first few days of their stay among these uncongenial surroundings, the old servant stood on guard twixt his masters and the world, warding off Juffrouw Donders's exuberant kindliness. The Baron seemed not ill-content. "This time, thank Heaven, there are no debts," he said. "And here I trust we shall live and die in peace."

Wendela looked away in silence. The house was dark, with the darkness of a great city's evil heart. It was stuffy. If you lifted the sash, the smell from the canal came streaming in. "A healthful smell," said Juffrouw Donders. "Just see what it has made of me!" Gustave having departed to look after the sale of the furniture, the good woman fell on Wendela, like a feather-bed, with endless laudation of her brother and disparagement of her departed husband. The birth of the one and the death of the other she considered the two chief blessings of her life. She had had a hard time of it with many mouths to fill. "Yet my own was never empty," she said, with a pat on her portly frame " though God knows I filled it last."

" Life is hideous," said Wendela more resolutely than ever, and she buried herself in the glorious past. She would draw her chair beside her mother's and ask for the tales she had heard as a child. " Wanda, Wanda," the Baroness murmured in gentle reproof, " Heaven alone is steadfast. The pomps and vanities fade away." " I know that," said Wendela bitterly.

Yet the lodging-house was not all noisy loneliness to the country-girl. A day or two after her arrival, as she was coming down-stairs earlier than usual, she met a young man who shrank aside with unwilling mien. The light from a little dusty window fell full upon his face ; his eyes were irresistibly drawn towards hers, and as his blush deepened to the old familiar apple-red, she recognised him. " Piet!" cried impetuous Wanda. Then she stammered : " I beg your pardon. I thought you were someone else," and stuck fast.

" I *am* Piet," said the young man. " I am glad you recognised me, Freule."

She leant up against the banisters, and it amused him to see how little changed her manner was. " However came you here?" she said. " I shall want you to tell me all about it."

There was not very much to tell. Having made his way to the capital, with the intention of " going to sea," he had met with good people who had kept him as their errand-boy. One day he had run up against Gustave, who was living with Juffrouw Donders, during the Baron's absence at Cleves, and Gustave had procured him a garret in the lodging-house. " And here I have been ever since," concluded Piet, " and wasn't it good of him to look after me, Freule ? "

" But why didn't he tell us?" questioned Wendela, bewildered. " And oh, your mother, Piet ! "

"Mother knows I'm doing well. She don't know any more. I can't help it," Piet went on doggedly. "Mynheer Gustave agreed with me. It's all father's fault. You know all about father, Freule."

"Yes, I know," said Wendela gravely. "But I thought that we all should be subject to our parents." She greatly admired herself for the propriety of this sentiment. She also admired herself for the faithfulness with which she practised it.

He looked grieved but not convinced. "I'm doing well," he said in self-defence. "Better than I should have done at home, though I've not made the fortune I had hoped to make. I am clerk to a solicitor, Freule."

She said she was very glad to hear it. He must come and see her father. And she continued her way, confused by the strangeness of this meeting. "He is just like a hundred other clerks," she told herself, but in her heart she thought this handsome, well-grown youth as superior to other clerks as her boy-lover had been superior to other peasant-boys. "He is just Piet," she said.

"A solicitor," said the Baron anxiously, "is the very person I am most desirous to meet, but one fights shy of them, especially after knowing Strum."

Piet Poster appeared before the Baron and Baroness. His manner was that of a page in the presence of his lieges.

"And what is the name of your solicitor, Piet?"

"Mynheer Spangenberg, landheer. Everybody says he's amazingly clever."

"So much the better. And where does he live?"

"He has his office on the Prinsengracht, landheer."

"I want you to ask him when he can receive me." Wendela looked up in protest. "Yes, my dear, yes; I can go in a cab."

"O Lamb of God, that takest away the sins of the world," repeated the Baroness with her back to the others.

"There's only one thing, landheer," began Piet, awkwardly fingering his pot-hat. "Master's a very great radical. One of the extreme Left, he calls it."

"Ah," said the Baron. Then he added, after a thoughtful pause, "I dare say there are honest men among them."

"And you, are you of the extreme Left?" asked Wendela, with laughing eyes.

"I am a clerk, Freule," he replied quickly.

"Hush, Wendela. Please, if possible, make an early appointment for me with your employer, Piet."

Wendela followed the young man into the passage. "You must no longer call my father 'landheer,'" she said.

"Oh but, Freule, I can hardly help it."

"You must help it. The landheer out yonder, forsooth, is Count Rexelaer!" She stamped her foot and then, ashamed of this ebullition, retreated hastily to the sitting-room. Juffrouw Donders's voice was heard downstairs, soundly rating the maid of all work.

CHAPTER LI.

LITTLE PARADISE.

"ANOTHER poem from Volkert," said Spangenberg, advocate and editor, tentatively dangling the manuscript in question over the editorial waste-paper basket.

"And who is Volkert?" asked the editor's companion, an untidy old man with a peaked beard, like a goat's.

"Your question proves what no longer wanted proving," replied Piet Poster's master, laughing, "namely, that you poets recognize no contemporary colleagues. This Volkert is a mysterious young gentleman at the Hague, of perfect manners—he has been here once or twice—and evidently of gentle birth. He is also a Priest and Prophet of the People, but then all the great poets are that nowadays."

"*I* take no interest in the lower classes, and you know it," replied the other, leisurely warming his knees. "Odi profanum vulgus, et arceo."

"I forgot," said the young editor carelessly. "Volkert does, a poetical one. He signs his contributions to my 'Cry of the People' with a single enigmatical P. By-the-bye, that might stand for 'Profanus.' Now what shall I do with his latest? The basket or the bays? Surely an editor's responsibility is unique under heaven!"

"Let me judge it," proposed the untidy man, sententiously, and he took up the paper. In a very short time he laid it down again. "Nicht einem jeden ward des Sänger's Kunst gegeben," he said.

Spangenberg's honest face twitched with sudden resentment. "I shall put it in," he declared coolly.

The poet rose, majestically gathering his dressing-gown about him. "You should not have asked my opinion, Christian!" he said with superb unreason, and stalked towards the door.

"No, but, look here, Mynheer Morèl!" cried the good-natured editor. "This is really fine; just listen! One would like its author to proclaim it in the 'salons' of the Hague!" But the other was gone.

The office of "The Cry of the People" was situated at that time in a little court just off the public thoroughfare. Since then it has been removed to more commodious quarters, but Spangenberg is still editor of the paper, Spangenberg the Socialist. Yes, he is a clever man, unfortunately. But Piet Poster was mistaken in vaunting the extent of his law-practice. People who employ lawyers possess property, and only a poor man makes money out of an "ism."

The name of the court was "Little Paradise." Hyperbolic that name may have been, but we know so little of Paradise. It is long since our ancestors lived there, and families which have "known better days" are too apt to exaggerate. Present Paradises go by comparison. The street was very narrow, very noisy, very dirty, and redolent of all the vegetable produce of Jewry, "given away," from slow hand-carts to thanklessly haggling Gentiles by hook-nosed, rag-bedecked benefactors. All day long the street was a babel of cucumbers and oranges. You were glad to escape from that bawling, brawling crowd, through a neat brick archway with a cheerfully grinning Death's head over it, into a little square of houses round a grass-plot and a central bed of roses. Mevrouw Morèl had begged the roses from Juffrouw Spangenberg.

The whole place belonged to Christian Spangenberg's parents, who lived in the substantial house alongside the archway; in fact, they had turned their unprofitable garden into an Eden of rent-producing bricks. Their back-windows looked out on the cottage-like buildings, which were low, like the rents, so that Heaven appeared nearer in the trim little court than in the tall, loud street, outside. The distant, deadened yell of "Cheap! Dirt cheap!" only beautified the silence, and Mrs. Spangenberg would let the children play upon the grass-plot, when Spangenberg was out. And children, romping on a grass-plot, will laugh and shout, even in the Jew-quarter of Amsterdam.

Mevrouw Morèl "thanked her Maker" for bringing her here. But, then, she was a thankful soul. She "thanked her Maker" constantly, and also "her stars," and "goodness," and even "herself," so there may not have been much in the gratitude she scattered so freely. She knew well enough what she meant when she thanked Mrs. Spangenberg. She meant eggs for the ailing, cakes for the diligent, kindness for all. There were nine Morèls, including parents, in one of the cottages, whom Spangenberg would never have accepted as tenants—only think of the woodwork!—but for Mrs. Spangenberg's broad admiration of the "dear little golden-haired, pale little dears."

Not that Spangenberg was by any means a hard-hearted man. He was a contractor; I do not know what he contracted in the course of his money-making except a gruff manner, but it certainly was not his heart. He made money, and his wife liked that, and they enjoyed it together in a solid, substantial, middle-class way; they had been poor together once. They sent their clever only son, who was always "wanting to know," to the Grammar School and then to the University, but when even this latter Babylonic Tower of Learning (as vast and as confused) still failed to supply young Christian's need, they began to fear that he wanted to know too much. There had been a daughter, much older than the late-born darling, who had married "against them," as they called it, and, sailing to the Indies with her husband, had dropped out of their lives. Henceforward Mrs. Spangenberg had a fretful dread of "thwarting," which maintained itself even when Christian (æt. 20) began to rant about the Rights of Man! "Don't put his back up, John," she constantly pleaded. "If we'd let Jacóba see more of her Arthur, perhaps she'd have found out what a duffer he was." The father unwillingly acquiesced, partly because of a manner young Hopeful had of throwing back his head as soon as the "thwarting" began. The worst blow befell the old man when his go-ahead son deliberately plunged into the sea of social miseries and thence sent up his "Cry of the People." The young advocate called himself a socialist, because with that party alone he found sympathy, political, with suffering. In reality he was one of the few whose pulses beat quicker when they hear of injustice—to others. His gorge rose against incompetent nepotism and pampered monopoly, against the sweating of women and the torture of children, things we all disapprove of theoretically, in our slippers by the fire. But Christian Spangenberg was an incipient Dutch Kingsley, with the poetry left out. He started a people's Mission and Social Club in the wretched quarter near his own respectable home. Furthermore he edited the "Cry of the People," thereby stamping himself a "Socialist" at once.

And his unfortunate father possessed money in the funds. The mother—desperate with the horror of a childless old age—flung her love between these combative elements and effected an armistice. Christian was to remain in the house and continue his law business. But his socialism must be banished to one of the cottages in Paradise Court, there to be left under lock and key when he rose to go home. The "Cry of the People" was never heard within Spangenberg Senior's doors. All the relations and connections, hard-working, hard-fisted burghers, looked on Christian as crazy. The chamber-cloaked father sat over his strong-box of evenings in property-laden snugness; the

25

eagle-faced son trod the boards of his Office at the back, denouncing the "gilded obesity of the bourgeois." And when they met at supper, sincerely affectionate, they got on very well.

It was Mevrouw Morèl's birthday, the greatest event of the year in Little Paradise, far greater even than Juffrouw Spangenberg's. For, if this latter good- and heavy-natured body was the Lady of the Garden, bright, clever little Mrs. Morèl was its Guardian Angel.

In the morning—"at dawn of day," said the poet—the seven children, six of whom had spent the night packed, like sardines, in boxes, gathered outside their parents' bedroom, the baby having been fetched out previously, to complete the surprise, while mother pretended to be asleep. And a surprise it was—as it had been for the last half-a-dozen years—when the whole lot of them, led by the baby, struck up an Ode to the Day. She came hurrying out and stood in the doorway, smiling upon them with the comeliest of faces, in her night-cap and woollen shawl, this mother of seven and an eighth baby coming, and she kissed them all round, on both cheeks, when the song was completed, and then had to kiss them again, because she had surreptitiously given Peterkin, the lame one, an extra hug and the others had seen it. Only her husband hung back, just a little ashamed. "It wasn't my own," he said with some hesitation; "I had not time to complete it. Next year, if I am spared, they shall sing you my own."

"I know, dearest," she said, "I recognised it. It was Pottema's. Yes, next year, please God; and then it will be the finest ode that ever poet sang."

"Do you think so?" he questioned dubiously. "I tore up what I had done. Pottema's poetry has faults, but, on the whole, it is not undeserving."

She sighed a little passing sigh. Lina, fifteen and her mother's right hand, had been a little toddling thing when

Homérus had first spoken of that ode to his wife. "She will not be able to repeat it, dear," the mother had said.

But the poem was not yet ready; none of Homérus's poems ever were. "Not for want of the power," said his wife, and perhaps she was right. Homérus Morèl was a seer of visions and a dreamer of beautiful dreams, his vast brow bursting with ideas, all in motion for an exit, like gases, a man full of thought, and yet often incapable of thinking. His father, an indolent scholar and gentleman, had given him a luxurious education, while spending the boy's small inherited fortune; in those days Homérus had only been Hendrik, the change was a late inspiration of his own. He believed himself the one supreme poet of his epoch, but he suffered from terrible spasms of doubt. With an artist's perception of the greatness beyond him, he would suddenly tear up whatever he had written, and sob out his weakness on the breast of his faithful spouse. And that lady would comfort him and send him for a walk in the Court. Once there, he could trudge round the grass-plot for hours, his lank body drooping forward beneath his knotted hands, his balloon-shaped head uplifted, with its pointed nose and beard. "There goes the poet," said some busy neighbour, at her lattice, "then it can't be twelve o'clock."

For punctually at noon Mevrouw Morèl would call: "Homérus, come to dinner!" She never bade him come and hold the baby, even when her own three hands were more than full.

She must have had at least three hands, for she looked after all the children, including this year's and last year's baby, and she even found time to have a girl-help and look after her. Moreover she looked after her husband and kept him as comfortable, though she could not keep him as tidy, as the rest. Incidentally she also supported the family, while the poetry was getting ready which was one day to enrich it. The whole lot of them believed in this beautiful con-

summation, even the smallest, who, having no inkling what
poetry was, were certainly least to blame. Father was their
gold-mine; some day he would be famous, and then there
would always be plenty to eat. They nudged each other,
at their play, suddenly hushed by the sight of the poet at
his desk. " What is riches, mother? Only money?" little
Homer, his father's namesake, had asked one day. The
parents looked at each other, struck to the soul. Mevrouw
Morèl had been down-hearted that morning, and had
grumbled somewhat. She kissed both Homers for only
reply.

The mother supported her family by writing children's
gift-books to order, the order mostly including the moral of
the tale : " To illustrate the evils of greediness, about 15,-
000 words. Little girl must have curly hair, and greengage
jam must be medium of punishment, as per picture. Ready
by 15th of next month." It was easy, and not unprofitable,
if only you wrote two stories a month.

The little woman's deepest depth of soul, however, was
not centred in her tale-concocting nor even in her house-
keeping ; those leisure moments which she had in common
with all intensely busy people she devoted to the composi-
tion of a many-volumed work on " The Social Position of
the Child in the Development of European Civilisation."
For she had been great since her childhood in the science
of sociology, of which her father had been professor and she
his favourite pupil. *Her* book will be finished some day,
you may be sure. " Scientific works do not sell," she would
say to her husband. " Not like poetry, first-rate poetry, of
course. Not as yours will." She apologised for her hobby.
Other luxuries she had none.

" Good morning, Mother; many happy returns of the
day," said young Spangenberg, looking in on Mevrouw
Morèl. " I couldn't come sooner, being detained by law-
business on the Prinsengracht."

" You mustn't call me ' mother ' any more, Christian, as I told you last birthday. I am getting too old to be pleased with a grown-up son."

" You old ! " the young advocate laughed merrily. " Your youth is as perennial as the Child's of which you write. What says baby ? Grandma ? "

She joined in his laugh, as she bustled about among her dinner-things.

" I wanted to ask," Christian Spangenberg went on, " would you let me bring Volkert this evening ?—I have spoken of him recently—you remember—the poet ? "

" Oh, you may bring him of course. But is he one of your Socialists, Christian ? Because, you know, I do not believe in your Socialists."

" Nor I in sociology, Mevrouw, you remember. Good-bye, then, and thanks, till to-night."

" That boy does too much," remarked Mevrouw Morèl, hurrying from the table to the oven.

" A man cannot do too much," said the poet, from his arm-chair by the fire.

" But he can do too many things at a time," protested the housewife, who mostly did three.

" True ; he should give his whole mind to one," responded Homérus, " would he excel."

CHAPTER LII

VOLKERT.

SPANGENBERG rushed on to his office—his editorial office. "Anyone been, Wonnema?" he asked of the single clerk.

"Only a man with some copy. Mynheer Volkert's up-stairs." The clerk, a meagre-looking individual with ever-lastingly hungry eyes, handed a packet across to his "chief."

"All right. You can go and have dinner." Spangen-berg ran up to his den. "Hallo," he cried on entering. "Glad you managed to come. Doing nothing, as usual?"

"I was thinking," replied the individual thus addressed, without altering his lazy position by the stove.

"That need not have prevented your keeping up the fire. Or supposing you had looked through this stupid pile of newspapers—but that was expecting too much."

"True," said the other. "Don't bully me. You know I've no head for practical politics."

"Practical politics unfortunately have but little to do with the 'Cry,'" muttered the young editor, pausing, with a very satirical grin, by his over-loaded desk.

"But look here," began Volkert suddenly, "I really had something to occupy me. I found this on coming in." He flung across a paper to his friend.

It contained these few words in a firm feminine hand:

"Your poem last week was noble and true. Go on; you are doing a great work."

Spangenberg turned the paper round, then he looked

hesitatingly into Volkert's handsome expectant face, and burst into a shout of laughter.

"Of course she is young!" he cried, "and very beautiful. I don't wonder you are charmed."

"I don't care about that," replied the poet earnestly. "I have touched a human heart."

"Can you pardon me, if I inquire what particular verses the lady is alluding to? She has taken her time about writing, and I grieve to say I forgot."

"It's the one called 'Noble Nobles,'" replied Volkert, sullenly staring at the neglected stove. "You remember, the one beginning:

"'They are not noble who but bear the name,
    While deeds and words a bastard's birth proclaim;
    But they whose heart and intellect have fed
    Upon the truths for which their fathers bled.'"

"Quite so," said Spangenberg. "And do you know exactly what it means?"

"Why did you insert it?" asked the poet with spirit.

But Christian, his eyes upon the letter, musingly repeated Volkert's first two lines. "I have it," he said slowly. "Some poor little shop girl or sempstress, ruined by a sprig of the aristocracy, 'whose words and deeds a bastard birth proclaim.' *Now* she finds out he won't marry her. Poor little creature: I wish I could help." He got up and came and stood in front of Volkert: "Yes," he said, "you have beautiful thoughts. It is very nice and pretty to have beautiful thoughts."

"It's not that," replied Volkert. "Here is a human creature whose heart I've touched. It's a wonderful experience. I have touched some grateful stranger's heart. I never felt anything like it before."

"It *is* grand," said Christian, solemnized by the other's evident emotion, "to know that one man can help another by something else besides a copper tossed in the dirt. Did you never feel that before? Gifted, graceful, graceless sleeper, you feel it—do you?—at last?"

The "mysterious young gentleman from the Hague" spread a pair of white hands towards the sooty stove. "I suppose I had not your opportunities," he replied, a little moodily.

"The more you feel it the better," cried his youthful Mentor, unheeding. "I wish I could trample the feeling deep down into your heart. Don't mind me or the mistakes I am making. Go down on your knees to whatever God you believe in and vow, at this crisis of your soul's existence, never to let the new feeling slip away. Give yourself in the future, not your money only, not only your beautiful thoughts. Give your position which I believe to be high; give your talents which I know to be great. There are so few of us who think as you do. Give yourself in the fight against oppression and injustice, against ignorance and crime."

"I will," cried the other. "I have always wanted to; it sounds so beautiful. But I am waiting for my opportunity; some day it will come!"

"Look through these newspapers then," replied Christian, pushing forward a pile; "mark all passages alluding to the trial of the boy Smits for insulting the Minister of Justice. Poor little fellow! they had imprisoned his father for speaking the truth. There; that will do for to-day. To-morrow will take care of itself." The poet pulled a face, but he drew up his chair to the table and began doing as he was bid.

Presently Spangenberg looked up from his own work: "For doing only is the true believing," he quoted. "Somebody says that; I forget who."

"Why, it's in one of my sonnets," said Volkert. "You know it is."

"On my honour, I did not. Oh you poets, you poets!"

In the evening the two men met again at Spangenberg's law-office, on their way to the Morèls'. "I must just look in at the 'Club,'" said Christian, as they emerged into the street.

The "Club," then the first of its kind, would be considered a poor affair nowadays. It stood in a back street of one of the humblest parts of the city; the double parlour downstairs being occupied by workmen smoking and drinking beer over their newspapers or chess-boards; while in one of the upstairs rooms a reading-class was going on for street-arabs over twelve. Everybody knew Christian, the founder of the whole concern, and several men expressed regret that to-night's weekly lecture had been postponed. The subject was announced: "Why and how must we reach the North Pole?" Last week's had been "The Follies of the Paris Commune."

Piet Poster was the teacher of the upstairs boys, a disciplinarian sturdily jolly and strong. As the young men entered his class-room, a dirty ragamuffin came slouching in behind them; the poet drew hastily aside. "Coffee," called out Poster, "go downstairs again immediately. You know you mayn't come up till you're washed."

The boy hesitated. Spangenberg turned quickly: "My dear Volkert," he said, "it's late already, and I must be busy a few minutes with Poster. Take this urchin downstairs—there's a good fellow!—and wash him."

The couple departed—it would have been too silly to refuse. As they wound down the narrow staircase, Volkert, anxious to cover his embarrassment, commenced conversation.

"Why do they call you 'Coffee'?" he asked.

"Because of what came off when I washed first," said the boy.

They found a pantry in which stood several tubs of tepid water, under a flaring gas-light. "I won't," said the boy, when he saw them, and hung up, dogged and dishevelled, against the whitewashed wall.

The young dandy opposite twirled his cane and felt ashamed of his orange gloves. He resolved to try argument: " Why not ? " he said, persuasively.

" 'Cos it makes one feel cold," replied Coffee.

" But then you can't go upstairs again. Don't you want to learn to read ? "

" Yes, I shall too," said Coffee. He stared intensely. He was lost in contemplation of the gentleman's gold chain. The Lover of all Mankind grew weaker than water before this refractory brother, but vanity recoiled from an unwashed return to the class-room. " Look here," he said, " I'll give you this silver florin, if you'll clean your face and hands." The effect was instantaneous. " You needn't mention the florin," said Volkert, as they wended their way upstairs again. But at the door he halted, ashamed. " Say what you like," he whispered. A cheer greeted the vanquished Coffee, who stole silently to a seat. " I congratulate you, Mynheer," said Piet in an eager aside to the visitor. " For days I have been regretfully sending that boy away. You manage them better than I." Volkert coloured. " I gave him a florin to do it," he said.

Mevrouw Morèl's frequent evening-parties would have delighted William Wordsworth, for their material pleasures were " plain," and their " thinking " was " high." This occasion of her birthday, however, was always distinguished by mixed company, and drinks. Spangenberg Senior's annual contribution consisted of a bowl of punch, and his wife sent a cake from the confectioner's which the children declared vastly inferior to their mother's homemade.

There was little Miss van Dolder in her grandmother's brooch and a black silk which might also have been her grandmother's. Miss van Dolder represented Hereditary Wealth in Little Paradise, with an income, from somewhere in the funds, of nearly a hundred pounds. She had seriously considered the duty of removing when the "Cry" first arose in the Court, but she dreaded the possible damage to her grandmother's inlaid cabinet. She professed an inherent distaste for all children and manifested a consistent affection towards the seven little Morèls. And there was Balby, the poor old lodger at the dressmaker's, Homérus's especial protégé, because he devoted whatever remained to him of life to the silent accompaniment of the poet on his interminable walks round the square. Homérus discoursed of all things in heaven or on earth, or beneath the abysses of the sea; if he halted for breath, his companion would remark, with a shake of the head: "It is marvellous indeed" or "It sounds quite incredible," and the poet would complacently proceed. One day he had been telling how a famous contemporary had acknowledged his genius: "And what do you think of that?" he inquired. "It sounds quite incredible," said Balby, meditatively eying the pump.

And there were the parent Spangenbergs, upon whose arrival the extra candles were lighted. Miss van Dolder remained anxiously debating with herself whether she had taken offence at this on the previous occasion. Spangenberg, on his part, was considering, for the fiftieth time, if the hostess was entitled to "my dear" the wife of the owner of the property. Fortunately Homérus sat oblivious of these doubts. Was it not "*Mevrouw* Morèl" and "*Juffrouw* Spangenberg"? Only a Dutchwoman can fully fathom that distinction.

Presently Christian put in his head. "Good evening, everybody. Good evening, Miss van Dolder," he said, "how solemn you all look. Might I ask you something, Mevrouw?"

She came out to him on the landing. "I was just mixing the punch," she said reproachfully.

"Oh, it can't spoil under your hands. I've got Tipper,

the tailor-evangelist I was telling you of. May I bring him up as well as Volkert? He isn't as tiresome as you'd think."

" But what's the use of bringing all these people here, Christian?"

" Oh, I want them to know you. It does them good."

" True," said the little lady thoughtfully. " Any-one might consider it a privilege to listen to Mynheer Morèl."

" Exactly," replied Spangenberg, bounding downstairs.

" But your parents will object," she hissed over the ban-isters.

" They always do," sang back this graceless product of parental love.

Volkert, immediately on his entrance, held all the ladies' hearts in the hollow of his unconscious hand. In that humble little company he shone unassumingly, like a still, white star, his one unattainable desire to remain unnoticed and give no trouble. Tipper on the other hand, a good young man and first cutter to a tailoring firm, shrank back, fussy from shyness and irregularly assertive on principle. It was his religious belief he asserted, not himself.

The clock ticked slowly, and the respectable company sat in a circle of boredom. Juffrouw Spangenberg praised the eldest daughter, Lina, to her blushful face, causing the damsel's mother to wriggle on her chair, and the contractor tediously told a lengthy story, which everyone had read the day before in the *Amsterdam Gazette*, about an Emir of Blucherstan (as he called him) who, travelling on a tour of inspection in famine-stricken provinces, had requisitioned provisions from the starving inhabitants and been fed upon roast child under the designation of veal. The little hostess cast terrified glances at the wall behind which five of her own offspring were sleeping; the advocate murmured a " pereant! " over his punch.

" It was one of that family that conquered Napoleon?"

suggested the dressmaker's lodger, speaking for the first time.

"Of course, Balby," replied Christian heartily amid the general hesitation. "So I thought," said the lodger, taking snuff.

But it was not till the elder Spangenbergs had departed, accompanied by Miss van Dolder (in a flutter of irritable self-reproach for having once more forgotten to rise before the contractor's wife) that the simple enjoyment, such as it was, of the evening began. Half a dozen men drew their chairs round the bright fire and the plenteous punch-bowl, and little Mrs. Morèl sat down to her squeaky piano and played them Chopin. Then Spangenberg sang a couple of songs, and one of these brought a thrilling surprise to the stranger; the words were his own, a lament from the "Cry," set to music, by whom? The tears stood in his big dark eyes. "Magnificent eyes," whispered the little musician to Christian. But Christian was busy proposing her health in terms of abundant laudation and trying to get Tipper, the teetotaler, to drink it in a glass of the golden fluid. Then a silence fell upon the company that Mynheer Morèl—they all called him "Mynheer"—might have his share of the fun and orate, which he did, warmly and well.

"You young men are mistaken, as I often tell Christian," he was saying to the new-comer, "in striving and straining, for a millennium. History should tell you that a nation's greatness, like an individual's, is absolutely dependent on present suffering and future hope. I trust, I sincerely trust, that the human race will never live contented. Fortunately there is now less chance than ever of that."

"The people——" began Spangenberg.

"Don't interrupt me, Christian. Pah, the folly of your talk. You are shamed by the Greeks or the Jews, who, like you disbelieving in a future life, at least believed, unlike you, in the joys and griefs of the present. Almost I would prefer the patient Man of Sorrows, with his glories of adversity and his 'yet a little while.' At least, experience can never disprove his ideals, as it speedily will yours. And although we may think that he grossly exaggerated the ethical value of suffering——"

The quiet tailor stretched his arm across the table as if warding off a blow. "I cannot hear my Lord and Master spoken of like that," he said.

Homérus started, uncertain what to do, and turned to Balby to hide his confusion.

"It is truly marvellous," said the lodger, waking up.

"Well, well, I am doing all the talking," continued Homérus, "which is uncivil"—O sancta simplicitas!—"you young men ought to furnish me with novel ideas. I have often contemplated writing a poem on 'The Coming Creed.' In fact, I have begun one, but the subject is momentous."

"Surely the coming Creed will be Love," ventured Volkert.

"Ah, young man; that is no novel idea. It is the old one which each good man newly starts with. Have you ever heard, you youngsters, of the love which speaks through pain? Love?—what do you, what do I know of love? Some of us, the best, the highest, are struggling to read, in the blinding sunlight, a few letters of that sacred Name, and to shout them down to the chattering, chaffering masses below. These are the poets, the prophets, on the uppermost rungs of the ladder. One of them, soaring beyond the power of eyes to follow, has cried back into our darkness: 'God is Love!' There we may leave it, in the inmost heart of Heaven." He stopped abruptly, and with a hasty, unconscious fervour, swept his long hand across the tablecloth.

Spangenberg leaped to his feet. "Erós! Anikate Erós!" he cried, "I am not a poet, like Mynheer or like Volkert; I am only a common-place mortal, but my heart sings the pæans my lips are unable to speak. What fitter

temple than this to recite the praise of the Prince who
holds rule here, a merciful tyrant? Gentlemen, hurrah for
Love in this house, where he gilds every day with his
presence. Hurrah for a sun that ascends through the years
without danger of setting. Gentlemen, I fancy I am talking nonsense. Hurrah for Mevrouw Morèl, the Queen of
Love in her own little kingdom! Hurrah!"

They all shouted and emptied their glasses, and soon
after that the little party broke up. Not, however, before
Christian had told Volkert about the hostess's wonderful
work on the "Social Position of the Child."

"A study in evolution," added Mevrouw Morèl, blush-
ing. "Thank you, Christian; I have reached the Mero-
vingian period. I should progress faster but that I so seldom
find time to go to the library for books."

"Couldn't I fetch them for you?" asked Volkert im-
pulsively.

The little lady blushed with pleasure. "Oh, I couldn't
really——" she began, but Spangenberg cut her short.
"That's right, Volkert," he said. "He's got oceans of
time, Mevrouw, and you've nobody else"—a quick glance at
the white-headed seer, who was gazing abstractedly into the
lamp—"He can come to you about it to-morrow."

The young men took leave. At the door the tailor
stopped, irresolute, and then faced round. "There is——"
he began, "I—I should just like to say this. You have
been kind in asking me here. I—perhaps we shall never
meet again. You have been speaking a great deal about
human happiness and the King of Love! Oh the King of
Love!"—he clasped his hands. "If only you knew him!
He leads his servants in paths of perfect peace. He is *my*
King. Would to God the Lord Jesus ruled in every heart
here present to-night." He had spoken the closing sentences quite fluently. He gave them all a sort of little farewell bow and was gone.

Christian and Volkert followed more slowly, passing in

silence across the desolate court. By the Spangenbergs' door they halted, under a solitary gas-lamp.

"Mynheer Morèl talks well," said Christian. "He has beautiful thoughts, like you, and he has talked about them all his life."

"And this is what you call a convivial evening?" asked the other young man.

"Yes," replied Christian, latch-key in hand, "this is what I call pleasant intercourse. Would you prefer a ball?"

Volkert went on alone. For a long time Christian's words kept ringing in his ears, but gradually they gave place to the other strange impressions of the evening: Mevronw Morèl, Mynheer Morèl, that humble home of valiant love and lofty effort. How they loved each other, these two, how they understood each other! This, surely, this unity of love and art was *life*. And was it the poet's fault if poetry doesn't pay?

Then he remembered Tipper and smiled. Yet deep down in his heart lay the tailor's solemn message: "He leads *His* servants in paths of perfect peace."

"Well," he mused, "I shall have to spend the morning in the University Library. After that I must hurry back, for I am due at my aunt's 'At Home.' Christian is right, but he sees only his one side of the question. I made a fool of myself at his 'Club.' A gentleman's duty is to remain a gentleman. Then what right have I to break loose? I accept my dull weight of 'Fortune's favours,' and drag on alone."

CHAPTER LIII.

THE WILL.

"Who is that?" asked a passer-by, as the brougham with its beautiful grey thoroughbreds swept at a sharp angle out of the Noordeinde into the square before the Palace.

"His Excellency Count Rexelaer," replied his companion. "Doubtless on duty. One can see you are a stranger in the Hague."

"Of course I am. And who is Count Rexelaer? One of the Rexelaers of Deynum?"

The other laughed aloud. "And who is King William?" he said. "And who is the Pope? It is something, at least, that you know there are Rexelaers of Deynum."

The "provincial" was nettled. "That is altogether different," he said. "Everyone knows that; it is a matter of history. But as for distinguishing each little mannikin at Court——"

"Hush, hush! you are still in the Hague. Keep those sayings for when you get back to Friesland. He is *the* Rexelaer of Deynum; will that suffice you? And moreover, or perhaps on that account, My Lord the High Seneschal."

"Well, at any rate, he had a nasty, sneaking sort of face," said the Frisian, as they walked on.

Count Rexelaer alighted from his carriage and passed through the great glass doors. The doorkeeper checked him deferentially.

26

"There is a foreign gentleman waiting to see your Excellency," he said.

Count Rexelaer found the foreigner in his bureau. He was a tall man, correctly dressed and neatly shaven, a man with a settled expression of worry on his smooth, pale face. Count Rexelaer measured him at a glance. One of those persons whom everybody but a gentleman, even a Royal doorkeeper, mistakes for a gentleman. Count Rexelaer was a gentleman and knew.

"My name is Loripont, Excellency," said the stranger politely, in French, "Antoine Loripont, at your Excellency's service. I can hardly flatter myself that your Excellency remembers it."

"No," said the Count, "I do not." After a moment's indecision he waved his hand in the direction of a chair.

Loripont took no notice of this permission. All through the interview he remained standing in a "correct" attitude by his Excellency's writing-table.

"I was valet," he continued, "to the late Monsieur the Marquis de la Jolais-Farjolle de Saint-Leu et de Deynum" —was it deference which prompted this final addition, or rather a desire to annoy?—"I was with Monsieur the Marquis at the time of his death. Shortly after, I wrote to your Excellency."

"Ah, *that* I remember," said the Count. "I replied to your letter by asking for fuller information, which was never received."

"It is so, Monsieur le Comte. Most humbly I hope for your Excellency's pardon. From the tone of the reply I too rashly concluded that further attempts would be useless. And so I gave the matter up."

"If it was ' chantage' you meditated," said the Count frigidly, "as I believed at the time, your efforts were indeed superfluous. They would be so still."

"It was not ' chantage,' Monsieur le Comte, if your Excellency will forgive me. I have no wish to extort money.

The Deynum Notary told me, immediately after my lamented master's decease, that the document was valueless. When your Excellency answered me that you were willing to perform whatever the law of the country required of you, I said to myself: I can do no more. The good God must look after his own."

"You showed judgment," said his Excellency, with downcast smile, drumming his polished finger-tips on the table. "Has time rendered you less discreet?"

"Not so, Monsieur le Comte, but time has taught me better. Perhaps the Deynum Notary did not know; perhaps he did not want to know. I have discovered that the document was not absolutely valueless. It is a valid will and testament."

Count Rexelaer looked up with an oath. "That is a lie," he said shrilly. "An infamous, blackguardly, blackmailing lie. Not a penny shall you get." Then his gaze sank slowly down again, upon his polished finger-tips.

"I must beg of your Excellency not to swear at me," said Antoine; "it awakens too painful recollections. I was about to remark that, in my country, the will was perfectly valid. I am speaking the truth. It would have been valid, even had there been no witnesses."

"It was not binding in Holland," said the Count, "and that is enough."

"The paper," continued Antoine, without heeding the interruption, "cancelled the Dutch will the Notary had just drawn up, and directed that the entire estate of Deynum and the sum of two hundred thousand francs should pass to the Convent of Crévort, to the little sisters of the poor, to be spent exclusively in charity. Madame the Countess, your lady, was again completely disinherited."

"Had this 'paper' been of any value, you would have turned up eight years ago," said the Count.

"Three years after the decease of Monsieur le Marquis I learned, from a Belgian lawyer, exactly what its value was. We could not have touched your Castle, Monsieur, which—luckily for you—lies in Holland, but the Belgian money should never have been paid. That was a mistake."

"Mistakes are often difficult to remedy," said the Count with a smile.

"Surely that depends upon who was erroneously benefited by them?" suggested Loripont, who had always been perfectly at ease in the extremes of servility and insolence. "Your Excellency has received from Belgium two hundred thousand francs to which you had not even a legal claim. Had I shown my little paper sooner, you would never have received them."

"Are you come to ask them back?" asked the Count.

"As for that, I am come to ask everything back."

His Excellency cast a quick glance at the bell-rope.

"There can be no doubt that your Excellency is not entitled to Deynum. My master left his property to the Church. I am only a valet. I ask you, a Christian and a nobleman: Have you a right to retain it?"

"The property," replied the Count, "is both naturally and legally mine. Allow me to say that my time is much occupied. The Marquis, just before his violent death, cannot have been responsible for his actions, and that paper, if it be genuine, represents a crazy whim. Good morning."

Loripont did not stir from his respectful pose. "As for whims," he replied boldly, "the first will was no less a whim than the second. But I hardly dared to expect that your Excellency would give back the estate. With the money, however, it is a different matter. That was paid in legal error. I am told it cannot be legally redemanded. I am not a judge of such matters. To me your law, which sets aside a dead man's wish, seems monstrous."

The Count veered round in his chair, politely contemplative. "On the contrary, my good man," he said. "Allow me to explain. The Dutch law is exceedingly judicious in requiring the assistance of a Notary. Were the rule generally introduced, a contested succession would become an exceeding rarity. In this country such cases are almost unknown."

"I understand nothing of these matters, your Excellency. But one thing I know. That money is not yours. It belongs to God."

"Is that why *you* come and ask for it?"

"Monsieur le Comte, I do not ask a penny for myself. I can no longer bear the idea that the owners have been defrauded through my negligence. That idea haunts me night and day."

"Nevertheless, I am unable to employ you as a go-between in paying my dues to the Almighty. That is final."

The Count blinked irritably and pushed about his writing-things.

"Monsieur le Comte," Antoine laid one hand on the table, "it is the religion—can you not understand? You know how my master died; I have kept my oath to him, and Brussels does not. For pardon he gave it all in that desperate moment—to buy pardon for his crime. And now it is useless, and a curse must rest upon it, while, perhaps, he endures the pains of purgatory. Do you dare to leave him *there?*"

Once more Count van Rexelaer smiled. "My friend," he said, "you are melodramatic. You can hardly expect me to purchase a release for all my relations whom their own misbehaviour may have landed in hell. But these are superstitious ideas, the outcome of a corrupt religion. With us Protestants Hell or Heaven is a question of grace, not of gold. There; of course you cannot understand. To come down to business: How much do you want? You were long my uncle's valet and, once in a way, I do not mind assisting you with a couple of hundred francs, but, take notice, you mustn't come again."

"My God, it is hopeless!" exclaimed Antoine, and fell back with a lurch, and stood silent.

" Yes, my offer is conclusive. It's no use trying these things on with me, my man,"—the Count held out a bank-note—" Here, thank me, and get you gone."

" Listen, you!" the quondam valet bent forward eagerly. " I used not to care so much about being quite sure. But as a man gets nearer the end, he wants to doubt on the right side. When your wife's uncle killed himself (and I hadn't grown rich in his service), I paid money to have masses said."

" That was very wrong," interrupted the Count. " It is a foolish, futile superstition."

" Listen, please. From this paper "—he tapped his breast—" I knew the suicide had hoped to spend his thousands where I could but give hundreds. I could not help that. Three years later I learned that I *could* have helped it. O my God, what a thought! It was my fault, then, that the money had not been paid! I have a small business; my wife is frugal and it prospers, but every penny I can scrape or save I bring to the priests in payment of my debt. My wife does not comprehend and our ménage is disunited. I shall never pay it off. I shall die before it is done. I also have a complaint "—he clutched at his chest; his words came hoarse and fast—" I am dying. I *dare* not die with that unpaid debt. I dare not meet the dead man, beyond, perhaps, in those flames in which my fault has chained him. Voyons, Monsieur le Comte—you are a mighty Noble—even you, you do not *know*."

An awe-struck silence sank upon the little room. The sick man stood panting, his eyes fixed, in eager doubt, on the other's face. The Court Favourite was calming his fretful nerves. At last he spoke, smoothly enough : " Your religious ideas are all wrong, my good man," he said. " I wish I could get you to speak to one of our pastors, for I see you are in earnest. You are the victim of a system which trades upon human credulity. Were the sum but a trifle, my scruples would forbid me to squander it on priests."

"I have refunded forty," said Antoine doggedly. "It has taken all these years. And a hundred and sixty remain."

"So you say. But this wonderful will, I have not even seen it!"

A flash of hope played across the suppliant's face, as he softly inquired: "Is your Excellency near-sighted?"

"No. Why do you ask?" But the Count knew why, and even he winced under this menial's measureless contempt.

Antoine fell back a few paces: "I am not as strong as I used to be," he said apologetically. Then he drew a paper from his breast and held it aloft with one hand, while the other remained concealed in a bulky side-pocket, which, the Count felt convinced, contained a revolver.

"It is the Marquis's crest," said Antoine. "If you knew his eccentric hand, you will easily recognize it."

"I cannot read it from here," replied Count Rexelaer indifferently. "Besides, the matter is of no account. You may take your hundred florins——" he got up and rang the bell.

Antoine Loripont put back his paper, buttoned his coat, and folded his arms across his chest. "And now," he said in accents of desperate restraint, "it becomes 'chantage.' I will make you do it. In the organs of the opposition, in the socialist journals, I will publish this valid will, valid but for a fluke. Now, will you listen?"

"In the papers of the opposition, the socialist journals? My good friend, pourquoi pas? I do right in upholding the law of the land. There, admit my incredible good-nature, in a man of my exalted position. Monsieur my departed uncle's would not have held out so long."

Steps were heard in the adjoining anteroom. Antoine Loripont pressed close to the Head of the Household, who

involuntarily shrank back. " I will tell," said the man in a
clear whisper, " what I know—it is not much, but it is
enough—of the wealth of Mademoiselle Cochonnard.
Now, Monsieur the Court Dignitary, here in the Royal
Palace I ask you again : Will you pay back the money or
not?"

For the second time during that interview the Count
swore a fierce oath. " D——," he said, " I knew it was
black-mailing all along. How much do you want? Will
five thousand florins do?"

" All or nothing," answered Loripont, retreating to the
door.

The Count started up and came running after him.

" Ten thousand," he hissed out hurriedly. " I can't
make it more than ten thousand. Twenty thousand francs.
Consider. Nobody would offer more."

Loripont opened the door and left him.

CHAPTER LIV.

THE SLOUGH OF DESPOND.

An hour later Count Rexelaer quitted the August Presence renewed and refreshed in all the tissues and fibres of his moral being, as by a bath of sunlight. For we all of us are strengthened by a draught from our Source of Life, physical or psychical, and the Court Functionary left the Court Atmosphere, refilled, re-corked, re-labelled and re-polished, a bottle full of sweetest Essence of Orange-flowers, with a soft little kidskin mask and a ribbon. Not that it wore the ribbon to-day, but it always felt it there.

"I may as well look in on Elizabeth," he said to himself, as another flunkey was helping him on with his coat. "Perhaps Gratia will be there, and that will save me a visit." Gratia was his old, unmarried sister, come to stay for a week with some quiet friend of her own.

He satisfied himself, on entering, that Gratia *was* there, and a great many other people also. Mevrouw Elizabeth, in her hospitable, comfortable life, liked to see her spacious rooms well-filled. Hilarius was an unusual visitor at her receptions; she received him with effusion.

"How is Jane's baby?" he asked, from the tips of his colourless lips. "Accept my congratulations."

"As for congratulations, my dear Hilarius, his abominable father has again cut them down."

"Fathers can't live for ever, not even old Simmans," the Count said lightly. But the words struck back, cold, with a swift reminiscence: "Even your Excellency, who is a great noble, does not *know*."

He glanced across at his own son and successor in spirited conversation with a voluminous somebody in a prominent pink boa, the Russian minister's wife. Then he edged away to his sister, whom he found the centre of an amused little group. "Doubtless, making a fool of herself," he reflected, as he greeted her. "I am sorry we so seldom meet, Hilarius," said the timid lady. "We were wanting to ask you to dinner, but we thought Margherita would hardly care to come?" The Count murmured something about pressing duties, and Reinout also came lounging up, dodging a beautiful woman who was evidently seeking to attract his attention—you remember the Duchess de Vañhas Vermillanas and her recent infatuation for Scriccini, the tenor? Well, twenty years ago, in the full flush of her beauty and her scorn for the Duke, she was deeply in love with Reinout van Rexelaer. His portrait still stands on her toilet-table, amid rouge-pots and essences. She bought it when he became famous.

"Hilarius, I want your subscription, too," said the Freule. "And Reinout's as well,"—she turned to the lady beside her, a Privy Councillor's wife—"it has really done excellent work"—she looked up at her brother. "I am speaking of the Society for furnishing Layettes——"

"Fie," said his Excellency, holding up a playful finger. There was a general giggle. How witty he was, his Excellency! "What a subject," he continued, "for an unmarried lady!"

"Hilarius!" she looked at him for a moment with her gentle, guileless eyes; then she turned to her nephew: "We only supply, to the poorest of the poor, what is absolutely indispensable; I assure you the work is good."

"I believe it," he said, and her face quite brightened under unaccustomed sympathy. He was written down a member on the spot, though declaring himself unable, to his father's disgust, to produce the humble florin of membership. Half an hour ago he had emptied his purse, with the old unthinking generosity, into the hands of a woman overflowing with woe.

His immediate neighbour stood twitting him with his novel duties. " You will have," she said, " to take the baskets round, yourself, and "—she screamed with merriment—" you will have to pin on the—the things ! " Plump Rolline, an early matron, drew nearer to enjoy the joke. " Oh, how funny ! " she said. " I should love to see the dear little baskets, with the dozens of little caps and chemises all done up with coloured ribbons and frills. I must ask Aunt Gratia to put me down for a florin too."

In another corner of the room George, looking handsomer than ever, was telling a story to an admiring circle of girls, amongst whom sat, in a clumsy, crimson heap, his own especial Miss Kops, the single untitled person in the room. The story, in spite of its silver-gilt wrappings, had dirt at its core. Reinout stood watching for a moment ; two of the girls who were listening belonged to the half-a-dozen from whom he was expected to choose a wife. He flushed scarlet as he turned away.

" Your cousin is evidently a wit," remarked Monsieur de Bonnaventure at his elbow. " When young ladies smile in that unwilling manner, the joke is always to their taste. I regret the more that I cannot speak the language."

" You know languages enough already," replied Reinout with a sneer, " to speak to women in."

The attaché smiled. " What will you have ? It is part of the profession, as you will learn soon enough. Have you any idea where they are going to send you ? Your father spoke of St. Petersburg. The climate is cold, but not the ladies. At any rate it is never dull."

Reinout, already several paces off, stopped and eyed the Frenchman from head to foot. " You find the Hague dull ? " he said slowly.

" I ?—forgive me, but yes. Wherewith should I amuse myself ? "

Antoinette, who was standing in a corner with the Count, here beckoned to her cousin to join them.

"Fallait endormir le petit," muttered the Frenchman as he sauntered away to take leave of the lady of the house, with tenderest enquiries after her venerable parent, whose wonderful health formed, in all Dutch society, a subject of amused admiration.

"Come here, Reinout," cried Topsy. "I am trying to get Uncle Hil to admire these verses. They are in the same review as those which Jane read out the other day, and by the same writer. I see that he signs 'René,' a namesake of yours. They are so good I wish you had written them; but uncle Hil doesn't care a bit."

The Count was looking bored. "Thank Heaven he has not," he said with awakening fervour. "One poet in the family is quite enough. No, Topsy, our future diplomat is certainly not poetical."

"Father, are you going away soon?" asked Reinout, detaining him, "because I should like to accompany you home."

"In a quarter of an hour," replied the Count. "Ta, ta, Antoinette. Don't read too much."

"Reinout," said his cousin, "come out into the conservatory for a minute." She passed into a little glass passage, bright with greenery and azaleas, and there stood silent, gazing down upon the open page. "Blessed are the pure in heart," she said presently. The French poem before her, some five and twenty lines, bore this title: "The Pure in Heart." The words of the close—but is poetry not untranslatable?—might be inadequately rendered as follows:

.   .   .   .

Eyes that would soar—Almighty God, Thou knowest—
Unto the whitest secrets of Thy breast,
Must they still sink, from lower depth to lowest,
By their own weight depressed!

Hearts held enchained by weeds and muddy coating,
Shall they not burst their bond,
And rise at last, in Thy pure sunshine floating,
Like lilies on a pond?

"For they shall see God," murmured Antoinette.

She looked up and gave Reinout her hand. Her eyes were full of tears.

"You will not betray me?" he asked, breaking the silence.

"Of course not," she answered. "But why 'betray'? Don't you want, at least, to pluck your laurels?"

"In there?" he asked, pointing to the crowded room from which they had just escaped. There was such a world of misery in his voice that she dropped her eyes again. "My father and I," he added, inconsequentially, "in our own way, we *do* love each other."

A commotion had arisen meanwhile among the gay company inside. Rolline appeared in the framework of the window, filling it with her healthful prosperity. Even at that moment a flicker of amusement played over her perturbed features at sight of the pair in the greenhouse.

"Oh, Topsy, haven't you heard?" she said. "Grandmamma's had a fit. Isn't it dreadful? She's dead."

Ten minutes later Count Rexelaer and his son, side by side in the silence, were driving rapidly home. They had nearly reached their destination before Reinout began:

"Father, this is what I had wanted to say: Monsieur de Bonnaventure comes to the house too much."

"Surely, Reinout, I am the best judge of the question whom I think fit to receive."

"Father, I only wanted to say this: Monsieur de Bonnaventure comes to our house too much."

"It is an improper thing to say, a ridiculous thing. Oblige me by speaking of something else, or holding your tongue."

" You will remember—will you not ?—that I said it ? "

" No, I will try to forget."

They did not exchange another word. The carriage stopped. Reinout was nearest the door. He got out first and hurried up the steps. In the entrance-hall he paused and faced his father. A well-known hat and stick lay on an oaken seat. Their glances met and dropped away. The servant who had opened the door stood motionless, at attention, with his eyes fixed on the buckles of his shoes.

CHAPTER LV.

HUMILITY AND HUMILIATION.

THE Canal of the Roses, despite its fragrant name, is not a pleasing water whereby to pitch one's tent; the roses smell too strong. Yet when Vrouw Poster sent, as a farewell gift, a great nosegay of "Baroness" blossoms, "What shall we do with these?" said the old lady to her daughter; "take them away."

The Baroness was now completely dependent on Wendela's care. The landlady's advances she repelled with chill hauteur; she would have no sympathy, not even from her daughter. "God withholds all His mercies," she said between her prayers, "even death."

With part of the produce of the Deynum sale the Baron repaid Gustave's loan and at the same time he dismissed him. "I cannot even afford," he said, "to give you the pitiable wages you at present receive."

"Yes, Mynheer the Baron, I understand," said Gustave, standing very straight.

"I shall not insult you by praising your faithful service. I heartily thank you. Give me your hand."

Gustave took his master's worn fingers gently in his own, looked upon them for a thoughtful moment, and then deferentially laid them down.

"Mynheer the Baron," he began, "it has always been my intention, on leaving your service, to settle down with my sister. I suppose this need make no difference?"

"I would not disturb your plans for the world," said the Baron.

"My sister has a hard struggle to make both ends meet and it is only fair I should assist her?"

"But a rich man like you, Gustave?"

"I beg your Nobleness not to speak of my miserable money, which is really more yours than mine. I would not live on it for the world, and, besides, I should be so dull." He had made a will, in fact, in which he had ventured, with due circumspection, to leave the produce of his speculations to the daughter of the man who had lost where he won.

And so Gustave quitted the Baron's service and waited on his sister's lodgers.

"I must go and see this Mynheer Spangenberg," said the Baron day after day. "I shall be better to-morrow and then I shall go."

Meanwhile some means of subsistence would have to be devised; for hours together the Baron sat revolving this problem in his weary brain. On one point his mind was made up. He would accept of no man's charity.

"You have, in fact—forgive my saying it—been living all these years on Count Rexelaer's bounty." The words burned in his heart. "I must prove them a falsehood before I die," he said, throwing back his grand old head. "I have borne everything and kept silence. I will *not* bear that."

He did not wish to see anybody, but John Borck came. "Papa, here is Mynheer Borck," said Wendela, and, before anyone could object, their former antagonist was in the room. "I wanted to consult you about a horse, Rexelaer," began the lord of Rollingen. "I hope you won't think I intrude, but I happened to be in Amsterdam and I remembered that nobody in all our country-side is as good a judge of a horse as you. I wish you would give me your advice."

"Gladly," said the Baron, much gratified, though not altogether the dupe of the excuse.

"I bought a horse here a week ago——" began Baron Borck, and soon his companion was very much interested.

"And now, I wonder whether you would forgive me, if I said a few words about something else?"

A troubled look came over Mynheer Rexelaer's face.

"Of course this business of 'the Dole' is infamous. I cannot understand—excuse me—your acquiescing in what is practically robbery. The money no more belongs to that gin-seller's son than it belongs to me. Yes, don't look at me so; I know what I am saying. Have you any idea why my Lord Count was so anxious to drive you from Deynum? They say he was afraid of your lovely daughter's charms."

The Baron checked the fierce words that came rushing to his lips. "We never met," he said simply. "I was glad of that, though my wife has always had a foolish softness in her woman's heart for the unknown boy whom they call Reinout Rexelaer. My daughter, if ever she marries, will marry one of her equals, I hope."

"He will be hard to find," said friendly John Borck. "But, look here, you must recover this money. Frankly, Rexelaer, I want you to authorize me—me, Borck of Rollingen—to undertake this lawsuit. Not on your behalf, but in the interest of us all. The thing ought to be known. There; I have set my heart on this, and I hope you won't refuse."

"My dear friend, I must. As soon as I am able, I shall speak to a lawyer; the money is undoubtedly mine. As for these Rexelaers, whose story you appear to know, I have allowed them to call themselves my cousins and to parade as such even at Deynum. I have never—God is my witness! —shewn up the sham, while scandal alone would have been the result. But, now, it is they who have forced the revelation upon me; I must defend my wife and child."

"I am delighted to hear you say that," cried Baron Borck, rising. "As a favour, I hope you will let me do what I can. By the bye, I bought the historical articles at

27

your sale, to complete my collection. And, before coming here, I slipped this into my pocket. It has no value for us; my wife would burn it. I thought perhaps yours might care to have it. My respects to her. Good-bye."

The Baroness had not put in an appearance. She could not bring herself to think kindly of "the Atheist."

Baron Rexelaer opened the parcel his visitor had left on the table. It contained the costly fifteenth-century livre d'heures, with its beautiful initials and miniatures, which has ever been the greatest treasure of the Châtelaines of Deynum. They call it "the Lady Bertha's Closet-book."

But you cannot make bread out of books, except you sell them,—not even then, unless they are not your own. And the means of procuring bread were growing scarce; they all three knew it, while hiding it from each other.

One evening Wendela came back to the Baron, after helping her mother to bed. Even this depth of sorrow could not bring father and daughter together, while between them lay the angry shadow of their loss.

"Wanda," began the old man, "I have been thinking of late I should like to find something to occupy my time instead of moping here all day. I feel much stronger. I have made up my mind to have in some little boys to teach them"—he went on hurriedly—"I shall teach them French. I have spoken about it to Juffrouw Donders, who is a very sensible woman and quite sees what I mean. She has been most kind about finding me the pupils. I mention this to you, because they are coming to-morrow morning, and I should wish you to explain to your mother what it is, when they are come. I will have them in the bedroom; that will do very well."

Wendela sat opposite her father, gazing, without response.

"They are little Jew-boys," the Baron continued musingly. "I cannot help wishing they had not been that.

But the feeling is one of foolish prejudice; I am heartily ashamed of it, and I daresay it will wear off in time."

" Did you say they were coming to-morrow morning?" asked Wendela in a constrained voice.

"To-morrow morning at nine. They are quite small children, and I apprehend no serious difficulty. I consider it better to tell you that I am to receive—remuneration, so that we must not look upon the lessons as a favour we are doing them. I am to receive tenpence per hour for each child."

" Tenpence per hour," echoed Wendela.

" I admit that I myself did not consider that very much. But then we must take into account how little I have to offer. Speaking a language is a very different thing from teaching it. And I have never taught." He said these last words in a tone of apology, for himself, or his patrons, or both.

Wendela did not reply, and they sat opposite each other, neither disturbing the other's thoughts, beside the gloomy lamp.

At last Wendela rose. " Good-night, Papa," she said, and held out her hand.

" Good-night, my dear. God bless you."

She turned away and moved slowly to the door. She had reached it and laid her hand on the knob; then she came back and, without a word of explanation, sank on the floor by his knees and covered his hands with her kisses. " Voyons, voyons," he said, his lips trembling under his white moustache. " What is it? What is wrong? Voyons."

But she did not reply. She gathered herself up slowly and left him to his thoughts. They cannot have been so very dismal, for he smiled.

Next morning, the four little Jew-boys being shut up in the bedroom with their new preceptor, Wendela went down to the basement to look for Juffrouw Donders. She found her in the kitchen, making a pudding with her own dumpy hands. Much ruffled by the Freule's intrusion on her privacy, Juffrouw Donders was eager to explain that she never demeaned herself by household work—no, never; only once in a way she had tried a new receipt, which her cousin, the pastry-cook, had sent her. She was accurate and voluminous in this assertion of her dignity, Wendela, meanwhile, standing by in patient disgust, conscious of her father's occupation upstairs and her own errand at the moment. Juffrouw Donders was not as charmed with her poor, proud lodgers as she had been three weeks ago. Her brother's reticence annoyed her. "Give them of your very best," was all that Gustave said.

"Juffrouw," said Wendela resolutely, "do you happen to know of anyone who wants to learn to sing?" She had sought out that sole accomplishment all through the sleepless night.

"Good gracious, I can't find pupils for the whole family!" said the landlady. After a moment she added a little more civilly: "You might advertise," and then she resumed her pudding-making, leaving the Freule to appreciate, slowly and fully, the beauty of a humble heart. Wendela crept upstairs again.

An advertisement attracted two families, one with an only daughter and one with a brace of girls. A young man also presented himself, but him the Baron vetoed. Ultimately the only daughter—a cheesemonger's—agreed to pay the stipulated price of fifty cents * an hour, but the mother of the pair of pupils—a butcher's lady—after having requested the singing-mistress to shew her powers ("First a serious piece, please, and then a gay one") declared very decidedly that she could not give more than eighteenpence the two. Wendela came away from that interview a differ-

---

* Equals tenpence.

ent creature. Till now her innocent wrongs, endured in isolation, had hardened and, if the word be permissible, haughtened her. For the first time humiliation struck her straight, soiling her soul with mud. Where now was the glory of this sordid shame? A hot flush melted the pure proud ice, and, as it melted, she saw it turn to mire. At last she understood that no greatness of ancestry can save *us* from disgrace. And her heart was emptied, of all but bitterness.

In the shelter of her early girlhood it had been easy for so high-souled a nature to fly from the hateful present into the calm splendour of a mythic past. The woman, face to face with life's vulgarity, laughed aloud. Knight Pilgrim, riding away into the darkness, never even turned to look back.

"Mine are at least Gentiles," she said to her father, fiercely.

"Hush, Wanda. They are very nice little boys." When the first lesson was over, the Baroness had called softly to her husband. "Come close," she said, and as he bent over her: "Mon ami, you are still so weak!"

"No, it was quite necessary," he answered. "But when I have settled with the lawyer, all will be right. I cannot make any more debts. I cannot. You must not mind."

"Mind?" she repeated wistfully. "I cannot be prouder of you than I am, Reinout. As for lessons, Louis Philippe gave them, and he was not even a gentleman."

Two days later the Baron called on Spangenberg. "I will look into the matter as soon as possible, Mynheer," said the busy young lawyer, "and I earnestly hope we shall be able to set it right."

"I should like to know whether the expense to be incurred—in no case should I care to incur great expense."

"Oh, never mind the expense," said Christian.

The Baron drew himself up stiffly. "No, but I must

beg of you," he said, "if possible, to furnish me with an approximate estimate——"

" Ten florins," said Christian. The Baron gave a great gasp of relief. Why, his watch must be worth at least a hundred !

" I am much obliged to you, Mynheer the Advocate," he replied with his old-fashioned bow.

In the street, as he went limping home, he twice repeated to himself, " There is nothing more humbling than being a man to whom all men may shew kindness. Yet, had I been truly a good man, I should never have found that out."

CHAPTER LVI.

A CLANDESTINE CORRESPONDENCE WITH THE LOVE LEFT OUT.

VOLKERT duly fetched books from the University Library for Mevrouw Morèl. After a time he began to think she required a good many. He brought them to "Paradise" in cabs, for he was not yet accustomed to walking the streets with a parcel.

"Tell me honestly," said Spangenberg one day, "does not Mother Morèl's gratitude cause you greater pleasure than any number of letters admiring your beautiful sentiments?" "I like the letters too," replied his friend. "You are jealous because you never got any." "Forgive me, Volkert; remember I am your officially appointed Mentor." "Yes, but I did not say you were always to be on duty." "True," said Spangenberg, holding out his hand.

Still, in his heart of hearts, Volkert would have been obliged to admit that his first endurance of personal inconvenience, after twenty-four years of facile generosity, friendliness and almsgiving—had brought him a completely new sensation. He recalled with a sneer at himself, how, before his meeting with the editor, all men about him, himself not least, had praised him for being so "free of his money," so "condescending to inferiors," so "good." And for the first time in his life, in some strange revulsion of reasoning, he gave the cabman who brought him and his books from the library no more than his legal fare. "Charity," he began to feel, meant something of which he had never heard.

"Spangenberg is exceedingly busy," said Mynheer Morèl. The old poet had got hold of the young one as an agreeable substitute for Balby. "And that too is a good work," reflected Christian. "And what a privilege for Mynheer Volkert," said Mevrouw Morèl, running to the window to catch a glimpse of the perambulating pair. "Spangenberg is exceedingly busy," said Mynheer. "It is his mission to be always doing something, as it is some men's to remain apparently inactive. The latter are the more important class. Believe me, my dear young friend, the world owes most things to its laziest men. Conquerors and statesmen are rockets and catherine-wheels. The courses of the human race are guided from the thinker's easy-chair."

Volkert liked Mynheer Morèl, not only for this affinity which caused Christian such alarm. He liked the gentle, reposeful courtesy of the philosopher, the avoidance of all that was coarse and loud. In the midst of the turmoil of his tiny home the old gentleman sat composed, and motioned his visitor to a chair with quiet dignity, as if unaware of the hole in its covering which even Mevrouw Morèl's dexterity could no longer conceal. To the young man, lapped in luxury, it was delightful to discover how utterly careless of creature comforts some of the world's best and wisest can be. He had never before met with men of education and refinement who could not distinguish vintages or who did not cavil at the taste of their cheese.

He enjoyed being present at the harum-scarum tea among a tumbling crowd of healthful children. There was not always enough to eat, but who shall say when seven children have enough? "Mevrouw," said her guest on one occasion, "with your permission I shall present to Freddie (æt. 8) your book on 'Amanda's Appletart or the Fatal Effects of Greediness.'" "I never go in to Mevrouw Morèl at meal-times," explained little Miss van Dolder to her more fashionable friends, "the feeding of the children is too painfully distressing." With this dictum Mevrouw Morèl would have agreed, as she wiped her pen at two in the morning. Juffrouw Spangenberg had no patience with her. "Why, indeed, must she write about the convolutions of the child? The medical men knew all about them already, for Juffrouw Spangenberg's own Christian had had them as a two-year-old baby, and their doctor had pulled him through!"

Meanwhile "The Cry of the People" continued to publish the young poet's effusions, still signed with a single "P." And letters addressed to that "P" continued also, at fitful intervals, to arrive at the office, always anonymous, always written in the same female hand. Gradually, in these letters, the soul of the writer began to reveal itself before the poet's fascinated gaze. It was a delightfully mysterious manner of making an acquaintance. He answered, as best he could, through the columns of "The Cry."

In the beginning the letters had been completely impersonal; the first half-a-dozen did not contain a single "I." The fair writer admired the poems and frankly said how and why. "The present is hideous," she wrote, "the past is dead. Oh the relief of meeting, in this world of tranquil, smiling evil, with a soul that believes in the future, with a heart that burns red, like a beacon, in the light of the coming day." Christian would have objected: "Her metaphors are mixed." Mynheer Morèl would have declared 'She is young.'" Volkert felt: "Such beautiful thought must belong to a beautiful face."

In the seventh scrap—they were all short, a rare merit—the "I" put in its appearance. "I have suffered wrong all my life," it said, "but I have always believed it divinely ordained. From the 'Cry of the People' I have learned for the first time that wrong is wrong and may be combated, that men *must* combat it so as to leave to those who come a better world than ours."

For reply he took the economist's pleasant maxim " All

is for the best in the best-regulated of worlds" and, in burning verses, tore it to shreds.

"I am trying to understand," said the next letter. "My parents have always believed that God guides and orders all things, and of the most monstrous injustice which befalls them they say: 'It is His will.' The world is divinely based on law and justice, wealth and poverty, sin and suffering; only change is evil. Wrong is right because it *is*. Devout Christianity seems so like Mohammedanism, with a little personal appeal thrown in to make all suffering worse. But I am bewildered; I have always rebelled. Is it possible, as you think, that an era is approaching, when our snug, smirking society will stand out in the face of God, a naked lie? If so, if in the far-away ages a new world were possible, then the life of each stone on the path were worth living indeed. God bless you; you have given me *hope*." His next poem was entitled "Kismet."

But her answer was in quite a different tone. "You are still young,"—the words startled him; he was somewhat ashamed of the keenness of their pang—"When you have suffered as much as I have, you will not cast your self with such glowing confidence on 'the Rock of God's Right.' The shipwrecked are afraid of rocks. No, let us give up demanding our own happiness, analyzing our own sufferings. To work for others; that is the task. The glory of the world's future; that, *perhaps*, may be the reward. So much you have taught me; I can never thank you enough for it. Strange that I should have selected your scarce-launched vessel to tow my broken hulk into port."

The poet did not like the "broken hulk" at all. It sounded suggestive of an old maid with a miniature, an upward glance of the eye, and a cat.

Spangenberg, on the other hand, was delighted with "Kismet." "You are actually beginning to see some good in 'to-day,'" he said. "That is encouraging. No benefactor of the human race was ever made up entirely of wrath."

The letters now ceased for some time. Volkert reflected, ungratefully, that they had been written by an elderly sentimentalist to a boy. And he remembered how frequently of late his thoughts had reverted to the beautiful image of his " Muse." Well, she was straightforward, and had stopped him. By-the-bye, he had signed his last verses in full: " Pelgrim," and this he now continued to do. " A charming name!" said Spangenberg, " I had always thought your P stood for Peter or Paul."

About this time, unfortunately, Spangenberg fell ill from over-activity and was obliged to stop at home, fretting, for so do busy men rest. The " Cry" not being allowed to enter his father's house, he could not even see what a mess his sub-editor was making of the business. But his mother brought him some excellent jelly and coddled and cuddled him in a flurry of tranquil enjoyment.

CHAPTER LVII

THE STORY OF RI-KSI-LA AND THE DEY NOUM.

UNDER these depressing circumstances Volkert stopped away longer than usual from " Little Paradise." None of them knew what became of him during the intervals. He followed no profession; he appeared to be possessed of liberal means. " Have you a mother?" Mevrouw Morèl had once asked him in the ordinary course of conversation, with a gentle lingering over the word. The young man had paused, as if for a moment's reflection; then, abruptly, he had answered, " No."

One morning he remembered with sudden compunction how pathetically Mevrouw Morèl had complained, the last time they met, of the absence from all the public libraries of that absolutely indispensable work, Schlafenmützel's Kinderjahre der Deutschen Kaiser. He had searched for it everywhere in vain. He now telegraphed for a copy from Leipzig (in eleven quarto volumes) and had it addressed to the office, whence he fetched it a few days later, carrying over about half as a foretaste, to Mevrouw Morèl's door. Finding this open, he bumped his way upstairs and staggered into the lady's presence, there suddenly to halt in awkward and annoyed surprise. For a woman, a stranger, lay with her head on the table, completely thrown forward upon her hands. Her shawl had slipped back and hung loose, revealing a beautiful neck; she was dressed tawdrily, vulgarly, not as good women dress. Little Mevrouw Morèl stood beside her, smoothing, with one affectionate hand, her coils of chestnut hair, and speaking rapid, earnest words meanwhile. The woman, who was sobbing convulsively, lifted her head with a frightened jerk, and the unwelcome visitor let all his books drop in a crash on the floor. The face was unknown to him, it must have been a pretty face once; now it was oh so despairing in its practised effrontery. The young man stammered a few words of apology and fled; Mevrouw Morèl followed him out to the landing. "It is nothing," she said, "but oh the books from the library! I hope you have not injured them!" Volkert, as he walked back to the office, rejoiced in the picture of her surprise.

The hungry-faced clerk was seated at his desk as usual, his protuberant nose inclined across his work. The office, like the clerk, was gaunt, unkempt, aggressively wretched. It looked as if it had never been new, the clerk as if he had never been young.

"Wonnema," began Volkert, "do you know a young lady"—his socialism largely consisted in calling everyone a "lady" or "gentleman"; with some people it takes that form—"do you know a young lady who comes to see Mevrouw Morèl in a light-green shawl?" He was not ashamed of his inquisitiveness; the poor bold, sorrowful face had fully aroused his pity.

"Has the 'lady,'" asked the clerk with a sneer, "a red face and pale-blue eyes?"

"Yes."

"Then I can tell you about her, if you really care to know. That girl is called Dora Droste. Ten years ago she was a kitchen wench in the Royal Palace; she was ignorant, foolish, and honest. Nowadays she is none of all three. If you want to account for the change, you must ask one of the king's great lords, but I fancy you will experience some difficulty, for he is a very great lord indeed. I have asked him twice without receiving an answer; the last time I did so I had the satisfaction of knocking him down. I think that's about all."

" Not all," objected the auditor, putting together the remaining volumes of Schlafenmützel which lay beside their box on the floor. " I don't see how the nobleman was responsible for what she is now."

" Nor did the noble man, as you correctly style him. This noble man was at the head of the Royal Buttery-department; she was under him. He dismissed her with contumely, when her disgrace was consummated, seeking, and finding, safety for himself in the vehemence of his persecution. The girl's future was irremediably ruined. She came to me—I also was a slave in the Palace at that time—and I lost my situation for taking her in. But she had a proud spirit and would eat her own bread. My lord of the Buttery had left her but one way of earning it."

" And what has Mevrouw Morèl to do with her ? "

" Mevrouw Morèl, were she wiser, would leave her in peace. She lives near us; I don't mind her, nor do the children. It's not she that's to blame." He ground his heel into the floor.

" You must not blame the noble too much," said Volkert. " He was like other nobles. He didn't know."

" Not know ? I took care that he knew ! " cried Wonnema. " I appealed to him for her, for the child, which is long since dead ! He laughed. I believe he said the child was mine. Not know, indeed ! An easy excuse ! "

" I only meant to say," replied Volkert, pausing by the staircase, " that you cannot understand. That class looks upon these things so differently. I have no doubt but this lord of the buttery is, according to his lights, a most honourable man."

The words seemed to infuriate Wonnema. He thrust back his desk. " An honourable man ! " he cried violently. " And you venture to say that here ! " He flung across a newspaper. " Take that upstairs with you and talk about honourable men ! "

"I did not mean to offend you," said the young man calmly. "How long ago did all this happen?"

Volkert went upstairs to the editor's room with the newspaper in his hand. It was the most recent number of "The Cry of the People"; he threw himself on the sofa and leisurely looked it through. First he read his own verses and was annoyed by an awkward misprint, and then his eyes dropped to the paragraph immediately beneath them which he saw marked with a pencil cross. It was named: "Two Stories about One Gentleman" and ran as follows:

There was a great Chinese Mandarin called Ri-Ksi-La, the first favourite of the Emperor. His wife's uncle died, and Ri-Ksi-La succeeded to a vast estate bequeathed by the uncle to the niece. But soon after came a priest to the Mandarin and said: "O Lord, here is another will, a later one. And it proves that my Lord, your Lady's dead uncle, wished all his possessions to pass to Buddha, that good might be done with them." "Let Buddha come and fetch them," said Ri-Ksi-La. Buddha has not come yet, and Ri-Ksi-La is still first favourite of the Emperor.

There was a great Turkish Pasha, called the Dey Noum, and he was first favourite of his master, the Sultan. He had a beautiful wife who had brought him all his money. And one morning there came a stranger to his divan and said: "O Dey, your wife's father was a slave-merchant in the far markets of Asia, and the slaves whom he sold were white." And the Dey Noum made answer: "I know it. The markets are far, and the money is near." The money is still there, and the Dey Noum is first favourite of the Sultan.

The young man from the Hague sat a long time motionless, with the paper in his hand. Presently Wonnema looked in. "Can I have that paper back?" he said. "I had marked it. I am going to send it to the great noble we were speaking of just now."

"What farrago of nonsense is this!" the other burst out. "You know how vehemently opposed the chief is to personal scandals. The thing will cost you your situation, as likely as not."

"I have thought of that," replied the clerk with quiet intensity. "When, after ten years' waiting, a man's revenge falls ripe within his reach, he does not withhold his hand."

"And what proof have you," cried the young man passionately, "of these covert charges against Count Rexelaer van Deynum? Probably none at all."

Wonnema produced a couple of documents from a locked cupboard. "Be careful, please," he said, with a white flicker in his fierce eyes. "I have seen the originals. They were brought by a foreigner. He will be here again to-morrow, and you can speak to him if you like."

CHAPTER LVIII.

A HUNTED HARE.

"I cannot understand Mamma," said Jane, arranging her tea-cups. It was evening, and Rolline was having tea with her. "Nor need I. As for me, perhaps because of the failure of her attempts to enrich me, I do not think money is everything. And I would rather not have had it than sit opposite Miss Kops."

"Oh, he needn't sit opposite to her more than he chooses," replied Rolline, gently stretching herself in a lady-like manner, and admiring her feet, the only part of her person which remained resolutely small. "And I must say I envy him the way Papuum succeeds. My husband says that they use it at the Palace. It has just been introduced into England, where ten thousand pounds are being spent on advertisement. They've got two Tatua Papuas there in some public building, the Westminster—Westminster Hall,* I believe, and everybody's allowed to come and tattoo them all over and rub out the marks again. And every night all the Harries of London come and scribble their names over the wretched creatures' arms."

"I know, I know," said Jane impatiently. "Well, I may be old-fashioned, but for me there is honourable and dishonourable money still."

"And what do you call honourable money?"

"Inherited money," replied Jane promptly. "Like

---

* Aquarium?

Uncle Hil's, for instance. Or Cousin Borck's of Rolfin-
gen."

"You are less tolerant than poor grandmamma, who
ought to have known. Did I tell you what Monsieur de
Bonnaventure wrote in my album?"

"No. I don't like Monsieur de Bonnaventure."

"Nor do I, but I asked him to write in my album.
Everybody does. And he wrote: 'Mon expérience de la
vie se résume en un seul mot: L'or dure.' It was very
nasty of him and in execrable taste."

"I wish," said Jane meaningly, "that people would not
speak so much of Monsieur de Bonnaventure."

Rolline modestly dropped her eyes. "As for that," she
said presently, "there are a good many things I wish people would not speak so much about. What do you say to
the two little stories in the 'Cry of the People' which have
been all over the place?"

"I say, as my husband does, that nobody ought to have
read them. People ought not to know such a paper exists."

"People didn't, but this number, they say, is out of
print. I go out more than you do, and I assure you I see
the story in everybody's face. My husband made me a
terrible scene, as if it were any fault of mine."

"Pleasant for Reinout," said Jane, beginning to wash
up.

"Oh, it won't hurt Reinout, for the will is undoubtedly valid here. It is worst for Aunt Margherita, but one
can't pity her, she makes such a fool of herself. The best
thing she could do would be to retire definitely among her
cockatoos and canary-birds and never be heard of again.
But she goes out more than ever—tight-laced, over-dressed,
powdered and rouged—since this thing got about."

"And it is this money which Mamma wants Topsy to
marry."

"Poor Topsy, I don't think she has a ghost of a
chance."

"She knows it," said Jane angrily, "and she doesn't care."

"Jane——"

"Well?"

"I wonder whether Uncle Hil knew when he married her."

But the baby cried out in the adjoining room, and Jane went to look at it. When she came back, she said, pursuing her thoughts: "I pity Reinout all the same. He is an honourable man."

"Oh, I don't pretend to understand Reinout; he is different from everybody," said Rolline.

"Reinout's education was destined to deaden every feeling but worldliness; with most men it would have succeeded, and what a success! He might have been a Talleyrand, as Uncle Hilarius once said to me. But other feelings have survived and caused the whole man to fail. He is like those two life-long prisoners released from the Bastille who did not know what to do with their freedom. He knows that he ought to feel nobly, and doesn't know how and yet can't live without it. I believe he is a miserable man."

"Nonsense, Jane, how excited you are! Quite a romance about poor, good-natured Reinout. I meet him constantly —at least I used to before this scandal; it looks rather cowardly in him to hide. He always seemed to enjoy himself and he flirted a good deal, I fancy. He is going out to Russia in a month or two, and he will die an ambassador, covered with stars, at his beautiful seat of Deynum. Poor Reinout, indeed!"

"All that is true," replied Jane, "the worse for him. He is hedged in on every side. Nobody can understand what that means, until he has tried to break loose. Supposing you and I were suddenly to wish to become Roman Catholics——"

"I?" cried Rolline, sitting up. "How preposterous you are, Jane!"

"It is only by way of comparison——"

"Conrad's family would never allow it."

"That is just what I mean. Perhaps our husbands would threaten to deprive us of our children, and we might end by becoming Catholics on the sly. I imagine that Reinout, deep down in his heart, lives a life of his own. The life that we see is his father's."

"You talk of him as if he were a cat," said Rolline. "I don't want to hear anything about any man's two lives, and I think it's rather a shame of you to suggest such things of Reinout. I should sooner think it of Guy from the horrid tales that I hear."

"Guy!" said Jane with ineffable contempt. "I don't know what set me talking to-night. I have never mentioned the subject to anyone but Antoinette. I will tell you something about Reinout, though. One evening, more than a year ago, when everybody had been speaking of his brilliant prospects, he came up to me suddenly and burst out, 'I would give it all to be a *man!*' He was strongly moved, as I saw, but he walked away immediately, and a moment later was laughing with Dolly Foulise."

"He isn't a woman," said Rolline sulkily, but Jane did not heed her. "Perhaps these revelations will help him," she thought to herself, over her tea-tray. "Perhaps!" Aloud, she changed the subject: "As for Guy, it is to be hoped he will marry Cécile and settle down at last."

"She will hardly make him a good wife," said Rolline. "However, Mamma is set upon it, and has not left Cécile an hour of peace since the poor thing went to live with them."

"Cécile is certainly a 'poor thing,' but she deserves a *nicer* husband than Guy. However, she is nearly thirty and must look after herself. But I suppose she's been bullied too long by Grandmamma not to have forgotten how to say no."

"Come, Jane, you, who had never been bullied by Grand-

mamma, forgot how to say no, when Mamma nagged at you
from morning till night."

"True," replied Jane, and a slight flush spread over her
sallow face. "And you, who were less strong-minded than
I, yet got your own way. Perhaps Mamma would tell us
she never was shortsighted."

After that Rolline looked cross, and neither sister was
very sorry when the cab came at half-past nine.

Jane remained thoughtful, with her pointed chin on her
hand, in her poor little drawing-room. She was musing on
the irony of life, which always grins at you, even when it
hurts you most. At first, when she had married a husband
she did not care for, she had comforted herself with the
thought of all the pleasant things his father's death would
bring her. She would buy any quantity of costly books and
have a "salon" and invite the clever people whom her own set
never saw. There was one man who daily passed her father's
house with whom she had long desired to pick an acquaintance, a man with flowing hair and a pale, thought-laden
face—perhaps an artist; she had even been a little "smit-
ten," as a girl. She would give private theatricals—pretty
little pieces, purposely written—and the papers would speak
of them. And, above all, she would have a real studio and
devote herself in earnest to what Rolline was wont to call
her "nasty, sticky painting-mess." Girlish fancies: in her
plain-spoken manner she had stipulated for these things,
and the thought had reconciled her to marrying Simmans.
That was eight years ago and more: her father-in-law was
now eighty-two. She loathed herself for desiring his death;
the idea was the misery of her life. Yet she knew he would
not die. He would never die. Nor would it matter much
now if he did. She had got to like her husband; she was
overburdened with children; her painting, and poetry, and
all the rest of it, had died away from her life long ago. She
hardly found time, nowadays, to read a good book, when

she could get one. It had been her life-long desire to possess a complete Thackeray; Mevrouw Elizabeth only paid for dress; Simmans could not always pay satisfactorily for that. If any lover of literature and the human race (are the two not one?) read this page and be able to do a good deed at no great sacrifice, let him send a cheap edition—the green cloth one will do—to Mevrouw Simmans van Rexelaer, Bankastraat, the Hague. Last Wednesday was old Simmans's birthday; the old gentleman gave a family dinner-party, and Jane had to go.

A ring at the house-bell; Jane glanced towards the clock—a quarter past ten. She did not expect her husband till eleven. It was not her husband; the maid announced in accents of mildest astonishment: "The Freule van Borck," and Cécile came hurriedly in.

"What has happened?" cried Jane, starting up. "Papa?" All the children van Rexelaer liked their quiet father best.

Cécile sank down on a chair. Her face was white, her whole manner distraught. She could not speak, but with trembling fingers she fumbled at the clasp of her heavy cloak, till it fell from her shoulder, disclosing her soft white dinner-dress.

"What is it?" cried Jane, now thoroughly frightened. "Which of them is ill? Why can't you speak?"

"Nobody is ill," gasped Cécile. "Oh, Jane, you must help me!" and she burst into hysterical weeping.

"Hush, hush," urged Jane tenderly. Hers was not a nature that easily showed pity, either to herself, or to others. She stood awkwardly beside her cousin till the latter's sobs subsided. Then she said: "Now tell me."

But Cécile did not lift her face from the hands in which she had hidden it. Once or twice her throat moved vainly, and at last she whispered through her knitted fingers: "I can never go back again." Jane bent low to catch the words; she was utterly at a loss to understand.

"I can never go back to your mother's again. Oh, Jane, I am not safe there;" and now Cécile began to cry afresh, but quietly, with that heart-broken continuance which comes of a lasting wound.

"If Guy has insulted you," said Jane with horrible perspicacity, "why didn't you tell Mamma, instead of running away here?"

"I don't know," replied Cécile without altering her attitude. "Don't let us speak of it. Only you must help me, that is all."

"But if I am to help you, I must understand," pleaded Jane. "What do you want me to do?"

"Hide me. Shield me. Oh, Jane, perhaps I am very foolish. I have never been accustomed to look after anything. But I can't marry him."

"Well, then, tell him so plainly."

"I have done that, more than once. And I told Aunt Elizabeth—I really did—that she might have all my money, but she only grew very angry and said I had insulted her. And—and"—the Freule's voice again failed her—"I *can't* go back," she burst out passionately. "Antoinette helped me to get away and told me to come here. I ran all the way. Help me, Jane."

Jane rose from the floor, on which she had sunk to listen, and stood pondering. "It is my own mother," she said at last, "Henry is just expecting his promotion, and we are looking to Papa to help us through with it. If Mamma knew I had thwarted her, she would never forgive me."

For the first time Cécile lifted her terror-struck face.

"You are not going to desert me?" she cried. "I have nobody. Topsy said she felt sure you would help."

"Let Topsy speak for herself," replied Jane; she felt goaded. "Of course I will help you," she added more kindly. "Yes, I *will*. This, I think, will be best. My Aunt Gratia Rexelaer is staying with her friend the Freule van Weylert; I will give you a letter to her. You are so agitated, perhaps you had better spend the night with them, and, if to-morrow morning your impression remains the same, well, you are of age, and nobody can force you to return home. I should advise you, in that case, to consult with Cousin Borck of Rollingen."

Her calm, strong voice did not lose its effect on the fluttering soul. "But Aunt Elizabeth has always said," Cécile began timidly, "that, as I am not yet thirty, my guardian can force me to marry whom he likes."

"Mamma confuses two different laws," replied Jane firmly. "You have no guardian and, your parents being dead, you are free to do as you will"—an immense expression of relief came over the poor girl's anxious face—"Dear Cécile, you will have to look after yourself a little; none of us must trust too much to others to look after them."

"I must try," said Cécile desperately, "but I haven't any money. Nothing but the few florins in my purse, and even that I left on my toilet-table."

Jane smiled. "That excuses Mamma's saying Papa must take care of you. Now I shall send for a cab. You can't go much farther in that dress."

"Won't you come with me, Jane? I hardly know your aunt."

"I can't: I don't want Henry to know; he is already sufficiently worried about his promotion. It is as likely as not Aunt Gratia will tell, for she can't keep a quiet tongue in her head. But we must risk that. I really think it is the best thing for you to spend the night in a neutral house. Why, they may be here at any moment, inquiring for you!"

"They may," screamed Cécile, starting up, as if she already heard footsteps in the street. "Save me, dearest, for your children's sake! Oh, Jane, how long the cab is coming!"

"I have sent for it," said Jane soothingly. "I daresay Topsy has told them you were in bed with a headache."

"I couldn't lock my own door," said Cécile, and then silence lay heavy between them till the cab came lumbering round.

The Freule Alette van Weylert and the Freule Gratia van Rexelaer were sitting quietly and comfortably in the former's softly lightly, thickly curtained, darkly furnished back drawing-room. Each elderly lady had her knitting beside her and in front of her a costly old Japanese plate, from which she had just partaken of her nightly flavourless "pap." The knitting was missionary kniiting. The Freule Rexelaer was very thin and frail, the Freule Weylert broad and substantial. At the Freule Weylert's elbow lay a great gilt Bible from which she was about to read a chapter before the two ladies retired to rest. The Freule was looking for her spectacles. The gilt clock on the seventeenth-century mantelpiece sang out the hour of eleven, and its great Dutch comrade in the hall boomed adhesion.

When Cécile was introduced, the reposeful room, the kind faces of the two old maids, above all the open Bible, seemed to inspire her with confidence. She gave Jane's letter to the Freule Gratia. The Freule Gratia read it in silence and passed it on to the Freule Alette. The latter looked up at Cécile, over her spectacles, and nodded, but a firm expression settled about her chin.

"You can certainly stay here if you wish, child," she said. "Sit down, my dear; ring, and I will tell them to pay the cab. It's no use wasting money."

"I promised Jane to ask you to tear up that note, Freule," began Cécile, addressing the Freule van Rexelaer.

"Oh but, Cécile, I must read it again."

"But you will, after that—won't you?—because I promised Jane to see it done."

"Now, I like that," remarked the comfortable mistress of the house, "always keep your promises and don't make any you can't keep. You are right to come here, my dear.

Will you have some pap? No? Well, I must tell them to air you a bed. I am afraid you will have to put up with my maid's things. Mine would hardly fit you." She smiled.

"And to-morrow she will have to come down to break-fast in that dress!" said the Freule van Rexelaer, folding her hands. This idea seemed especially to preoccupy the quiet little lady.

"She can send to your sister-in-law's to-morrow and she can stay here as long as she likes," answered Freule van Weylert, searching for the place in her Bible.

"It is very kind of you, Alette. And quite right. Only, I am sorry. My sister-in-law will be so vexed."

"You cannot help that, nor can I. Some one of my relations has been vexed with me all my life. You cannot endeavour to act right and please relations who want you to act wrong."

"No, no," said the Freule Gratia hurriedly, "poor Cécile!"

The mistress of the house settled her spectacles on her nose, and once again shot across one of those sharp glances at Cécile.

"My dear," she said, "I am very rheumatic. Would you come here for a moment? I should like to give you a kiss." And, as the young girl bent over her, Freule Alette, looking up into her troubled face, laid one hand on the open volume.

"Do you know, at all," she asked, "where to look for comfort in the sorest trouble?"

"Yes," said Cécile very softly.

CHAPTER LIX.

THE BARON'S CONFESSION.

WHEN "Pelgrim's" correspondent had not written for three weeks he began to find out how much he missed her letters. "I am vain," he said to himself, as we sometimes do, liking ourselves for saying it. But this poet was not spoilt by over-encouragement. Literary men did not see "The Cry."

He felt quite glad one morning to find the familiar handwriting awaiting him. "I do not know why I write," said the letter, "I had made up my mind not to address you again, but how often have I not done that, and torn up the page! There seems some bond between you and me; you have robbed me of my old reliance; I am looking to you for future strength. I am weary of the old dead greatness; you, the plebeian, though you cannot understand us, you have taught me that each man's own soul is his only pride or shame. There is no outward splendour, no adventitious sorrow, there is nothing in all the world but this naked ' I ' and God. It is naturally a lesson for a man of the people to teach.

"For that you are a man of the people all your poems prove. That you are no longer young I knew when first I wrote; for a moment I was led to doubt, but your last verses again proclaim me right. I can now say frankly that I like you. I am sure you are a good man."

The poet smiled as he folded up the sheet.

"She jumps at conclusions," he said to himself. "Poor old lady, she is charmingly prude!"

Spangenberg was up again and hard at work. His first week was spent in alternate disapproval of Wonnema and commendation of Piet. "I should certainly send Wonnema about his business," Spangenberg confessed to Volkert, "if I could take away his children's appetites first." So Wonnema stayed. "I've had my say," said the clerk unrepentantly. Like so many, he was a "personal" socialist, made such by personal wrong. His master, on the other hand, was a practical, hard-working idealist, striving by all the means in his power to embody his beautiful hopes. Piet Poster, poor fellow, was devoid of political opinions. He saw the nearest duty and did it.

He was working desperately hard just now for his Law-examination. "And when you are a notary and a gentleman, Piet," Spangenberg once said to him, laughing, "you can propose for the hand of your Frenle." "Don't, sir, please," said Piet, scribbling hard. The lawyer was going to add something about a better-dowered bride, but a look at the young clerk's face suddenly checked him. "My illness has thrown back the Baron's business," he merely said as he turned away.

Certainly Wendela would not prove a well-dowered bride. "Fifty cents an hour," declared the butcher's lady, "is more than sufficient remuneration in the case of a young person who is more remarkable for her airs than for her tunes." Wendela had a hard time of it with the butcher's lady, but she honestly did her best, and fortunately she was too proud to feel offended at the woman's vulgarity. "The girls don't improve," said the butcher's wife, "in spite of their exceptional talent." "Would you wish to stop the lessons?" asked Wendela, lifting indifferent eyes to the fat, red face above the piano. "No, Juffrouw, but for you to take more pains," said the woman, glorying in the deeply Dutch insult of that "Juffrouw" to the daughter of the Rexelaers.

Wendela hurried home to build up the imposing struc-

ture of her mother's snow-white coiffure. It is a ridiculously small detail, but it came back every day, remorselessly.

"It can't be helped," said Wendela. We never say that
till the spirit of protest awakens within us. But hers sank
to rest again as she looked across at her father and heard
him telling how pleased he was that one of his little Jews
had repeated the verb "aimer" without a single hitch. Yet
again she reasoned: "He has brought his trials on himself.
I am innocent." That thought was the long sorrow of her
life, worse, a thousand times worse, than the loss of all the
rest. She was angry with this estimable, this beautiful old
man; and in the daily presence of his virtues she hated her
bootless wrath. From a few careless words, caught up at the
time of the loss of the Castle and erroneously interpreted,
she had gained an impression that her father had wasted his
property. She did not know what "speculation" meant,
but she knew it to be a very wicked sin. Was her mother
aware of her father's crime? She fancied not. Even in
her childhood she had hidden away his guilt and wept over
it and prayed till all faith in prayer died away in her heart.

The Baron tottered feebly across the dingy room, from
his chair to the window, from the window to his chair.
"It is quite amusing, my dear," he said, "to watch the
movement on the canal. Human activity, after all, is
more interesting than stones and trees. Let me wheel you
into the sunshine." The Baroness roused herself with an
effort. She hated the canal. "It smells"; that was all
the impression it conveyed to her, even while March winds
still kept the windows closed. But when spring came
round, the slow Dutch spring, and the watery sun peeped
out from time to time and a couple of consumptive trees
began to swell a little at their finger-tips, what did she say
then? The overpowering odour of garbage penetrated
everywhere, and yet it was but a herald of the fœtid oppression which summer would bring. Even the Baron
grew sorrowful with the approach of the mild weather. He

had been contented in the city while nature still lay dead. But the breaking of the poor grey-green shimmer over the canal-trees seemed to stir him in the depths of his soul. He would sit looking out for hours, but no longer at the bustle of human activity—at green fields, perhaps, and golden buttercups? "I should like to see some grass again," he once said, not to his wife or daughter, but to a new friend who came in of evenings, the landlady's only other lodger, besides Piet. And one day he brought home a little pot of pale mauve crocuses; mother and daughter looked up in amazement at such extravagance. But next morning he gave it away again, to one of his little Jew-boys.

Juffrouw Donders's other lodger had been with her for thirty years, as she was proud of repeating to all and sundry. He had gone, fresh from the Amsterdam "Athenæum," to teach Greek and Latin to the lowest form at the Amsterdam Grammar School, and he was teaching there still. Boys might come and boys might go, but he went on for ever. On that evening when the crocuses were spreading their promise of summer all over the place, this gentleman dropped in for a chat. "Oh—ah, flowers!" he said. "I find they vitiate the air so." He knew the way from the Canal of the Roses to the Grammar School and round home by his five-o'clock ordinary. He must have been aware that the world was bigger, because he himself had been born on the other side of Amsterdam, and Amsterdam is a large city, but, if he knew, he kept the secret well.

Between the Baron and his fellow-lodger, who, by-the-bye, had mistaken the crocuses for tulips, there was nothing in common but the house they lived in, a strong bond in itself. The two would sit smoking their pipes together, and once the old gentleman treated his guest to a glass of "the King's Wine." There were only half a dozen bottles left, which the Baron had refused to sell.

And they would converse on trifles. The Baron rarely reverted to his brighter past or dwelt upon his present troubles. If anyone spoke of troubles, it was the old school-master, who had never been able to manage his class—surely no creature on earth is worthier commiseration. "It must be so hard to teach bigger boys," said the Baron sympathetically. "My little fellows were tiresome at first, till I told them very seriously how sorry I should be if we did not get on well. Big boys, of course, would have paid no attention to that."

Though the Baron did not speak of his fallen greatness, Gustave proclaimed to all the neighbourhood what a very great man the Baron was. The neighbours would look up, in vague curiosity, for a glimpse of where he sat, behind the small-paned window, scrupulously tidy and venerably white. And some of them would take off their hats. That reminded the Baron of Deynum, and hugely delighted him. "The world is full of good people," the Baron said.

"Is it true, Mynheer," asked Dr. Barten, the school-master, one evening, "that 'Ipsa glorior infamia' is the motto of your noble house?"

"Yes," said the Baron curtly, shrinking from the subject.

"Then, it ought to have been 'ignominia,' Mynheer."

The Baron was very much taken aback. "Why?" he asked, and his hand trembled.

"Infamia is used of some inner, moral shame," expounded the pedagogue with great relish, "Ignominia of an outer perceptible blot. The latter is evidently intended."

"I am very sorry," said the Baron sadly. "It has always been infamia."

"Yes, it is a pity; with dead languages we should be particularly careful, for they cannot look after themselves. But, whether in ignominy or infamy, undoubtedly, dear Baron, the right to glory is yours."

"No, no," said the Baron disconsolately, "so even that is wrong."

A couple of days later he came to the Baroness after his morning's lesson. "My dear," he said, "the little boys are not coming back any more. I do not think it is right to take money for teaching them and then not to do it. The last few times I have not been able; my head gets too tired. They are very good and do their best, but this morning I told them they must not come to-morrow. I was sorry, and they cried. But I must write to their parents. And God will take care of us."

The Baroness looked up at him but did not speak.

"And, my dear," he went on quietly, "there is something else I want to tell you; I can choose no better moment. Your own money, dearest, I used it—in speculation —to avert the sale. It was very foolish of me, very wicked. I have seen of late how surely my pride has worked my ruin. Lest disgrace should fall upon my head, I have heaped it on my soul."

He stopped speaking, his voice tremulous, his head bowed. "I knew it," said the Baroness.

The words startled him in their calmness. "Knew it," he stammered.

"I knew," continued the Baroness simply, "that the money had been there and I saw it was gone. Never mind, dear; it was not much."

"Gertrude," he murmured, "you will love me to the end—will you not?—as you have always done. It is only a little way."

And then the old lady began to cry. The husband had to find her pocket-handkerchief and wipe the tears from her stiff, pale face. There was rain beating against the windows. The lodging-house room was full of a murky mist.

Next morning the Baron did not get up, and Wendela, in the pauses between her lessons, had two of them to nurse.

CHAPTER LX

"I FEAR the contents of this letter will surprise and vex you. I entreat you to believe that not for one moment did I foresee the possibility of asking you a favour when I began our correspondence, if correspondence it can be called.

"Yes, I am asking you a favour. You are a literary man, an associate of literary men. Could you procure me copying or translation or some such work? You can judge of my hand-writing. It is true, as I told you, that I am a woman of high rank—doubtless, you dislike me on that account—but I am also a woman in great poverty, struggling to earn a livelihood; and for that you will think none the worse of me. I am not ashamed to claim your help; if you can assist me, appoint some place of meeting, but promise on your word of honour never to find out my name or address."

Volkert placed an advertisement in the following number of "The Cry." "Come to Mevrouw Morèl's, 5 Little Paradise, to-morrow at noon." "She will be surprised," he thought to himself with a smile, "to see her kind old man." His interest in his unknown admirer definitely sank under her request for "literary work." He could easily picture the kind of creature, ringletted, mittened, melancholy, old-maidish.

At the appointed time he went to Mevrouw Morèl's.

" I am so thankful you are willing to protect me," he said, " I feel horribly nervous." " And to protect the lady, eh?" retorted Mevrouw. " Quite so," said Volkert gravely.

Punctually at noon a ring at the street-bell announced the aspirant for hard labour on bread and water. " I like that," said Mevrouw Morèl, " you can do twice as much, if only you are precise." A quick footstep was heard ascending the stairs; the room-door was thrown open, a tall, striking-looking girl appeared on the threshold, stopped, gave a sharp glance at the couple who rose to receive her, turned and fled downstairs again, flinging-to the door.

Mevrouw Morèl remained staring at her companion, with round eyes of amazement.

" Wendela!" said the young man aloud, to himself, in utter discomfiture.

" What is it? I don't understand. How absurd! Tell me quick," cried little Mevrouw Morèl, her comely face alive with curiosity.

" I have met that young lady before," answered the poet. " More, dear Mevrouw, I myself do not understand."

Piet Poster, standing expectant outside, every nerve on the " qui-vive," was terrified to see the Freule van Rexelaer come rushing down, her face aflame.

" But, Freule," he burst out, " what has happened? You promised to warn me immediately. You haven't been gone ten seconds. Let me run up and punch——"

" No, no, Piet," cried Wendela, " nothing is wrong. Only come away quick, I beg of you. I don't want to remain in this place one moment longer!"

So this time Piet Poster did not demolish the enemy. In the silence of their rapid homeward walk the Freule once only interrogatively ejaculated: " Pelgrim!" and Poster, shyly glancing sideways, saw fresh blushes mantle her crimson cheek.

The young poet walked across to the office, altogether bewildered, and sat down in Spangenberg's room. Vainly he knit his eyebrows over this new experience; he could understand nothing of the Freule van Rexelaer's need. But an immense pity and kindness filled his impulsive heart.

Presently Spangenberg arrived in a state of supreme elation. "Hurrah!" he cried, as soon as he saw his friend. "Can you keep a secret, a secret which all the town will know in a day or two?"

"Of course I can keep a secret," replied the other testily, thinking he knew too many already.

"No, but mine is one worth knowing, one I enjoy so much I want you to enjoy it too. We have heard—too much of late, and little thanks to Wonnema!—of the Mandarin Ri-Ksi-La, His Excellency the Count of Deynum, Lord of the August Household of our sovereign Liege, the King."

"We have," said the other. "Too much. Let us talk of something else."

"Stupid fellow, luckily for you I know and forgive your surly humours. You deserve to miss the story. Well, this chief of one of the oldest, noblest families of Europe—the van Rexelaers are that,—are they not?"

"Of course," acquiesced the other wearily.

"Quite so—is the grandson of an innkeeper in a hamlet near the frontier, a gin-shop-man called Rekselaar"—he spelt the word—"just simple Mathew Rekselaar, not even connected, as you see, by name with the great historic race."

"Another lie of Wonnema's," said Christian's companion calmly. "One would feel for Count van Rexelaer, if only on account of this vulgar persecution. For shame, Spangenberg, you are as bad as your clerk!"

"His Excellency is a worthy object of your sympathy," began Christian in a scornful tone.

"He is," burst in the other with unexpected violence.

"Do I not say so? But, Pelgrim, you should not presume that I find such delight in slander. I had excellent reason to sift this matter, and thereby do yeoman service to a worthy man, a real noble, as it happens—I, Christian Spangenberg, is that not a freak of fate? It appears there was an error in the register at first, the fault of some rustic clerk, and his present Lordship's father quietly added the 'van.' Nothing easier, as everyone knows, than to effect an erroneous entry in the registers, nothing harder than to get it remedied later on. This family, you may be sure, has never filed an application. It was the gin-seller's son who worked himself up the backstairs into the palace; he had an exceedingly handsome wife, a haberdasher's daughter—there are nasty stories why he got his Countship, but that's slander; I stick to business."

"Well, the title is genuine then, at any rate," cried the Count Rexelaer's champion, turning a hot face, for one moment, towards the lawyer.

"The new title is genuine, of course. Nothing surprises one more than the ease with which upstarts start up. Besides half a dozen genealogists, whose hobby is quite out of fashion, who knows that this Holy Roman Count is the coarsest of shams? What, then, will his Lordship say to see his gin-selling, tape-selling grandsires uncoffined and his own name published in print, corrected and revised up to date?"

"I said too little," declared the other bitterly. "You are worse than Wonnema."

"And why have I ferreted out all this? The great lord who arouses your pity, not content with stealing the real Rexelaer's name and acquiring his property you know how, has used the confusion obtained by fraud to seize on a revenue due to the head of the house, for he poses as such. He has brought down his innocent rivals from honourable poverty to honourable privation. Whilst rolling in his filthy prosperity, second only to the Sovereign, honoured, flattered and envied, he is stealing their last crust from these people who have never even risen against the lie of his life. Evidently he hates them; perhaps for that reason. It is said that his wife is no better than he. It is said there is a son. Poor fellow, I pity him. Perhaps he will never find out the truth; let us hope, if he does, he will take after his father sufficiently not to care. God help him, else"—the young editor was violently excited—"I would rather be one of my match-boys in the streets of Amsterdam than that man's pampered, envied, blood-and-dirt-nurtured heir!"

"For God's sake, stop!" cried the other, facing round. "I am he."

CHAPTER LXI

"HE LEADETH ME IN GREEN PASTURES."

"LET us go at once and tell him," said "Volkert" ten minutes later. "Let *me* tell him; it is my right. I am sure my father will refund the money, as soon as he understands." Spangenberg let this view pass; he had never pitied Pelgrim Volkert half as much as he pitied the Jonker Reinout Rexelaer.

"Yes," he answered, "the fact that the different spelling can be proved nullifies any claim to 'the Lady's Dole.' It was not so easy to unearth the evidence. Piet Poster has done the greater part, travelling round from village to village, till he found the right place and right entry at last. He could not have worked with greater energy, had he been working for himself."

"But if these things were so," protested Reinout, "I cannot understand the Baron's not showing us up before."

"You would, if you knew him. He would never have stirred even now, had you left him bread to eat. He told me himself: 'Count Rexelaer's family history is his business, not mine. I need not expose its seamy side because his wife was her uncle's heiress.' That's the kind of man the Baron is."

"But the pedigree in the hall at home," groaned Reinout. "I have known it since my birth. All our ancestors up to Rovert, the Protestant, who joins on to the main line with Ruwert, his Catholic brother? I cannot believe you.

It is all worked out and printed in the Archives of the Nobles of Holland.   It is matter of history."

"History will be none the worse for a few lies more or
less," said Spangenberg, smiling sadly.   "As for you, you
will be a Count when your father dies.   You must be content with that."

Reinout lifted his eyes and slowly fixed them upon his
friend.   Their depths were swelling with mute despair.

Christian rose hurriedly, unable to endure more.   "Dear
old fellow," he said, unsteadily, "no one can help you but
yourself," and then he hurried away, lest the other should
see him break down.

When he came back several hours later, in the evening,
he found Reinout sitting just as he had left him, moodily
pensive, with folded arms.   At the noise of the opening door
the Jonker roused himself.   "I want to go—at once—" he
said, "to Baron Rexelaer.   Christian, you must take me
there."

"Very well," acquiesced Spangenberg, secretly delighted.
"I was going to-night, in any case, to tell of my success."
So, presently, they started together.

"There's a little waiting-room," said Christian, as they
neared the house, "where you'd better wait a minute while
I ask permission to bring you in.   But first I must tell him
about the 'Dole.'"

The pair passed down the long, ill-lighted corridor.

"That's the door," nodded Christian.   "There's never
anybody there.   I'll be back in a minute."

Reinout turned the handle and found himself once more
—in a little box of a room—face to face with the Freule
Wendela.   The girl was concocting some mess or medicine
she needed for her invalids.   She put down the cup on the
table.   "And so this is the way," she said, trembling, "in
which you keep your word, Mynheer?"   He paused on the

threshold, secure in the thought that she could not pass him. "I had no idea," he stammered hurriedly. "I beg of you to believe me. I came to see your father. You misjudge me; it is only natural, but I swear that you misjudge me!" The spirit lamp boiled over in a spreading splutter. He bent to extinguish the flame, and she caught up her cup and left him without another word.

He heard her speaking to Spangenberg outside. "I thought you were the doctor," she was saying. "You will find him very ill."

Reinout waited for several minutes in the bare little room, which was not much more than a cupboard for hats and cloaks. The pale wall-paper had lost its pattern; the blind hung torn and crooked, there was a hole in the shabby oil-cloth where the boards came staring through. He stood beside a bright-green, varnished table, full of stains, a very epitome, it seemed to him, of vulgarly pretentious poverty. That dirty, gaudy table brought home to him his father's guilt as nothing else had done. He turned away from it to the open window. A mean little back-yard with tall houses close behind it, a couple of brilliant flower-pots on lofty window-sills, enhancing, not amending, the misery around, here and there an overhanging towel or a barefaced sponge, the whole of it gaunt and squalid under the early-fading light.

The weather was soft and warm; after a mild May-day of fruitful rain the clouds were lifting, and under slowly gathering shadows the slumbrous earth lay hushed, heavy with the travail of nascent life through every fibre of her being.

Christian opened the door and looked in. His energetic countenance was solemnized into repose. "Come," he said, "I have told him about you. He is willing to see you." Reinout followed into an adjoining chamber, and there, propped up on the pillows of a green-curtained lodging-house bed, he saw lying the gentle yet haughty face he had so often admired in silence at Deynum. Seated at the head of the bed was the Baroness, straight and still; behind her stood Wendela; the Freule had been weeping. And at the other end of the small room, in the background, Reinout noticed, with a touch of surprise, Father Bulbius, the parish-priest from " home."

That morning the Baron had asked them to send for Father Bulbius. " I did not want to ask too soon," he had said, " but I want to ask to-day." When the telegram came, Veronica had of course said : " No." Her rule seemed absolute now-a-days, and she at once explained to the Father that he was hardly feeling well. " I should go if I were dead," Father Bulbius had answered fiercely, and the pimple on his face had openly scowled at Veronica.

All through the day the Baron had lain quiet, waiting for his old friend. His wife thought he was dozing. Towards evening he roused himself and called to Wendela. " There is a paper in my desk I should·like to have," he said, " under several others, in the left-hand corner. Yes, thank you. That is it." He waited until once more alone with the Baroness, who sat immovable by his side. " Gertrude," he then began, " you know this parcel. The statement it contains of Count Rexelaer's conduct towards us is accurate, and, I honestly believe, impartial. I have resisted your suggestion to send it to the King and now I can tell you why. I had always intended to do so at my death, hoping that from it some provision might result for you. That is my one great sorrow that I must leave you like this. But now the moment has come, I don't want to seek help for you and Wendela by what, if not exactly an evil action, is at least an ungenerous one. Gertrude, I want your permission to tear up this document. God will provide."

The Baroness could not answer him. " May I ?" he asked, holding up the papers. She bent her head. An expression of great relief came over the sick man's features as he sank back in his pillows and lay slowly destroying the memorial on which he had spent many laborious hours. He had always been sluggish with his pen.

He was able to speak quite calmly with Father Bulbius, when that gentleman arrived, towards evening, hot with travelling and anxiety. "It was like you to come at once," he said. "I believe, dear Father, that I have not long to live. Since my last stroke, three weeks ago, I have been very tired. Yes, I had another stroke, or fit, or whatever the doctors call it; fortunately Gustave alone was with me and I warned him not to tell. I am ashamed to remember how tired I was, but to-day I am not tired, and so glad to rest. And I am quite willing, Father, to do all that the church requires of me. I myself cannot think that God expects much more from us than humbly to cast ourselves upon His mercy. And I should not care for masses to be said on my behalf. But I do not wish to be wiser than others, so tell me what you would have me do?"

"It is not the last sacrament you are asking for?" said the priest, forcing back his emotion.

"When the end is come," replied the Baron quickly, "we must not shrink from the end."

Later on he did not talk much with anyone, but he suddenly beckoned to Bulbius. "You are a cleric," he said. "You must be a scholar. Tell me, is it 'ignominia'?"

"What do you mean, dear Baron?" asked the priest with troubled brow.

"Infamia, you know, glorior infamia? They have been telling me that it was ignominia. The—the outer blot, I think. I do not quite understand. Is it that?"

"No, indeed," replied the priest, with warmth. "They who speak like that know little of us. Obloquy and outer degradation, smears that shift with every phase of thinking, what are these to stir a Christian's pulse? With your ancestor it was indeed the inner humiliation, as the children of this world must ever deem it, that revealed itself to him as the hidden glory of God."

" I am glad of that," said the Baron wearily. " It has been my comfort all through life ; I did not like to think it wrong. But the things that I have gloried in are after all but follies. I have been a poor, erring creature. God forgive me. It is better like that."

And then Spangenberg brought the news that Piet's quest had at last been successful and that, in the face of accumulated evidence, the money would be restored. The Baron said little, but his eyes wandered vaguely towards a side-table on which the torn fragments of paper yet lay. " I am glad the news has come to-day," he said. " Mynheer the advocate, I am deeply grateful for your aid." He was quite willing to see the son of his rival; they brought Rein-out to his bedside.

The poor fellow threw himself down on his knees, not knowing what he did, in a passion of useless contrition. All the blame of his father's actions seemed to weigh upon him, the heir, and to crush him. On all sides, wherever he turned his gaze, nothing but infamy !

" Forgive me," he murmured, " say you forgive me. I ask your forgiveness for us all."

" My poor boy, you have done me no hurt," said the Baron gently.

" We have, we have; I cannot separate myself from— them. The shame is ours; the curse is ours. Say you forgive us. I have no right to ask, no right but my exceeding need. I just want your forgiveness, and then I will leave you in peace."

" Surely, if there be anything to forgive, I gladly forgive," said the Baron in trembling accents. Spangenberg drew Reinout away; he was exciting the feeble old man too much by the violence of his regret. " I should like them to give me a little wine," said the Baron, " I should like Gustave to give it me." The old servant brought, with bent head and unsteady hand, a glass of the King's Wine. His master drank half of it. " Take the rest," said the Baron.

"You remember, Gustave? In '30, eh? God save the King!" Gustave saluted silently, unconsciously, as he lifted the wine-glass to his trembling lips.

Outside, the shadows were beginning to deepen. A confused murmur of traffic came up vaguely from the Canal. Someone had opened the window a little, for the room was close with the hot May air. The stifling Canal smell, rendered all the heavier by the day's moisture, came spreading over them all. Even the dying man seemed to perceive it. He moved restlessly once or twice.

Presently he beckoned to Wendela. "I should like," he whispered, "to shake that young man by the hand before he goes. I should like him to make sure—no malice! And there is still one thing I should like to ask."

And so Wendela led Reinout to her father and joined their hands. "With the others?" murmured the old man, eager interrogation in his eyes. "In the Chapel? Both. If ever you have the power." "Yes," said Reinout firmly. "Let us go," whispered Spangenberg in his ear, and the two friends crept out of the room together.

The Baron sank into a long, calm stupor, holding one of his wife's hands all the while.

It grew quite dark in the room, dark and stifling. Toward midnight he opened his eyes and fixed them full on the dear, white face. "In fields," he said, "in fair green fields." And that was the end.

Wendela and her mother remained alone. There were three of them in the room still, and yet there were only two. All the immensity of the change is *there*.

It was long before either moved. At length said the Baroness in a firm voice:

"He was a perfect man. Without reproach."

Even at that moment Wendela lifted a quick look of surprised inquiry to her mother's face. It was only a flash, and immediately she dropped her eyes again. But the Baroness had seen it.

"A perfect man," she repeated steadily. "Sometimes I have asked myself if you fully understood that. All the actions of his life lie patent before me. There is not one of them, even when they caused me the most serious loss, which was not perfectly honourable and upright."

Wendela sank down beside the dead man. Her mother knew, then, knew far more than she did, and approved. "Oh, if I had only understood one day sooner!" she cried in a sudden tempest of tears. "Only a day sooner! Father, father, I shall never be able to tell you now."

And so, at last, Wendela's peace of mind was bought by a lie. For it was a lie, one of those falsehoods by which noble-hearted women shame the truth.

Reinout, on his way home to the little hôtel where he was in the habit of staying under his assumed name of "Volkert," hurried along unheeding, swayed to and fro with the tumult of his thoughts. He did not notice where he was going, as he passed along crowded thoroughfares, noisy with the hundred vulgarities of every-night sale and barter, or turned into little narrow by-streets, desolate beneath their solitary lamp. Presently he emerged upon a quiet square, on one side of which a little crowd was collected. Under a gaslight a man stood preaching; Reinout, looking aside carelessly in passing, recognised the evangelistic tailor, Tipper. He slackened his pace for a moment to listen, and, as he did so, the words fell clearly on his ears: "It's no use. You can't escape from yourself. No man can. You *must* have peace with yourself. And you can't make peace with yourself till you make it *in* God."

"Three for a penny," said a Jew hawker close in front of him, "and warranted to wear."

CHAPTER LXII.

NO THOROUGHFARE.

"Come back immediately, Reinout. What does this masquerading mean? I have just got you nominated to Vienna, but the Minister wants to see you first. Not knowing where to find you, I was obliged to open your bureau. I am disgusted to discover that you are doing things which require an alias. I command you to return at once.

"Van Rexelaer."

"Dear Father,—I am not coming back. I am never coming back. Do not be angry with me, I entreat of you. I cannot act otherwise. Your life and mine lie so wide apart it is no use trying any longer to link them together.

"René."

The two papers lay spread out before him on the lodging-house table, his father's summons, received that morning, and his own reply, ready, with the ink still wet.

As soon as he had recognised the hand-writing of that "Den Heer Volkert, Café Monopole, Amsterdam," he had understood that the decisive moment, too long kept at bay, was upon him and held him by the throat. The idea, even as he gasped beneath it, brought him relief; he was glad. There are those of us who decide quickly, mostly wrong. There are those who decide slowly, mostly wrong also. He was one of the few who decide slowly and right.

Since the horrible discovery—two days ago—of his

father's conduct in connection with "the Lady's Dole," he had lived in the consciousness that he had reached the parting of the ways. He had seen it growing plainer as he journeyed on, but now he had climbed up to it, and was standing still. You cannot stand still long. Happy are you if you can go on straight. Reinout could not. He hesitated, yet from the first he felt—thank God!—that he would turn to the right.

But it is an awful thing for any human heart to cast off all its outer clothing, be that clothing soft or cumbrous, and to stand out naked in the light of a laughing day. Reinout looked back down the past. He recalled how the first flash of light had struck across his velvet-curtained soul when, mazed with the beauty and sick with the sorrow of the wondrous world they were hiding from him, he had first learned, through a girlish gift, in a poet's prophetic promise, that mystery which unlocks all mortal mysteries, the Law of fraternal Love. To love his neighbour as himself—to do good. After all, that is not so very hard! but immortal mysteries rise beyond. To some little vision of these also he had struggled through the thickness of the easy years. To love the Lord thy God with all thy heart and with all thy soul—to do right.

And, long ago, the prisoned song within his breast had awaked, at the sound of other singing, and fluttered its wings on high. He *could* not have sung in his cage.

He recalled his first meeting with Spangenberg. After the acceptance of several of his enthusiastic poems by "The Cry of the People," its editor had printed a request to their author to call. He had gone to Amsterdam, retaining the pseudonym under which he had written, and had naturally become known in "Little Paradise" as "Volkert." He had found there a fresh and healthful and honestly-aspiring life; but his course lay elsewhere. A gentilhomme devoir fait loi.

And he loved his shallow, friendly father, all whose yet

unfulfilled ambition was centred on the son and heir. His mother—hush, he paused before that sepulchre and flung away the key.

Of the story of Dora Droste he could think more calmly. He saw that Wonnema's account of it was coloured by personal spite, and he therefore refused to accept the discharged servant's conclusions. The Count treated such matters as all his acquaintances treated them. With a bleeding heart, Reinout could excuse him.

Against Loripont's accusations, also, he felt that he could at least partially defend his father—in the heat of his yearning to justify him altogether. After all, the hurried scrawl of a man pain-maddened to suicide was not a reasonable will; after all, it might be presumed, might be hoped, that the Count had been ignorant of the source of Margherita's fortune ; after all——

But no: " I cannot live any longer on that money," he said. " It is no use reasoning about it." Nor was it possible to smudge away the clear-cut truth of Spangenberg's revelations. For the first time he beheld his father's unvarnished nature. And at the same time his own nobility fell from him. All the chivalry of his youth in a clatter of tin.

From the life, then, to which he had dutifully clung, while it only seemed distasteful, he now must break away, because God had proved it evil. A gentilhomme devoir fait loi.

He sat down and began a letter to his father; he began several times, with new confidence, after every false start. At last it was finished, a lengthy document, summing up all his difficulties, his doubts, his grievances, tacitly exonerating his parents from any share in causing them. The writing it all down in orderly sequence, the thinking out the tumult of his thoughts, did him good. " It is no use reasoning about it," he repeated when all was over. " I cannot live on *that* money, and that settles the matter."

He carefully read the letter over again. Then he drew

from his breast-pocket a small morocco case and sat looking at the two portraits it contained. His father, with the nervous, shifty features and silken whiskers, all the well-known illustrious orders scattered over neck and chest; his mother, handsome still with a certain conscious comeliness, stout and décolletée—too stout and far too décolletée—in her laces, diamonds and flowers. Slowly he closed the case and hid it away again. Then, with weary hand, he took up the letter and tore it across.

Ten minutes later he had written the few lines of answer recorded above and posted them in the letter-box at the corner of the street. It was done, then. You let go the last tip of the envelope and "it" is irretrievably done. He walked briskly away in the direction of "Little Paradise." His thoughts were of Vienna, at first, and the ultra-covetable small balls at the Hofburg: "I hope you like our society, Monsieur de Rexelaer?" "Your Majesty is too gracious; who would not be charmed?" And then he drifted away to Deynum Castle, and the Chevalier—how sorry that good old man would be!—and the Countess, his mother, among her birds and flowers. Amarinda was dead; Florizel still tottered on three rheumatic legs. After all, the starry career was his; he had been born to it, educated for it: his whole life had been lapped in its supercilious luxury. The home was his, the beautiful resting-place of that illustrious race which had been his from the cradle. The great lady, the Countess, was his mother. In all separation we cry out, there. It is no use casting away keys, when lock and chain hold firm.

He turned into "Little Paradise" and nodded up at Mynheer Morèl. "Will you come and take a walk with me round the square?" the old man called down. "Presently, Mynheer," Reinout answered back. "Please begin without me. I must have a long talk with Spangenberg first." The Master frowned; he was unaccustomed to the most indirect of "no's."

30

"For the moment, I am going to stop here," Reinout said bravely to Christian. "I am not going back to the Hague. But that means that I must earn my own livelihood. I have been wondering whether, if Poster passes his examination and leaves you, you could engage me on trial in his place? You know, I have taken my law-degree."

"My dear boy," cried Christian, "you are welcome to whatever help I can give you, but you're too good for my law-work. Why, with your education and your languages —half a dozen at your fingers' ends—you can get a much better post than that! Don't you remember what I said to you when first you came to me? Well, you *can* earn money; be thankful for it."

"I believe that I could perhaps get something better, but, Christian, I want to have just this. I want you to take me for one year only and to let me earn what Poster earns. At the end of that time I shall probably go away. You see I am perfectly frank with you."

"And then?"

"That is my secret. A fresh secret. Not a very important one."

"But why don't you rather try literature?"

Before Reinout could answer, a pebble struck the window; Father Morèl, having twice completed the circuit of the grass-plot and being big with sublimest thoughts, stood making impatient signs.

"Yes, yes; in a minute," nodded Reinout; "Literature!" he repeated, turning again to his friend. "Do you seriously recommend me to earn my bread by that? Look here, I will tell you a little story. Three or four years ago, while I was a student at Leyden, a thin volume of poetry appeared, entitled 'The Morning of a Life.' The name was not very original; the book was a modest one. Have you ever heard of it?"

"No," said Christian.

"Nor has anyone else, except the man who paid the bill.

His name was 'Pelgrim Volkert.' When the little book first came out, he watched anxiously—oh so anxiously!—for the opinion of 'the literary world.' Sometimes he thought that little book contained the baldest rubbish ever penned; sometimes he fancied it so full of heartfelt beauty that none could read it without tears. In his inmost confidence he believed it would create a stir. Had it done so, I am not sure whether there would not have been a student less at Leyden, next term. Well, several weeks passed; then there appeared a long review in a provincial paper, saying —I don't mind telling now—that the book contained some of the most exquisite poetry in the language, and repeatedly asserting that here was a new light at last in the waste of Dutch literature. I suppose that the light was a Will-o'-the-Wisp. The rest is silence. Three copies were sold, and six months later the author paid the bill. I remember that, on the evening of that most eventful day, he told his father: 'Yes, he should like the Diplomatic Service very much indeed.'"

"Quite so," said Christian.

"And you propose to me to live by literature?"

"I was thinking of the by-ways, not the high-ways," replied the editor, "reviews, articles, studies—journalistic, compilatory, biographical work. But you are right. I don't think you could make a living out of literature. At least, not in this small country. And do you know why?"

"Why? I should think I did."

"No, but let me tell you what I mean. I think you can stand it to-day, and, moreover, you deserve it, after what you have gone through this morning. Don't laugh. You are a genius. That is all."

Reinout staggered, almost as if he had received a blow.

"I—I don't think so," he stammered, stupidly.

"But I do. And I have seen a good deal of your work in the 'Cry,' and I am a better judge than yourself. There, that is enough for to-day. Now go and walk with Father

Morèl. He's another. But, then, fortunately, he has Mevrouw to take care of him."

Reinout found the poet vexed by having been kept waiting; he was not good company. Said his fond wife to herself as she laid down her endless darning to watch them
turn in the little square: "There the good man goes, scat-
tering all his diamonds, as usual, for another to pick up and
set in his crown. Well, I'm glad the other's Pelgrim Volkert. He's a genius. Like all geniuses, he will live alone,
and be buried by a crowd."

CHAPTER LXIII.

ALONE.

A FEW days later Piet Poster successfully passed his third and final examination. Immediately afterwards he sought a situation as assistant-Notary in the Southern Provinces and, being a zealous Catholic, easily obtained one. He wanted to leave Amsterdam, he said.

He wanted to leave Amsterdam, although his Patroness, as he persisted in calling the Baroness, still remained there. The widowed lady had declined Father Bulbius's renewed offer of the Parsonage. " No indeed," said Wendela, " we must never go back."

Besides, the Baron lay buried,—temporarily?—in the public cemetery at Amsterdam. In spite of its modest adjuncts, his funeral had been a quietly imposing one, for a large number of his old colleagues of the States Provincial had come up to attend it, as well as many members of the Order of Nobles of the Province, headed by Baron Borck. Not one of them but had remarked with astonishment among the mourners the young heir of the new lord of Deynum.

A white cross was to be erected on the grave. The Baroness could afford it; what a vulgar, all-important little point! But even the ditch into which sorrow sinks has to be duly paid for, as also the stone which affection puts up to remember the spot by. " I should like to stipulate," Count Rexelaer had said to Spangenberg, " that the family do not return to Deynum." " If the money is refunded im-

mediately," Christian had replied, "there will be no prose-
cution." Shortly afterwards capital and interest were paid
over to her who was now become, indisputably, the last of
the Ladies Rexelaer. Count Hilarius said that he hated
the appearance of injustice and would rather err on the side
of too great generosity. He retained his opinion that the
testator had intended the money to go with the Castle, but
he rejoiced that the benefit of the doubt enabled him thus
delicately to succour the aged Baroness, of whose destitute
condition he had not been aware. Spangenberg was a
bright young fellow, as we have seen, but when he left the
presence of the Lord of the Household, he could not have
told you whether his Excellency, prior to this visit, had
been aware of that little inaccuracy in the spelling of his
noble name. "My father was very exact," said Count
Rexelaer blandly. "I can not understand a slip on his part
in so weighty a matter."

"Yes, Freule, I'm going to-morrow," said Piet. "And
you know who's to have my old room, don't you?"

"No," replied Wendela indifferently. "Who?"

"Don't you really? The Jonker Rexelaer."

"Indeed!" said Wendela in the same tone. But the
news was distasteful to her. She had not seen Reinout
again since the day of the funeral, nor did she wish to see
him.

"Before I go, Freule," said Piet Poster, awkwardly
standing by the open door, "I wanted to thank you for all
you have done for me."

Frank Wendela cried out, "It's the other way," she
said.

"Please don't say that," replied the young man hurriedly. "I haven't been able to do anything, really. But
one thing I shall always be glad and proud of, that it was I
who was, indirectly, the cause of Mynheer the Baron's em-
ploying Mynheer Spangenberg. Do you know, Freule,

when I ran away from Deynum, I had made up my mind
to sail to foreign countries and come back in a year or two
with barges full of gold-dust to repurchase the Castle, as
people do in story-books. I found out soon enough what a
fool I was; I haven't been able to repurchase the Castle,
but—but——" he hesitated. "The Jonker van Rexelaer is
a good man," he said.

"He told me," said Wendela, "about the beating you
gave him, when a boy."

"Did he, Freule? Those are not the kind of beatings
that hurt. I hope he will be happy some day, and I hope
you will be happy, Freule, very happy, and sometimes remember how we used to play together, how you used to
play with me, I mean, when we were children at Deynum."

"Goodbye, Piet," she said, holding out her hand. "I
shall not forget. I hope that you, too, will be very happy."

He gently took the extended hand and bent over it. He
would have liked to lift it to his lips, but he was a Dutchman and, above all things, dreaded making himself ridiculous; he checked the impulse and drew back. "Goodbye,
Freule," he whispered, and went away.

After his departure complete monotony settled down
over the house on the Canal of the Roses; there was monotony in everything, even in the landlady's voice as she
harassed the slavey. "Your father was perfect," the Baroness had said, yet there was an endless monotony in her
prayers for the dead man, and her sorrows for his sufferings
in purgatory. And for this worry of her mother's Wendela
could feel nothing but half-repressed disgust; she rejoiced
in her new-found relief from the load of her father's guilt.

She tended the invalid as one nurses a little child, and
bore, without complaint, the placidity of her pleasureless,
painless existence. Surreptitiously she continued to buy
the "Cry of the People," which she had first seen, by the
by, through Piet Poster. She would meet Reinout on the

stairs, and from time to time he paid a formal evening-call. He was very quiet, and apparently very busy. Juffrouw Donders informed the Freule that he used to sit up quite late into the night. And the landlady's opinion carried weight, not only because she controlled the consumption of paraffin, but also because of her habit of walking the house at all hours, to superintend her lodgers, if possible, through the key-hole.

After the first tornado of protest, things also settled down into comparative calm at the Hague. In answer to discreet inquiries the police had informed His Excellency the Lord High Seneschal that a person called Pelgrim Volkert was well known to them as a writer of seditious verses in that obscure newspaper, the "Cry of the People." The police always know so much, they seldom care to know all.

Count Rexelaer's supreme dread now was lest they should find out who Pelgrim Volkert was. What would become of a Court Official whose son was proven a socialist? Yet he felt that such degradation was fast clouding over his coroneted head.

With this horror upon him he hazarded a wild effort to get Reinout declared insane. It failed; even the closest of nets must have meshes. Whereupon he wrote him a letter damp with tears, a father's heart-broken appeal, the prayer of a man who was losing what he best loved on earth. "Dearest, dearest father," the son wrote back, "let us give up this infamous fortune, and the Castle, which is not even ours!" Everyone noticed how gray and worn Count Rexelaer was looking. He spoke angrily to Margherita. "The boy has covered with infamy the noble name which he bears," he said. "It is your fault with your poetry and nonsense. It is your roturier-blood. A hundred times rather I had wished he was dead." "My poetry was always sensible," retorted Margherita. "It is your ridiculous education that has ended like this. And as for my blood, what is yours, Monsieur le Cabaretier? Do you not think I know *now*—from your dear sister Elizabeth? Leave me in peace with my terrible sorrow. You are insufferable; only yesterday Monsieur de Bonnaventure was remarking how irritable you have grown."

The Chevalier wiped a tear out of his bleared old eye with a silk handkerchief. It was given out that the only son of the Rexelaers had gone abroad for his health; Mevrouw Elizabeth, who was exceedingly put out by Antoinette's disappointment, added that the poor young fellow had always been a little wild. People touched their foreheads significantly. Oh, the instability of human greatness! Everything, yes *everything* that Fortune could bestow. And now *this!*

During all these months Reinout kept on very quietly. He did his daily task for Spangenberg, and occasionally, though more rarely, contributed a few verses to the "Cry."

" You never send me a letter now about my poems," he once ventured to remark to the Freule van Rexelaer.

" No," replied that young lady shortly.

" Perhaps you have given up reading them?"

" No."

" Or do you, having glanced at them, pay no further attention to their contents?"

" Oh no." But this last "no" was ambiguous.

Antoinette had faithfully kept her cousin's secret; no one knew of his writings in the French magazines. The literary circle in "Little Paradise" looked upon him as a Dutch writer of genuine genius, doomed to hopeless obscurity by the very language he wrote in. But even such recognition as Holland can bestow they never expected to be his. He was not a "popular" poet; the artisans who read the "Cry" skipped his poetry, which had not even a chorus. Besides the Dutch, great in painting, are dead to poetry. Even in painting imagination is a sin. It was by imagination that our common mother fell. Had she been content to perceive that an apple is an apple she might have been in Paradise at this hour, as many a substantial Dutch burgher-mother is. Woe to him that distinguishes apples of discord and apples of Sodom and golden apples of the Hesperides, in quest of which latter, perhaps, he sails away into the Unknown. We live both comfortably and right-eously in Holland—nowhere more so—but we do not live by admiration, hope and love. We live by the fear of God and the care of our purses. And we all of us, except the poets, despise a poet just a little for not being something else. Reinout, therefore, was singularly fortunate in having happed on the Morèls.

He knew it, and thoroughly enjoyed those Sunday even-ings—much Poetry and a little punch—which now formed his sole recreation. Of the company which gathered about Homérus none but Spangenberg was acquainted with the de-tails of the new-comer's story. They had heard that he had broken loose from old moorings in a comfortable haven to row with his brothers against the stream. They also knew that " Pelgrim Volkert " had been a literary pseudonym, but they never connected its bearer in their thoughts with that great historic house of which the Mandarin Ri-Ksi-La was the acknowledged head.

Sometimes an allusion would cause the young fellow to wince, as when Homérus, having discoursed on the limits to man's self-sufficiency, wound up with the words: " No human plant ever fully recovers from transplanting. No organism has more than one 'home.' The uprooted heart, whatever may become its future surroundings, goes through life alone."

Reinout pushed back his chair into the shade.

" When my father and my mother forsake me," began the tailor.

" Then shall I be forsaken indeed," concluded Spangen-berg.

" Then the Lord shall take me up," said the tailor.

"That is finely put," remarked Reinout's voice.

"It is from the Bible," replied the tailor. "Have you who are, I believe, an orphan never found it there?"

"No," said Reinout awkwardly.

"Perhaps you have never looked for it, or for anything else. If you have not got a Bible, I should be very glad to send you one."

"I will get one," said haughty Reinout, and then instantly repented: "I mean," he added, "that I should not wish to trouble you."

"It will be a very simple one, mind you—outside. The jewel's the same, whatever the casket."

"Thank you very much indeed," said Reinout.

CHAPTER LXIV.

SUCCESS.

WHEN Reinout abruptly brought his clerkship to an end, his year of probation was only ten months old. April had come around again with premature joys and uncertain promises, foreshadowing a fairer, though not a fresher, sunshine in broad cloudsweeps of wind and rain. It had been a bright, breezy day, full of the turmoil of Nature's restless awakening, with sudden gusts of movement and floods of warmth, one of those days on which all the young world seems dancing merrily, from the bare trees and bold clouds up in heaven to the dead leaves and swift brooks down on earth. A great ripple of jollity spread over creation, the clear wind played up to the dancers and the sly sun laughed down on the dance.

Reinout had spent his day as usual at the office, doubled up over the endlessly useless entanglements of the law. Spangenberg, who hated the systematized robbery of his profession with a constantly increasing contempt, had gone off early to his editorial business, and his clerk was glad enough, at four o'clock, to shut up shop and betake himself to the Canal of the Roses. They were a queer pair of lawyers, and the greater part of the business of the office consisted in unavailing attempts to protect the defenceless.

At his lodgings Reinout found a foreign letter awaiting him. This letter, which he had been daily expecting for weeks, he now tore open as if his life depended on a hundredth of a second of time. His eyes flashed through the contents, and he was out of the door again and off to "Little Paradise." "Good gracious!" cried Christian, looking up from his desk. "Is the Prinsengracht in flames?"

"No," gasped Reinout in joyous breathlessness, "but it will be, Christian, when I have set the world on fire!" And he spread out his open letter in front of his friend.

Spangenberg read it and looked up with his brightest smile.

"You only lose a bad clerk," said Reinout.

"Exactly," replied Spangenberg.

After a moment he added: "So this was your secret. What a linguist you must be!"

"Oh no; I have always spoken more French than Dutch at—home. But don't think that this bird has come falling into my mouth ready-roasted. It has taken a lot of labour and patience to catch and to kill. I've been hard at work for years, trying to get things inserted in the Parisian reviews. Nobody ever knew anything about it, except, quite towards the end, a dear little cousin, who hid away my secret as soon as she had discovered it. It used to be so funny, sometimes, people asking me, for instance, whether I ever read the French reviews?"

"How can people find out if you don't tell them?"

"True, but I couldn't. Nor would you have turned the love of your bosom naked into a dancing-room. There, I'm growing coarse and accurate. Do you think it wrong of me to write in French?"

"No more wrong than for the pastor of a small country-parish to accept a call to a great city-church. Dutch is at the best but the language of one family, with a large proportion of deaf-mutes among its children. French is the language of the civilized world."

"That's what I have always thought, and I considered my efforts in Dutch altogether secondary, but of course others may judge differently; I can't help that. Well, it has been a hard struggle, but success, or something very like the beginning of success, has come at last."

He took up his letter and read it over again. It was a communication from a well-known Parisian publisher to whose review he had already frequently contributed some trifle. The publisher wrote that he accepted the manuscript novel which had been sent him, though suggesting a change towards the close, and that he offered for the copyright, not the enormous sums we so often see set down in the story-books, but a bona fide price of nine thousand francs. Out of the pure goodness of his heart he added some sentences of warmest commendation, both of this work and of former contributions to the "Revue."

"Yes, I have come down to prose," said Reinout sorrowfully. "It's no use, nowadays."

"But, dear fellow, do you know what makes me so happy?" cried Spangenberg with beaming eye. "When fame comes to you, as I am sure it will, world-wide fame, they will be proud of you over yonder, in the Hague! They will be jealous—fiercely appreciative, perhaps, but still appreciative."

"Do you think so?" asked Reinout, in the same sorrowful tone. "I do not. How little you know, Christian, the classes or the 'social conditions' your paper makes war against. With the people from amongst whom I came out the smallest bit of ribbon of Franz Joseph's giving at Vienna would far have excelled the laurel-wreath of Shakespeare himself. I might have done anything vile, composed in my leisure moments the bawdiest of love-songs, but not preached sedition! My own father will weep to think I have not failed. He will endeavour to forget me. Perhaps he will succeed."—Reinout's voice faltered.—"I am told he has sent for my cousin to Deynum. Listen. Only a few months ago I met in society the grand-daughter of an illustrious French poet, a woman who had just bought, with her honour, the title of 'Princess.' Unwisely I talked to her about her 'immortal grandfather'; can you guess what she answered me? 'Immortal indeed, there is no escaping from my grandfather. "Ce qu'il y avait d'infime dans son origine et d'infâme dans sa vie" is writ down in all the dictionaries of Europe.' His life had not been disgraceful in any sense, as you and I read the word. But he had been a revolutionary, a passionate lover of freedom, a scorner of kings. And his origin had been of the humblest, that can never be denied. They will hate me all the more when I call evil evil, because I am one of them."

"I observe," said Christian, referring to the letter, "that you have called this book of yours 'Gloire Infâme.'"

"Yes. When I first began it, I still thought I was entitled to the motto which has been the secret strength of my life. Let the title stand. No one, I have taken care of that, will recognise the story. But it is none the less an autobiography."

Reinout returned home earlier than usual that evening, cherishing, all along the brightened streets, his triumph of the moment and the prospects, financial and other, which it opened up before him. Some perhaps might have feasted so auspicious an event, but it is ill feasting alone.

As he was passing the Baroness's parlour door, the sound of Wendela's singing arrested him. He stood spell-bound on the landing, in the half-light; the spacious alto, clear and warm, he knew and loved; it was not that which now enchained him. But never had he heard it singing to that plaintive air those words of his own: air and words such as Christian had sung them on the first night at the Morels'.

> "The white doves brood low
> With innocent flight.
> Higher, my soul, higher!
> Into the night!
> Into black night!

" Beyond where the eagle
    Soars strong to the sun.
  Nought hast thou, if only
    Earth's stars be won.
    Earth's stars are won.

" Beyond where God's angels
    Stand silent, in might.
  Higher, my soul, higher !
    Into the light,
    Straight to God's light."

Why had she never sung these words to him. Why did she choose for this singing the moment when she believed him to be away? He knocked boldly and entered. "Mamma is not very well to-night," said the young Freule, rising hurriedly from the piano. " I have been rubbing her; she is trying to sleep."

In that sentence the long patience of her life of quiet sacrifice stretched before him. She stood there, under the cold, blue April sunset, in the beautiful perturbation of a pure and haughty woman. No pretty darling this to be won by an embrace. He went straight to the dimly-lighted window and spread out his letter, as he had done for Spangenberg, and asked her to read it.

" This will not mend matters at the Hague," she said.

" No," he replied quietly, " I understand that. And so do you. You and I, Freule, we *know*, at least, what is this ' world ' of which men speak so much. We have held it in the hollow of our hand. Earth's stars are won."

They were standing, looking out, beyond the still canal between its smutty trees, beyond the heavy house-tops, up into the pallid heaven, at solitary Hesperus, white and hard.

" And there is one glory terrestrial," she said; her voice had altered. He turned in astonishment and—oh marvellous sight to him !—he saw that there were tears in those strong brown eyes. " And another glory celestial, and the glory of man is as the flower of the field."

With a sudden impulse he drew forth a shabby little brown volume. "Do you remember this?" he asked eagerly. "Do you remember giving it me, half a dozen years ago? It was a revelation, in my sordid existence, of a love of something else than gold and gilt. You told me, when you gave it, that it was the greatest treasure you possessed."

"I should not say that now," she answered, taking from the top of the piano a smaller, yet more faded book. She held it out to him; it was a Catholic copy of the New Testament. "My father left it me," she said simply, and then, with splendid scorn: "Bulbins told mother I ought not to have it."

Reinout broke the moment's thoughtful silence. "And do you remember," he continued, "the night in the chapel, and your bidding me choose, beyond all earthly splendour, the glory of God-sent disgrace?"

She turned fully upon him, in the gathering darkness. "Yes," she said in a firm voice, "Knight Pilgrim," and then trembled and shrank away.

"I used to think," he went on, "that surely it was my duty to remain where God had placed me, turning my back on the life I really loved, and working for the best. But, perhaps because he saw me sinking, he has called me, by the voice of *shame*, from the Slough of Despond. Not all men are compelled to choose as I was. I trust to God I have chosen well."

"You will be rewarded," she said, still gazing at the star, "by the good you will do in the future."

"Dear Freule," he answered earnestly. "In some other way, in the old way, perhaps, I could have done as much, and more. But this also I believe that God has taught me: He does not ask us to seek to do most good, but only to do right to-day."

"No, no!" she cried vehemently. "You will do more! A great career will be yours; an immeasurable sphere of usefulness. The God who gave you genius has wonderfully

31

prepared you for the use of his gift. Enthusiasts are ignorant of life, and those who know life are no longer enthusiasts. From a child, as you said but a moment ago, you have held in your hand this bauble of Greatness and Glory and been schooled to appraise it. You can tell us what it is worth, as you cast it away."

She had spoken with her old impulsiveness: she stood panting. " The whole world will listen. We all shall be your family !" she said.

He looked up quickly, with a sad smile: " It is very lonely," he answered, " the human race, and nothing nearer. One feels that, perhaps, most in a moment of success. And my work is only just beginning. You see what this man says "—he pointed to his letter—"' Your story is not finished ; the career of your hero is left incomplete.' He has seen clearly, too clearly. Unwillingly, I fear, you have borne your large part in the chapters already written. Wendela, can you join me willingly, if we try honestly, cleanly, to write the rest ? "

CHAPTER LXV.

RESPICE FINEM.

THE carriages came creeping up in an apparently end-less succession; cavalry and police were keeping the crowd back, pushing and prancing amid protests and exclama-tions, occasionally of admiration, more generally of envy or ill-will. One by one, slowly, in a consistent monotony of variety, the landaus and broughams turned cautiously into the square, their horses' heads gradually taking shape under the gaslights with a glitter of harness and champing of bits, to the soft guiding voice of the coachman; some-times there would be a pair of horses, sometimes a single one: bays, greys, the President's old white mares—oh what a big black beauty goes there!—then several chestnuts, one after the other, but always the same big frightened eyes, looming in the damp mist, and the tall servants behind, anxious also, under the steady rain, and a blurr of bright opera-cloak or gold lace against the panes, and then fresh champing and fresh glitter—steady! steady!—and another pair of horses, wet and worried, and the lines of smeared lamps down the distance, not a whit shortened or altered, and another carriage—way there, way!—as the wretched spectators splash back into the shining puddles, and the stream comes flowing on to that wide blaze of light under the awning by the Entrance.

There was a great Reception at the Palace to-night, a "raout," as they call it. Nearly a thousand invitations had been sent out, and such members of the "Everybody" as ought to have been invited and were not, were weeping their eyes out in the bitterness of home.

In the great hall and on the staircase there was decorous confusion. For the flutter which is inseparable from Palace receptions caused all these birds of beautiful plumage to ruffle their feathers in the fear of such ruffling, and many a biped, provided with a third leg by way of ornament, went stumbling and grumbling over that glittering appendage on his passage upstairs. It must be a melancholy consideration for Royalty that nobody ever comes to its entertainments for pleasure, but only to avoid the pain of not having been there. It had done everything in its power to welcome its guests, neither overheating its saloons nor overcooling its wines, and yet everyone was anxious to be home again and frankly confessed as much to everyone else. "Delightful, is it not? So well managed," said one old man, miserable in a stiff gold collar, to another rickety creature in perfectly disgraceful calves. "Yes, Rooseveldt understands his duty; I shall be glad, though, when it's over." "So shall I;" the collar-tortured individual turned to a bright-looking girl by his side. "Ah, Freule van Rexelaer!" he said. "Now you, doubtless, would like such an evening to last for ever? Very natural, my dear. So should I, when I was your age, so should I."

"No indeed," replied Antoinette, laughing. "I detest these crushes. I am here to chaperon Mamma."

"Antoinette, come here at once," commanded Mevrouw Elizabeth in a flustered whisper. "Are my feathers right? Pretend not to be looking. I feel all crooked. I knocked them against an overhanging palm."

"I think your hair's coming down," replied mischievous Topsy. "Hadn't we better go back?"

"Topsy, how can you be so provoking? I am especially anxious for you to create a good impression. I don't want you to remain on my hands for ever, though it's beginning to look as if you would. What you meant by refusing the two eligible *partis* I procured for you, nobody knows but yourself, and since that infamous boy behaved so disgracefully——"

All the naughty merriment died out of Topsy's eyes. "Yes, yes, I know," she said impatiently. Mevrouw Elizabeth cast an aggrieved glance over her ample shoulders, but she let the ebullition pass. "I am anxious to get near Christine," she said. "I told George that his wife was sure to have all the best men about her. She is so uncommonly attractive."

"Which means," cries Antoinette, "that she flirts so shamelessly she amuses them all."

"Well, at any rate she amuses them, which is more, my dear, than some people seem able to do."

Antoinette did not answer. She never crossed the first barrier of her mother's outspokenness, and so managed to live on the outskirts of peace.

The rooms were filling to overflowing, literally, for a crowd was swaying to and fro between the great doors. Gauzes, and diamonds, and animated faces—bored ones also, and vexed and freely perspiring—and an overwhelming abundance of uniforms under the candles and greenery in a blaze of colour and a cloud of perfumery amid the incessant rustle and buzz. "It is horribly hot," said Rolline, when she happed upon Guy in the press. "Not a bit," replied that gentleman calmly. "You think so because you are anxious about your dress." "Anxious:" that was the prevailing impression; the anxiety which is always attendant upon the Sovereign, the fear of "something going wrong."

The great folding-doors were thrown wide apart, and a crowd of gilded officials came trooping through. Then, in the opening, there appeared, alone, a man clad in a hussar uniform, with a great orange-gold band across his breast, a man of magnificent bearing and commanding mien. He paused suddenly, and turned to the courtier who stood nearest:

"And your son, my dear Count," he said in French. "He is better, I hope? He is here?"

Count Rexelaer bent in reply as only they can bend who have no backbone:

"Sire," he said, "Je n'ai plus de fils."

THE END.

APPLETONS' TOWN AND COUNTRY LIBRARY.

PUBLISHED SEMI-MONTHLY.

41. *Passion's Slave.* By RICHARD ASHE-KING.
42. *The Awakening of Mary Fenwick.* By BEATRICE WHITBY.
43. *Countess Loreley.* Translated from the German of RUDOLF MENGER.
44. *Blind Love.* By WILKIE COLLINS.
45. *The Dean's Daughter.* By SOPHIE F. F. VEITCH.
46. *Countess Irene.* A Romance of Austrian Life. By J. FOGERTY.
47. *Robert Browning's Principal Shorter Poems.*
48. *Frozen Hearts.* By G. WEBB APPLETON.
49. *Djambek the Georgian.* By A. G. VON SUTTNER.
50. *The Craze of Christian Engelhart.* By HENRY FAULKNER DARNELL.
51. *Lal.* By WILLIAM A. HAMMOND, M. D. (Cheap edition.)
52. *Aline.* A Novel. By HENRY GRÉVILLE.
53. *Joost Avelingh.* A Dutch Story. By MAARTEN MAARTENS.
54. *Katy of Catoctin.* By GEORGE ALFRED TOWNSEND.
55. *Throckmorton.* A Novel. By MOLLY ELLIOT SEAWELL.
56. *Expatriation.* By the author of Aristocracy.
57. *Geoffrey Hampstead.* By T. S. JARVIS.
58. *Dmitri.* A Romance of Old Russia. By F. W. BAIN, M. A.
59. *Part of the Property.* By BEATRICE WHITBY.
60. *Bismarck in Private Life.* By a Fellow Student.
61. *In Low Relief.* By MORLEY ROBERTS.
62. *The Canadians of Old.* An Historical Romance. By PHILIPPE GASPÉ.
63. *A Squire of Low Degree.* By LILY A. LONG.
64. *A Fluttered Dovecote.* By GEORGE MANVILLE FENN.
65. *The Nugents of Carriconna.* An Irish Story. By TIGHE HOPKINS.
66. *A Sensitive Plant.* By E. and D. GERARD.
67. *Doña Luz.* By Don JUAN VALERA. Translated by Mrs. MARY J. SERRANO.
68. *Pepita Ximenez.* By Don JUAN VALERA. Translated by Mrs. MARY J. SERRANO.
69. *The Primes and Their Neighbors.* Tales of Middle Georgia. By RICHARD MALCOLM JOHNSTON.
70. *The Iron Game.* By HENRY F. KEENAN.
71. *Stories of Old New Spain.* By THOMAS A. JANVIER.
72. *The Maid of Honor.* By Hon. LEWIS WINGFIELD.
73. *In the Heart of the Storm.* By MAXWELL GREY.
74. *Consequences.* By EGERTON CASTLE.
75. *The Three Miss Kings.* By ADA CAMBRIDGE.
76. *A Matter of Skill.* By BEATRICE WHITBY.
77. *Maid Marian, and Other Stories.* By MOLLY ELLIOT SEAWELL.
78. *One Woman's Way.* By EDMUND PENDLETON.
79. *A Merciful Divorce.* By F. W. MAUDE.
80. *Stephen Ellicott's Daughter.* By Mrs. J. H. NEEDELL.
81. *One Reason Why.* By BEATRICE WHITBY.
82. *The Tragedy of Ida Noble.* By W. CLARK RUSSELL.
83. *The Johnstown Stage, and Other Stories.* By ROBERT H. FLETCHER.
84. *A Widower Indeed.* By RHODA BROUGHTON and ELIZABETH BISLAND.
85. *The Flight of the Shadow.* By GEORGE MACDONALD.
86. *Love or Money.* By KATHARINE LEE.

Each, 12mo. Paper, 50 cents; cloth, 75 cents and $1.00.

New York: D. APPLETON & CO., Publishers, 1, 3, & 5 Bond Street.

MANY INVENTIONS. By RUDYARD KIPLING.

Containing fourteen stories, several of which are now published for the first time, and two poems. 12mo, 427 pages. Cloth, $1.50.

"The reader turns from its pages with the conviction that the author has no superior to-day in animated narrative and virility of style. He remains master of a power in which none of his contemporaries approach him—the ability to select out of countless details the few vital ones which create the finished picture. He knows how, with a phrase or a word, to make you see his characters as he sees them, to make you feel the full meaning of a dramatic situation."—*New York Tribune.*

"'Many Inventions' will confirm Mr. Kipling's reputation. . . . We would cite with pleasure sentences from almost every page, and extract incidents from almost every story. But to what end? Here is the completest book that Mr. Kipling has yet given us in workmanship, the weightiest and most humane in breadth of view."—*Pall Mall Gazette.*

"Mr. Kipling's powers as a story-teller are evidently not diminishing. We advise everybody to buy 'Many Inventions,' and to profit by some of the best entertainment that modern fiction has to offer."—*New York Sun.*

"'Many Inventions' will be welcomed wherever the English language is spoken. . . . Every one of the stories bears the imprint of a master who conjures up incident as if by magic, and who portrays character, scenery, and feeling with an ease which is only exceeded by the boldness of force."—*Boston Globe.*

"The book will get and hold the closest attention of the reader."—*American Bookseller.*

"Mr. Rudyard Kipling's place in the world of letters is unique. He sits quite aloof and alone, the incomparable and inimitable master of the exquisitely fine art of short-story writing. Mr. Robert Louis Stevenson has perhaps written several tales which match the run of Mr. Kipling's work, but the best of Mr. Kipling's tales are matchless, and his latest collection, 'Many Inventions,' contains several such."—*Philadelphia Press.*

"Of late essays in fiction the work of Kipling can be compared to only three—Blackmore's 'Lorna Doone,' Stevenson's marvelous sketch of Villon in the 'New Arabian Nights,' and Thomas Hardy's 'Tess of the D'Urbervilles.' . . . It is probably owing to this extreme care that 'Many Inventions' is undoubtedly Mr. Kipling's best book."—*Chicago Post.*

"Mr. Kipling's style is too well known to American readers to require introduction, but it can scarcely be amiss to say there is not a story in this collection that does not more than repay a perusal of them all."—*Baltimore American.*

"As a writer of short stories Rudyard Kipling is a genius. He has had imitators, but they have not been successful in dimming the luster of his achievements by contrast. . . . 'Many Inventions' is the title. And they are inventions—entirely original in incident, ingenious in plot, and startling by their boldness and force."—*Rochester Herald.*

"How clever he is! This must always be the first thought on reading such a collection of Kipling's stories. Here is art—art of the most consummate sort Compared with this, the stories of our brightest young writers become commonplace."—*New York Evangelist.*

"Taking the group as a whole, it may be said that the execution is up to his best in the past, while two or three sketches surpass in rounded strength and vividness of imagination anything else he has done."—*Hartford Courant.*

"Fifteen more extraordinary sketches, without a tinge of sensationalism, it would be hard to find. . . . Every one has an individuality of its own which fascinates the reader."—*Boston Times.*

New York: D. APPLETON & CO., 1, 3, & 5 Bond Street.

ADA CAMBRIDGE'S NOVELS.

MY GUARDIAN. 12mo. Paper, 50 cents; cloth, $1.00.

" A story which will, from first to last, enlist the sympathies of the reader by its simplicity of style and fresh, genuine feeling. . . . The author is *au fait* at the delineation of character."—*Boston Transcript.*

" An interesting English story of ' The Fen Country.' It is a novel out of the usual order. The reader will be absorbed in the fortunes and history it records, and the easy, graceful style of the author will be found thoroughly enjoyable."—*Chicago Inter-Ocean.*

" The *dénoûment* is all that the most ardent romance-reader could desire."—*Chicago Evening Journal.*

THE THREE MISS KINGS. 12mo. Paper, 50 cents; cloth, $1.00.

" An exceedingly strong novel. It is an Australian story, teeming with a certain calmness of emotional power that finds expression in a continual outflow of living thought and feeling.'—*Boston Times.*

" Sure to obtain favor from the reading public. The descriptions of life in Melbourne are highly interesting to us on this side of the world; and as for the three Miss Kings themselves, they are simply charming."—*Halifax Critic.*

" The story is told with great brilliancy, the character and society sketching is very charming, while delightful incidents and happy surprises abound. It is a triple love-story, pure in tone, and of very high literary merit."—*Chicago Herald.*

NOT ALL IN VAIN. 12mo. Paper, 50 cents; cloth, $1.00.

" A worthy companion to the best of the author's former efforts, and in some respects superior to any of them."—*Detroit Free Press.*

" The author has had a story to tell, a very interesting and unusual story it is, and she has kept to it with an amount of self control that is as rare as it is gratifying to the reader. Its surprises are as unexpected as Frank Stockton's, but they are the surprises that are met with so constantly in human experience. . . . A better story has not been published in many moons."—*Philadelphia Inquirer.*

A LITTLE MINX. 12mo. Paper, 50 cents; cloth, $1.00.

" A thoroughly charming new novel, which is just the finest bit of work its author has yet accomplished."—*Baltimore American.*

" The character of the versatile, resilient heroine is especially cleverly drawn."—*New York Commercial Advertiser.*

" Another of the Australian stories for which this author has attained so just a popularity."—*Boston Beacon.*

THE ENGLISH PRESS ON ADA CAMBRIDGE'S BOOKS.

" Many of the types of character introduced would not have disgraced George Eliot."—*Vanity Fair.*

" Ada Cambridge's book is rendered attractive by the kindly spirit and fine feeling which it evinces, by the wide and generous sympathies of its author, and no less by her remarkable literary ability."—*The Speaker.*

New York: D. APPLETON & CO., 1, 3, & 5 Bond Street.

New York: D. APPLETON & CO., 1, 3, & 5 Bond Street.

www.ingramcontent.com/pod-product-compliance
Lightning Source LLC
Chambersburg PA
CBHW032011110726
47901CB00004B/1049